WILL YOU STILL LOVE ME IF I BECOME SOMEONE ELSE?

JOTHAM AUSTIN, II

Will You Still Love Me If I Become Someone Else?

Jotham Austin, II

RHETASKEW PUBLISHING
UNITED STATES OF AMERICA

COVER AND INTERIOR DESIGN

© 2021 - Flitterbow Productions

(cover illustration courtesy Jotham Austin, II)

All characters, settings, locations, and all other content contained within this book are fictional and are the intellectual property of the author; any likenesses are coincidental and unknown to author and publisher at the time of publication. This work and its components may not be reproduced without the express written permission of the author and Rhetoric Askew, LLC.

ISBN-13: 978-1-949398-49-6

© 2021 – Jotham Austin, II
ALL RIGHTS RESERVED

for all those that remember

and still love me . . .

PART 1:
BRIAN'S STORY

CHAPTER 1

Brian:
29 Days after Event

I have not slept for days. What if I close my eyes—even blink? Could I become someone else? Someone who I cannot control. Someone who will replace me. Someone who will take her from me. I can't live like this much longer. I must sleep—

Must fight against them—

For her—

I squeeze my eyes closed. The darkness is unsettling. Blackness resting like a heavy weight on my chest. My heart is beating fast. My arms start tingling. Pins and needles stab my feet. Angry white noise fills my head. Am I dying? Are they trying to kill me? I jerk up, eyes scanning the fuzzy darkness. I'm still me. The tension in my shoulders releases, my head rests on the pillow. I close my eyes again.

I'm leaving that plane when their minds, all one hundred and ten of the other passengers on that plane, merge into my head. Their faces flashing like one of those old projector movies. Their memories stuffed into the catalog of my own life. Their faint, agitated voices haunt me for a release I don't know how to give them.

The film ends and strobes of hot, white light explode into sparks of color on the backs of my eyelids. My heart thuds against my chest, throat, neck. Or is it the vibrations of them pounding on my mind?

Above their chatter, I fixate on the white noise of her breathing. She is real; she is my anchor, and they will not take her from me. I snuggle closer, inhaling her lavender scent. Their voices fade further from my mind. A gray fog begins to swaddle me. The fog becomes thicker and tighter, until all the space around me is forced into a matte black darkness, and there I find myself, alone.

A hand grabs me, my arm breaks out with gooseflesh. "Wh-What?"

"You're okay, sweetie."

"What?"

She sighs. "You were tossing and turning."

"Sorry, crazy dream."

"What about?"

I close my eyes and—like studying a fuzzy and faded photo—her pale, freckled face and delicate lips, framed by fire-red hair, come into focus.

"What about?" she repeats.

I blink my eyes to clear the image. I study my fiancée's face. Her long brown hair, full lips, eyes like golden-brown marbles, and that flirtatious smile—her name pops into my mind—Brenda.

"Were you dreaming of her...again?"

"No!" I blurt out the lie.

"Tell me the truth."

"Yes."

Brenda puts her hand onto my chest and rubs small circles with her fingertips. "I still love you."

"Yeah."

Brenda clears her throat.

"I love you, too—" I have to sort through a flood of names to remember hers. "Brenda."

Her lips curl into a cheeky smile; she always has that smile when I say the wrong thing. I kiss her on the cheek. Brenda rolls over, and I swing my legs off the bed. Brenda's long, curvy body fills my space.

I smack Brenda's dangling foot. "Time to get up, or you're going to be late."

Brenda grins as I step out of the room, her voice pleading after me. "Five more minutes. Put the coffee on, please."

As I sit down to eat my breakfast, I look to the clock and think, *Is Brenda getting out of bed this morning?* The bedroom door opens. "You're alive. I thought you were going to sleep the day away."

Brenda sticks out her tongue, rolling her eyes.

She moves around the kitchen, studying every detail—every movement labored and exaggerated, like a wind-up doll. She glares at me while grabbing her coffee mug from the cabinet. She sniffs the air, walking to the coffeepot.

"What are you eating, sweetie?" Brenda yawns while pouring the steaming coffee into her mug. Her sideways glances and jerky movements are annoying, but I'll hold my tongue.

"Eggs and sausages," I say, stuffing a fork full of the greasy food into my mouth. "And two pieces of toast and some coffee."

"Hungry, are we?" Brenda sits at the table and begins poking through the *Chicago Tribune*. My head is filling with anger, the way she attacks the pages, popping the seam, crinkling the paper in half, releasing that inky newspaper stink. She mumbles as she reads the article—pausing, she slurps her coffee.

Annoyed, I answer, "Yeah, just a little. Why, what's it to you?" Small toast crumbs and spittle project out of my mouth.

"Didn't your mom tell you not to talk with your mouth full?" Brenda laughs like a scolding mother, grabbing a napkin to wipe my mouth.

I smack her arm away. "What the fuck is wrong with you, girl?"

Brenda cradles her arm and snaps, "What's wrong with you?" She pushes away from the table, towering above me. Her eyes burn through me, eyebrows raise into the angry wrinkles forming across her forehead.

She mumbles something and spins on her heels, walking away. A cabinet door opens and slams shut. The ice machine clinks ice into the glass. Water turns on, the drone of the mechanical pump drilling into my head. She walks to the table, plops into her seat, and gulps her water.

I drop my fork onto my plate. "Do you have to drink so fucking loudly?" I shake my head. "Drinking like an animal."

Brenda huffs. "I'm going to ignore the fact that you cursed at me and point out the total weirdness that's going on."

I put the last forkful of runny eggs and sausage into my mouth. "Like what?"

"Well, first, you're eating eggs and sausage."

"And?"

"Well before the event, you barely ate any meat, and you absolutely hated eggs." Brenda swirls her glass, making the ice clink against the sides.

"Can you stop that shit?" I stand with my plate, walking to the sink. "Nothing but clink-clank with the ice, and nag-nag about what I'm eating. Who the fuck made you queen of the kitchen this morning?"

"Please, calm down and relax."

"No, I'm fine. Just trying to have breakfast without my mom analyzing my every movement."

"I'm not trying to be your mom." Brenda looks into the glass and sighs. "I'm just bringing it to your attention. Maybe you can discuss it with Dr. Shirley today."

"Oh, I see what this is about. You and Doc have been talking behind my back." I throw the plate into the sink. "Well, fuck both of you."

Brenda walks to me, shaking her head. "I have not spoken to Dr. Shirley yet, but—"

I step into Brenda's space. "No fucking buts. Don't talk behind my back. I eat what I eat, and you and that quack doctor can suck on these—" I gasp as the chill of icy water splashes on my face. Brenda pushes me out the way as I rub my eyes. My vision blurs. I grab a dishcloth and blot my face. The odor of fried meat and grease makes me nauseous. I throw the cloth down. The kitchen is a mess of pots and pans. I see Brenda's coffee mug.

"You want me to put your coffee in a travel cup?" I turn and start fumbling in the cabinets, the *tap-tap-tap* of Brenda's heels on the hardwood floors growing louder.

"Are you trying to drive me crazy?" Brenda's voice is soft and shaky.

"What?"

Brenda moves closer to me, pulling me into a tight hug. "I keep telling myself how much I love you, how much I care about you, but you're not going to drive me crazy."

She holds me by my shoulders; if she lets go, my muscles will dissolve away, and I'll collapse into a puddle of nothing.

I whisper in her ear, "I'll not let you go." She nods then pulls away. I wipe the tears filling her eyes. "I'm sorry. I'm trying my best to control them."

Brenda shakes her head. "Do you even remember how you treated me just now?"

"I have to visit Dr. Shirley and then go to the clinic."

"What? Why do you have to go to the clinic again?"

"Nurse Marci asked me to stop by."

"I don't trust, Marci."

"She's the only person I trust there."

"I don't like any of this."

"I'm going to pick up Granny and take her as well."

Brenda swirls her finger between us. "You need to stop worrying about Granny and those people in your head, and focus on me." She leans in and kisses me on the cheek. "Focus on us."

"Yeah, right... But those people are me now."

"No, sweetie. They are just memories, and memories can be forgotten—"

"Recuerdos llenan el vaćio," I blurt out.

"What does that mean?"

I hunch my shoulders. "No clue."

"You have to—"

"Brenda, these people want to get out." I point to my head. "And I'm afraid of losing control of them."

"Just..." She kisses me on the lips. "I love you." She turns and walks out the door.

It takes me a few minutes to realize she is gone. I look at my watch. I have to leave if I'm going to make my appointment with Dr. Shirley. I stare at myself in the mirror. I'm still me, right? My reflection nods in agreement as I walk out the door.

CHAPTER 2

Brian:
29 days after Event

I hate the idea of meeting with this shrink, Dr. Shirley. This is part of my "memory rehabilitation" process, learning to compartmentalize my memories. A waste of time, sitting in a dim office that reeks like a vanilla candle had sex with a leather couch. The *tick-tock* of a clock in the room adds rhythm to Dr. Shirley's dry monotone voice drilling into my head. As if I'm not crazy enough. She commands me to lie on the soft leather couch and close my eyes. Concentrating on that *tick-tock*, white sparkly caterpillars nibble the black of my vision until I'm surrounded by the white fog of memories. The doctor's voice resembles a siren, calling from the ether.

"So when was the last time you flew in a plane?"

I push the hot air out of my lungs, vanilla fills my nose, and the answer emerges from the white. "The last time I flew was from Philadelphia to Chicago."

"Do you remember what time the flight boarded?"

"The flight boarded at 2:57 p.m."

I have always wondered why flights board at off times. Must have something to do with departures and arrivals of other flights. And yet you still have to sit on the tarmac, twiddling your thumbs for thirty minutes, making small talk with your seatmates.

"What was the flight number?"

"2164."

I wonder how many people remember the number of the last flight they took. The last flight I took from Philly to Chicago was flight 2164. It departed through the purple-red haze of a summer sunset, landing as perfect as can be expected for a tin can with wings and giant rubber tires going hundreds of miles an hour.

"Welcome to the city of Big Shoulders," the captain announced. He spent five minutes droning on about weather, connecting flight information, and how much he appreciated us flying with him. Do people remember that stuff when they land?

Her voice cuts into my internal monologue. "Who were you sitting next to?"

The question startles me; it's as though she is reading my thoughts. Who was I sitting next to? Never a cute, long-legged underwear model with a face that appears airbrush perfect. Or an independent filmmaker who falls in love with your life story. At best, somebody falls asleep on your shoulder, snoring in your ear; and at worst, a bratty kid whines that their iPad is not loaded with Dora episodes. In other words, no one you'd care to remember after the flight lands.

The most interesting person I sat beside was this guy going to a science convention, some years ago. We had some beers in the airport with his lab friends. He worked on using nanotubes to transport DNA to specific cell types. Most of what he talked about was more advanced than my introductory college biology classes but gave me a lot of promising ideas for the novel I was working on. I did get the number of this cute girl who was part of their group, but we only went on a few dates. Her face fades as Dr. Shirley clears her throat.

"Do you remember who you were sitting next to?"

"On one side was a grandmother who smelled like she bathed in medicated muscle rub. But what a sweet lady. She smuggled a bag full of homemade chocolate fudge onto the plane. While we were sitting on the tarmac, she pulled out the parchment-wrapped candies and offered me one."

I can remember her saying, "Here sweetie, have a piece of fudge..." She smiled as I took the candy. "You look just like my grandson, Ralphie."

"Thank you." I unwrapped the candy and popped it in my mouth. In all my twenty years flying, that was the closest thing to a mile-high experience I have ever had. That was a damn good piece of fudge. Sexual Chocolate Granny, the stuff airplane fantasies are made of. If she were thirty years younger, she could have passed as Pam Grier's younger sister. She gave me another piece of chocolate after I dropped that compliment on her.

She was sitting in the window seat and spent most of the flight rambling on about her grandson, Ralphie. I remember her silver-white hair that framed her brown-skinned face, each wrinkle well-earned. She had a gold cross, studded with tiny diamonds, lying on her chest. An oversized knit sweater, red with white stripes. She wore track pants, blue with a white racing stripe running the length of her leg, ending in a pair of diabetic thick-soled black shoes.

"Like I said, a typical granny that had no sense of style, but had a bag full of damn good fudge—"

"She sounds like an interesting woman, and you became friends with her after the event. I'll make a note to talk about her in a later session. But who was sitting on your other side?"

I smile at the image of the gray-haired man coming into focus. "On my other side was Dan 'the businessman' Smith."

Two first names, that toothy grin, and his ethanolic cologne battled with Granny's medicated foot rub for control of my nasal passages. After our initial hellos—and him guessing at my net worth—he appeared to realize that whatever he was selling, I could not afford. He fell asleep before we pulled out the gate.

"Very good Al—" I open my eyes and glance at Dr. Shirley, who says, "Sorry, Brian."

"No worries, a lot of people have been stumbling over my name recently. Even I forget sometimes." I laugh at the idea of someone with all these memories forgetting his own name.

"Thanks for understanding, Brian. Let's get back to the questions. How many people were on that last flight you took?"

"Yeah, now that's a tough one." I close my eyes and let the fog surround me again. I sense everyone on the plane, their voices calling out. I count one hundred and six passengers (including myself), three flight attendants, and the two pilots. So what is that?

"One hundred eleven people on that plane." I answer.

"Very good, Br-Brian. Do you remember what gate the plane parked at?"

"Thirteen... Gate thirteen."

"Anything you remember happening when you landed?"

I shake my head. "No, Doc, the plane came to a complete stop. There was the harmony of clicking seatbelts unlatching, the overhead bins popping open. Joints cracking, groaning, cellphones dinging to life, bits of conversation ending, pleasantries, and true goodbyes."

"Interesting—"

"Doc, I have thought a lot about this. Think about how many people you see again after a flight. One hundred and eleven people on a plane and you never see these people again. It's always hello, fly, land, goodbye forever. Crazy when you think about it. You say goodbye to Granny and businessman Dan, wishing you got that fudge recipe and could call Dan's company to hear about what he is selling, but you never do. Is it because you don't care? Or just too lazy to bother? Or too busy dealing with our own life? All the above?

"You just shuffle your way off the plane with 'excuse-mes' and 'you-go-aheads,' pouring out of gate thirteen, staring at the folks in the terminal. That momentary lost feeling, like you fell into a maze. Should I go right or left? Then it clicks that you need to get your luggage.

"You stare at the monitor and see your stuff should be on carousel two. You see the arrows pointing left. You see familiar faces from the plane. All one hundred and eleven of us disperse from gate thirteen into the world, hopeful and blending into the larger hive of humanity. Then, these fleeting faces and conversations are lost from your life forever."

"Brian, what happened when you got to the carousel?"

I think about walking to that carousel. The steel-gray fog explodes with colors, and their faces swirl into focus. Their bodies, like mannequins, hands outstretched, grabbing at me—

"I got to carousel two and saw the same faces. Staring at me like we're long-lost cousins meeting for the first time. Never speaking, just standing there, staring. We were all just standing there. The cattle bell rang, and bags began pouring out of the hole in the ground. Mindlessly, we all gathered around the spinning belt, everyone just staring, hesitant to grab a bag."

"That must have been frightening. What did you do, Brian?"

"I did what I always do, think about my bag. Except my mind flooded with other thoughts—"

I grow silent, remembering the voices in the fog. They had started to call out, *Is that mine with the red bow tied to it, or did I use green ribbon? No, my bag is black. I had two bags...*

"Brian, go on, please. What happened?"

"Doc, it was horrifying. One hundred and ten other voices and thoughts entered my mind. That was the first moment I knew something was wrong."

Dr. Shirley's pen scratches across her pad, sending a shiver down my spine. "How did you know something was wrong?"

"Because, when I closed my eyes and thought about Granny, a green suitcase with flowers on it flashed in my mind. I grabbed it—"

"Why, Brian?"

"Because it belonged to Granny. But Doc, how did I know that? Then I saw a black suitcase with a green stripe down the front. I grabbed it with confidence. I read the tag, confirming it had my name on it. I would have just walked off, but I had Granny's bag also. I wheeled it around to her, and she smiled the way grannies can. She thanked me and said I was her favorite grandson. I smiled and turned to walk away. And then she started whimpering."

Colors creep through the fog like caterpillars, until Granny's face appears in the fog and I reach out to comfort her—

Dr. Shirley's voice calls out from the ether, "Tell me more about your interaction with Granny at the carousel?"

"She was confused, but I knew so much about her..."

"Such as?"

"Like where her grandson Ralphie lived. Strange thing was, Granny didn't tell me that Ralphie would be a few minutes late picking her up. I took Granny to where Ralphie would meet her. Once again, strange that I would know such a thing, but I followed the voice in my head. I told Granny to wait here, I was going to get the car. She smiled, and I walked to the information desk."

"Please continue."

"Yeah, Doc, I told them that Mary Collins was waiting for her grandson. Strange thing, Doc. How'd I know Granny's real name? She never did tell me; I always called her Granny. I knew something was weird, and I had to leave the airport quick. The lady at the information desk said she would send some help. I turned and walked off, patting myself on the back for doing a good deed."

The scraping of the pen is annoying me. That *tick*-fucking-*tock* like the *click-clack* of Brenda's ice.

"Brian, stay with me. What happened next? Did you leave as planned?"

"Doc, you know I didn't fucking leave as planned."

"Please take a few deep breaths, Brian, and contain your emotions."

I take several gulps of the vanilla-soaked air. "Sorry, Doc."

"Are you ready to continue?"

"Sure, Doc."

"Tell me what happened as you were leaving the airport."

"Okay, as I'm leaving, I see eighty or so people milling around carousel two. The luggage is pulled off the belt. An overworked TSA guard checks everyone's ticket and ID, pointing them to their luggage. I looked at the faces, and names started popping into my head. Their luggage seemed familiar, and then voices and memories filled my mind—"

Granny fades into the dense fog and faces flicker like an old-time projector. The voices in my head start shouting at random, and I shout back,

"Is that mine with the red bow tied to it...?

"...did I use green ribbon?...

"...no, my bag is black...

"...I had two bags—"

Dr. Shirley's voice cuts in, "Brian, are you okay?"

"Yeah, Doc, just... reliving that day is hard, and—"

"You're doing great, Brian. We can stop if—"

"No, Doc, I want to get this out."

"Okay, when you're ready."

I take a deep breath and continue. "So I ran past the luggage carousel and down the corridor leading to the parking lot, head pounding with thoughts. I stepped out of the elevator into the parking lot. It was hot and humid. Typical Chicago summer. I closed my eyes, panting, swallowing the thick air, trying to catch my breath. Then I heard them, one hundred and ten voices, and thousands of memories.

"Their memories. Memories about their cars, their wives, their girlfriends, their boyfriends, their puppies, their jobs, their children, their appointments, and all the other B.S. that filled their one hundred and ten lives. I opened my eyes, hoping their voices and memories would go away. But there they were, luggage in hand. Searching like lost children, the passengers from my flight, flight 2164."

"So you recognized them?"

"Shit, Doc, I not only recognized them, but I knew their names—or at least, names popped in my head like when you see an old friend. My head was throbbing, my heart pounding, the thick air wrapping around me, suffocating like a wet plastic bag. I dropped my suitcase and fell to my knees, screaming at the top of my lungs. I sat on the ground for seconds, minutes, maybe an hour—who knows? My head was a fog of other people's random thoughts and memories. I could sense their bobbing heads crowding around me, searching for their identity. I started shouting names at them as I pushed my way past.

"Every time I said a name, a face would light up, eyes widen, and a hint of a smile would form. But it would fade into a blank, confused look—"

"So you were shouting the names of the other passengers?"

"That's what I fucking said, Doc."

"Calm down, Brian. I'm trying to clarify the facts. Count to ten and establish your mental images, as we practiced, and go on with the story when you're calm again."

I sigh, and that artificial vanilla clears away the hot, white, strobing lights. At the count of ten, I'm wrapped in my dense, fog-like cocoon.

"Once I was free from the tangle of arms and mumbling voices, I ran to my car, ignoring the faces, the cries for help, the voices in my head. I just got into my car, and silence. Driving fast, trying to forget the one hundred and ten people from flight 2164 from Philly to Chicago that landed at Midway gate thirteen on that summer night."

A brilliant light pierce the fog in my mind. The hot white melts the visions away. I open my eyes to Dr. Shirley's smiling face.

"So what do you think happened to you, Brian?"

I lift myself to a seated position. "I don't know, Doc, and no one can tell me what happened. How did one hundred and ten people get amnesia, and I get all of their memories?"

"I don't know, Brian, but we are going to work on getting things straightened out."

"Doc, do you think I should start visiting these folks and give them back their memories somehow?"

Dr. Shirley sits her pen and pad on the side table and leans closer to me. "And how will you give them back their memories? Do you know which memories belong to who? And would you give all the memories or just the positive ones?"

"You cannot imagine all the crap that fills other lives. Maybe these people don't want some of these memories back; maybe they want a clean slate. I know I would, but would it be fair for me to filter their memories?"

Dr. Shirley raises her eyebrow. "Oh, I have a pretty good idea of the crap that fills other people's lives."

I smile. "I guess you're right, Doc."

She looks at her watch. "Well, we went a bit long, but you were finally opening up. Hopefully, we can work through the bad—"

"Doc, it's not all bad. On good days, I can speak random languages, but I may not know what I'm saying. I can play several different instruments, but my hands are small and fingers short. I know how to perform heart transplant surgery and tie a French braid. I can fly several types of planes, and I even know Granny's secret fudge recipe. I know a lot of things now, but it's choppy. I can't control the memories coming in. I have even less control over when they fade out and I'm left with just me."

"Try to stay positive."

"Don't get me wrong, the bad is bad—a lot of regrets, missed opportunities, and tragedies. Think one hundred and ten other people's baggage, one hundred and ten lives of failed dreams, dark secrets, and misplaced talents."

"I can imagine, and we will work though it all, Brian."

"And poor Brenda—"

"Who?"

"My fiancée, Brenda."

Dr. Shirley reads her notes. "Oh, yes, Brenda. We will work on managing all your relationships." Dr. Shirley glances at her watch again.

"I guess that's the purpose of these sessions, to talk out all their crap and then 'compartmentalize it.' Whatever the hell that means."

"Very good, Brian. We made some substantial progress, so let's call it a day."

I walk out the office and reflect on what we talked about. Maybe if I could control the memories, I would have at my command more information and talents than any human on the planet. A "gift from God" is what the newspaper called my situation. A "tragedy" is what the newspaper said about the others. In my opinion, they had their terms mixed up.

Jotham Austin, II

At the end of the day, I want my life back. My simple life. Where I wake-up, kiss my fiancée, work on my novels, sleep, and repeat. I would give them all up, give up all of this knowledge and talent, and forget flight 2164. Forget Granny, Dan, all one hundred and ten of them. Why couldn't I be one of the one hundred and ten? No matter how hard I try—and trust me, I have tried—all I can do now is remember.

CHAPTER 3

Brian:
29 Days after Event

The worst thing about Chicago in the summer is the humidity. Ninety degrees, ninety percent humidity. That hot, relentless sun reminding you that the worst thing about a Chicago summer is walking outside. I step out the car and a wave of thick, moist air smothers me. A few steps and I have to wipe the sweat tickling my brow, pulling my fingers through my hair.

We should have debates about global warming on days like this. Instead of trying to convince people about changing weather patterns in the snowy winter, they should be here, saying, "See, it's hot!"

I walk past an empty spot, and kick myself for not parking closer to Granny's house. Well, not Granny's house, but her grandson Ralphie's house.

***

I met Ralphie once, a week or so after the event. He was not tall but built like a linebacker. I remember his face; his smile full of white, perfect teeth, his wide brown eyes pulled you into his hello. His arm extended, and our hands met. The firm handshake demanded attention.

He did not say much at first, except a mumbled thank you for the call at the airport on the night of the event to retrieve his grandma. I followed his hand, pointing at Granny. She sat ramrod straight on the edge of the chair, hands folded on her lap. Her cheeks sunken, skin like wrinkled leather, brown eyes wide and gazing into space.

"I saw you on the news last night," Ralphie's deep voice startled me.

"Hopefully I didn't make an idiot out of myself."

"No, you did great."

"Thanks."

The silence grew awkward between us. I started to bounce around, shoving my hands into my pockets, playing with my keys. Avoiding eye contact with Ralphie. I noticed the whitewashed brick walls, caged lights dangling from thin cords and exposed steel beams, like this building was some sort of factory in its prime. I studied the other people from the plane. Their faces like Granny, expressionless. Eyes—brown, black, blue, and every shade in between—lost in space. Lost in the vacuum of their own thoughts. Their eyes in stark contrast to the probing, aware eyes of their caretakers.

"More tests today, you think?" I jumped a little as Ralphie's voice cut through the mumble of noise.

"Yeah, I think so."

"Granny doesn't mind, but taking these days off from work is going to get me fired."

"What do you do?"

He raised his eyebrow and smiled, revealing that childish gap between his two upper teeth. "Landscaping engineer," he said, followed with a sarcastic chuckle. "What about you, boss?"

I was about to answer but had to pause as a flood of occupations entered my head. A pounding sensation of unfiltered noise. I covered my eyes with my hand and tried to calm myself like Dr. Shirley suggested.

"You okay, buddy?" His hand squeezed my shoulder, steadying my shaky knees.

I sucked in air, like I had been running. The stale air mixed with spicy cologne, fruity perfumes, and the dank-humus scent on Ralphie's hand caused me to gag. Metallic bile burned my throat. I swallowed hard and focused on the fog forming in my mind until my stomach settled. I opened my eyes, and my spinning world settled.

"I'm a writer."

Ralphie's mouth opened, but no words came out. He hunched his shoulders and started to fuss over Granny.

"What type of stuff you write about?"

It took me a second to find an answer. "Science fiction novels."

"I knew your name was familiar."

"You read sci-fi?"

He nodded his head. "Yeah, I like reading sci-fi. I go to the Chicago Comic Con and everything. I'm a big nerd."

"Zombies."

"You write zombie novels? Which one? I probably read it."

"I wrote *Zombie Night!*"

"Oh my gosh, you wrote *Zombie Night!*" He smacked me in the arm. "I love that book. When is the second part coming out, *Zombie Day*?"

His eyes probed for an answer, and my mind spun to find one. The title seemed correct, but was I writing a second book? Was it a trilogy or a longer series? I shook my head.

"I'm writing away, but my agent says I can't give any details."

"Come on. Really?"

"Yeah, you know to build anticipation... It's a marketing thing. Sorry."

"I understand." His mouth twisted into a smile.

"Hey, maybe you can be a beta reader or get an advance reading copy."

He flashed that childish gap-tooth smile, nodding his head yes. The loudspeaker announced several names.

"Hey, man, that's us!" He reached for Granny, helping her out of the seat. "See you around."

I nodded as he walked away.

"Hey, Ralphie, if you need someone to take Granny to appointments, let me know."

He nodded back.

"Oh, and I'm going to hold you to pre-reading my book."

He waved over his shoulder, keeping his attention on herding his grandma to the exam rooms.

For some reason, I was always last. The last to be questioned. The last to be examined. The last to be hooked to machines and beeping devices. The last to be poked and prodded. Why'd they make me wait all alone in this empty, whitewashed lobby?

The same nurse always greeted me, Marci Jenowski. She didn't look like the other nurses; she wore heels, always had a serious grin smeared across her face, and she would give orders to the doctors.

"Brian Watson, come on down!"

"Finally."

She pulled my medical folder close to her chest. "Brian, my favorite patient. How are you doing?"

"Okay, just tired of coming here for tests." She rolled her eyes. I added, "No offense to you or the doc, just the last few weeks have been exhausting."

She grabbed my arm and gave it a little squeeze. "I understand, but no tests today. Just some news."

She walked ahead of me. Her long, straight black hair was tied into a ponytail, swaying side to side.

"So...good news, I hope."

Marci glanced at me, and her full red lips formed a smile. A hesitant smile that told me the next words out of her mouth would be a lie.

"Nothing to worry about...Brian." She grabbed my arm again and pulled me into the exam room, locking the door behind us.

"What's going on?"

She laid the folder down, loosened her ponytail and stepped closer to me.

"I just wanted to talk with you about things first. Just wanted to make sure you're doing okay." She wrapped her arms around me.

"Uh, okay... Thank you," I said, taking a long whiff of her fruity shampoo. Her perfume, teasing with its vanilla and caramel hints. I squeezed my eyes tight, her scent enveloping me. My hand slipped around her waist, grabbing at her firm, familiar butt. I nibbled on her ear, she moaned.

"I've missed you so much." I whispered into her ear. She wiggled her body closer.

"You remember me?"

"Oh, my sweet baby, how could I forget you?"

Her hands pushed against my chest. "We should stop."

I pulled my hand off her butt and staggered away. "Oh my gosh...what?"

"No, I'm sorry."

I sat on the exam table, confused. She pulled her hair back into a ponytail, straightened her blue top and fumbled with the door. She stopped, spun on her heels and with two quick steps she wiggled between my legs. She leaned in and combed her hand through my curly hair, pulling my head until our lips met. I resisted, but some part of me relaxed as I tasted her salty, bumpy tongue probing inside my mouth. I opened my eyes, and my hands had found their way into her top, squeezing her breasts.

I pulled away enough to talk. "Marci, what the hell is going on?"

"You remember me?" She smiled, buttoning her top again. "He's in there, and I need to get him back."

She picked up the folder and walked out the door.

A few minutes later, Nurse Marci and Dr. Greene came into the room. Marci stood near the door pretending to read the notes she was holding, and Dr. Greene patted my leg. "So Brian, how are you?"

"Confused."

"Marci said you were feeling good."

"I'm sorry, it has been a long day on top of a long few weeks." I faked a yawn. "I just want to sleep."

"Okay, I'll make it short." He flipped the pages in the folder, pausing to read some notes. "Our tests are inconclusive. We found some densities in your brain scans—"

"Densities?"

"In neurological diseases such as prion disorders, Alzheimer's, or Huntington's, there have been studies showing densities—plaques—forming in brain tissue. These plaques, under certain conditions, can be transmitted between humans."

"What?" I mumbled.

Dr. Greene patted my leg again. "Don't get too wound up." He chuckled, then continued, "Alzheimer's and Huntington's plaque transfer were only in lab experiments..." Dr. Greene's voice faded to a mumble. His eyes swept the room. He swallowed hard then continued mid-thought, "But prion disorders, like mad cow disease, are transmittable and fatal."

"What are you saying? I'm going to die."

"No, no. Your condition seems stable, but we should test those you've had contact with since the event."

"That could be hundreds of people. I have been on talk shows and at this clinic, out buying coffee."

"No, just those you had, um," Dr. Greene smiled, "close physical contact with."

"What?"

"People you're around a lot, and people you've had...intimate contact with—hugging, kisses, relations, etcetera."

My eyes darted to Marci, who was scrutinizing the papers she was holding.

"Why?"

I was watching Marci, but Dr. Greene answered, "It's probably nothing, but we just want to do some scans and cross anything we can off our list." He squeezed my knee to get my attention.

I stared at his face as my hands balled into fists. "Could you stop touching me?"

Dr. Greene jerked away, and mumbled under his breath, "Sorry."

"This is some bullshit. I come down here thinking I'm going to get some answers to why my head is filled with all these memories, and y'all talking about some mad cow disease."

"Please, calm down," Nurse Marci pleaded with me. "We are just trying to help and understand what is going on."

"Calm down? I want some answers."

Marci stepped closer, reaching to touch me but stopping short. "Brian, we need you to work with us. We are getting answers as fast as we can." She rested her hand on my leg. "Please, can you help us?"

I nodded my head. "Okay, I'll make a list."

Dr. Greene yelped. "Great, coordinate with Marci. She's your personal medical assistant, and personal contact."

I raised an eyebrow. "Nurse Marci..."

"Don't worry, she doesn't bite." He laughed. His hand hovered over my knee, but he yanked it back and walked out the door.

After the echo of Dr. Greene's footsteps faded into silence, I glared at Nurse Marci. "Why?"

She folded the paper she was reading and stepped into my space, forcing her body between my legs. Her hands rested on my thighs as she leaned closer, a thin layer of air separating our lips.

"Because I need him back." She pecked me on the lips before I could protest, "So make that list, and we can get together soon. Maybe you can remember more and give me back my Alexi." She pressed that piece of paper into my hand.

"What if it doesn't work like that?"

"I'll get him back one way or the other." Marci winked and, before I could say anything, walked out the door. The paper said, "Call me, anytime" above a phone number and address. I glanced up and could imagine Nurse Marci's crooked grin. That convinced me I could remember for someone and give them their memories.

***

Ralphie's voice pulls me from the ether of memories. "Hey, Brian, you just going to stand there in this heat?" The screen door screeches open. "Come in?"

After a few seconds, Ralphie's face emerges from the fog of the flashback images. It takes Ralphie's hand, squeezing hard on my shoulder, to clear the memory of Marci's deep, long kiss.

"No, I'd love to come in." We shake hands as I step into the dim house.

"Granny is excited to see you." Ralphie looks away.

"She remembers me?"

"No... She thinks you're my dad." Ralphie shakes his head, and points to a photo on the fireplace mantle. "Or you resemble him."

"Oh."

"I don't see it, but I've stopped trying to figure out what's going on."

"Well, hopefully these new tests will help."

"Yeah, hopefully..." His voice fades into awkward silence. "Thanks for taking her. I really appreciate it." He smiles and pulls a twenty-dollar bill out of his wallet. "For gas, Brian. Take it."

"No need. Buy me a beer sometime."

Ralphie pats my shoulder. "You're a good man. Count on that beer!" He waves at the couch. "Have a seat. Let me get Granny."

"Okay." My eyes follow him into the dark shadows of the house. I think of Marci and consider the idea of transferring memories by intimate contact.

Could it work with Granny? Would I have to French kiss Granny?

I close my eyes and imagine the scenario. An image starts to form out of the darkness—

The room was hot and steamy. A hand wiped through the fog and across a steamed-up bathroom mirror. It's Granny; she is younger, standing there nude, posing in the mirror after a shower.

Another figure appeared behind Granny, a tall darkskinned man (not the one in the picture), who wrapped his arms around her.

His voice tickled her ear. "You don't have to come with me. Your parents already hate me enough. If something happened to you..."

She turned and kissed him on the lips. "I'm a grown woman. I want to do this with you."

"But your pops would—"

"Shut up, you fool. You're ruining the moment."

I could feel his calloused hands rubbing along my body, squeezing, pulling me closer to him. His mouth kissing my neck, kissing my breast, kissing my—

"Hey, man, what are you doing?" Ralphie's voice clears the fog, and the vision dissolves into Ralphie and Granny eyeballing me. I follow their gazes and see the pulsing against the fabric of my gym shorts. My hands cover the tent I've pitched.

"I'm sorry, just thinking about—" I catch myself, unsure how to explain what happened. "Um, my wife."

"Not judging, but the bathroom is that way, man. First door on the left." Ralphie's lips curl into a smile. "The water is cold, too."

I spring up, pulling at my shorts, hands covering my crotch. How do you explain this? Getting a boner imagining someone's grandma when she was twenty? Am I a peeping Tom? Ralphie's baritone chuckles echo down the hall after me, as I step into the bathroom. This may be the most embarrassing moment in my life. I shake my head no. There was the rope climb in ninth grade gym class. I close my eyes, allowing the memory to play out—

We were all sitting on the floor, legs crossed, silent, waiting for the gym teacher, Miss Jenkins, to call our names. Janice jumped to attention and her hand brushed the top of my head as she passed. Was this on purpose or an accident? Either way, my heart started to beat faster. Her perfume, fresh cut watermelon on a cool summer day, eddied around me.

I studied her long, muscular legs contracting and relaxing as she climbed that rope. The bell at the top rung out and, before the echoing ding faded from my ears, her body had slithered to the ground. She winked at me and tickled the top of my head as she passed. Her scent filled me with an unknown pleasure.

The smile on my face must have drawn Miss. Jenkins' attention. Her croaky, sharp voice called my name, disrupting the pleasant images of Janice in my head. I stood and leapt for the rope when the pull in my shorts caused my knees to buckle. I stumbled, grabbing the rope for stability. Miss Jenkins covered her mouth to hold in a laugh and pointed.

"You, um." She waved in the direction of the locker rooms. "You should go cool off."

Miss Jenkins' face was beet red. The gym filled with laughter as I duck walked, pulling my shirt down to cover my erection. How could I ask Janice out on a date after this? Our eyes met—could I still ask her out?

She winked and licked her lips. That was enough of an answer. I turned and waddled to the locker room followed by a trail of laughter—

Three knocks on the door pull me back to my reflection. The memory fades and Ralphie's voice booms through the door, "You okay in there?"

I splash ice-cold water on my face. "Yeah, I'm okay."

I study my reflection. No, that was the most embarrassing thing that happened to somebody else; I never got a boner in gym class. I splash another handful of the ice-cold water on my face and wonder if I could crawl into their bathtub and hide forever.

CHAPTER 4

Brian:
38 Days after Event

As I open my car door for Granny, the odor of greasy hamburgers and French fries wafts out. Granny scrunches her nose, shaking her head no like a defiant child.

Ralphie rubs Granny's back. "Come on, Granny, I don't have all day. Plus, you need to see Dr. Greene and Nurse Marci." Ralphie wipes the beads of sweat on his forehead with his hand.

Granny's eyes widen and her lips curl into a smirk. She is wearing makeup, red lipstick applied with artistic precision, mascara, and eyeliner, hair combed straight. I think back to the days after the event and her lifeless expression. Maybe these sessions at the clinic are helping. I wonder if she is remembering how to do those things or if Ralphie does cosmetology in his spare time.

"Hey, don't be making eyes with my grandma!" Ralphie laughs, breaking my study of Granny's face. I duck into the car while Granny and Ralphie fuss at each other. Ralphie leans in and brushes the seat with his hand.

"What happened to your car, you fire the maid?"

"Sorry it's a mess. Been busy."

"Yeah, with all that strenuous typing on your secret novel."

I snap, "Something like that."

"Hey, I'm just jiving you." Ralphie lifts out of the car and helps Granny slide in.

Ralphie kisses Granny on the cheek. "Call me after the appointment, and I'll come back home. Understand?"

Ralphie stands as Granny nods.

"I can take her to lunch." I shout after him.

Ralphie leans back into the car.

"Why?"

"To give you more time, if you need it."

"Okay... Still, call after the appointment."

"Sure."

Ralphie nods and kisses Granny on the cheek again. "You be good, Granny!"

Ralphie wags his finger. "And no funny business." Before I can respond, the door slams shut. I wonder if he will say that every time I give Granny a ride.

Granny does not say much. She gazes wide-eyed out the window. Is she trying to remember? Remember what happened to her life? I whisper to myself, "The event happened, Granny."

I stop at a red light, and the car in front of me blurs. I squeeze my eyes closed, and a vision starts to form.

***

I remember that night, getting home, seeing Brenda at the door. She backed away when I reached for her. My body disjointed from my mind. Every time I glanced at her, she was someone else. My stomach churned, legs buckled, gravity yanked me to the ground. My head drummed on the floor. Her face, her screams were swallowed in a sea of rising darkness.

The scene shifted to faces of nurses and doctors, hovering over me and asking questions.

"Who are you?"

"Brian Watson."

"How old are you?"

"Thirty."

"Who is that person there?"

I looked at her face. The woman smiled like a long-lost friend. Names swirled in my mind. The doctors started scribbling on their pads, and I became even more nervous.

"Brenda. Brenda, my fiancée."

The doctor nodded and squeezed my hand. "Good, good. One more question, then we will let you rest." I nodded. "What else do you remember?"

I shut my eyes and contemplated, what does anyone remember? I was going to be snarky and say, "My life," but flashes of memories hit like a video on 4x. Frame after frame. Experiences lived. Voices filled my head.

"I remember everything!"

"What do you mean everything?"

I squinted, and the faces hovering over me stepped back. My head throbbing, I yelled, "I remember them all!"

The scene fades to black.

***

Granny is tapping on my thigh. "Sweetie."

"Yeah."

"It's green."

I study the light, lift my foot off the brake, and the car lurches forward.

Granny giggles and rubs her hand along my thigh. I pat her hand still.

"Thanks, Granny."

She giggles while moving her hand into her lap. She starts singing.

"You remember anything about the event?"

Granny seems to be in a trance, singing or mumbling to herself. I stop at a red light.

The red brake lights fade, and the white sterile walls of the hospital room swirl into view. A high-pitched voice taunts me.

***

"What do you remember, Brian?"

It was confirmed that I had more memories and voices in my head other than my own. Whose voices was the issue, or was I going bonkers from hitting my head the night before?

The doctor laid pictures out on the table. "Do you recognize any of these people?"

I lifted out of bed a bit and studied the photos. They were various family members and friends. Mom, Dad, Brother, Brenda sticking her tongue out. The doctor cut in. "Why was she doing that?"

"She was being a brat." I could tell by the doctor's twisted smile the answer was not sufficient.

"It was our second date. We were walking down Michigan Ave downtown, and I asked if she was having fun. She turned and said, 'Anything we do together is fun.' I laughed and said, 'You say that to all your dates, I bet.' I took my cell phone out and snapped her picture. I told her I wanted one to remind her she would always have fun with anything we did together. And she stuck her tongue out being a brat."

I glanced between the photo and the woman sitting in the room. I would have never guessed that the smiling woman in this picture was the same one sitting in the corner, alone, forehead wrinkled with worry. Was she the same Brenda, or was this some elaborate prank?

The doctor flipped the picture and read the writing. "Very well." He put the family pictures away and pulled out a thicker stack. Picture of faces in various states of distress or confusion.

"Any of these look familiar? Take your time and think."

The first picture was of Granny. "Mary Collins!"

The doctor flipped the photo. "And where do you know her from?"

"She sat next to me on the plane."

"And she told you her name?"

"No."

"So how'd you know her name?"

I hunched my shoulders.

"How about this one?" The doctor held up another photo.

"That's Dan Smith."

"Are you sure?"

"Yes, he sat next to me."

The doctor murmured as he wrote notes on the photo. He showed me photo after photo, and I answered with a name, an occupation. It didn't matter where they sat on that plane, I knew. The doctor stopped after about twenty photos. He straightened the pile of photos by hitting them against the table. The sharp noise of the photos aligning stung my ears.

"So Brian, it appears something unexplainable has happened."

"What?"

"You may not know this, but everybody that landed with you last night has amnesia."

"Okay, but I'm fine?"

"Yes, you seem to have your memories intact." He cleared his throat and leaned in. His coffee-tinged breath irritated my nose. His whispered, like he was telling me a secret, "You seem to also have everyone else's memories. We need to do more tests, but..." His words faded out and the silence grew as he pulled his face away from mine.

Someone knocked on the room door...

***

The knocking fades into cars honking. I blink my eyes clearing the vision.

Granny pats my leg. "Sweetie, the light is green."

"Yeah." I massage my brow. "Sorry."

Granny responds by tapping on the dashboard and singing, a bluesy kind of tune:

I got my new lover, and he don't know.

I got my new lover, and he don't know.

I'll try to stay the course.

But when he opens his eyes,

I may be at another lover's side.

I park the car at the clinic. "We made it."

Granny stops tapping and pats her rhythm along my thigh. I study her face. Her red lips bend into a smile. Her wrinkles and thinning gray hair fade into that younger woman I saw stepping out the shower—I concentrate on the images forming...

A surge of excitement tingled along my spine. I was afraid my heart would pound out of my chest. I was leaving my home in Chicago with my boyfriend to go tempt fate on that mighty Mississippi river and join the movement. My parents thought I was going to work, but I was passing on the job my dad got me at the meat-processing factory. Passing on the life of a content black woman making life work. Passing on making babies. Struggling to make it by pretending we are living by our own free will.

The makeup compact snapped shut and revealed his smiling face ogling me. I glanced away from his intense gaze, into my lap, smoothing the fabric of my dress along my legs. His hand reached into view and laid on top of my hand, stopping my nervous tugging at the dress. Our fingers interlocked, squeezing together as the Greyhound bus pulled away for trouble.

CHAPTER 5

*Brian:
56 Days after Event*

"So how's it going at the clinic?" Brenda's voice is a whisper above the drone of the car's engine.

"Okay"

"You've been going for several weeks and nothing but okay?"

"Time flies."

"What?"

"Well, Dr. Greene had some ideas..."

"Such as?"

I think about the idea Dr. Greene had, or was it Nurse Marci? Brenda's face is a blurry haze. My eyes keep following the fleeting specks of light floating past. The yellow glow of the streetlamps swirl into a kaleidoscope of storefronts and people ducking in and out of the shadows. Do I know them? Probably not—

"Brian, stop it! You're freaking me out." Her voice, sharp and loud in the small space of the car, cuts through the fog. I have to blink several times for her face to come into focus.

"What?"

"You were zoning out..." She exhales with a puff. "Again."

"Sorry, just going to the airport... It kind of brings back memories."

"Maybe you can leave them there."

"Tried."

"When?"

"Does it matter?"

"I guess not."

The car fills with that low, relaxing drone of engine noise. I think about Nurse Marci—

"So what did Dr. Greene say?"

"That idiot. I have the feeling that Marci has all the brains... And she's easier on the eyes."

"What?" Brenda slaps my arm.

"It's true."

"Well, I don't want to hear about—"

A car cuts us off. "Asshole," Brenda yells as the car jerks to a stop, then squeezes my thigh. "I'm sorry. Just been a long week. Please, tell me about your appointments."

"Just the same shit."

"What kind of stuff?"

"You know those memory tests, scans, and I have to drink that god-awful imaging slurry."

"I'm sorry you have to go through all that."

"Yeah..."

"You said they had a theory."

I consider the last couple visits with Marci and that wet, long kiss. I should tell Brenda. I rub my arm, but this does not seem like the moment.

"Well, the theory is that this memory thing may be infectious or something."

"What?" Brenda turns toward me, wide eyes searching for the punchline. I glance away from Brenda's probing eyes, and a sea of red brake lights fill my vision.

"Watch out, babe!"

My body jerks forward, caught by the seatbelt. The odor of burnt rubber fills the car's interior. Our headlights glow like small yellow suns, inches away from the car in front of us.

"That was close—"

"Infectious?!" Brenda shouts, ignoring the fact she was inches from smashing into that car.

"Yeah, I thought Marci would have called you about coming to the clinic and getting scanned."

"Scanned?" The car creeps forward.

"Yeah, you have to drink that rotten egg drink, and they put you in a MRI type device."

"Marci hasn't talked to me about anything."

"Maybe it's because I told her we've not had relations since the event."

"Relations?"

"Sex."

"Oh... Who the hell calls it relations?"

"Dr. Greene."

"Maybe last time he got some, that's what they called it." Brenda giggles and sneaks a glance at me.

I grin, thinking about the last time we had sex. Has it really been months?

"Well, I can talk with Marci."

"Yup." My mind is still calculating the last time I made love to my fiancée.

Silence grows between us. When was the last time we kissed? The last time our lips embraced? Lips parted, exchanging silent secrets. According to Nurse Marci and Dr. Greene, exchanging memories.

"So were you like making out with everyone on the plane?" Brenda snickers. Her hand slides up my leg and rubs my crotch. "We will work on this lack of relations when I get back."

The car comes to a stop. I lean over to kiss Brenda on her cheek, but she turns her head and our lips meet. I can taste her minty breath as our tongues exchange memories. My hands wiggle under her shirt and squeeze her breast.

She pushes my chest and our mouths part. "It will have to wait, lover boy." She adjusts her top and slides out the car.

Walking to the driver's side, I force myself in between Brenda and the trunk. Our bodies brush together, and she giggles, taking a defensive step backward. I grab her and pull her to my body.

"Have fun with Dr. Shirley tomorrow." She winks.

"Relations?"

She smacks me across the chest. "Stop flirting with your female health professionals."

"I'll try."

She pecks me on the lips and walks away. "You better save all that for me." She blows me a kiss. I catch it and press my hand to my lips. I wait to leave until she disappears into the mass of bodies. I drive away from the airport into the night.

Like that night, the voices in my head chatter all the way home.

The house is quiet, unlike my mind. How long will the voices torment me tonight, without her? I go to bed early. Without Brenda to fill her half of the bed, I toss and turn. The darkness wraps around me. It takes me all night to unknot myself.

***

I only slept a few hours last night, and I have to resist falling to sleep once I lay on Dr. Shirley's couch. The room darkens, and she starts counting in that *tick-tock* monotonous voice. My muscles relax, and the gray fog pulls me into comforting darkness.

"You've not gone to sleep again?" Dr. Shirley's voice cuts through the darkness, and I realize she is several feet away.

"No, just trying to acclimate to the darkness, fixing the room in my mind like we talked about."

"Good, let me know when you're good and comfy."

In this state of visual deprivation, every noise is amplified. Dr. Shirley's feet scrape out of her shoes, toes scrunching in the carpet. The *tick-tock-tick-tock* of that clock punctures my skull like a pile driver. The leather on the couch crinkles every time I move a muscle. I can hear my heart thumping, drumming faster against my breastbone.

"How are you feeling?" A woman's voice, not Dr. Shirley's, echoes between my ears.

"Who said that?"

"Over here."

A woman is sitting in a rocking chair, backlit by the orange-yellow hues of a rising sun peaking over the horizon.

"So you finally come back to see me," she calls out.

I squint, trying to make out the figure. I rub my eyes. The sun dims, and I can see her.

"It's me, Jeni."

"I don't know anybody named Jeni."

Jeni smiles, tapping her head. "Think, I'm still in there."

Jeni floats off her chair. In a flicker, the distance of a fingertip separates us. She places her cold hand on my shoulder, and a flood of images flash in front of my eyes like a movie being rewound. The scrolling images stop and the memory plays—

Everything happened so fast, the car fishtailing, screaming, yelling, a utility pole, silence except for the tat-tat-tat of rain on the car and the crackle of thunder in the distance. I laid my head against the headrest. Lungs heavy, but the pressure relieved itself as the airbag deflated.

Jeni was laughing or sobbing. I grabbed her arm, but my seatbelt kept her out of reach. Jeni's head rotated, and she smiled at me. The windshield was spider-webbed. Lightning illuminated the car's interior and seconds later the thunderclap caused Jeni to yelp.

Even though the car was totaled, there was no motivation to get out of the car and get wet. Figured it was best to stay put and enjoy the tat-tat-tat of rain and the sha-boom, sha-boom of the passing thunder. I released my belt and squeezed Jeni's arm. I coughed and gasped, trying to clear the white airbag powder from my throat, I could taste the electrified air and something else—the pungent, sweet aroma of gasoline.

I opened my eyes wider, trying to focus on the black snakes slithering along the road. Fire-orange tongues forked in and out against the inky black sky. The dancing snakes mesmerized me, twirling pinwheels of sparks, sparks getting closer. I was getting drunk on that smell of gasoline. I rubbed my hand over my eyes, realizing those were no snakes. I would have to get Jeni and myself out of this twisted mound of metal.

With all of my strength, I climbed out of the car, falling out of the window onto the hot, wet mud. The cool rain washed the sticky, copper-tasting blood from my head into my mouth. The stink of gasoline watered my eyes as I moved around the car. Jeni's body was motionless. I pulled on the door but, like mine, it was stuck. I leaned through the window, struggling to get her seatbelt undone. In hindsight, I should have done that before walking around the car.

The rain was falling faster, raindrops beating into my skin. My hands nervous and wet, I pushed and pulled the belt buckle until it unlatched. I pulled Jeni through the window. Her dress snagged on something. I pulled harder, and she was released into my arms.

I laid her on the ground as I rested my tired arms, taking in a deep lungful of gasoline vapor. Jeni was on the edge of unconsciousness. Her leg was cut, or maybe something worse; with every flash of lightning, the bottom half of her torn yellow sun dress stained redder. In between claps of thunder, she whimpered, "Get moving." Maybe it was the rain-soaked wind whispering in my ear.

I lifted her stiff body—resisting gravity, resisting me. But as I cradled her in my arms, her body went limp. I carried her across that abandoned corn field, heading for old Magee's long forgotten farmhouse—

A voice in the ether asks, "Why were you out in a storm with your lover?" The scene starts to play again.

I search the flood of memories, and I'm still not sure why I decided to bring her out here. Jeni was pregnant, and I remember this may be our last chance to be alone. Something about being spontaneous, romantic, and re-kindling our passion like in the movies; where the black night sky is cloudless, and a bright, hot-white gibbous moon makes romance easy. But even before we spread the blanket and opened the bottle of sparkling grape juice, I should have noticed those ominous clouds creeping in the distance. The sudden rain caught us kissing, running to the car. Soaked, but laughing, and that kiss...wet and furious, like the approaching storm. Driving fast, trying to make the moment last. Rain. Thunder. Lighting. Car spinning. The images fade into black—

"Well, Doc, you know the rest."

That voice again calls from the ether. "No, tell me what happened after you pulled Jeni from the car."

The vision continues—

The wind whispered in my ear, calling me a damn fool—or was that Jeni? I stopped and listened. Nothing. Her limp, lifeless arm stiffened, reaching around me, grabbing onto my shoulder, as if she were carrying me. Carrying us. I told her everything was going to be okay, and we were close to shelter. Jeni smiled, resting her arms on her round belly.

As the rain pounded harder, I stumbled through weedy, unattended volunteer corn stalks and vines that seemed to grab and tug at my feet. Once we made it to the cover of the porch, I laid Jeni on the weather-worn wood planks to work on opening the door. Pushing on that old wooden oak door, which opened with unexpected ease, released an uninviting, stale, musty, dry air. But I had no choice.

I carried Jeni into that house. I kicked the door shut with my foot, and the house became quiet as mausoleum except for the crackle of thunder, the rain, and Jeni sobbing or laughing.

Exhausted, I sat on the floor holding Jeni. As I relaxed, studying the dilapidated house, Jeni's body convulsed, and I could barely hold her—

Explosions fill my ears. A flash of lightning floods my vision. My eyes open, adjusting to the light, and there is Dr. Shirley hovering over me, shaking me awake.

"See, you did it to me again."

I blink my eyes a few times, still adjusting to the intense flood of light. "What? Where am I?"

"You're still in my office. You were going on a bit about Jeni and a car crash. Then you started snoring." Dr. Shirley laughs.

"What? I don't know what you're talking about," I say, rubbing the sleep out of my eyes.

Dr. Shirley raises an eyebrow. "So you have no clue who Jeni is, or anything about a car crash?"

"No, I don't know a Jeni." Dr. Shirley scribbles something on a pad. Anxiety fills my voice. "Funny, I don't ever remember meeting a Jeni."

Dr. Shirley pulls a folder out, scanning through several sheets. I catch a glimpse of the flickering sheets and their photos.

"Are those the people from the plane?"

Dr. Shirley nods and closes the folder.

"How is Brenda doing with your memories?"

I avoid Dr. Shirley's intense gaze.

"She is adjusting."

"Adjusting?"

"I'm all over the place mentally. One day I'm depressed, the next anxious. I can't sleep." I grin. "Except when I'm on your couch."

Dr. Shirley smiles. "Your sense of humor is intact." She pulls a pad out of her desk drawer. "Listen, Brian, I want to give you some medicine that will—"

I spring out the seat and wave my arms. "No medicine. I don't want to be a mindless drone."

"Brian, sit down, please, and let me finish. I want to give you medical marijuana."

I fall into the soft couch and consider how it would feel to get stoned. It's been years, but memories of playing poker, smoking a bowl with several friends fill my mind.

"Here you go. There's a dispensary around the corner." She slides the paper across the desk.

"No, I don't need that."

"So what do you need?"

"Sleep, food, and creative love."

"Take this prescription, and I'll guarantee the first two." Dr. Shirley smiles, adjusting her thick-framed glasses and pulling a rebellious blonde curl behind her ear.

I take the prescription off the desk. The paper is chalky and thick. I fold it and shove it into my pocket.

"Okay, so let's meet in two weeks. Bring your recordings."

"The recordings are dumb." I roll my eyes.

"They will help us compartmentalize your visions and make sense of them."

"That will help me make sense."

She follows my extended finger to the folder of photos. She shakes her head. "I don't think that would be good."

"Yes, maybe putting a face to memories could help with the compartmentalization."

Dr. Shirley taps her pen on the desk several times. "Okay"

"Great—"

"Not so fast. I'll give you a copy of the photos, but you promise to talk to me about the visions. Under no circumstances are you to visit the folks you find in here."

"I promise!" I blurt out too fast.

Dr. Shirley raises an eyebrow. "Don't make me regret this."

"I won't visit anyone without your consent." I give her a soldier's salute.

"Okay, go wait in the lobby. I'll have Sandra make a copy for you."

I wait until I'm in my car to open the folder. On top of the photos is a yellow sheet of paper. Big, looping cursive words are scribbled across the lines. I read them out loud, "Call me before you do something stupid. Unlike what the newspaper article said, you're not a superhero!"

I crumple the note, throwing it to the floor. I study each picture, small three-inch images. Confused faces, hollow eyes like bottomless pits, haunting me. There is information below each face: name, address, caretaker, etc.

I turn the page; there she is. The girl in my dreams. I found you. I close the folder and drive away.

CHAPTER 6

Brian:
56 Days after Event

I'm not sure why Jerry—my manager, wannabe movie agent, and childhood friend—would pick a place I hate to have lunch. He does this to gain an advantage with clients, but me? Jerry's logic is that if you hate the food and the highbrow service, he will seem like a true gem.

I pull into the parking lot. I should have refused to meet him here, but I've been spending too much time in the house working on my novel and could use the distraction. A loud cackle breaks the silence. I recognize that laugh. Jerry is flirting with the waitress.

I hate this thick Chicago heat laying on me, like a blanket, more than I hate gastro-pubs. Gastro, molecular, and pub don't belong in the same sentence, much less the same title. In my opinion, it's a way to charge one hundred percent more for fifty percent less beef on a stale bun. But the bun was incubated with healthy gut bacteria dipped in liquid nitrogen. Translation, I pulled it from the freezer and wiped it on my butt to thaw it. What a joke, but hey, Jerry is paying. So overpriced, frozen butt-wiped buns it is.

I pull hard on the gaudy brass handle, swinging the fake barn door open. A rush of cool air, and a pungent citrus fragrance tickles my nose once I enter the dim interior. The citrus mingles with a raw meaty metallic aroma. As my eyes adjust, the kitchen comes into view—a white chef hat floating around like an ocean buoy. A large meat cleaver swirls, glinting, above the chef's pudgy smiling face, his large horse-like teeth, his eyes small but round. The cleaver drops with a swish and a solid wet thud.

"A table for one?" a voice calls at me. I spin around, and a tall, frail woman appears out of the shadows.

She calls again, her voice filled with excitement or disgust. Maybe both, "Table for one?"

"No, I'm meeting someone." I take another step. My mouth salivates as I inhale the smoky, aromatic alliums.

"Do you know if the person you're meeting is already here?"

I glance around. The small entryway opens into a large, cavernous room with about twenty tables, a long bar hugging the wall.

The restaurant is empty, except for the two men dressed in suits at a corner table. One of them notices me watching. He hushes their conversation and hides his face behind a menu. Through the patio windows, I spy Jerry's silhouette.

"He's out on the patio."

"Great. You can go out, and I'll let your waitress know."

Have I been here before? The way the filtered light illuminates the tabletops. The negative space created by the oversized chairs and their geometric arrangement. The random beams of overhead light give way to shades of purple and deep red flooring. The lines of repurposed wood frame the patio windows. I wish I had my camera. I swallow gulps of air, letting the raw meat, fruit, and spice fill my lungs. Homestead, the perfect name for this place. Smiling, I pull the large wrought iron patio door handle, flooding the space with thick hot, summer air and light. I embrace both and step out onto the patio.

Jerry turns as I get closer to the table. His oval, too-small-for-his-face, neon orange glasses sit on top of his nose. Skin bulges under the pressure of the eyeglass temples, accentuating his fat, blushing cheeks. His face looks like a ladybug; again, I wish I had my camera.

Jerry stands with a huff, extending his hand. His fat, stubby fingers are full of gold rings. Jerry looks like an overweight, semi-retired, 70s porno star, minus the pork-chop sideburns. His floral print shirt bursts with black curly hair escaping at the top. Too much man to contain. Too much man, indeed.

The waitress's upper lip rises on one side, and her hands are on her hips. Her full lips are vivid red. Jet black, straight hair frames her round face.

"Take a picture, it will last longer." She winks, and her lips twist into a smile.

I look away, sitting in my seat. Jerry plops down with a grunt and rubs his hands together. "Like I was saying, sweetheart, do me and my friend right and I may give you a few leads in the biz." His loud bird cackle of a laugh fills the small patio space.

"Yes, Sir."

"You can call me Big J."

She smirks and cuts her eyes to me. "What are you drinking, honey?"

I'm trying to place her familiar face. Where do I know her from? "What's good?"

She leans over the table to grab the drink menu when she jerks up squealing. Jerry cackles, his hand retracting from her butt. She steps away from us and taps Jerry on the shoulder. "You stop that!" Her voice raspy but feminine.

"Come on, Jerry."

Jerry waves his hands. "I'm just having a little fun. Right, babe?"

"Yeah." She rolls her eyes. She squeezes my shoulder. "We have several craft beers on tap." She smiles, teeth perfect, straight, and white. Her voice has an artificial sharp twang to it.

A party flashes in my mind. An art opening in Las Vegas. That's where I recognize her from. But, funny, I have never been to an art opening in Vegas. Or have I gone and forgotten?

"You're a model, right?"

Her smile grows. She puts her hand on her hip and winks. "Who told you that?" She asks Jerry.

"I saw an art show in Vegas." She steps into my space. Her scent is earthy and has a pleasant cinnamon aroma.

"You know Rodriguez?"

I raise my eyebrows and shake my head and mumble, "Doesn't sound familiar."

"Sorry, his first name is Eduardo."

"Maybe."

"Has to be him. That's the only artist I ever modeled for. We were..." Her voice fades into mumbles as though she is convincing herself. "We are partners."

I smile. "He has a lot of talent."

She twirls her hair. "He is a genius. I mean, his mind was—is—so beautiful."

"In what way?"

"In every way." She giggles. "If you know what I mean." Her hand massages my shoulder.

"Yes, I think I do." I close my eyes. Her scent, her fingers kneading the knots out of my muscle. Did we know each other? Did we make love in a garden? Hands remember—

"Hey, I want a little of that action." Jerry hoots.

She wags her finger at Jerry. "I'm keeping my eyes on you."

"Just the way I like it." Jerry moistens his plump lips with a rotation of his fat red tongue.

"So what are you two having?"

I glance over the menu. "House Margarita."

Jerry snatches the menu from me. "I'll have this IPA."

"Great, I'll be back with these drinks and can take your order."

Jerry whistles as she walks into the main dining room. He reaches his hand out. That fat hand full of rings whose fingers violated Angela—a good friend, a good lover, of mine. I refuse to shake Jerry's hand in protest, interlocking my fingers so they don't betray me.

"It's like that now?" Jerry rubs his hand.

"Come on, man. You want respect, you have to show respect."

"What the hell are you talking about?" Jerry pulls his glasses off and squints, studying me.

"Don't give me that look, Jerry."

"I just want to know what your deal is. Since that plane thing, you have been a real asshole."

"I'm the ass? You're the one pinching Angela's ass. You know how I feel about my muses."

"Who the hell is Angela?" Jerry whines, like an apologetic child.

"Angela is our waitress, and we—"

"Our waitress? I didn't know you two—" Jerry leans a bit closer and starts whispering, "You dog. How long have you been hitting that? Behind Lee's back?" Jerry holds up his fat hand, balled into a fist. "I knew you were a player, but damn. Leave some hotties for the rest of us."

I frown, shaking my head side to side.

"Oh, you're going to leave me hanging? It's like that."

Why does the name Lee sound familiar? My fiancée is Brenda. I want to ask who Lee is, but Jerry grabs my arm and starts whining—

"What? You want me to say I'm sorry for flirting and pinching the ass of your muse?" Jerry shakes his head and folds his arms across his chest. "Okay, I'm sorry." He lifts his hand into a fist. "Bros before hoes."

I shake my head and tap my fist against his. "Just don't do it again."

Jerry grunts, "I mean talk about the pot calling the kettle black. You're the asshole having the affair."

Jerry squeezes his glasses onto his face. Minutes of silence pass. The sweltering air fills the void. The sky is a warm blue with a few wisps of milky white clouds. I enjoy days like this.

Angela walks onto the patio with two drinks. Her stride is long and exaggerated. Her hair, now braided into a ponytail, swings over her shoulder. Watching her move, I am overwhelmed with an intense desire to create, my imagination wild with colors and landscapes. I pull my notebook out and start writing fast.

"Hey, that's what I like to see my artist doing—getting inspired after calling me an asshole!"

Angela sits the drinks on the table. "Hey, what you writing?"

"He is writing you a love poem, I bet," Jerry's heckles with a snorting laugh grabbing his drink.

"That's sweet." Her cold hand brushes my neck. The sensation shocks me. I stop writing and jerk my head up.

What the hell am I doing here? I glance at Jerry's grinning, ultra-white teeth. We are having lunch, but why is the waitress massaging my neck?

"Oh, I'm sorry." Her face turns beet red as she jumps to attention. "I thought it was okay to read it." She steps away. "But I know how you artist types can be."

"No, it's not that. I was just zoning out."

"I'm sorry if I messed you up."

"Never."

Angela's lips curled into a smile. "You sure I didn't mess you up?"

"No worries."

"Promise?" Angela's hand squeezes my shoulder.

"I'll let you read it when it's finished."

Jerry clears his throat. "I'm sure Angela knows all about these artist types, and how to get them in the mood." He slaps the table and reaches for his drink.

Angela spins on her heels. "Enjoy your drinks. I'll be back for your orders in a second."

I look at the beer. "I thought I ordered a margarita."

"I think you will like this better." She winks. "It's Eduardo's favorite." Before I can say anything, she disappears into the dining room.

I lift the glass to my nose, sniffing the dank, grapefruit aroma. I hate beer, but I take a long, slow sip. I swallow, and Angela was right I do like this.

Jerry lifts his glass in a toasting gesture. "Cheers."

Our glasses clank. Jerry takes a swallow of his drink, shakes his head, and says, "So you and her are an item?"

"Where the hell would you get the idea that I was doing anything with her?"

"You just told me she was your muse, and you were offended that I pinched her butt." Jerry pulls his glasses off. "You okay, buddy?"

"Yeah, I'm fine." A sharp pain pings behind my eyes. I rub my temples. "I just have these intense visions of other people's memories when I come in contact with some trigger."

"Trigger?"

"You know, music, a face, a smell, a touch, or a place. You know that saying, 'This song really takes me back?'" I put the notebook away. "Well, that happens to me, but I just get random flashbacks of memories, and personalities take over."

"Man, that's wild." Jerry slaps the tabletop. "We should be tapping into this for a new book or something."

"No, it's not that easy. What I want to do is find these people, make things right, and get these people out of my head."

"That's why you should write the book."

"I don't know." I scratch my head, contemplating what Jerry is proposing. "Maybe, but the memories are too random. It's hard to put a face to the experience."

"What do you mean?" Jerry takes a sip of his drink and bobs his head in approval of the taste. "This drink has a bitter asparagus taste to it. Not bad though."

"Unless the person is staring in a mirror or a reflective surface, I have no clue who the memory belongs to." I take a sip of my drink.

"So you must see a lot of naked women, men, and sex. That would be better than a porn website."

"It's not like that." I shake my head, hoping that's not the way it works. That could explain getting random boners like a horny sixteen-year-old. I should check, but I bet there were a few teenagers on that plane.

Jerry's voice cuts into my thoughts. "So how are you going to piece things together?"

"Well, I got this." I pull out the folder Dr. Shirley gave me and hand it to Jerry.

"I think I see. As you remember things, you will try to assign a face to it."

"Yup!"

"Anything interesting?"

"Yeah, Mary Collins. Or, as I call her, Granny."

"Why her?"

"Been spending the most time with her and her family, I guess."

"What, did you dig up some juicy dirt? Could use that to get some extra payouts if someone important was on the plane." Jerry starts flipping through the photos, "I'd bang her—"

I snatch the folder from him. "Stop fucking around. This is serious."

"Okay, okay!" Jerry releases the edge of the folder and takes another sip of his drink.

I read the notes I scribbled on the photos as I remember the disjointed story. "So Granny was on a bus to Mississippi with her boyfriend. They were going to join a sit-in or rally. At some point, the bus stops at a rest station. She goes off to use the colored-only bathroom. When she flicks the light on, there are three hooded men waiting in surprise. They beat—"

I stop reading as Angela approaches the table.

"You guys ready to order?" Angela glances between Jerry and me. "You guys need a few more minutes?"

"No, we can order. I was just telling Jerry to stop pinching asses, or we couldn't be friends anymore!"

Angela grins. "That's good advice, or else you never know what could happen." She winks at me. Jerry and I order food and wait for Angela to leave us alone on the patio once again.

Jerry leans in. "So what happened to Granny?"

"She went back to Chicago, recovered in some time, and lived out her life."

"Why is this interesting?!"

"Well, that's a different question. In the bathroom struggle, Granny managed to pull the hood off one of the attackers. Now this is where it gets strange. I was seeing the memory through Granny's viewpoint until she pulled the hood off. Then my viewpoint switched to that of the attacker. I felt his youthful anger and misunderstood rage toward the changing world. He was trying to prove a point about his power and place in the world. Crazy, right?"

"Yeah, I guess. Not sure I follow."

"Granny was on the plane, and I got her memories. I see through her eyes. The fact that my viewpoint switched, and I got a new set of emotions and visions, means that person was on the plane."

Jerry runs his hand through his curly, golden-blond hair as the wheels in his head make the connection. He points to the folder. "That means you know who this fucker is that hurt Granny. We can make him pay."

"What? No. I mean, I guess."

Jerry waves his hand like he is swatting at bees. "What do you mean, you guess? You—" Jerry waves his hand between us. "We need to make those assholes pay for the crimes they thought they'd get away with."

"Jerry, calm down. It is not that simple."

"Oh yeah, it is that simple. We find this guy and beat the crap out of him or call the police."

"And what, Jerry? Ask him if he remembers beating up a black woman in a bathroom in the 60s?"

Jerry huffs. "Yeah, I forgot he doesn't have any memories."

"Exactly, Batman!"

"We have to do something," Jerry whispers.

"Yeah, it gets a bit more complicated. I googled him, and he is" I shake my head "no, was a lawyer."

"Ah, we definitely need to fry his ass."

"Jerry, look what I found about him. He became a civil rights lawyer and activist. Here read this."

Jerry snatches the printed paper out of my hand, head moving as he scans the lines of text. The angry lines on his forehead smooth and his hand relaxes, letting the sheet of paper fall to the table.

Jerry's mouth hangs open, his dazzling white teeth contrasting against his red tongue.

"Jerry, you okay."

He pulls his glasses off and starts rubbing his eyes again. "You're right, writing a book is thinking too small. We should be thinking TV and movies. I know a few people, we could—"

I shake my head no. "You know I don't do things like that. I could not exploit these people like that."

"Come on man, we are talking big money." Jerry rubs his thumb and forefinger together.

"These are not my stories to tell."

"If they don't remember, maybe it's your job to do the telling. Maybe it's your superpower."

"I don't—"

Jerry reaches out and grabs my arm. "Just think about it. Forget the money! This may be the only way these people, their families, ever get their stories back." Jerry takes a sip of his drink. "I know if I had somebody on that plane and they lost their memories, I'd want to hear their story."

I consider Jerry's points. But how do you tell people? Should I skip the unpleasant details and just give the punchline? Maybe Dr. Shirley can help. I scribble these questions on the paper Jerry had and shove it into my folder.

"I'll think about it Jerry, but I'm no superhero."

"Call yourself anything you want, just think about it." He holds his glass up. "Cheers."

"Cheers."

Angela appears with two plates of food. As she sits them on the table, I remark in a sarcastic voice, "Thanks, Sugar-pop!"

Angela cocks her head and raises an eyebrow. "How do you know that? I mean, only a handful of people know my nickname."

"It's a long story."

"Aren't they all?" Angela pulls a chair to our table and sits down. "Your friends inside left a few minutes ago, and you're my only table, so let's hear this long story."

Friends inside? My mind jumps to the two guys in suits. I try to remember their faces, but I get nothing.

Angela stuffs a French fry from Jerry's plate into her mouth. "Go ahead, I'm all ears."

"So you remember that plane that landed and everyone forgot their memories?" Angela nods her head yes. "Well, I was the one guy who remembered everything."

She mumbles into her hands that are covering her face. "Those guys were not lying... My Eduardo."

I push my plate aside and flip through the photos. Eduardo. I stop and scribble artist on his picture. Angela's name is underneath, listed as caretaker.

She whispers in my ear. "So my darling Eduardo is in that mind of yours?"

CHAPTER 7

Brian:
83 Days after Event

I sweep my arm across the bed, and Brenda is gone. I jerk up and call out her name, but no reply. I relax as the numbers on the clock form into recognizable shapes. I realize that she has left for work. I overslept, or has she been avoiding me by leaving early? Or am I avoiding her by waking later? She goes to bed early, and I am a night owl. I do my best writing at night. Are we drifting apart? Should I say something?

My head spins with information and random memories. I have a strong desire to spend time with Granny. Her smiling face brings clarity to my scrambled brain. Her voice, that song she sings, *I got my new lover, and he don't know...* drowns out all of their voices. I need her like a shot of whiskey. What excuse can I use to spend time with her?

I could call Ralphie and say we need to go to the clinic, but then Ralphie will ask about Dr. Greene and Nurse Marci. Those two irritate me. Their hushed whispers. Constant note taking. The strange make-shift clinic they have me meet them in. Tests done, but they never deliver results. But there was that wet, deep kiss. Maybe I should schedule an appointment with Nurse Marci again. Test her hypothesis about memory transfer being a disease that can be passed with deep, wet kisses that taste like minty toothpaste and lattes.

What would Granny think? What would Brenda think? What would they think about Angela? Maybe I should call

Angela and we can have a long philosophical conversation about art, camera lighting, and deep, wet kisses.

I throw the covers off me. The chill of the room hits my nude body. Why don't I have clothes on? The fabric of the bed scratches my skin. I search the floor for my underwear. I have a desire to go for a run, a long run along Lake Michigan. A run where my muscles stretch and contract to the soundtrack of my thumping heart.

I dress from the scattering of clothes littering the bedroom floor. I sniff the socks before putting them on. Why? The faint stink of corn chips is not a strong enough motivator for me to find a new pair, plus it's getting late and I don't enjoy steaming under Chicago's summer sun.

I dig through my dresser drawer searching for my dry-fit shirts, but all I can find are cotton blends. My compression shorts are also missing. Is it laundry day or should I buy more running attire? I squeeze my shoes on, toes are pinching, there is no arch support, and the compression in the sole is gone. I did not realize my running shoes were overused.

I tap on my smartphone. Where are my running apps? I scream in frustration and slam the door closed.

It must have rained last night. That petrichor sweet scent of wet concrete hangs in the damp air. My muscles are tight. I bend, stretching, my hands reaching, holding my shins before the rubber band of hamstring resists. I hold the pose for a count of ten. I take off east for the running trail along Lake Michigan.

I have only run half a mile to the lakeshore path, and my legs are starting to cramp. I did not hydrate myself this morning. I slow my pace. I stop and stretch out the kink in my calf muscle. I find my stride and pacing once I get to the gravel trail closer to the lake's edge. The water sloshes over the rocks and the cool spray is refreshing. The skyscrapers of Chicago jut into the lake shore. The noise of the city fades away into the squawks of seagulls gliding over the turquoise water. White puffy contrails crisscross the sky, fading into the blue.

I pass the one-mile marker, my muscles loosening, and my breathing steady. I quicken my pace. The steady flow of air through my nose and out my mouth is relaxing. The lake path is busy.

Runners, sweaty and hot. Faces flush with red. Tired arms pumping the lake-cooled air. The freshest runners wave with their entire arm. Their hand is an extension of their stamina.

The spent runners nod or wiggle a few fingers, gulping for air.

There are folks on bikes—skintight outfits, tight butts spilling around small, uncomfortable plastic bike seats. A courtesy warning, "On your right" or "On your left." A nod and a blur of neon outfit fading into the distance.

There are dog walkers, lazy and slow.

Stroller walkers with curious children pulling against the buckle—a shaken bottle of energy ready to pop. A polite hello from a stressed mom, praying the restraining stroller straps will hold.

The lake path is busier than I imagined or remembered, maybe both. Then I remember, today is Thursday, and the path is always busy on Thursdays. Something about the weekend approaching and getting a few extra laps in before the weekend binge.

As everyone buzzes past, I spend the most time concentrating on their faces. I used to play the game where you pick a person and create a story about their lives. I'm afraid to do that since the Event because the story may be real.

All the faces seem familiar, like memories waiting to be revealed.

A shirtless man passes with an energetic wave. His face is familiar, and I return the gesture. His smiling face lingers in my mind. Do I know him? Maybe he has one of those familiar faces. I stop torturing myself by studying the lake's corrugating surface.

I pass the two-mile marker. Two miles finished. Another two and I'll make the turn for home. As I gaze out at the lake's horizon, the noise of footsteps crunching loose gravel pulls my attention to the path. Someone is running in-stride with me. He has an attractive face. Attractive? He winks at me, and my face flushes with heat.

I slow my pace a bit and let him pass. I study his arms like glistening pistons moving with the same tempo as his smooth stride. His tanned skin accentuates his well-defined back muscles. My eyes study his tight running shorts. His tight, firm, familiar butt.

He slows his pace. "Have we met before?" His voice is deep, New York or Philly accent. "You look familiar." His hazel eyes scanning up and down my body.

"What?"

"The way you looked at me when we passed earlier, I thought maybe we knew each other." He grins. "Hopefully, we have not..." His voice fades into the crunch of gravel underfoot.

"No, I don't think we have."

Have we met before? My eyes follow the contours of his face. I would have remembered this man.

"So what is your name?" he asks.

"My name is—" I'm drawing a blank on my name. The pause is a second but seems like minutes. "George!" I blurt out the first name that enters my mind.

"I know a George that runs...well, used to run this trail every day almost. He has a running group. Good guy." He studies my face. "Different George for sure. He is white, shorter, and not nearly as handsome as you."

My cheeks tingle as I try to stop myself from smiling. "And your name?"

He runs ahead a bit, and I call after him again, "What's your name?"

"Oh, I'm sorry, just thinking about poor George and his accident." He shakes his head. "My name is Larry." He slows his pace and extends his arm. His hand is sweaty, soft, and warm.

"Nice to meet you, Larry." An image pops into my head. "Not Larry Cotton, by any chance?"

"Yeah, my last name is Cotton. How'd you know that?"

He runs off the path and slows to a walk. I chase behind, I can feel my lungs burning as I catch up. Gulping air, I can taste his spicy cologne. I stop walking and close my eyes. His image in my mind forms out of the gray fog—

I was at a party, a black-tie fundraiser. He winked at me from across the room and motioned his head for me to follow him down a hallway. The scene shifted to the dark hallway. Our bodies pressed against each other in the tight space. He leaned down to me, his mouth opened, and his tongue is rough, tasting like pepper and gin. His hand squeezed my butt and pulled me closer into his space—

"You okay?" his voice calls from the ether, and I remember his face.

"Yeah." I take another gulp of air, of his scent. "We met at a party. A while back, remember."

"Party? I think I'd recall a handsome face like yours." He grins.

"Well, it was a while ago."

He steps closer. The minty alcoholic vapor of his mouthwash tickles my nose. "Well, I want to finish my run, but a few of us are meeting at the smoothie place by Montrose Harbor." He gives my shoulder a squeeze. "Maybe I'll see you there."

I nod. "Yeah, maybe."

He brushes against me as he starts to run the other way. "See you soon, George."

I nod again, smiling and waving. I gaze at his flexing muscles for a bit until he disappears into a group of runners.

I turn, running, excited about meeting Larry at the smoothie place. Two miles or so to go. I run faster, hoping to get there early and have time to wipe off the sweat. The passing faces are undefined blurs as I daydream about Larry. That night, that fleeting embrace. That morning waking tangled in his arms, legs, and warm soft blankets.

The happy memory fuzzes out into tightening pain across my chest. My heart is pounding, pounding its way out of my body. Stabbing pain spider-webs along my left calf. I hop off the path, grabbing at the tight ball of muscle, rubbing hard to work out the knot. Leaning against a park bench, the thump of my heart pounding in my head. The murmur of concerned voices nagging at me. Gulping air, chest burning, rubbing my calf harder, my stomach clenches and I fall to my knees. The fresh cut grass smells like a slice of ripe watermelon. A puff of grass clippings and pollen tickles my nose.

Unable to catch my breath, combined with the allergens in the grass, I start coughing—bile burns my throat—gagging, puking. I spit the frothy strand of saliva spooling from my mouth into a watery mess on the ground. The acidic stink makes my stomach clench again. I close my eyes and concentrate on relaxing my body. A scene starts playing—

I was in a room lined with tall bookcases. A large window overlooked the city. I was sitting behind a large wooden desk. Marci and Dr. Greene walked into the office. They began pulling off their lab coats and hushing their conversation. Marci grunted and pushed past Dr. Greene, her heels tapping on the floor. Marci stood by the corner of the desk, hands on her hips and glaring at me.

"What's wrong with you now?" I asked.

She leaned in and whispered, "You think you're funny?"

"About what?"

Marci sat on the desk. Her short, pleated skirt rose revealing the lacey band of her thigh-high stockings, and a peek of skin. "The master files have been encrypted; you know we have a meeting with investors."

"And...?"

Marci folded her arms across her chest. "And they will want to see something. Not everyone has a cushy faculty job to fall back on."

I rolled my eyes, taunting in a sing-song voice, "Marci and her flunky, Dr. Greene. Up shit's creek without a paddle." I chuckled and continued with a parental tone. "You two got one fat check and now need to deliver on something you did not have the right to sell. That's why you don't make deals with the devil."

Marci's face twisted with disgust. "Alexi, my sweetie," Marci laid her hand on top of mine and gave it a squeeze. "Listen, we are so close, and with this infusion of cash we can move things forward."

"No, you listen. I think the idea of reading memories and helping people deal with repressed memories or traumatic events is incredible. But now we have stumbled on the power to have memories transmitted, to then manipulate their memories without them knowing. Doesn't that freak you out a little bit?" I glanced at Dr. Greene playing with the buttons on his lab coat. "You have any objections? Or did you already pad your pockets?"

His head jerked up. "What?"

Marci crossed her legs. "Alexi, you always have to be a good guy. Maybe that's why it didn't work out between us." She winked and un-crossed her legs. "There's always second chances, right? I know you can be bad." Her foot brushed against my thigh.

I pulled away. "Stop it Marci! Here's the deal: I set up an RSA encrypted folder, all three of us will have passcodes, and we all agree what to do with this technology."

Dr. Greene snorted and hunched his shoulders in a cartoon sort of way when he caught Marci's glare. "What? Sounds good to me."

Marci shook her head and mimicked Dr. Greene's words in a high-pitched voice. "Sounds good to me." She flicked her hand at him. "You're nothing but a spineless bastard."

"Kids, let's get along. Marci, enter your passcode please." I scooted my chair away from the computer to give Marci plenty of room, but she leaned her butt into my space anyway.

"No peeking." Marci pressed the 'enter' key and stood, brushing her hands along the sides of her skirt. "Was that good for you?"

"Your turn, Mark." I stood and let Dr. Greene have the chair.

While Dr. Greene was contemplating his passcode, Marci leaned into me. Her face was close to mine. Dr. Greene coughed and Marci pulled away.

Dr. Greene stood. "So what now?"

Marci grabbed my hand, but I pulled away. "Yes, Alexi, what now?"

"We finish the controls and uncover the full power of what these nano-transmitters can do."

Dr. Greene started for the door. "Sounds like a reasonable plan, but how do we know you won't hack those codes?"

"Ha, look it up; RSA prime factorization-based encryption is as close to hack proof as possible. We would need every supercomputer in the world to calculate the code, and that would be for just one code."

Marci smirked and taped my temple. "You will reveal all your secrets to me."

I held in a laugh. "A little melodramatic. All you have to do is play nice. I have never held any secrets from you."

"Yeah, what about Leslie?" Marci winked. "Have you told her about any of this?"

I glanced between Marci and Dr. Greene. "You leave Leslie out of this," I said, pointing at Marci, "especially you."

Dr. Greene snorted and adjusted his glasses. "She will stay out as long as you don't get in the way of our thirty-million-dollar research center."

"What did you say?"

Marci spun, glaring at Dr. Greene. "Get the hell out of here, loudmouth!"

"I'm sorry, Marci, I thought..."

"No one asked you to think." *Marci extends her arm,* "Out. Grown-ups need to talk." *Dr. Greene held up his middle finger and walked out like a scolded puppy, slamming the door.*

"Marci, what the hell have you two been doing? You know we have a pending defense contract, and they're crawling all over your lab."

"Alexi, calm down. I have everything under control."

I studied Marci's eyes and wondered if I could trust her. "No more games. Those files stay locked until we know what we have."

Marci huffed. "Are you still going to make your secret nano-constructs for us to test, or are you going to make me get on my hands and knees and beg?"

"Please don't. I'll make it, but you're playing with fire. I'm doing this to make sure none of us get burnt. Until we know how—"

"That's bullshit, Alexi. If this works, the only things I don't know are in those files and in your head. Just say it, you don't trust me."

"Marci that's—"

Marci pushed her finger to my mouth. "Don't, it was a rhetorical statement."

"I'll have the solution ready for you soon. I'll fly out to your lab and I can supervise."

"Yes, Dad."

"Stop it. You know I'm right."

Marci waved her hand. "So are we still going to have those drinks tonight?"

"You never stop trying."

She turned and looked at me. "Can you blame me? I messed it up between us. I'll always love you." She folded her hands. "Are you going to make me beg for a little bit more of your time before you leave tomorrow?"

I should say no, but I have to figure out what her play is. "Sure but promise to drop this schoolgirl seduction stuff."

I held up my hand, wiggling my fingers. "No more, I'm married now."

She smiled. "Can't blame a girl for trying. I promise to play nice."

I shook my head as Marci walked out of the office, and the scene faded to black—

My eyes open, my head's pounding. I am on all fours, gasping to catch my breath, hovering above a slimy mess. Why am I kneeling on the ground?

Voices murmur behind me, a hand touches my shoulder. I start to stand. Hands grab my arms, stabilizing my body.

"Whoa, buddy. You okay?"

"Yeah, I think so." I wipe my mouth.

"Here drink this you look dehydrated."

I take a gulp of the water.

"Whoa not so fast, just sip it."

"Where am I?"

"Did you hit your head?" A woman asks.

"No. Just not sure what I'm doing outside." I hand the water bottle back. "No, you keep it."

I nod my thanks. "Must have walked down to the lake." I study the faces of the group. Two men and two women. Faces familiar. My running group? My running group from high school track? I have not run in ten years at least. What the hell am I doing?

"Hey, you're going to be okay. Just pushed yourself too hard." The man that helped me up squeezes my shoulder.

"Yeah."

"Take it slow just starting out. Maybe you can join our running group."

"What?" I gaze at the lady's familiar brown face, brown eyes, curly hair cut short. "I'm sorry... What group?"

"George's running and support group."

"My name is George, and your name is Jeff." I blurt out.

Jeff steps away from me. "What the hell? What kind of game are you playing?" He looks at the women. "What, you guys set me up on one of those hidden camera shows?"

I shake my head no. "It's me..." *Is my name George?* I shake my head. "No, I'm mistaken. My name is Brian."

Jeff laughs. "Is this a joke, man?"

"What?" I ask.

"George saved all our lives, one way or another, and now he is suffering without his..." His voice trails off. "Forget it. Let's go, guys."

They all turn to run except the girl with the freckled face. "What you're doing is mean. George is my—"

"Brother," I say, cutting her off. "He is your brother, and your name is Sara."

"How do you know that?" Jeff balls his fists.

I hold up my arms in surrender. "Wait! I'm sorry, let me explain."

Sara pushes me. "No, we told all you press people we're not talking or giving a quote or an update of my brother's status," Sara yells, swinging her arm at me. "He's my brother, not a fucking feature story or guinea pig."

She sobs and Jeff pulls her into his chest. His eyes are like daggers stabbing through me.

I'm still trying to figure out what I'm doing here, but I owe them a bit of explanation.

"I'm not sure how I got out here this morning, but my name is Brian Watson."

"I don't care who you are. Leave me alone!" Sara yells.

"I was on the plane with your brother."

She gasps at that.

Sara looks at the rest of the group before studying my face. "It's you. You were at the clinic..."

"Yeah, it's me."

Sara steps close to me. "I'm sorry about lashing out at you. It's just been so..." She shakes her head, tears welling up in her eyes. She continues, "Maybe we can go somewhere and talk?"

"Yes, that would be good. There's a smoothie place a mile or so up the trail we go to."

"No, not there." I rub my leg. "That's too far for my poor legs. There's a breakfast place close to Michigan Ave."

They nod in unison, and we walk into the shadows of the city.

After breakfast, Sara offers me a ride home since my legs are tight and still cramping. The ride to my condo is uneventful.

Sara talks a lot. Talks about dealing with her brother. Talks about how much she misses talking to him about her life. She expects me to fill in for her brother, but my head is spinning with abstract memories combined with the pain from my legs.

I'm a poor substitute. Sara is frustrated with my memory not cooperating. I explain to her that memories come and go.

She nods as though she understands. But how could she? She asks if we can meet again to talk and maybe I can sit with her brother. She says that could jog my memory. She winks at me, laughing at her silly pun.

As I get out of the car, I notice the shades moving in my condo. I spy the retreating silhouette.

"It will be okay. We can work through this together." She pulls my hand to her chest. I let my body follow, and she wraps her arms around me.

Her hair smells like cherries. She must still use the same shampoo as she did when she was a kid. An image of the bottle pops into my head.

"You still use that cherry-smelling kid shampoo?"

Her eyes swell with tears as she nods. "Call me. We have a lot to—" Her voice cracks, and she turns away from me.

"Yeah, I'll do that. I promise."

I step out of the car into the heat of the noon sun. The car pulls away into the hive of the city. With the humidity pressing on me, I limp up the steps. The door buzzes before I can get my key out. I enter the condo, and Brenda is standing at the door.

"I've been hustling out early these past couple mornings, working late so I could come home early today and take tomorrow off to enjoy the afternoon and long weekend with you." Brenda sucks her teeth, flailing her arms. "Shit! Not only are you not here, but I see you getting all huggy with a girl in a car."

"Brenda, I can explain. She is the sister of one of the passen—" She cuts me off, waving her hands, pushing past me, out the door.

"I don't want to hear your explanations. I don't want to hear about passengers anymore. I need to take a walk and—" She runs out the door.

I chase after her, but my leg cramps. I lean against the wall paralyzed in pain. I call out, hoping my words can stop her.

"Brenda, wait!" I yell at the closing door.

By the time I rub the cramp out, Brenda is gone. I try her cellphone, but it goes straight to voice message.

"I'm sorry, Brenda. I'm sorry for all this."

CHAPTER 8

Brian:
83 Days after Event

My body shrinks into a ball of tight, throbbing muscles. A voice in my head is telling me to stretch, but I'm tired of listening. Ignoring the pain, I crawl into the house and curl against the door, knees to my chest. The lemon fragrance in the floor polish Brenda uses is making me nauseous. I wrap my arms around my legs and pull myself into a tighter ball.

The house is quiet, except for faint sobs. I lift my head and listen. Who's there? The house is empty as a school classroom in the summer. I concentrate on the sobs and realize I'm the source. Strange not to recognize your own voice. I rub my face. My hand smears the wetness from my eyes. Why am I crying?

My muscles are pins and needles, painful and tight. Sitting on the floor like this is idiotic, but I don't have the strength to change position. There is some comfort in the pain, or is the comfort in not confronting the pain of changing positions?

I let out a puff of air and start stretching out my leg. I can hear the molecular tearing of my quads and hamstring resisting. I let out a yelp and freeze as the pain paralyzes me. Among the chatter of pain pinging in my head, there is a taunting voice pounding against my skull. My voice? Their voices?

A deep, drunken, slurry voice drowns out the rest. "Stop crying, you pussy!"

The word "pussy" startles me. I have never been called that or used that expression. It's a funny word. Rolls off the tongue. I repeat it in my head in my own voice. "Pussy, pussy, pussy." I smile, finding a burst of energy.

I uncoil my legs. Hands on the cool hardwood floor, I push upward, pressing hard against the door for support. Standing, I shout, "Pussy, pussy, pussy!" The words echo through the condo like a cleansing.

I take a deep whiff. My own sweaty funk overwhelms me. I pull at the cotton shirt that's drying to my chest. Like Velcro, the shirt snags my chest hairs.

I throw the damp shirt on the couch. I step out of my shorts and underwear, legs aching with every movement. I walk nude across the living room into the kitchen, stopping every other foot to bend and twist my muscles loose.

I open the refrigerator, and the cool air blows onto my naked body. Gooseflesh on my arms. I grab a beer, pop the top, and take a long, slow swig. Beer seeps out of the corner of my mouth, running down my chin onto my chest. I jiggle the bottle and take another drink, finishing it. I grab another and walk to the bathroom.

The bathroom stinks of lavender and bleach. The white floor tiles are cold and textured on my warm, sweaty feet. I turn the shower on. The spray of chilly water tickles my skin. I take a swig of beer, hand in the stream of water. First cold, then warm, then perfect.

I toss the empty beer bottle at the garbage can five feet across the room by the door. The bottle rotates end over end, spilling the last dribbles of golden goodness on the floor, on the wall, and into the can. The weight of the bottle causes the trashcan to wobble out of its perfect place, but it does not tip. I throw my hands in the air and shout, "Nothing but net!"

I step into the shower. The warm water eases the pain in my legs into a comfortable numbness. I wish Brenda were here. I close my eyes, and her face appears—

I ask the vision, "Tell me why you're so stressed?"

She speaks to me, "Wedding plans!"

I open my eyes. How could I forget that? A thing like that should be unforgettable. Yes, we are getting married in three months. I have been dealing with... We've been dealing with the event so much I forgot about it. I must talk with Brenda.

Like a ghost calling from the ether, she is shouting, words slurring into one monosyllabic phrase. "Brian, what the hell, where are you?"

"I'm in here, sweetie." I call out.

The bathroom door slams against the wall. Brenda's shoes *click-clack* on the tile floor. She yanks the shower curtain with a violent swish. Brenda's eyes are red and swollen. Hair jetting out of place. Perspiration squeezing out of angry wrinkles on her forehead. Face pale and exhausted.

"Brenda?" I whisper, not recognizing her. It's not the well-made face of Brenda in my mind, but a tired, sad face.

Eyes wide and dazed, she shakes her head side to side.

"Brenda!" I call out trying to get her attention. The spray dampens her shirt. I turn the knob, quieting the shower. "Brenda, what is—?"

She raises her hand, composing herself, eyes welling with tears. "I don't know if I can do this anymore." She holds my sweaty clothes out toward me, then drops them on the floor. Her head drops, following the clothes. Her body sways, tempted to follow and rest on the cold floor.

"Bri—," she shakes her head, hand covers her mouth. Anguished words stumble out, "I love you, but I just don't know if I can..." Brenda turns from me, sobbing.

I step out of the shower, my hand grabbing Brenda's arm, slipping, grasping her hand. She shakes her hand, my hand clutching onto her finger. "Brenda, wait!"

"Let go!" she yells, struggling to escape my hold on her fingers. As I pull on her fingers, she slips on the wet tiles. I catch her, like a trust exercise, but she starts to wiggle out of my grasp.

"Let...go...of me," Brenda yelps, smacking my arms, twisting her body and kicking her feet.

"Brenda, stop. Please." I wrap my arms around her, squeezing our bodies together.

The garbage can tips and falls during the struggle. The beer bottle clanks on the floor, spinning and making a grinding noise against the tiles.

She stops struggling, resting in my arms against my wet body. We stand still, frozen in time, mesmerized by the bottle's buzz. The cold air prickles my wet skin.

Brenda stands straight and turns into me. I pull her closer to me, holding her. Her muscles unspool into me. Her weary head rests on my chest.

"Brenda, I love you." I kiss the top of her head. Her hair smells like a summer fruit salad.

Her body regains its strength, and she straightens again. Spine cracking into place, she stands stiff and rigid. Our eyes meet.

"I don't know how long I can keep this up." She drops her head. "The mood swings, the slobbery, like beer spilled on the floor in the kitchen, and the women."

I glance at the brown spots trailing to the trashcan. Brenda shakes her head, tears streaming out of her eyes. "Seeing you in that car with God knows who, just, just—" She wipes her hands across her face and looks at me.

She sucks in a breath, then continues, "Remember what you promised me when you asked me to marry you?"

The room becomes a vacuum like my mind. Air pulls out of my lungs. Maybe I should exhale, but I may lose the threads of my own memories. My mind spins, empty of information and thoughts. The trickle of water dripping from the showerhead fills in the silence.

As the seconds *drip-drip* past, Brenda's sighs. I try harder to remember, my mind spins through memories. It's like sorting through spilled photo books that belonged to a random group of people. All the thousands of photos on the floor, and one by one I inspect the faces, the scenes, snapshot of memories. A thousand words are spoken, but without context they have no meaning.

I close my eyes, concentrating on the flickering images. I can hear Brenda breathing. How much time has passed? How long does it take to access one memory? One important memory, to me? To someone else? Can I remember this for Brenda? I'll love her forever and would never hurt her in any way.

We stood at Buckingham Fountain on a cool Chicago summer night—a gentle breeze filled with summer rain, grilled meat, loud conversations, and alcohol-fueled drunken courage. I was on one knee, ogling Brenda, who was backlit by that, pale full moon which observed her like a curious father.

Brenda tugged on my shoulders. "Get up, Brian. You're going to embarrass yourself." She giggled. "You're embarrassing me!"

I held the small black ring box out. Her laughter faded into faint whimpers of joy, a hand covering her mouth, a hand wiping her teary eyes. Her head nodded yes, our mouths kissing. Our bodies pressed into an embrace—

"Honey, what is going on?" her voice calls from the ether.

I wipe the tears making their lazy trail down the sides of her face.

"Brenda, with this ring, I'll love you forever and will never hurt you in anyway. Please be my wife?"

Brenda wraps both arms around me and squeezes hard. Her face presses into my chest. "I love you."

"I love you, too." She shivers, and I wrap my arms around her.

"And you better keep your promise!"

"I promise to do my best."

"You have to do better than your best."

"I'm trying."

"I know, sweetie." She pulls out of my embrace.

"So you think we can have those relations now." I wink at her.

She raises her eyebrow at me.

"Sorry, I was just trying to be funny."

She shakes her head no. "You don't remember this morning?"

The memory of waking up naked floods back. That explains that, but... We had sex?

She nods my head yes, and smirks. "I must be losing my touch if you're sleeping through our relations. I'd better get some more practice." She winks, walks away stripping out of her shirt.

She disappears into the bedroom. I start to follow and kick the beer bottle across the bathroom.

Brenda calls out, "You better hurry. You're ruining the moment!"

"One minute, cleaning up the mess you made."

"Forget the mess and get in here, or I'll start without you." Brenda starts making fake moaning noises.

I stand the garbage can and collect the discarded tissues and bathroom disposables that scattered across the floor. I glance in the can, and at the bottom there are empty medicine boxes for morning sickness and multi-vitamins. What does this mean? I pick up the box. Does that mean Brenda is preg—?

"Brian, let's go!"

I drop the garbage and cover the boxes back up. I walk to the bedroom. A flood of voices enters my mind. When did she find out? Is it my baby? I'm so excited to be pregnant! Why didn't she tell me? Brenda is pregnant?

I repeat that last voice, my own concerned voice. I walk into the bedroom and smile. Brenda's body is spread across the bed, I study her belly, and my mind fills with my own thoughts.

"I love you!" I say to Brenda as I fall into bed snuggling next to her, falling into a long deep kiss, falling into my own skin. I close my eyes, enjoying the sensation of her hands rubbing on my chest. Her vanilla perfume fills every breath. I can taste her pheromones. Her beautiful, well-made face smiling at me. Her weight on top of me, the pressure comfortable.

Enjoying the moment, I can make out her voice in my head. Her faint, quiet voice in my mind, saying, "Help me."

The weight shifts in a steady gyrating motion. I am floating. No, I'm falling, falling, falling, Brenda's face falling away from me. I throw my arms out to grab onto something in the black, bottomless void—

Her face appears, the girl in my dreams. She is in trouble. I push against the weight of the vision, my muscles tensing up. The pain of my muscles cramping eases into the pleasure surging through my body. The weight lifts, and my body jerks up.

I blink my eyes studying the room in a state of déjà vu. Strange be in a familiar place and not recognize anything. There is a nude body stretching out in the bed, her arm wrapped around my waist. Who is she? What is her name?

"Brenda?" I whisper.

She frowns at me and reality rushes in. But why are we naked and in bed? Were we making love? Did I see morning sickness medicine in the garbage? Did Brenda tell me she was pregnant? Who was the other girl in my head? Is she pregnant? I lie down, and Brenda curls onto my chest.

No, Brenda never told me about being pregnant. We need to talk. My thoughts drift from the hypothetical conversation with Brenda about marriage and babies, to the strange woman who has been haunting my dreams.

I have to get these people out of my head, starting with this woman. I remember the folder. Maybe I can visit her tomorrow.

"For you, for us, for the baby," I whisper into the top of Brenda's head.

CHAPTER 9

Brian:
92 Days after Event

A sharp electrical pop in the distance jerks me awake. I blink my eyes several times to clear the haze of sleep. After a few fuzzy seconds, my eyes scan the last few lines of text I'd typed. Must have fallen asleep while writing. The tight muscles in my neck confirm, along with the random string of letters where my head lay awkward on the keyboard. I close my eyes and rub my forehead.

My hand slides to massage the knot out of my neck. Another crack of thunder makes me jump. My ears ring like a slap across my face. I hold my hand on my cheek, it's raw and sore. Another boom, and I flinch again. My hand is on the other cheek, and the sting of pain fades like lightning.

I have never been afraid of thunderstorms, but my heart is racing. I'm jittery like a trapped animal. My reflexes at the ready, ready to defend, ready to attack. The air in the room has become thick with humidity and the pungent odor of ozone. A sharp pop stings my ears, followed by an electric sizzle, and the glow of the monitor fades. I am surrounded by darkness.

I push away the desk chair. I stand, walking, arms sweeping at the dark space, reaching for something familiar. My foot catches the bottom of the couch in the office, and pain shoots up my body. Lightning flashes—illuminating the room, the couch, and the door—then darkness. The thunder drums seconds after, mirroring the pulse of pain coursing through my body.

I fall onto the couch, pulling my legs into a tight ball. I rock myself, rubbing my foot, my face. Another flash, another boom. My heart is thumping, fast and hard against my chest. I close my eyes, start to pray, and a vision comes—

I realize it's the woman who I have been dreaming of. I study her face—expressionless and fragile, pale white and dotted with millions of freckles. Her red hair is curly and long. Her eyes are white pearls with a center of sky blue. The perspective is different than before, and it takes me a while to realize I'm staring in a mirror holding my stomach. Maybe I have been kicked or punched. Who hit me?

Another crack of thunder forces my eyes open. The low, deep rumble and the soft tap of rain against the window become less menacing. I wipe my face, wet with tears. I lunge for the desk, hands probing the surface until I find it, the folder of photos. The power is still off, so I grab my cellphone and use it as a flashlight to flip through the folder Dr. Shirley gave me.

I flip through several pages of faces, and on the last, there she is. She is smiling, happy. Her name pops into my mind before I read it, Amanda Conner. There is an address and number. I smile and turn off the flashlight.

The *tap, tap, tap* of the rain has passed. The house is still dark, but I make my way to the bedroom. The bed is empty. Where is Brenda? I remember that Brenda has gone to visit her mom again for a few days. I hate sleeping alone. I close my eyes dreaming of Amanda.

***

I wake up rested and clear headed. I must visit Amanda. Brenda's warning not to do something stupid while she is gone lingers in my ears, but Amanda may be in a dire situation without her memories. Dr. Shirley's reminder that my superpower is not to remember for everyone also jogs in my head. What does she know about superpowers?

The icy water of the shower stings my warm skin. My cocky optimism is replaced by fear as a shadow moves across the shower curtain. My nose fills with fresh mowed grass and the stink of fertilizer. My heart is beating fast, pulling from my chest.

I close my eyes, trying to calm myself. A blurry vision, in the faded sepia and dark shadows of a horror movie, plays in my mind—

Hands grabbed at me. I struggled, but my soapy body rubbed against him and his sweaty onion stink. My screams drowned his words out. My arms are pulled behind me. My body is bent into an awkward position, water gagging me, drowning me. I held my breath. He's in me, thrusting and pushing all the stale air from my lungs. I screamed—

My eyes open. My legs buckle, and I fall to the shower floor. My stomach clenches, and acidic bile fills my mouth. I shake my head, crying. I have to see Amanda. It's my duty to make sure she is not suffering.

The drive to Amanda's house is short. The temperature is mild for this time in August, in the mid-eighties. The car fills with that pleasant aroma of late summer flowers and mowed grass.

As I step out of the car, there is a cool breeze blowing off the lake, and the cloyingly sweet floral fragrance of laundry hanging on a clothesline fills my nose.

I grab my folder and find Amanda's house number. There is not much variation between the row of houses. Each has a flight of concrete stairs leading to a porch. Various outdoor furniture litters the small spaces. Some of the lawns are green, and some are decorated with colorful fall flowers, manicured daily.

Not Amanda's house. Her lawn is brown and dead. The concrete steps are cracked and worn to loose gravel in some places. I grab onto the wooden railing but realize I'm supporting its wobbly, decaying frame more than it's supporting me. The wooden plank porch, covered with a threadbare AstroTurf rug. I step with caution across the porch, like walking out onto an icy lake.

I ring the bell. Boots stomping and muffled cursing causes my heart to thump against my chest. The red wooden door swings open and there he is.

"What the fuck you want?" he yells, spittle and crumbs flying after each word.

"Is this Amanda Conner's house?"

He looks into the house, sucks his teeth, and glares at me. "This is my house, blackie. What you want with Amanda?"

"Is she okay?"

"You people are like cockroaches." He pokes me in the chest. "You get rid of one and another shows up. After Mom and Pop died, I told that dirty slut not to mess around with" he pokes me in the chest again, and sucks his teeth, "*you* people, and now look at her."

I realize it was a mistake coming here. I take a step away from the door. "I'm sorry. I was on the plane with Amanda, and I remembered something about her."

"Yeah, I don't care who you are. You don't know nothing about me or Amanda. Just another one of Derrick's brothas demanding shit." He lunges out the door, punching me in the chest and spitting at my feet.

"No, I don't know Derrick." A face flashes in my mind—a man with a wide friendly smile, hair cut short, hazel brown eyes. Emotions pull at me, a sense of compassion, understanding, caring, and love. I realize Derrick is Amanda's lover.

"Don't lie to me, man!"

"No, I'm the guy from the plane. I can remember things the other passengers forgot, like your sister."

He eyeballs me, sucks his teeth. "Shit, man, you think I'm dumb. No blackie can remember shit. If you're this airplane dude, tell me one of Amanda's memories." He leers at me like he is reading my mind.

I look away at my feet; I have no clue what to tell him. I remember the scared, fragile Amanda, being abused by her brother. Stepbrother. By him! Tell him that and World War III could break out. Tell him I know about the shower, and he may kill me. The silence must have lingered too long.

He clears his throat and says, "That top step behind you is a bitch."

Confused, I follow his outstretched arm, turning my head to glance at the steps behind me. "Yeah, it could use a little work," I say, turning my head around.

He growls at me, "You fucker!"

I realize he is throwing a wild left hook too late. His fat calloused fist strikes me, knuckles sharp against my face. I bite my tongue. Salty, metallic blood flows into my mouth. Before I can raise my hands, another punch lands on my lips. Another punch to my eyes blurs my vision. Instead of turning into a mutant when aggravated, I'm getting my ass kicked.

He lands an uppercut on my chin. My vision blurs to black and a vision starts to play like a movie—

Her clothes were ripped and torn away. His limbs were swinging with furious purpose, catching parts of her face with each blow. Her skin was raw and swollen where his fists landed. He shoved her onto the floor, calling her a slut, a dirty blackie-loving slut. She screamed for him to stop, but her voice faded into hopeless quiet, like falling with your hands tied behind your back—

My eyes blink the world back into focus. He is standing on the porch, and I am lying on the sidewalk. A sharp stab of pain in my chest forces the air out of my lungs as I move to stand.

"Get off my property, blackie. Tell Derrick not to come around anymore. The judge said I'm family and can care for my baby sister. Thankfully she forgot about him, and we can be together again." He laughs, spinning on his heels. I watch his blurry figure fade into the house, and the door slams shut.

Pain shoots through my chest with the smallest movements. I clench my teeth and lift myself off the ground. My head still throbbing, I stumble trying to pick up my folder. The photos and my notes flutter out onto the ground. Bending to collect the pictures before the wind takes them, the ground vibrates, and I fall to my knees.

"You okay, sir?" The arm is meaty and muscular, wrapping around me. "You got into it with Danny. Nothing but trouble, that boy."

Her accent is a mix of Irish and Polish. I gaze at her face, wrinkled and leathery. Iron black, wavy hair spills off her shoulders. She is short, but she is supporting my two hundred and twenty pounds like I'm a toddler.

I grit my teeth and whisper, "Thank you."

"You need to get sweet Amanda out of that house." She pauses, clearing her throat, clearing the sadness. "He used to be sweet, too. After their mother died, Danny became a monster."

"What do you mean?"

"He did things to his sister. Evil things. I could hear her scream..." We stop walking. Her name pops into my mind, Grace. She helped Amanda hide from Danny. Her eyes watering as she says, "Evil things...but I helped her get it out."

Confused and struggling to manage the pain of every movement, I contemplate the meaning of what Grace said, "Evil things." Stabs of pain jab along my chest as I exhale. I remember Amanda being pregnant. Impregnated by her stepbrother or Derrick? I lean over as a wave of nausea hits me. I close my eyes, embracing the fog, and count to ten. The memories of being tortured and molested flicker like an old movie in my mind. The memory of being pregnant makes me think of Brenda. Did she tell me she was pregnant, or am I seeing images of Amanda?

"Breathe, sweet boy."

Grace's fat fingers are massaging my back. She lifts me to a standing position, and we start walking.

"After that horror, that sweet angel moved to my house. And with the help of this sweet lady lawyer, Danny stayed away. Amanda got a job and met a boy." Grace laughs. "He was different, but his soul was good. He loved Amanda and swept her away." Grace laughs again. "I missed my angel, and then she invited me to dinner. Belly full of love." Grace stops talking.

We've made it to my car. I'm leaning on the hood. "What happened, Grace?"

"She got a second chance with Derrick. He saved her. I was a little disappointed they didn't wait until marriage to have a baby. They called me old-fashioned. They are so happy together." Grace smiles. "Their baby is beautiful. Amanda named her—"

"Tylie." I take the name from Grace's lips.

Grace helps me into the driver's seat. My happiness is momentary as Grace leans in and whispers her secret. "Danny took her from the plane and is doing things—terrible things—to her. You must help her get back to Derrick."

Thinking about the recent ass kicking I received moments ago, I whisper, "How?"

"With the guidance of God, he has led you here. He will lead your next step." She pushes a paper into my hand and kisses me on my forehead. "Go to the hospital. Your ribs may be broken." After she gives me directions, she walks to her house and disappears into the door with a final wave goodbye. I reach into my breast pocket for my cellphone and pull the bent and broken device out.

"Smartphone becomes a flip phone." I laugh, big mistake, as pain explodes in my chest. I exam the paper Grace gave me. I recognize the handwriting as Amanda's.

I read it out loud, "You're invited to dinner at Derrick and Amanda's house..." This is the note Amanda gave to Grace.

As I drive away, another stab of pain radiates around my chest. Dr. Shirley's voice echoes in my head. *You're not a superhero.*

I spend the entire afternoon and night at the ER. When I get home, the house lights are off. The faint aromas of meatballs and baked apples fill my nose. A wave of guilt stabs me, remembering that Brenda came back home today from her trip. I should let Brenda know that I am okay, but I am starving.

I walk into the kitchen, thoughts of meatballs and apple pie filling my head. The plastic bowl with dinner is on the top shelf of the refrigerator. I tighten my chest muscles—bracing for the pain—and reach out my arm, keeping my other arm pinned to my fractured ribs. A jolt of pain travels from my chest, along my spine, and pounds my head as my hand latches onto the bowl. I exhale, resting for a second then letting the pain subside.

I press my lips together and gnash my teeth, inching the bowl off the shelf. The weight of the bowl, heavier than I expected, drops as gravity pulls it out of my weak grip. Reflexes forces my other arm to reach for the dish. The pain is blinding. The bowl of pasta hit the floor. I stumble backward, clutching at my ribs.

The bedroom door bangs open. Brenda's feet pounding on the hardwood floor. She flicks the overhead kitchen light on, hand covers her mouth, muffling her gasp.

Tears start to well up in Brenda's eyes. "What the hell happened to you? We couldn't find you. My God your face. Oh my God, is that blood all over you?"

"No... Not blood...sauce." I wheeze for air.

Her eyes scan the kitchen floor. "What happened?"

Still wheezing, I grab for her arm. "I'm...sorry..."

"Stop talking, honey, I'm here now. I should've never left you," she says scraping a chair across the floor. "Sit down and take slow, deep breaths."

She guides me to the chair. I sit while holding my arms close to my chest. The piercing pain subsides as I settle into the chair.

"Now, what happened, sweetie?"

"It's a long story." I pull a bottle of pain medicine out of my pocket.

Brenda hands me a glass of water, grabs a towel off the counter, and starts to clean the food spilled on the floor. She turns her head and says, "I told you, we're not going anywhere."

CHAPTER 10

Brian:
119 Days after Event

Where am I? I study the shadows that are dancing along the walls. My bedroom? I'm tangled in sheets. The familiar bedroom looks smaller. I blink my eyes. Now it's even smaller. The walls are moving, squeezing together, squeezing out the light. I remember to breathe. I exhale, the walls push out. I inhale, walls suck in a little. Another breath out, and the walls push out a bit further. One last breath, and the walls set into place. The room is as I remember it.

My arms stretch out into the world, searching for someone familiar. No Brenda, so it must be late morning.

This room is stuffy and hot. My chest still radiates a dull pain with every sip of air. How many days have I been laying in this bed—drugged and healing? I brace my arms on the bed, clench my mouth close, and lift myself, sitting on the edge of the mattress. Feet flat against the cold wood, I hold my breath and stand.

The room wobbles, the walls push in again. I reach out, trying to push against the wall before it smacks into me, but my eyes deceive me. I push against the nothing. Falling, my head knocks against the floor.

The coolness of the wood floor is comfortable. I close my eyes, letting the squiggles in my vision come to a stop. I breathe in the hot, thick air, breathing out even hotter, stale, used air. Breathing in. Breathing out. I count to ten breaths. My eyes flutter open on the last exhale, and the room is not spinning. I pull myself to a kneeling position. The room is still.

I use the bed to stabilize my wobbly legs as I stand. I stand in place for a count of ten—nothing. I walk to the bathroom. The room is not breathing. The walls are not undulating with the irregular rhythm of a dying heart. I stare at myself in the mirror—face still bruised, lips still swollen, and left eye still blackened. I don't recognize myself.

The vanilla, lavender, lemon, and cinnamon fragrance of the condo have become irritating. Brenda's scent has become irritating. Do I belong here? Should I leave Brenda? I need something to take the edge off. I remember Dr. Shirley and that prescription she scribbled on thick, chalky paper.

I step out of the condo for the first time in several days. The hallway is filled with a sweaty, corn chip aroma. I swallow hard tasting bile and hurry to get out of the building.

I walk a familiar path. I find myself heading to the lake, but not today. I am going to The Joint. A silly name. A perfect name. A joint is what the doctor ordered. I laugh at my own joke.

At 10 a.m. the place is bustling. Bodies are hovering over glass display cases. Fingers pointing invisible lines to the products on display. Hands fan the musky tang of dried cannabis buds. A short, stocky woman, her face full of metal and gems, steps out of the sea of bodies and smiles at me.

"Welcome back."

"What?"

"Brian, right?"

"Yeah, that's me, but—"

"I thought so. You were here a couple weeks ago."

"No, I think you have me confused."

She rolls her eyes. "My bad. What can I help you with?"

I hand her the prescription.

Her eyes scan the loopy cursive. "Ah okay, follow me. I have exactly what you need." She winks, walking to a display case along the wall. As we weave through the dozen or so bodies, I notice the dank aromas changing—fresh cut grass, to sharp mint, to the stink of patchouli oil.

"Here, smell this one." She shoves a dish of dried, dark-green floral bits at my nose.

"Whoa, that smells like... Lavender."

Smiling, she grabs the dish out of my hand. "Yup, the purple prince is a hybrid strain. It was developed so that—"

"I'll take it."

She presses her fist to her mouth, nods and takes the dish to the scale to weigh out my prescription.

I wonder what triggered my snap decision. Something familiar about the name purple prince. Have I been here before?

"You need a pipe?" Her voice buzzes my ears.

"Yes."

She grabs a glass, rainbow-stained pipe off the shelf. "This is the basic $19.99 model, but for a real treat, you should get a water pipe." She waves her hand at the fragile glass structures. "They start at about sixty dollars." She cuts her eyes at me, rests her hands on her hips, and snaps. "Or you can just get some papers for a couple bucks."

"No, the glass pipe is fine."

She hunches her shoulders. "Meet you at the front register."

I leave with the pot and a pipe. My stomach grumbles, and I head to a diner for breakfast.

A few minutes later, the waitress is sitting coffee down and scribbling my order on her pad, Special #1: four bacon strips, four eggs over easy, and a stack of hot cakes. I like the word hot cakes. Reminds me of the days I spent on the farm. Food my grandma made. Two sips into my coffee, a body plops into the booth.

"Hey, you!"

I watch him grab a menu and start reading. His body is lean and fit. His T-shirt damp. A runner. A name pops into my head: Larry.

"Just invite yourself to sit down." I smile and sip my coffee. His spicy cologne mingles with the diner's scents of fried bacon and warm cinnamon roll.

"You looked like you could use a friend" He reaches across the table and squeezes my arm. "How have you been? We missed you on the trails."

"I've been better. I broke my—"

The gray-haired, wrinkle-faced waitress taps her pen to the pad. "You want coffee, honey?"

Where did she come from? Another waitress took my order. I crane my neck peeking at her nametag dangling between her cleavage. "Tammy."

"Oh darling, I don't need honey. I take my coffee black." Larry winks and blows a kiss at Tammy.

Tammy's cheeks redden and her lips curl into a smile.

Her smile is familiar; maybe she is a stripper or a porn star. A little old to be in any porn I watch, but I recognize her face, her name, and those breasts. Maybe I'm a bit—

Tammy walks off and Larry laughs. "Tammy is the only reason I come here so often. She knows how to put a smile on your face."

I analyze his face. His intense smoky-blue eyes, like mirrors reflecting another me. As I stare at my face in his eyes, the tables, and chairs of the diner swirl into a fuzzy blur. Larry's face sharpens, and my reflection in his eyes becomes clear, more resolved. I lean forward to see my true face—

"You okay?" He waves his hand, breaking the trance.

"Sorry, just zoning out. Didn't sleep well last night."

His hand slips over mine. "Well maybe you need to relax a bit." His lips pull into a smile revealing his perfect white teeth.

I pull my hand to my coffee and lean away. "And how do you propose—I relax?"

"Well, if you don't stand me up again, I'll show you."

It hit me, the entire scene on the lake path. Damn, who was I? Who am I now?

"Sorry about that. I got a bit sick on the path. Pushed myself too hard."

"Yeah, I heard all about it, and now you can make it up to me." He winks into a sip of his coffee.

The scraping of plates, slurping and the noise of conversations spill into our booth filling the silence between us. I remember Dr. Shirley explaining that I should explore and compartmentalize these emotion-triggered memories. Without my folder of photos and notes, I don't know whose experience this is. Maybe if I play this out a bit longer, things will click, and I can make note of it. Am I finally gaining control of these people in my head? Maybe Dr. Shirley's compartmentalizing shit is paying off. Maybe I can slip into and out of memories, and personalities. Maybe if I remember, I can tap into and control this at last, and move on with my life, and with Brenda. Or maybe I could do more—

"What's on your mind, baby?" He caresses my hand.

The word baby makes me wonder how Amanda is doing. Finally, free from her demented brother. I did that, am I a superhero?

"I can leave if you don't want the company."

I focus on his face. "No, just a lot on my mind. I think I may be on the verge of figuring something out."

He pulls his hand away, grabbing his coffee mug. "Do you want me to leave?"

"No!" I shout at him. "Stay, it's nice to have someone—"

"Here you go, ladies!" The word, ladies, jars me from my own internal thoughts.

Tammy slings plates of steaming food on the table. Her name tag is gone. The top two button of her shirt are missing. She smiles a bit, following my eyes glancing at her exposed breasts.

She leans into me, whispering, "You men are all the same when it comes to boobs." Her mumbling voice hangs on the word boobs. Her lips brush against my ear. Her fruity perfume and maple syrup scent pull at a memory. Do I know her? Have we met before?

I study the way she is standing; her hands are on her hips. She puffs her chest out and licks her lips in a slow clockwise motion. I glance away to stop fantasizing about her boobs. Why is she still standing there? Is she waiting for me to ask, *How are we men all the same?*

She pats my shoulder. "You need anything else?" It was a general waitress question, but the way she was biting her lower lip, eyes searching for something... I put a forkful of food into my mouth and shake my head, studying the creamy sun-orange egg yolk oozing along the caramelized fried potatoes.

"Friendly, aren't we, Brian?" He picks a slice of toast and spreads jam on it. "Or do you want me to call you George?"

That name, George, causes the puzzle piece to click into place. A compartment filled. I'm becoming a master of domains. Maybe I can play this out and help Sara, George's sister. I found his profile in the files Dr. Shirley gave me, and maybe I can help return his memories. I have to play along, and maybe I'll fill in all the pieces and compartmentalize Georgie-boy once and for all. I'm in full control. A self-congratulatory tingle shoots along my spine.

"You can call me George if that does it for you. Oh, and hopefully it's not a problem but I have a fetish for middle-aged waitresses named Tammy!" I lick the salty remnants of yolk off my fork. Larry giggles and gazes down at his food.

He lifts his eyes. "What are you doing after this?"

"Something with you, I hope." I stab a fried potato on his plate and put it into my mouth.

"Hey, you got your own potatoes, buddy!" He laughs. "Well, I live around the corner. Wanna see if we can find trouble?"

The word trouble plays in a loop in my ear. I'm nodding yes, but thinking no. Thinking about her, but wanting him.

Maybe I have gone too far. Maybe I have found all the trouble I can handle for one day.

Like a suspicious parent, Tammy is hovering by our table. Larry gives her a nod, like they have a secret wager. Her face has a differential smile smeared across it. She nods and spins away. Seconds later, she hands Larry the bill.

"What's the damage?" I pull at my shorts for my wallet.

"Consider it my treat." Larry pulls bills out of his armband wallet. I follow his eyes to the brown paper bag I placed on the table.

He points. "What's in the bag, Georgie?"

The nickname pulls me further into this character. "What? This bag?" I shake the bag.

"Yeah, that one," he whispers in a low, deep voice, leaning forward.

"How much trouble are you looking for, Larry?"

He snatches the bag and peeks in. His eyes widen, and his lips form into a smile, like a flower blooming after a long winter.

"Purple prince is what they call it," I say.

"I can smell the lavender and grassy notes. Not very funky." He sticks his nose in the bag and inhales. His lips curl into a grin. "My favorite!"

"I'm glad. Maybe I'll share with you."

Larry folds the bag with care and slides it across the table. "What are we waiting for?"

He slips out of the booth and heads for the door. I ogle his tight butt and his muscular legs flexing with every step.

Tammy walks over to the table and scoops up the wad of money.

"Thanks. Have Fun." Tammy winks and walks away.

"You coming?" Larry yells at me over the noise.

"Yeah." I nod, scooting out of the booth, and there they are—sitting at a table in the corner, hiding behind their menus and whispering close to each other—the two men from the restaurant.

I shuffle up to Larry and tug on his arm.

"Whoa! Where's the fire?" He chirps.

"Just excited to, you know." I shake the bag.

"Yeah, right."

I peek back into the diner's window. Who are they? Why are they watching me? Following me? Am I just being paranoid? Maybe they are just two people in suits having breakfast—

His arm laces around mine, and pulls me—*no, I'm Georgie*—away.

CHAPTER 11

*Brian:
227 Days after Event*

I like eating breakfast at this diner. I like seeing Tammy, something familiar, comforting in her smile. I like it best when Larry shows up and pulls me away with him.

Walking through the familiar noises of the city—car horns, human chatter, and sirens wailing in the distance—blend into one harmonious symphony. My mind deconstructs the noise into their own singular threads, their own compartments. Familiar faces pass by. Do I know them? My mind whirls with familiar names. Where am I going? Why is this man pulling on my arm? I watch a figure in the distance. A woman and a baby. A laughing baby. A happy mom. Brenda? I shake my head remembering that Brenda is not pregnant, that was Amanda—

"Are you even listening to me?" His voice blurs into the surrounding noises.

I ponder his face—who is he? Larry. Have we done this before? Who am I supposed to be? Am I'm George, Sara's brother? No, I'm Brian pretending to be George, and I'm going to Larry's apartment to smoke a bowl and learn about George so I can help Sara.

"Yeah, I'm listening." I wink, pulling against his arm. He resists and I fall into him with a little bump.

"Hey now!" His laugh is deep, sincere, and familiar.

Like a drug, I am slipping deeper into this character, and I have no desire to stop the slide.

We walk close, hands brushing against each other. The city rushes past in blurry, broad strokes. Broken concrete and smooth blacktop. Smiles and smooth laughter. Broken bits of conversation—polite and otherwise. Car exhaust mixes with frying burgers and burning cheese. Honking buses mix with birds chirping overhead. Squealing breaks, squealing children, wheels in my mind squealing. Everything familiar, but I remember nothing. Who am I in this moment?

"So what do you think about that?" His voice pulls my attention to his face.

"What?"

"I knew you weren't listening to me." He bumps me with his hip.

"Ouch. You trying to hurt me?"

Larry raises his fist and shakes it. "Start paying attention to me. If you know what's good for you."

I nod, and we walk in silence for another block. Larry voice is muffled like my head is under water. He pulls my arm. A door opens into a bronze and marble decorated lobby.

"You okay?" His voice booms in the small elevator.

"Yeah, perfect."

His apartment is on the tenth floor. Open loft style, with dull, red bricks and shiny hardwood floors. I smell the aromas of clean—floral soaps, lemon polish, and vanilla. A wall of windows faces the mighty, corrugating turquoise-blue Lake Michigan flowing into the Chicago River, flowing into the people who, like ants, march along giving the city rhythm and soul.

"Make yourself at home. Going to take off my running stuff," Larry says. His New Jersey accent strengthens in the privacy of his home.

Larry disappears into his bedroom. I sit on the couch, wiping my sweaty palms down my pant leg, heart beating fast. I sink into the softness of the couch and close my eyes, trying to relax. I'm in control. I know who I am. I am Brian. My muscles unspool like a weight has been lifted from my shoulders. After all these months I can control these memories. I can now help all the other passengers. I can get back to my life with Brenda.

"You snoozing?" His body plops on the couch, hand caresses my leg.

I examine the sterile, empty space. Where am I?

"Am I that boring, Georgie?" The hand rubs in slow ovals between my knee and my crotch. I study his face. His wet hair, slicked back. Eyes wide and searching. Lips parted like he is about to say something or want to kiss. I wait, but words never come out and our lips do not meet. A name flashes in my head—

"Larry."

"That's my name, don't wear it out." He smiles.

I reach across him, grabbing the bag. He leans into me so that my head brushes across his chest. I put the pipe and canister of marijuana on the table and lean back.

"Why do I always have to start?" He reaches for the pipe before I answer.

I pry off my sneakers and kick the shoes under the coffee table.

He smiles and looks between me and my shoes. "Um, excuse me?"

"Oh, I'm sorry." I bend over to collect my shoes when his hand rubs my back.

"I'm just kidding. Relax." He laughs, a high-pitched, snorting laugh.

A fake laugh, to take the edge off his movie star face. To make him seem a little less perfect. I laugh, so I fit in.

He hands me the pipe and a lighter. I light the dried botanicals while sucking on the pipe. I watch the orange hot glow—fuel, heat, and oxygen. I suck harder, and the orange glow burns brighter as I pull more oxygen through the heat and fuel. Savory smoke burns into my lungs. Lungs fill with thick toxins. Lungs heavy and warm. I pull the pipe out my mouth and hand it to Larry.

"Take it easy." His hand rubs on my shoulders. "Save some of that sucking for me." A snicker sneaks out of his mouth as he kisses on my ear.

The spicy smoke in my lungs makes it feel like I'm holding my breath under water. My lungs are burning, but I'm afraid to breathe. Suffocating, I gasp. Hot, white puffs of air erupt out of me. The plume of smoke covers Larry's head in a fog of dank, stale, used air.

I start coughing, drowning in fresh air. Gasping. Choking. Lungs on fire.

"Breathe." His hand kneads my back.

I pat his leg. "I'm...okay."

He nods his head, holds the pipe to his pursed lips, and pulls air through the red botanical embers, filling his lungs with delicious smoke. A laugh sneaks out of my mind, my mouth. Another laugh. What is funny? Larry's face begins to vibrate. I rub my eyes. The room is vibrating. No, that's not right. I'm laughing so hard that I'm vibrating.

"What the heck is so funny?" Larry blows a white cloud of pungent smoke into my face.

"I don't know!"

Larry starts giggling. Contagious. I have not been this happy in months, not since... I can't remember when. A weight has been lifted off my shoulders. A weight that I had not realized was there until the voices in my head stop screaming. The hot-white, lavender smoke has replaced all of my worries. I wrap my lips around the pipe and take another lungful of smoke. I blow the smoke out, enjoying the quiet in my head.

"Now you're doing it right!" Larry takes the pipe. "Not trying to suck down the whole thing."

I start laughing. "Sucking the whole thing!"

Larry starts coughing. "You're too much, Georgie-boy!"

That nickname, Georgie-boy, startles me. A voice starts shouting in my head. The muscles in my shoulders spasm. A knot pulls my spine. A sharp pain jabs in between my ribs. "Breathe, Georgie-boy. Breathe," the voice whispers. "This is my favorite part."

Larry leans into me, face close. His scent fills me. His red lips are moving. I try to listen to the mumble of words coming out of his mouth. Something about Tammy. Or was it?

Our lips meet. His face wavers, vibrating into Tammy's. Her flirtatious smile, maple flavored breath, large pale breasts. I close my eyes, imagining I'm kissing her. Her image fades into blackness. An image starts to flicker into view—

Intense pressure drummed on my lips. A kiss? No, a punch. Punches. My lips stinging. I pushed through the fuzzy haze. The scene started to play.

I was packing. Why? Running away from home? "Eighteen going on thirty," was what my mom was yelling at me in the echoes of the house. I was running from a fight with my dad in the basement. By the end, my mouth would be sore, ribs would be sore. I was not going to get my ass whipped for thirty minutes. I understood what the red boxing gloves are for, leather cracked and grayed, holes covered with layers of duct tape. I would put those gloves on and hold my hands up to cover my face. A defensive position was best. It was easier to hide bruises on the arms. Any attempts to go on the offensive, like an angry wild jab deflecting off my dad's shoulder, would result in a barrage of fists and spittle, and refusing to put on the gloves would be worse. I learned that the hard way. A bare fist on soft adolescent flesh and a fractured wrist hurt like hell.

I was packing. I was running away. Running from my abusive dad. A tolerant mom. Mom and I had another fight, and Dad would be home soon, smelling like cigarette smoke and whiskey and, we would have to "talk" it out—but not this time. I stuffed clothes into a small bag, grabbed the five hundred dollars I had saved, and looked around my room for what I hoped was the last time.

I opened the window, shimmy to the ground, and bicycle off. If I keep going south, I'd be in Northwest Indiana by nightfall. Could go into a truck-stop diner, and hitchhike a ride east with a "Howdy do?" and a smile.

The scene shifted. I was hanging out at a truck stop somewhere between Chicago and the Big Blue World. The Hollywood romantic story that motivated me to run away was not well scripted. But you don't realize how weak you are until a trucker pins you in a restroom stall. If it was not for my high-

pitched screams for help, I was positive he would have done a lot worse than pin me over the sink.

My savior was the blonde, Amazonian waitress who burst into the bathroom with a rolling pin, chased him away with a promise, or a threat, of something more than pie and coffee. I was sobbing, my body shaking as I realized the world is full of abusers. She wrapped her arms around me and kissed the top of my head.

Her large breasts poked out of her tight uniform, and she pulled my head into her soft cleavage. I tried to resist, but with her gentle voice repeating, "It's okay, sugar..." and her hand rubbing circles across my back, I had no choice but to close my eyes and swallow her scent in. Sweet dough, maple syrup, and fried hamburgers mingled with her citrusy, ethanolic perfume.

I relaxed, muscles unspooling. If she would have let me go, I would have melted into the bathroom floor drain, but she held me tight, and the tighter she pulled me into her, the clearer my mind became.

Through the blackness behind my eyelids, still enjoying her aroma, a female figure appeared, nude pale white skin glistening, moving closer. With every step, the scene became a bit brighter, and I realized it was her, the waitress that saved me. Her large breasts hanging proud, resisting gravity. Her areolae were pink and large, nipples firm like—

A voice echoed, rippling the image, my body shaking.

"Hey there, we're getting a little friendly, aren't we?"

My eyes fluttered open, and I realized the waitress was holding me at arm's length, her face was flushed, and she was smiling.

"What happened?" I mumbled. I followed her eyes, to the throbbing in my pants. "Oh, I'm sorry. I just—"

"No worries, sugar." She reached out and caressed my face. "I have that effect on men of all ages. I'll get you some food. I get off in an hour or so. Maybe we can talk a little bit. Help each other out. You know what I mean?"

I nodded my head. She smiled and walked out of the bathroom door. She spun around in the doorway. "My name is Tammy. And your name is?" She held her hand out to me.

I adjusted my pants, grabbed her hand, and said, "Alexi."

"I like that name, kid." She let go of my hand and walked away.

I followed her into the main diner. I sat in a corner booth she pointed out, and as promised, she joined me when her shift ended. I should have said, "Thanks and see you later!" but the fragrance of apple pie and the size of her tits was too much to ask a horny eighteen-year-old, going on thirty, to resist.

The night at Tammy's was perfect. Her house was in the middle of three acres of wooded land, with a pole barn at the end of a gravel path at the edge of the woods. Like a picture in a child's storybook, the white moon hung proud in the starry black sky. She made a bed up for me and kissed me on the forehead. "Sleep tight. We will discuss our arrangement tomorrow, but I think it's going to work out nicely."

I smiled and nodded, thinking she was talking about chores on her land or a job at the diner.

The scene flickered and I was surrounded by noises. Moaning. The sharp crackle of a whip. I got out of bed and followed the noise. There was a chill in the fall air; I rubbed the gooseflesh on my arms. The house was like a maze. Lefts and rights. Three floors of long multi-room hallways. I poked into dark rooms, calling out in a soft voice, "Tammy. Tammy."

I stared out a kitchen window and noticed light spilling out of the barn door. I stepped outside. The cracks and moans grow louder. The pea-gravel dug into my bare feet. Where are my shoes? I eased my body through the barn door and covered my mouth to hold in a surprised yelp. Tammy was in black leather boots, her flesh spilled out between the tight black leather strands crisscrossing around her body. She had a flogger in hand, standing over a beet-red ass.

Tammy's voice was deep and sultry. "What I tell you about causing a scene at my diner?" The muted thwack of the flogger on the fat of that ass fascinated me. "What did your mistress tell you?" Tammy yelled out.

A mumbled response. His head turned. Our eyes met. It was the guy from the diner that pinned me against the sink. Glistening red ball gag in his mouth. He nodded his head in my direction. Tammy spun and walked to me, swinging the flogger, a crooked smile smeared across her face.

"Alexi!" Her voice was deep. Full of anger. Full of frustration. "Since you're curious, you need to strip."

"What?"

"I said strip naked and get over here!" She walked to the man and untied him off the modified pommel horse. With a quick snap of her wrist, the flogger smacked his ass, and he jumped, pulling on his clothes waddling past me.

"I'm not waiting much longer!"

I walked to her. The scent of leather filled my nose.

She laid the flogger on the pommel horse and pulled me into her. Her nails digging into the flesh of my butt. She lifted me off the ground. She smiled.

"I knew you would be a good boy. You like it rough, don't you?"

I nodded; eyes buried in her cleavage. I would have agreed to anything.

"Alexi!" I stared at her blue eyes, gold eye shadows and red blushed cheeks. "First rule. There are no free lunches!"

"What...?" My words are lost in her mouth as she kissed me, her tongue probing. She let me go, smiling. She pushed me away. Everything moved fast. She had something in her hand.

"Rule two. I'm the boss!"

In a blur, something clocks me on the top of my head. Her hand was holding a rubber club. Her shrill laughing, the world rushed past me, and my body smacked against the hard-cold earth. She stood over me and started disrobing. Her image started to fade.

Fading.

Fading into black—

I jerk awake, grabbing my head. Nothing. A dream. Where am I? Still in bed? Where is Brenda? A dank, lavender odor hangs in the air. I pull the covers off my body. Why am I naked? The room is unfamiliar and sterile. Am I in a hotel? Did Brenda and I go on a vacation?

I hear a man singing. I swing out of bed to investigate. The shower is running. I push open the bathroom door, and warm air fills my lungs. The baritone voice is humming a tune. I notice my naked reflection in the mirror. Why am I naked? Why is there a man in our hotel shower?

I put my hand on the shower curtain. I yank the metal rings across the metallic bar. The swish of the plastic curtain sprays my body with cold drops of water.

"What's...going...on." I stumble backward, trying to figure out the scene. Did we? I am naked, he is naked. I am hot, wet, and sticky. My throat dries. My tongue is like cotton, sticking to the roof of my mouth. He turns the water off.

"Hey, sleepyhead. I thought I worked you into a coma." He laughs. "Or you smoked too much pot."

"What?"

"You're the type that can keep a secret. I like that. A little birdy told me you were good at keeping secrets." He steps out of the shower. His naked wet body presses against mine. He grabs my hair. "You like it rough, wild man!" He kisses me on the cheek, gives me a sharp smack on my butt. The *thwack* of his hand on my flesh sounds like the crack of a whip.

"I know just how you like it." He grabs a towel. "Or is that just with older waitresses named Tammy?" He winks. "Your secret is safe with me."

"What?"

I gaze at him. Who is this man? Is he implying that we had sex? No. Impossible. There has to be another explanation.

"Hey, Georgie-boy. You okay?"

The name Georgie-boy, familiar. The name Tammy, familiar.

"What happened?"

This man pushes past me into the bedroom. He picks up clothes off the floor and flings them at me.

"Look, I don't want to play this game anymore. We fucked, okay. You seemed to like it ten minutes ago, and now you're playing the 'What did you do to me' game?" He points to the door. "I ain't got time for this shit, man. I'm a bit high, too, but—" He laughs. "Just get your stuff and get the fuck out."

I start pulling on my pants, shoes, and shirt. I follow the direction of his finger. Have we done this before?

"I'm sorry, but I don't remember."

"Don't give me that shit. You always play that 'I don't know' shit when it's time for you to leave. I know who you are. Tammy told me everything you are into, so you can stop playing the innocent part." He points again. "Out!"

I hurry across the cold, empty space of the apartment.

"Take all your shit."

I follow his finger to the baggie of dried herbs and the pipe lying on the coffee table. I throw them into the brown bag.

"Hey Brian, or should I say Georgie-boy! How was that rough talk? Remember now?" He winks. "Come back soon, Georgie-boy!" He starts slapping his butt, gyrating his hips, and laughing. That deep, deep mocking laugh follows me, along with the gross display of his flapping flesh.

I lean my head on the closed door. My mind swirls with faces. Georgie-boy. Tammy. Granny. Brenda. How many times have I played this game? How many times have I been chased out and stood in this hallway? Did I enjoy this? Do I enjoy this? A song starts looping in my head.

...I got my new lover, and he don't know... I got my new lover, and he don't know...

Are we lovers? My stomach clenches. I fall to my knees. I notice a yellowed spot on the carpet. My spot? Have I been on my knees here before? Disgusted, not by actions I can't remember, but by imaging the worst? The warm bile pushes past my tight lips. Regrets burn my throat and spills out of my body as a chunky, frothy mess. I wipe my mouth. I wipe away the strands of spittle, but the sour lingers in my mouth. Where am I? My heart starts to pound against my chest. I close my eyes and inhale and exhale like Dr. Shirley taught me. I can smell lavender. Her image forms in the fog of my mind. Her voice calls out to me.

I look at my watch, 10:19 am, no wonder my stomach is grumbling. I pull my phone out and text Lee.

"Wanna do lunch? "

"Sure, let's meet at our place."

"See you in 2 hours or so."

I pocket my phone. Where the hell am I? I see an elevator and run for it, leaving someone's past behind me.

CHAPTER 12

Brian:
227 Days after Event

What the hell is happening to me? What did I do? And who was that man? The doorman waves hello. His eyes are familiar. His smile is familiar. Have I been here before? Or is he in my mind? Someone else's past? Was he here earlier when I came in?

I don't want to acknowledge his presence. I start trotting, lunging for the door and into the world. The hot sun stings my eyes. I use my hand to shield my face, but sharp flashes of pale-red light pulse behind my eyes.

Running. The city blurs past me. The tall buildings close in on me. I run faster as the tall shadows surround me. Suffocating. My legs pound the concrete hard. I ignore the faces of the people I pass. Running faster, legs burning, lungs filling with stale air.

I stumble up my building stairs and push into the lobby. I wipe the sweat dripping into my eyes. The hallway narrows into the door of my condo. I'm expecting the sickly-sweet fragrance of Brenda's lavender and vanilla spice perfumes, but my lungs are filled with the sweet aroma of roses.

The odor of fresh cut flowers mingles with my own musky scent. I scan around the room and spot the large arrangement of red and pink long-stem roses. Drawn to the flowers like a honeybee, I push my nose into the sex organs. I wonder what the occasion is and read the small and sloppy handwriting on the attached card.

"To my sweetie, Happy B-Day! Love always, Alex."

The name Alex punches me in the gut. My heart pounds hard against my chest. A sharp pain stabs behind my eyes. Tiny white speckles and squiggles of light fill my vision.

"Who the hell is Alex? Why is he sending Brenda—?" Voices start screaming in my head. Who is Brenda? Is Brenda my wife or fiancée? Who is Alex?

I grab the vase and shake the flowers. The pungent stink of fresh-cut roses fills the air. I throw the heavy, water-filled vase across the room. The ballet of pink and red flowers and green stems dance in a perfect arc, defying gravity for a moment. The moment passes and they fall in a predictable way. The glass shatters like thousands of tiny cymbals clashing at once. The noise jars me out of my rage and directs my attention to the issue.

Had I forgotten my fiancée's birthday and someone else remembered? How can I, the keeper of memories, dreams, and nightmares, keep forgetting the most sacred of them all? Why can't I remember what is most important to me?

I contemplate the mess of flowers and glass, drowning in a pool of regret. Have I lived this moment before? Or has someone else?

Shattered glass and sickly-sweet floral vegetation thrown away and forgotten, I start to wipe at the mess. Large chunks of glass stab me as I collect the roses, but I try to pick around them. Rose thorns scrape across and into my flesh. Thin rows of scratches crisscross my hands. Tiny droplets of blood ooze out of the wounds. I throw the flowers to the floor again. Angry at myself for forgetting. Angry at the roses for reminding me they have thorns.

The vase cannot be fixed, maybe replaced. Maybe that's what Brenda is doing, replacing the mess in her life that cannot be fixed. My cellphone buzzes. It's her. I press the answer button—

"Hey there."

"Hey, you. I'm off today, going to grab some lunch and a drink or two, want to join."

"Yeah sure, Angela—"

"Where do you want to go? "

A flood of voices scream in my head. "Billy's Burgers and Beers. "

"That dump."

"That's our place. Right?"

"Yeah... Okay, see you there."

I glance at the clock on the wall. I have time to wash this sweet, pungent, smokey odor of my earlier transgressions off my body.

I start stripping off these skunky-stank clothes. The clothes still stink like him, and every whiff causes my stomach to clench and hot metallic bile singes the back of my throat. I ball the clothes and throw them into the garbage can, pushing them to the bottom, like memories best forgotten. I tie the bag, closing off the experience.

I open the bathroom door, and the cool pushes against the warm air surrounding my naked skin. I start the water for a bath. How long has it been since I took a bath? Letting my long limbs soak. Epsom salts melting the tight knots out of my muscles. The sweet calming lavender soap, the white noise of the water molecules colliding.

A calmness settles the voices in my mind. The water is warm. I turn up the heat. The bath is half full. I swirl the soap into the water. The water begins to froth with large white clouds of bubbles, and my hand melts into the scalding water like gallium. I slip into the water like a comfortable silk robe. I close my eyes, and I'm relieved as an image of Brenda flickers into my mind, the memory of how we met starts to play—

The blinding sun reminded me that I forgot my sunglasses at the hotel. The concrete radiated heat. Beads of sweat dampened my collar, too warm for an April day in Chicago. Hyde Park, to be exact, where I wandered around campus, lost, separated for my tour group. I was trying to decide if I wanted to spend five years of graduate school here or north of the city.

I snuck away from my tour group to meet with Professor Brice, who works on nano-constructs, and we started talking about potential projects. I met several other folks working in the lab who were all smiles and pleasantries. They promised to come to the recruitment party later that day but had to hustle to their laboratory benches like well-trained rats. Did I want this life?

After meeting Brice and learning more about the nano-project collaboration, the decision will be easy. I spotted my tour group a couple blocks away. I waved my arms and pushed my way through a rush of students, running across the street. There was beeping, brakes squealing, muscles tensing, and the pop of metal colliding with my body.

My legs buckled, and I smacked my head on the asphalt. My eyes blinked open, blinding sun. My ears filled with screaming. Maybe my screams echoed back from the heavens. I laid on a bed of pins and needles inching their way into my flesh. Everything was mute and moving slow. I squinted and followed the wisps of thin white clouds streaking across the limpid, sea-blue sky. I blinked, and the scene flickered with shadows crowding around me. Voices filled my ears. Darkness tunneled my vision as my body melted from the pain. Blackness swallowed me whole.

Hot, sticky air filled my lungs. Pressure... pressure... pressure, on my chest. My eyes popped open, and she was leaning in for a kiss, our lips embraced. I imagined we were lying on a grassy knoll enjoying the warm spring day. My eyes adjusted, focusing on her red lips, her tanned face, her brown eyes, flushed cheeks, and brownish-red hair pulled into a tight ponytail. Her lips were moving. Was she talking? Why don't my ears work? I tried to listen. I noticed other curious onlookers. My legs were on fire. I tried to sit up, but her hand pressed on my chest.

"Stay calm. Help is on the way."

It was her voice, her lips moving, those sweet, red lips. My lover's lips. I realized our first kiss was not a kiss at all. My face must have given away my disappointment.

"Oh, relax, I work here at U-Chicago." She stroked my hair. "You passed out and stopped breathing. I figured it was from shock."

"My...leg hurts...bad."

"It's not a bad break, should heal up nice. They will have you patched up in no time and back to the grind."

Sirens were getting closer, my time with her was ticking away.

"Name?"

She read the nametag on my shirt. "Your name is Alexi." She smiled. "Welcome to the university!"

"No, I know my name." I swallowed hard, ignoring the pain twisting the muscles in my leg. *"Wh-What is...your name?"*

Her eyebrows raised, and she nodded. "Marcina." She squeezed my shoulder. "Now relax."

I'd never forget that moment. I asked an angel her name, Marcina. Marcina, the name rolled off the tongue. A name I could've said forever. I love you, Marcina. *An ear-piercing noise broke my concentration. Sirens?*

The sirens stopped. Two men shoved Marcina aside and started to strap my head to a board. I realized Marcina's first name was not enough; what was her last name? I tried to use my arm to push the EMT guy out of my way, but intense pain shot across my body.

I yelled as loud as I can, "Marcina, what is your last name?"

Marcina poked her head between the EMT guys and looked at me.

"Marcina Jenowski." She smiled.

I relaxed. Our eyes met one last time as she poked her head in between the EMTs. "I'll see you around?" She touched the top of my head. "And when you get patched up, remember you owe me a cup of coffee and a brownie." She winked and moved as the EMT guys wheeled me off.

I lifted my hand to give a thumbs up. Even the intense pain could not keep me from smiling—

My eyes open. Image blurry. I jump out of the water. An alarm beeping fills my ears with noise. I cough, expelling soapy water out of my lungs. The annoying ring of my cellphone continues.

I slip out of the tub onto the cold floor, gasping for air like a bamboo shark swimming onto land. The stabs of pain push the last drops of water out of my lungs. The cellphone pulls my attention away from the involuntary act of inhalation. I crawl onto my knees, smacking the phone.

"Damn it!"

I get dressed and hurry out the door.

When I walk into the empty restaurant, she is lounging in a booth, feet dangling over the edge. I look at her smiling face. She swings her legs down to the floor, and I slide in next to her. Our bodies press close. Her cinnamon scent. My Angela.

"Sorry, I'm late."

"No problem, it was last minute." She leans in, kissing my cheek. "I'm just glad you came."

A round of drinks arrive.

"I know what you like."

"Cheers." I hold up my glass.

Angela taps her glass to mine and mumbles into her glass. "Cheers, Eduardo."

The door creeps open, and I cannot believe my eyes.

Angela coughs out words, "What is she doing here?"

I rub my eyes; another Brenda is standing at the table. I look at the woman sitting next to me, and her face is Brenda's. The disheveled, standing Brenda starts to wobble, fall—

I reach out to catch Brenda and ease her into the booth. She is talking, screaming, but my ears are not working. My mouth is moving but I cannot hear my own voice. Why can't I hear? Her eyes well up with tears and she storms off. Was that Brenda? I watch her walk out. Should I follow her?

My cell phone chimes. It's Nurse Marci.

"Hello."

Marci's shaky voice answers. "Who's this?"

"It's me, Brian."

"Great. Brian you have to come to the clinic."

"Why?"

"Because of Granny."

"Okay."

"Get here as fast as you can."

"Why?"

"We need to do another scan."

I nod.

"Brian, you understand?" Marci's voice is full of concern

"Yeah."

"Come as fast as you can to the clinic."

"I said okay."

The line goes quiet. I pull the phone away and the call has been ended.

Her hand rubs on my back. "Everything okay?"

I turn to look at her. Her face blurs. Is she Brenda? Is she Angela? Is she Granny? *I got my new lover and he don't know—*

"Sorry, I have to go?"

"Go?"

Her face stops vibrating.

"Sorry, Angela, I have to go to the clinic." I stand.

Angela grabs my hand. "Nothing serious. I can go with."

I shake my head. "No, just... just something with Granny. They need my scan."

"Oh." Angela's face twists into a scowl. "What's so special about Granny that she gets scanned all the damn time?"

I hunch my shoulders. "I don't know, but I better go."

She waves. Her voice is small. "Don't forget about me."

"Yeah." I do not turn around, walking out the bar thinking about Granny and her song, *I got my new lover, and he don't know...*

***

Driving to the makeshift clinic, a jumble of thoughts enters my mind. Marci and Granny. Their faces haunt the city streets. Voice chatter in my ears. Cars beeping. Light green. Thanks, Granny. Fuck you, Nurse Marci. I blink my eyes several times, trying to clear them out.

The cherry gum in my mouth reminds me of Marci's wet, sticky tongue. That kiss...familiar, but aren't all kisses? Wet, sticky, and familiar. A lover's kisses. You never forget those. Maybe I'm someone else. Or I can pretend. Pretend to love Marci? Granny? Brenda? Even Larry... Being serenaded by horns, I blink my eyes again. The light is green.

I pull into the parking lot. The cars are all familiar. Everything has become familiar to me. I'm in full control of myself, but my memories still elude me, the voids filled in by other's experiences.

The cool, antiseptic air flows out as I walk into the lobby. The white-washed hallway leads to the place it all started—that lobby filled with deadpan faces and empty shells of people robbed of their memories. Hopeful that they could get some part of themselves returned.

"Brian?" A voice calls out of the ether. I look up and see Nurse Marci. "Brian, so nice to see you again. Sorry you had to come in a hurry, but I don't think we need to do a scan today."

"Okay, I can still go say hi to Granny."

"Yeah, sure." Marci's body presses against mine. Her hand squeezes my butt. This moment seems familiar, but I'm uncomfortable and break the connection by stepping away.

"Sorry, Marci, I've had a really bad day."

Her brow crinkles. "Maybe we can go to my office and talk about this. Maybe I can cheer you up."

I shake my head. "I have something to do tonight. Maybe tomorrow we can meet."

"It will be over soon, I promise." She grabs my hand. "Granny is in exam room five."

Marci gives my hand one more squeeze. As I walk past, I notice her eyes are watering. Is she crying because of me? I grab the handle of the exam room and glance behind me but, like an apparition, she is not there.

I walk into the room, and Granny is standing there. Naked. I spin away.

"Oh my! Sorry, Granny!"

Her yelp fades into a sigh of comfort. "Why you keep calling me that silly nickname? Acting like you never saw me naked before."

I turn and study her face... Her young, smooth face. Why do I call her Granny? "Sorry, sweetie, you treat me so good like a granny should."

Her brown cheeks glow with a red blush. She wobbles putting her leg into her pants.

In one quick move, she is in my arms.

"My hero. Always there when I need you most." She says reaching her hand out, caressing my face.

I sit her onto the bed. Our faces are close. Lips too close. I taste the salty sweetness of sliced ham and baked beans on her breath. It takes me a second to register the flicking of her familiar tongue in my mouth. I close my eyes and enjoy my lover's kiss. *I got my new lover, and he don't know—*

Hands have a way of remembering. Even in the dark. Hands remember where they should be. Hands are not bound by time. They remember, like long, deep kisses. Time melts away, like the penultimate piece of chocolate. Swallowing the lump in my throat, trying to remember before the flavor fades away, and you are forced to eat the last bite.

I pull away and smile at Granny. Why do I call her that? She is young enough to be my lover. Is she my lover? I gaze into her eyes and remember—

We were at the hospital after the bus attack. Her body bruised and broken. Her family rushed in, accusing me of putting their baby girl in harm's way. "She could have been killed—" Her mom yelled, slapping me across the face. They were attacking me more than the folks who did the beating—

The vision fades as muffled voices yell outside the door. Granny is still kissing on my neck when the door slams open. We both start grabbing at our clothes to cover our bodies.

"Granny!" Ralphie yells as his smile fades into a balled fist. "You sick bastard!"

"Wait, I can—"

The thick, meaty fist collides with my jaw. Stars jog into my plane of vision. Granny screams, her body jumping in between us. Another meaty fist snaps my head back. Stumbling. Falling. Brenda steps into the horizon of my vision. What is she doing here? Nurse Marci pushes past her. They glare at each other. Nurse Marci kneels by me, grabbing my hand and yelling. She is yelling at me to concentrate. My eyelids are heavy with tears. She leans in close; her mouth is moving. I try to remember her red lips.

Her voice is distant, saying, "What is your name?"

Her face blurs in and out of focus. She was there that day. It was her voice, her lips moving, those sweet, red lips, my lover's lips. Dark shadows are swallowing my vision. A voice calls for me to focus from the void.

My own voice yells, "Recuerdos llenan el vacío."

The black fog starts to fold into me. "I remember now." The matte-black darkness swallows me, and there I find myself alone.

PART 2:
BRENDA'S STORY, MARCI'S STORY

CHAPTER 13

Brenda:
We Will Never Forget How Much We Love You

Falling, but I wake up in the same place
This defies logic
The act itself
Falling
Falling, suggests
You start some place
And end in another
A different place or position
That can be painful and undesirable
Falling down
Falling off
Falling into
Love may be the exception

CHAPTER 14

Brenda:
Day of Event

You never realize how much you love someone until they leave you, surrounded by all their stuff. The walls are filled with memories. Trinkets and mementos of their life fill the smallest of nooks. Every moment of silence reminds you of them. The quiet of night is the worst.

How did I live all those years? Single and alone, his breathing not here to keep me company, the warmth of his body. I miss my husband. A four-day trip away to a laboratory near Philadelphia. But not any lab. The lab of his former girlfriend. Marci. Ex-fiancée to be precise.

He told me not to let the past get to me. They were still friends. Research colleagues. She lives in Philadelphia. We live in Chicago. "Just friends," he reminded me when he left the house. "Just friends," he reminds me every time he checks in at night. "Just..."

The tubular ringing of my cellphone startles me. My heart is racing to hear his voice, like the first phone call from him. I lunge for my cell phone—

"Hey, you!"

"Hey. How was your day?"

My face tightens as a childish smile smears across my face, my free hand twirling the ends of my hair. "Oh, the usual. I don't want to bore you with the intricacies of legal speak. Just more clients in sad situations and—" I wipe my eyes, swelling with tears. "I don't want to talk about it. How was your day?"

"Oh, I'm sorry..."

"Don't be. Tell me how your day went."

"It was crazy busy! I gave an impromptu talk to a group at this luncheon that Brice invited me to about scientific writing and life balance."

"Who's Brice?"

"Oh, remember, he is the director of the Nano Institute in Chicago. I met him during grad school. He helped me with some research ideas, and we collaborated on that book..."

The phone goes silent. I can imagine him gazing at invisible words buzzing by his head, scanning the ether for the perfect words.

His voice breaks the silence, "Funny thing is, I haven't heard from him in years, and then I just ran into him at breakfast. It was Marci who saw him first."

I cough into the phone. "Marci was with you at breakfast?"

There is another pause. Here comes another "we are just friends" speech. Why does this bother me so much? Something about moving on from the past? Forgetting the painful memories of days gone by? Maybe it is more about my past relationships, trust issues, than about Marci and—His voice cuts into my thoughts.

"Marci is a good friend. I know we had a history, but that's in the past. We have some interesting research breakthroughs to talk about and wanted to maximize the time we got to chat about it. We had breakfast, I talked with Brice at the luncheon, and then I spent the rest of the afternoon in her lab. Besides breakfast, we had adult supervision. The whole time."

He pauses, swallows hard, but continues before I could start talking. "If it makes you feel better, a liter of salt solution was spilled on me, and I didn't have time to change before the flight. Looks like I peed my pants. But it's starting to dry and flake away. I rubbed the worst off in the plane bathroom."

He snorts a laugh. I love that laugh. A nerdy, high-pitched, squeaky laugh. I can imagine his lips parting, nose flaring. His whole-body jerks when he laughs. An awkward display of joy. A pure emotion.

"Just you and your science friends. How much trouble could you get into?"

"Yeah, like a team of superheroes. Just doing research wherever it takes us. Writing books and making the world a better place."

"Yeah, that's what worries me."

"Why?"

"Nothing, don't worry about it."

"Sure, you're okay?"

"So what did you get into this time?"

"Oh, Marci is working on the coolest thing. I mean, if it works, and we combine her idea with this new nano-construct I developed, it could transform the way we think. Literally! She has money pouring out of her eyeballs in this institute. And I want to make sure I have my space at the table, not that I care about money and fame. But check this out..."

His words run into each other. My mind flattens his excited, pitchy voice into a monotone *wah-wah-wah*. All I can hear is, "Marci, *wah-wah*. Marci, *wah-wah*. Research on, *wah-wah*. Nano-*wah-wah*. This will change the way we think. I mean literally."

The line goes quiet. He clears his throat. "What, you fall asleep on me?"

"Oh no, just letting the knowledge wash over me." I fake a laugh and hold my tongue as my mind fills with more sarcastic responses like, *You had to fly out to Philadelphia to hear about her research? A phone call or videoconference would not work? A four-day trip with lab buddies and ex-fiancée.* I exhale and stare at the clock on the wall.

I settle on, "Yeah, sweetie, that sounds fantastic. You and Marci are doing some great stuff. I'm glad you got to eat breakfast and talk with her about it." I pat myself on the back for taking the highroad.

The hands on the clock begin to wind around each other. The numbers blur into black smudges. I blink my eyes and focus. 4 p.m.

"Isn't your flight at three-something? Or are you spending the night with Marci?"

Why did I say that? I was trying to change the subject. I was trying to take the highroad. I hate those jealous wife types. But here I'm playing the part.

"What?" he answers in a concerned quiet voice.

"Nothing, just joking around with you."

"Um, yeah, it was supposed to leave close to three, but the plane was delayed. Been on the tarmac for almost an hour."

I'm glad he did not call me out on my stupid remark. That's what I love about him: his ability to read my emotions, to not take the bait—bait that I did not intend to throw out.

"What is your flight number again? I can track it. "

"I don't know. Who remembers their flight number?" He snorts a laugh. "Hold on one minute, let me ask Granny."

I can hear the rustle of papers and a quiet voice whispering.

"Thanks, Granny. It's flight 2164!"

"Who's Granny?"

"Oh, the sweetest person on earth—besides you. But she comes with delicious homemade fudge. I think she would edge you out by a hair."

Granny giggles and says, "Oh stop!"

"Good thing I found you first." What the hell is wrong with me? I would not consider myself a jealous type. Am I? Am I this insecure? Must be the hormones. One benefit of being pregnant, you can always blame the hormones. I should have told him before he went to Philadelphia. I need to tell him, but not over the phone. It will have to wait until he gets home.

His voice cuts into my thoughts.

"You sure you're feeling okay?"

How should I answer? Should I tell him about getting overly emotional over the smallest nothing? The puking sessions in the morning? The dull pain in my boobs that makes sleeping difficult? Or confess that I'm scared to death to become a mother? I remind myself that he does not know.

"I'm doing okay. I cannot wait to see you. Give you a big hug and kiss. Hold you close to me tonight."

"I miss you too. Maybe we can go for a walk and..."

His voice cracks and fades into silence.

"Yeah, that sounds nice. I have some news—"

Laughter erupts in my ear. How much fun could he be having with a grandma? "You said you were sitting by Granny? Is that a grandma or somebody's name?"

"Yeah, she is a grandmother."

"What's her name?"

"She introduced herself as Granny. She could be Pam Grier for all I know!"

Another burst of laughter. The giggling schoolgirl laugh like off-key violin strings plucking at my brain, and the string breaks when I overhear, "You stop it, you big flirt! You're just saying that to get more fudge out of me."

I curl my hand into a fist and punch the couch. My diaphragm swelling with anger, with heat; the burn of my last meal making its way up my esophagus. My chest is on fire. One more body change. One more thing I have to deal with. Seven and a half months more. At least after tonight, I will not be alone in this venture.

I whisper through my clinched teeth, "I have to go, sweetie."

"Oh. You sure everything is okay?"

I want to yell, *My chest is on fire. My boobs are sore. I'm jealous of some grandma giving you fudge. I'm mad that you're having breakfast with your ex. I just found out I'm a month pregnant. I'm freaking out about everything. Other than that—*

My voice trembles, "I'm okay."

The faint crinkle of static fills in between us. Or is that my imagination? My mind spinning its wheels.

"Okay." The pitch and tone of his voice fades into the crunchy static on the line. I strain to hear his voice. "I'll be home soon."

I hold the phone, listening for more. Nothing but that crunchy silence and that clock ticking on the wall. His voice is soft. "I'll be home soon."

I push out another lungful of air. "I'm fine. I love you. Have a safe flight."

I end the call before he can say anything else. I run to the bathroom, hot stabs of pain burning my throat. My knees slam against the cold bathroom tile. The water in the toilet has the faint smell of chlorine. I cough several times. Pump priming. The stringy, orangish, half-digested carrot and walnut salad stains the pristine water, like abstract art. I stare at the swirls of orange and green.

The acidic, sour-milk stink causes me to gag again. A series of coughs. The pump priming. My abdominal muscles clench, and my diaphragm spasms like an accordion. I grip the edge of the toilet. The cold porcelain cools my hot, sweaty hands.

I push my knees into the hard tile. My raw throat burns with every cough. Cough. Cough. Cough. A defiant strand of saliva hangs from my mouth, connecting me to my dinner. I spit. My hand reaches, gripping the cold metal handle. I pull with all my strength, flushing away the one meal that stayed down more than an hour today.

The spray of cold clean water against my clammy face is refreshing. I push away from the toilet and lie on the cold tile. My vision blurs with tears. I close my eyes. Stomach still grumbling. Throat raw. But the cold floor absorbs the heat radiating from my body and relaxes my tense muscles. I stretch out and rub my flat belly, imaging the bulge to come. I fade into sleep.

Darkness. Falling. Weightless. Falling. A soft tapping. Fingers tapping. Tapping on glass. Rain on a window. Tapping. Soft metallic tapping. Pain stabbing my side. Why am I resting on hard stone? Jagged concrete, rough stone. Body folded like a rag doll dropped from a great distance.

Uncurling, muscles pulling apart. Molecular tearing. The noise it makes, like Velcro underwater. Muscles contracting. Pulling into their lowest energy state. Pain accumulates again. I stretch out. The noise of the ripping and tapping forces my eyes open.

The room is dark and cool. A dim light throws unnatural black shadows on the wall. I blink. I remember. Throat still raw. Head pounding. Stomach growling. How long have I been on this floor?

The soft tap of a key on the front door grabs my attention. I shift my weight to stand and pins and needles stab my foot. I wiggle it, wiggle my toes, rotating the numb appendage to full function. The tapping on the door continues. Is someone trying to pick the lock?

I pat my pocket, where is my cellphone? I remember it's on the couch. I move into an awkward yoga-style pose. Muscles stiff, I get onto all fours and push myself into a standing position. I lean onto the sink for support. I splash water on my face. The sharpness of the freezing water is like a slap across my face. I stare at myself in the mirror, drying my face with my hand. I study my face in this dim yellow glow of the nightlight. I see a face that I don't recognize.

The tapping at the door pulls my attention. I start flicking on lights in the dark condo. "Who's there?" I yell.

Maybe I should have stayed quiet and called the police—or, at least, called the neighbor to take a peek. I grab my cellphone and begin dialing when he calls out.

Like a lost child, confused and whiny, the voice says, "Brenda, it's me."

I run to the door grasping the handle, but pause listening to the croaking voice calling for Brenda. He calls out for help, and throwing caution to the wind, I pull the door open.

I only recognize him by the scent of his spicy cologne. His eyes are droopy. His face sags, like he has lost weight. His shirt is half unbuttoned, curly chest hairs rejoicing in their newfound freedom. His bulky frame struggles with the weight of his small travel bag. He staggers two steps backward, lunges one step forward. A drunken dance. He holds out his hand. A bunch of keys hang onto his middle finger.

His mouth is moving, but his speech is slurry, mumbling. I lean in, his soft voice, words slurring, "You changed the locks. None of them work."

"Sweetie, what happened to you?"

The keys drop from his hand. They hit the ground, like shattering glass. His movements are in slow motion. He bends to pick up the keys, his arm reaching out, shoulder bag sliding off, pulling him to the left. He wobbles to the right. His leg kicks out from behind him like a cartoon character slipping on a banana peel.

I step backward to make room for this awkward display. I realize he has lost complete control of his body. His limbs pull in opposite directions, but gravity is pulling down. I reach out to stop his clumsy fall, my mind reacting one moment too slow. The sharp thud of his head hitting the wood floor stops my approach.

My hand covers my mouth, muting the loud squeak. I stand there mumbling to myself in disbelief as the rest of his body crumples into a heap of limbs. I am paralyzed, frozen in time, for seconds, minutes, maybe hours, until his body finishes its uncontrolled tumble. His head twists, closed eyes fluttering.

His fingers start to move. They start to vibrate. The vibration moves up his arms. His shoulders start to shake. His torso bobbing like he is a fish out of water. His legs start flopping around. His head drags on the floor.

"My husband is having a stroke," I yell. Yelling for help. I fall to my knees grabbing, his flopping body. Yelling. Yelling at him to stop. Yelling at the world for help. Yelling at the darkness funneling my vision. All I can do is yell and hope someone will wake me from this nightmare.

INTERLUDE

Brian:
Day of Event

Who am I? What's my name? Alex... George... Brian... Dan... Mary... Eduardo—the pressure is building in my head.

I blink, and there she is. My Leslie, or is her name Brenda? She kneels beside me, calling for help. I try to reach my hand to caress her face, but my muscles don't respond. How do you make muscles move?

Who am I? Faces and names flash like an old movie projector. Voices yelling, but no one is here except her, crying. Where are the voices coming from?

I try to focus on her face, my Leslie... Granny... Angela... Amanda? I squint and the blurry faces focus into her, Brenda. She leans in and kisses me on the lips. I close my eyes and the voices stop. A vision starts to play—

I was soaking in a bath. My muscles were tight and sore. The bathroom door whooshed open, drafting cool air around my body not submerged in the hot sudsy water. My skin broke out in gooseflesh. She sat down a bottle of wine, two glasses and stripped her clothes off. Her body pressed against mine as she slipped into the tub, on top of me. I rubbed my soapy fingers along the curves of her body. Her skin felt firm and smooth. My mind dissolved away into the glass of wine she was holding. She took a drink and kissed me. The bitter tannins lingered on my tongue. The glass was wet, slippery. It fell to the floor, a shattering sharp ting. Brenda jumped out of the tub, cursing at herself, at me. I reached out, grabbing, trying to hold on to Brenda and pull her to me—

The vision flickers into a gray fog that fades into a black emptiness. The voices flood back into the empty void. Who are they? Who am I?

CHAPTER 15

Marci:
Night of Event

At a certain age we all struggle, trying to reclaim our youth. The fountain does not spring eternal, but we keep searching for the streets paved in gold. Like Ponce de Leon, we will travel many miles to satisfy our dying flame's quest for more oxygen. Money, sex, beauty—we all have our own vices. Yet we all satisfy the craving in our own peculiar way.

I gave everything away for my career and here I am. Alone, drinking tequila, and waiting to salsa dance with strangers. My mind waiting to go numb. My body waiting to be enjoyed.

The bartender hands me another drink. As the first sip of tequila stings my tongue, I remember him—the way his arms wrapped around my body, his lips kissing along my collarbone—Alexi. These last four days we worked together it took every fiber in my body not to throw myself at him. What we could have been if I had not been in a hurry to get here.

My twenty-one-year-old self would be proud. I'm a team leader, institute builder, the "It" person on the cover of trendy magazines, *NPR* interviews, a comfortable level of wealth. So much to be proud of, but my ten-year-old self misses the white wedding dress, white picket fence, toddlers toddling, the faithful dog and husband. It should have been Alexi. I take another sip of my drink, and the sting of regret is already starting to fade.

I find myself here on Saturdays often to escape who I am. This small dive bar in the space between the polish and glam of Downtown Philadelphia and Penn's Landing. The narrow cobblestone streets always stink at night like a dank basement, but inside the bar, the tequila is cheap, the music is loud, and my space is filled with the ethanolic spicy stink of cheap lovers. Bodies pressing together, glasses clanking together, laughs, loud talking, kisses and flesh being shared in the shadows.

I have had two drinks; the band has been working this place into a frenzy of kinetic motion for the last half hour. I have been ogling him since he strolled in. He winks and starts making his way to me through the twirling bodies. We have met here several times the last couple months. I would like to say these meetups are random; they never are, but we pretend.

He leans into my space, and asks, "You want to dance?"

It takes me a second to remember his name—Eric—but I remember his face, his body. He's a good dancer. He is also good at... This night may have a happy ending, after all. I nod, close my eyes, and swallow the rest of my drink.

I stand and turn to order another drink, our bodies brush against each other. I lift onto my toes, stretching across the bar top, waving to catch the bartender's attention. The bartender mouths "another" and I wink, nodding.

My arm is being tugged into the swarm of bodies, and my asymmetrical pleated dress lifts. The air tickles my skin like I am flying, my body is twirled in rhythm to the singer rolling his r's, fading into the quiet caesura. The band members take a moment to wipe the sweat off their brow or a swig of beer. He holds my hand, arm extended; my body is balanced on the quality of my three inch, two hundred fifty-dollar stiletto heel—

The music drums to life, and he pulls me close. I inhale his sweet and fruity sangria aroma. He spins me away and twirls me close. I step in rhythm with his gyrating body. Strobing lights. His bronze skin glistens, thick gold chain swaying with his hips. The top three buttons of his silk shirt undone, curly black hair, his leather pants, tight—he pulls me into him again, and our hips join in a sensual dance of their own. I lean in close; our cheeks press together.

He places his hand on the small of my back and attempts to dip me. I resist. I smile, so he spins me again, but he does not pull me close. I step into his space; his eyebrows are drawn in, lips pursed, the face that men get when they realize they can't overpower you. But I want him to overpower me tonight, so I relent and let him dip me.

We press our bodies together as the quiet of the last chord dissipates into the lead singer saying they were taking a break and would return in fifteen minutes.

"You'd be a good salsa dancer if you didn't try to lead so much."

I kiss him on the cheek and retort, "You would be a much better dancer if you let me lead."

He wraps his arm around my waist, whispering in my ear, "Lead on, my lovely flower."

We grab our drinks and retreat to a quieter spot in the shadows of the bar. He is more talkative tonight. He talks with his hands and is trying hard to impress me with his status. A hedge fund guru, most eligible single, thirty-five or younger; he has a penthouse a few blocks from here and a car that can go fast. None of this impresses me, but I play along. I enjoy this manly display of his.

He keeps talking and I keep nodding, hanging onto every word. Maybe it's the tequila or maybe it's the past days I spent with Alexi, but I miss being held and comforted. I yearn to be desired. That starry-eyed sensation that curls your toes. To make love under the anonymous glimmer of shimmering lights, energized by the potential future. Then the night breaks into day, and you are twisted in the warm cuddle of your lover's body.

His breath is warm on my neck. "I'm getting a little worried that you're bored with me already. For someone who wants to lead, you're awfully quiet."

I take a sip of my drink. "There's a time to lead the moment, and a time to enjoy the moment." I take another sip and wiggle my glass, clanking the ice.

"Another?" he asks, grabbing the glass out of my hand, and I nod.

As he slips off his seat his hand brushes against my thigh, slipping beneath my dress. He squeezes and leans in for a kiss. Our lips meet, our tongues meet. My arms wrap around him, pulling, my hand squeezing his firm butt.

He leans away, but my hand is still locked on his ass.

He smiles. "Why don't I settle the check, and we can go to my place. The view is better, and the drinks are cheaper."

"Yes, I'd like that." I squeeze his ass one more time. He looks in my direction and nods. I slip off the stool; our arms interlock as we make our way to the bar, and out into the dank summer night.

First time we met, we went to a fancy hotel after dancing, better to stay as anonymous as possible. Several encounters later, we stand like a familiar couple. Our hands brush against each other, fingers tangle and untangle. I lean against his chest; his arms wrap around me until the car arrives.

As the car twists and turns, our bodies share space. Our mouths share space. Our hands share space—

The car slows, stops, and the door opens. We step out into the night and egress with purpose into a marble walled lobby. Into an elevator where a key is inserted, turned clockwise, the elevator jerks to life.

I study Eric's face in the polished metal elevator door. He has a victor's grin. I lay my head on his shoulder, his arm wraps around me.

"Having fun, my flower?"

I nod my head. He keeps referencing me as a flower. Maybe I'm a flower, and he is a bee. His stinger is sharp, and my petals are delicate, craving his tender caresses to release my sweet nectar. Maybe he is a chauvinistic pig and flower is his default term for women he has our type of relationship with.

The elevator dings, the doors slide open, and the sparkling lights of the city greet us. I move my head along the panoramic skyline. A wall of windows extend floor to ceiling, city lights illuminating the wide space. Dim interior lights begin to flicker on, guiding us off the elevator. He tugs on my arm—

I must admit this is impressive.

"Come on, my flower." Eric pulls my hand, and I step out the elevator. "Make yourself at home. Take off your shoes and relax."

Eric kicks his shoes off and shoves them out of the way. "Make yourself at home." He repeats.

I step into the warm glow of the dim lights, the fragrance of fresh cut flowers, roses or lilacs, and my muscles relax. My purse slips off my shoulder, and I sit on the little bench by the elevator to take off my shoes.

"Want the same thing to drink?"

I lift my head and smile. "That would be nice."

Eric disappears into his space, and I remind myself why I'm here. Not to fall in love with a magnificent view, but to clear the cobwebs of melancholy and soothe my lust for Alexi. I gaze out the window, and I can imagine myself sitting here at night with the lights out, a glass of a dry, oaky red wine—but that's not why I'm here.

I stand, the cold floor soothes my warm stockinged feet. I follow the clanking of ice in a glass and Eric's off-key whistling. I walk behind him and run my hand along his back.

"I like your place. Will I get a tour?"

Eric turns, handing me my drink. "Anything you want, my flower."

I take a sip. Eric loops his arm around mine and pulls me into the labyrinth of his abode.

I don't pay attention to much of what he is rambling on about. Midcentury this and imported that. I nod as though I am impressed by his stories of globetrotting and eccentric tastes in overpriced antiques and used furniture.

At some point he turned on music. Maybe it was that control box on the wall he was playing with, but Coltrane blowing on his horn wafts through every room. I take another sip of my drink.

"And here we are back where we started." Eric plops down on the midcentury, extra-long couch. He pats the cushion, but I pretend not to understand his gesture and walk to the window.

I close my eyes and wrap my arms around my chest, trying to comfort myself from the glare of those city lights beaming at me. Their eyes observing my every move. Criticizing my every mistake. I'm afraid when I open my eyes, I'll be that scared girl again running from her future. Except this time everyone will be watching and reminding me it was all a dream. Everything snatched from me. I'm shown to be a fraud, a failure, and cast back to nothing worth remembering—

My muscles tense, arms gooseflesh, when his hand slides across my ass, around me, and his body presses into me.

"Sorry, I did not mean to startle you, but the way the lights were reflecting off you..." He lays his head on my shoulder, kissing my neck and whispers in my ear, "I could not resist you if I tried."

I turn to face Eric. "You should not try so hard."

Our mouths meet and my hands yank his shirt. A button pops, but he does not pull away. *Pop, pop, pop.* I pull the shirt over his shoulders and run my hands along his muscular back.

He pulls away and our mouths release from each other. He makes a satisfied grunt. My hands tug his belt and he jerks forward, I kiss on his neck.

His hands fumble with the zipper on my dress. My hands work on undoing his belt. Our mouths have joined again, his tongue probing, breath hot like spiced rum.

The zipper releases and my skin tingles as the dress slips off my body. His warm soft hands drawing crooked lines along the sides of my body. Each hand squeezing one of my butt cheeks.

In one swift, well-practiced move, I'm lifted and carried through the noise of frantic saxophone runs. Through the aroma of roses and lilacs. Through this perfect place, this perfect time, my mind goes numb as he sits me on the soft bed.

I pull at his pants.

He pulls at my bra.

I pull at his boxers.

He pulls at my panties.

His naked body, glistens like molten-bronze melting into me. I want to close my eyes. I want my eyes open. I want to resist. I want to lead. I want to be taken. I want to give. I want to be needed. I want to be loved. Respected. Enjoyed. Pleasured. Remembered. Forgotten.

I can hold my breath no longer. I scream out, and a small tingle shoots through my body. I can't resist smiling, feeling happy. I cannot resist digging my fingers into his flesh.

He grunts with pleasure and his thrusting slows and stops. He rolls off me and moans, exhausted. I roll onto him, laying my head on his chest. The lights of the city cast eerie shadows across the bedroom, and the noise of a piano playing blends into his soft snoring. I close my eyes and begin to drift to sleep when the soft buzzing of my cell phone nags at me.

A few numbers can ring through my Do-Not-Disturb setting, and none of them can be good at this hour. I lift off of Eric's chest and slink out of the bed without disturbing him. I dash out the room and around the corner to the bench.

My phone has stopped ringing, but I read his name.

"Damn it, Mark!" I mumble into the phone, trying to keep my voice a whisper and not wake—my phone buzzes to life.

"What is it, Mark?"

"Marci, we have a situation in Chicago."

"What kind of situation?" I start pacing the room when the lights of the city pull me to the window.

Mark lets out a sigh, and words spill out. "How fast can you get to Chicago?"

"Mark, please tell me what is happening. I was having a pleasant evening and—"

"It's Alex. He's in the hospital—"

I cut Mark off before he can finish. "Why didn't you start with that instead of all this mysterious bullshit? Now, what happened to Alexi?"

"Marci, it's hard to explain. You just have to come here and fast. We cannot lose containment of this situation." Mark's words begin to run together in a nervous ramble. "I think we can get access. This may be something big, but we need to have our story straight."

I close my eyes to relax and inhale the calm of those fresh cut flowers. "Mark, sweetie, please calm down and tell me what is going on, or I swear I'll reach through this phone and punch the shit out of you!"

"Marci, please it's hard to—"

"If you say it's hard to explain one more time! Now, just fucking tell me!"

The line goes quiet, except the noise of Mark wheezing air through his nose.

"Marci, everyone on Alex's plane seems to have lost their memories."

"What?"

"Yeah, 110 people have no memory of who or what they are—"

"And Alexi too?"

"That's the kicker, Alex seems to be fine. He's passed out into some sort of coma. The EMT said he was seizing at home. He made it further than anyone else on the plane, so I'm figuring that—"

I run into Eric's bedroom and start picking my clothes off the floor. "You figure? You better have a definitive answer by the time I get there."

"EMT said before he passed out, all he talked about was his wedding plans, and he said his name is Brian. I would have missed him if I did not go to the room and check on him. I didn't realize he was getting married, again. What happens to—?"

"Mark, I have no clue what you're babbling about, but stop. You're making my head hurt. Brian is Alex's nom de plume, but this makes no sense—"

"Sorry, Marci, but people are asking questions and I don't know what to say."

"Mark, listen closely. Don't talk to anyone about this until I get there. Play stupid if you have to. Nothing to no one. No spouses, no friends, and definitely no media or government agency. I'll be in touch once I know what flight I'm on."

"Okay, I understand. One last thing. What about Alex's fiancée, Brenda—"

"You mean his wife, Leslie, and what part of nothing do you not understand?"

I end the call before he could respond, tossing the phone on the bed.

"Trouble in paradise?"

His voice startles me. "I'm sorry, Eric. Something happened, and I need to get to Chicago fast."

He reaches out and grabs my arm. "Nothing too serious."

"I hope not, but I'm the boss and I need to do boss things."

"Maybe I can help?"

"Unless you have a magic carpet, not much you can do."

Eric starts laughing.

"What?"

"I don't have a magic carpet, but—"

"If you can get me to Chicago ASAP, that would be icing on a very nice time."

Eric swings his legs out of the bed, stands, and looks at me, "So are you staying for me or for my plane?"

"No, it's not like..."

"You were just going to sneak off, like at the hotel?"

"It's not like that."

"Like what?"

"I had things to do, and I didn't want to complicate your life—"

"Don't you dare, Marci. Just admit it was a booty call."

I lean into Eric and peck him on the lips. "Not going to lie, at first I was planning to just leave again, but after—"

"After you found out that I have a private jet, you're now going to give me another date."

"I don't have time for this bullshit, either you are giving me a ride to Chicago or I have to go. I'm not begging." I pull away from Eric, but he grabs my hand.

"Marci, I'm confused by who you are and what you want. I like you. You're a big-time nerdy scientist, talk of the town that slums at dive bars looking for an occasional booty call—"

"What?"

I follow his gaze to the top of his dresser, and I see my face on the cover of a magazine.

"Okay, but why did you not say anything?" My heart pounds fast against my chest. I ball my fists ready to strike. "Why are you playing this fucking game with me?" I'm not sure why I'm getting mad. I'm the one that started the game. It is just a booty call, right? Why is my heart racing? Why can't I just get my shit together and leave?

"Marci, I was just going to be straight with you tonight and confess how much I like being with you. But part of my job is to read people, and you wanted to be anonymous tonight just like the other times we met. You just want to let your hair down and forget the weight of the world, and I wanted to do that for you. Not make you look silly or foolish." Eric steps into my space and continues. "I did not expect to fall for you so hard, but every time we are together, I miss you a little bit more after you leave. I knew I had to bring you home and make love to you. Show you I was serious about us."

"Life is funny that way. I kind of missed you too." I wrap my arms around him, and we squeeze each other.

I don't want to fall for him, but why not? Because I don't have time for love bullshit. I don't have time for figuring out how to be a couple. I don't—

"Marci, you have to let go of me if I'm going to get you to Chicago."

I let go of him and watch him walk into the other room to make the call.

I stare at those city lights. I see myself getting lost in those lights. I keep reminding myself why I'm here. I see Eric's reflection in the window—why am I here?

CHAPTER 16

*Brenda:
1 Day after Event*

Where am I?

I'm confined in a space. I am surrounded by darkness. Maybe I'm in a box. Where are the walls? I can't move. I struggle to comprehend my situation. Maybe the darkness itself is what holds me tight. Am I paralyzed? The stink of plastic and disinfectant fill my space, with hints of artificial fruit and coffee. My shoulders are stiff. My arms are folded across my body. I try to move them, but they are cemented to me, heavy, pressing into my chest. My legs are bent at uncomfortable angles. I can feel the lactic acid burn in my thighs. Voices, beeping machines echo from the ether. My mind returns to the pins and needles sensation stabbing my leg. I bend my head downward, a pinhole of light in the distance grows larger, brighter—

I jerk to an upright position, neck tight. I unbend my leg that is tucked under my butt. My knee pops as I straighten it out. I try to wiggle my foot, but this intensifies the stabbing pain. After rotating my foot in slow circles, the numbness lessens. I sense my toes wiggling in my black slip-on shoes and white running socks. My feet itch. Sweatpants scratch my legs.

I stare at my watch, the numbers blur. I close my eyes, wiping at the dry crust that formed in the corners. I blink several times more until I can read the numbers. It has been two hours since we arrived. I remember when I opened the door. Seems forever ago. I can visualize his face. His slack skin. Mouth drooling. Head drooping. And that fall. The hollow thump his head made when it hit the polished cherrywood floors. Blood flowing. Rust red blood. After that, everything blurs together.

I remember screaming. I remember the neighbors coming out and holding me. I remember the ambulance. Did I ride in the ambulance? I cannot remember how I got here. To this place. Cold and sterile white. Uncomfortable plastic, multi-colored neon chairs. A nauseating chalky chlorine odor hangs around my head. Mechanical whirls and beeps blend into blurs of hushed conversations. I'm in a hospital. I hate hospitals.

Two hours since I escorted the person impersonating my husband to the hospital. Two hours since he was transferred here and wheeled on a stretcher into an exam room. One and a half hours since they told me to wait here. I must have fallen asleep because I don't remember anything after sitting in this chair, exhausted and hungry.

I look around and see a head bobbing behind a desk. She stands, walks away, comes back, and starts typing at her desk. The scene plays several times. I stand when she stands. I need answers.

I stand by the nurses' station for a few minutes. They hustle around me. Arms reach around me, past me, through me, to grab a clipboard. Grabbing pens. Grabbing at the tray of doughnuts—broken pieces and crumbs. She sits, chewing on the cap of a pen. She has a round, pale, pin-up girl face. Her hair is jet-black, pulled into a ponytail. Her lips are red and glossy. Her smile, warm and inviting. Eyes, large blue marbles.

"What can I do for you, sugar?" Her voice, nasally and full of Southern twang, drags over "sugar." I expect her to say something else after sugar, like pie or baby, but she glares at me. After a few impatient pen taps, I realize it's my turn to talk.

"I'm wondering if there's any news about my husband."

She nods and taps the pen on the desk. She looks at the papers on the desk. Her eyes dart to the dinging computer. Her eyes squint, reading something on the screen. A quiet whisper of a curse escapes her pursed lips. She smiles at me and stands, shuffling through more papers. Another ding. Another squinting glance at the screen. She mumbles another curse word and someone's name between her clenched teeth. She looks at me, tapping a finger on her pursed lips.

"One second, let me check."

I follow her with my eyes. She stops and talks to a lanky man. A doctor, I presume. She points, and he looks at me. I wave. He shakes his head.

I can tell the news is not promising. Her head is down, shoulders slumping as she shuffles to me. Her red smile flattens into a hesitant frown. Her eyes dart between me, the floor, the dinging computer, and the pile of papers on the desk.

"I'm sorry, sugar. The doctor has no updates." Her lips have a sympathetic twist.

"Thanks."

I turn to the chairs in the waiting area.

"There's a cafeteria and waiting area on the second floor. The coffee isn't bad, and the chairs are a bit comfier. If you give me your cell number, I'll call you."

I nod and scribble my number on a paper. She folds the paper and stuffs it into her pocket. She twists her red glossy lips into a smile.

"Thank you," I mumble, walking away.

The cafeteria seats are as uncomfortable as the seats upstairs. The coffee tastes like burnt oranges. The muffin is dry and crumbles with every bite. Disgusted with this snack, I take note of this nook of a space they call a cafeteria.

The room is packed with ten long picnic-style benches. The wooden ones they have at a park. Except these are easy-to-sanitize durable plastic. Two walls are covered with floor to ceiling mirrors. The third wall is painted a mustard yellow that pokes out between artwork of puppies, cityscapes, and rainbows. The cafeteria is empty except for the table in the corner. A table of people in white lab coats, conversing in between bites of food. Laughter erupts from the group, and I stop picking at the muffin and walk out.

I follow the velvet rope line that leads to the hallway exit. I throw my half-finished coffee and half-eaten muffin in the garbage. A ping of guilt nags at me as I throw this food away. The guilt is fleeting as I remember that the coffee was burnt, and the muffin was several days old. I'm doing the starving children of the world a favor.

I walk along the deserted, whitewashed hallway. I was told to follow the purple line on the floor to the waiting room. Follow the green lines to the patient rooms. Or did they say exam rooms? Same difference, I guess.

The waiting room is empty. The same multi-colored neon chairs fill the room. Durable plastic. Sharp angles. There is a bench with a fat cushion along the wall. It's not pretty, but the puffy, fake, cracked black leather cushion is a relief to my butt.

The sign says family and friends. There are no families here. No friends. Just me and the ghosts of hospital visits past. A scent lingers in the room like a bakery doused in cheap lemon disinfectant. I poke at my phone. His face flashes on the screen. I lean against the wall, and my eyes close. A tight, warm darkness begins to surround me.

I'm falling. We are both falling. I reach out for him. His head is dangling. Dry crusted blood is streaked along his forehead. I stretch against an invisible tether for his hand. I grab it, wrapping my fingers around his hand. His hand is cold and heavy. He accelerates, unnaturally, and the weight of his fall forces me to let go of his hand. He slips out of view into the darkness. I'm still falling, all alone, hopeful to see him at the bottom.

A hand squeezes my shoulder. I smell him—the scent of fresh dug dirt, cut flowers, and rosemary—before my eyes open. His smile fills out his face. His friendly, toothy white smile, contrasting against his brown skin.

"Hey, your phone was ringing."

The once empty lounge is full of people squirming in their seats. How long have I been here?

"What? What's going on?"

He leans forward, pointing at the floor. I follow his finger and see my cellphone.

Nodding my head, bending to pick it up, I say, "Thank you."

"No worries, you have been here the longest. Maybe they finally have some information. Like why they sent us to this place."

I shake my head and mumble, "What?"

"You're here for one of the folks from the plane, right?"

All of their tired, stressed faces stop talking, holding their collective breaths and waiting for me to speak.

"No... No, My husband came home and started convulsing. Fell down and hit his head."

"Oh, I'm sorry..." He looks into his hands. "I just thought everyone in here was from the flight my grandmother was on. Kind of strange they would bring a stroke patient here." He raises his eyebrows.

"What happened on this plane?" I glance at the wide-eyed, concerned faces in the room again. Maybe forty to fifty people crammed in this small space.

He wipes the sweat off his forehead and tells me his well-rehearsed story. "I got a call from the airport saying something had happened. So when I get to the airport, everything seems cool. I walked around looking for the information booth, where my Granny called me from. And then I see folks in a room surrounded by nervous airport security. The scene looked suspicious, so I went to check it out and saw a bunch of people in a small room just mulling around. Bumping into each other. Like a scene from a comedy or something. The TSA folks were keeping them in there. They tried to chase me off, but I saw my Granny, pushed past the guard, and pulled her out. But she just..."

His words fade into the vacuum of space between us.

"What happen to your grandmother?"

"She went to Philadelphia for some sort of Civil Rights Historical Artifact Conference with an old boyfriend and some civil rights attorney she reconnected with recently. I didn't want her to go, but she read me a riot act, 'I'm a grown woman, Ralphie,' and she wanted closure to those memories." He looks at me, shaking his head. "Now, she has amnesia. My poor Granny can't remember anything."

Something in my mind clicks. "Does your Granny make great fudge?"

"Sure," he raises his eyebrow, "why?"

"Does she look like Pam Grier?"

"Not sure where you're going with this, but okay... Let's say she does resemble her."

A squeak escapes my mouth as I connect the dots. "My husband was sitting next to your Granny on the plane."

"How'd you figure that from fudge and a resemblance to Pam Grier?" He leans forward, "I thought you said your husband had nothing to do with the plane, but fell and hit his head? But now he was sitting next to my Granny?"

I wave my hands, ignoring his question. "I talked with my husband before he left Philly on the phone. They were stuck on the tarmac. It was before the flight took off, and they were flirting with each other."

He is nodding his head in agreement until I said the word flirting. He smiles, shaking his head in disbelief. "Um... Your husband was flirting with my grandma?"

"You know what I mean."

He hunches his shoulders and shakes his head.

"But I still don't understand why you're here."

He clears his throat. "I told you. Granny has amnesia." Glancing around the room he continues, "Everyone on that plane got amnesia."

Everyone starts nodding their agreement with his story.

"They all have amnesia..." My words fade into the buzz of my cellphone. I missed the call. I listen to the voicemail. I recognize her voice. That slow, Southern drawl.

"I have to go. They have news for me."

All the eyes in the room stare on me. He grabs my hand, squeezing.

"I hope it's good news."

"Thanks."

He lets go of my hand. I turn, walking through the tangle of shoes, legs, concerned faces, and worried smiles.

His voice cuts through the drone of chatter. "Hey, my name is Ralphie."

I turn, his face framed between his broad shoulders. His face familiar—head shaved smooth, chin sharp, hazel brown eyes serious. His lips fill out his face. Not a smile, not a frown. Even across the room, his scent like the ground after a warm spring shower tickles my nose.

"I'll come back down and let you know what they say." I give a small wave and walk out of the waiting room.

I walk to the nurses' station. I wave at the nurse with the pale white face and thin red lips behind the desk. "You called me?"

Without acknowledging me, she extends her arm, "Exam room 5, that way."

Several doctors push past me as I enter the room. My eyes fix on him. He is lying on the bed, tubes extending out of his arms. I study his face, ashen and clammy. He smiles at me. I wave.

"You okay?"

He nods.

"What did they—" Someone grabs my arm, and I spin to face them.

"We should talk first."

"Okay... Doctor, what's going on?"

"Can we talk outside the room?" He starts walking and I follow.

"Is he okay? Just tell me. Does he have amnesia?"

The doctor lets out a puff. "No, he doesn't have amnesia. Or I don't think he does. He seems to remember everything. He is a little worried that he messed up the wedding plans. I told him things would be okay. Seems like a nice guy. He will be okay, you should not—"

"What wedding plans?"

The doctor gives a suspicious peek behind him, and he continues in a whisper, "He might be a little confused. He did hit his head pretty hard. Some details may be a little fuzzy. Like he doesn't remember all the staff here, but I can't say too much about this. You will have to wait to talk with the project leader..." he rubs his head, "okay, never mind that. He remembers you and talks about you non-stop. He is worried you're going to freak out about the stitches on his head." The doctor squeezes my arm, and smirks.

My mind was still mulling over the word. "Wedding?"

"Yes, he has been talking non-stop about your wedding plans, how stressed you have been. He felt bad having you spend the night in the hospital."

A sharp pain throbs behind my eyes. I rub my forehead. "Doctor, we were married a year ago or so. And yeah, I'm a little stressed because we—" I remember I have not told him yet. "I just found out I'm about one month or so pregnant, and I had to spend the night sleeping on an uncomfortable plastic bench. I'm stressed because—" I close my eyes to compose myself. "I'm sorry, Doctor. I'm just worried about my husband."

The doctor's words replay in my mind, and I add, "One thing, Doctor, my husband doesn't work here."

The doctor swallows hard. Mechanical beeps and whirls fill the silence between us.

"Oh, that... Um... You will have to talk with the project leader. She will be here soon. I'll make a note of that." He scratches his head and scribbles something on a pad of paper. "You can go in and see Brian. At least you can tell him to stop worrying, and you can try to relax in a more comfortable chair."

"Who is Brian?"

The silence builds between us. The drumming behind my eyes intensify. Flickering white squiggly lines dance across my vision.

"Your fiancé. I'm sorry. I mean husband. Right?"

The pain behind my eyes is spreading, like my brain is being split in half. The doctor's mouth is moving, but I can't comprehend the words. The name Brian echoes in between my ears. I close my eyes and think about his name.

"Your husband's name is Brian." The doctor grins.

"No, my husband's name is—"

The floor begins to slant. Or maybe I'm slanting. I take a step forward to compensate for the tilting. Walls slanting. My body pitches forward. I stumble, catching my balance by leaning backward, but I arch my back too far. Falling. Falling away from the doctor. Arms flailing, reaching. Flashes of light whirling by. My fall stops. I'm suspended in air. The scent of fresh dug soil surrounds me.

"I gotcha, pretty lady."

He holds me, helping me steady myself. He walks me to the uncomfortable chairs with the plastic odor.

The doctor is yelling. Yelling for someone to get me fluids and check my vitals.

I wave my hand. "I'm fine, Doctor."

He squats to meet my eyes. "Just relax. It will be okay. What is your husband's name? Brenda, I need to know."

"His name is Alex."

The doctor pats my leg. I read his badge. Strange, it's from the Institute of Memory and Nano Technology. Where Marci works? Isn't Marci in Philadelphia? What hospital is this? The letters begin to smear together. I rub my eyes and read his name. Mark Greene.

"ABr. Greene. Who are you? Where are we?" I rest my head against the chair.

"Whoa, you gave me a scare. You need to just relax. A lot to take in at once?"

"I'm okay. I just want to know where we are." I grin at him and Ralphie.

"Okay, Brenda, I'm not supposed to say anything," Dr. Greene glances at Ralphie leaning in, "but you are at The Institute of Memory and Nano Technology-Chicago."

"Okay, but who's Brenda?"

Dr. Greene scratches his head again, like he is trying to sort out a lie. "That's what Brian said. I mean what Alex said your name was. I can't talk about this anymore. My team leader will be here soon."

My mouth opens to speak, but my mind freezes. I want to say my name, but I cannot remember. What is my name? I know my name is not Brenda. I try to think, but everything is moving too fast.

Hands paw at me. I try to focus on his face, but it's like peeking through a straw. I blink my eyes and the view widens again. Dr. Greene pats my leg. Ralphie is rubbing his hands through his hair—his wrinkled forehead and concerned brown eyes.

I blink again. Their faces blur into a kaleidoscopic swirl. I concentrate on the swirls and, for a brief moment, everything comes into sharp focus. Dr. Greene stands and yells for a gurney. His face melts away into flashes of light.

I remember my name—Leslie—as the light fades into darkness.

CHAPTER 17

Marci:
1 Day after Event

My brain is throbbing, reading the notes on my phone that Mark has been sending me. None of it makes sense, plus I had one too many tequila drinks last night.

I rub my temples and stare at Eric. He is reclined to a flat position, sleeping, arms folded across his chest, a blanket folded across his legs. I can tell he sleeps on this plane often, zipping across the world. I want to talk, but he has a meeting in San Francisco later. I choose not to disturb him. We have one and half-hours till we land at O'Hare airport. I recline my seat back to take a nap.

"About time you stopped working." I turn my head toward his voice, he continues talking when our eyes meet. "You were making me look like a slacker, and that's hard to do." He flashes a smile but does not laugh.

"Thanks, Eric." I return his smile.

"Enough talk. I need sleep."

He turns his head and the white noise of the engine fills the space between us. I close my eyes, but my mind is still spinning away. One hundred ten people lose their memories, and one does not. How can that happen? How do we fix it? What do I tell investors? What do I tell Leslie? What will Alexi say?

Alexi's laughing face pulls through the fog of my dream, and his face fades into Eric's. Eric is holding me tight, kissing me. Making me happy. Maybe it could work if I let him. Maybe—

Something pokes into my arm. His voice is calling my name, "Marci, Marci, Marci!"

I open my eyes, his face close to mine. "What?"

"Marci, my flower. We are landing soon."

I kiss him on the lips. "Thank you."

"Oh, don't break my heart—"

"What? I'm not joking about going on a real date. Plane or no plane. I had a good time last night."

Eric smiles. "If you didn't try to lead all the time, you could have saved that breath of yours."

I raise my eyebrows and start to speak, but Eric puts his finger to my lips.

"Shhh! Listen, it breaks my heart because I want to take you to breakfast and spend the days counting the grains of sand on the beach of Lake Michigan with you."

"Oh..."

"But I have a meeting this morning in San Fran. And you have boss work to do. Maybe tonight, I can come back to Chicago... If you're not too busy with boss stuff."

I smile. "Yes, I'd like that."

Could Eric and I be a couple? We met online, a site to explore fantasies. We are just two people that have fucked a couple times. Now he wants a real date—why not, Marci?

Eric grabs my hand. My mind still spinning. Why ruin a good thing? Just good sex and none of the messy relationship stuff. Why complicate things? His fingers intertwine with mine, and I squeeze our hands together. Could we make a good thing better?

A small voice calls within my ears. *What the hell are you doing, Marci? You don't have time for puppy love. You need to focus Marci, and not this. Get your head back in the game. This was just a good fuck. Nothing more. Check the box and move along. Like you planned.*

I turn to the window and watch the clouds drift by. I ignore the voice and watch the sleeping White City growing larger on the horizon, back dropped by purple hues of the approaching new day.

One of my favorite things in the world is flying into a sunrise. The hues of orange and purple smearing into the black of night, always fill me with inspiration and wonder.

***

Eric kisses me on the cheek as the plane lands. I squeeze his hand again, and I accept the fact that I'm falling for him. Like Alexi, it was that first kiss—

We hug and kiss our goodbyes on the tarmac. Eric's plane takes off, and I walk into the terminal. I grab a coffee and wander to the taxi stand, where a tall gentleman is holding a sign with my name on it. I wave at him.

"Marci..." He smiles at me.

"The one and only."

"Ma'am nice to meet you. My name is Bill, and I'm your driver during your stay in Chicago. Just call my number, and I'll be there to drive you from place to place." He extends his hand and we shake.

Still holding my hand, he asks, "That all you have?" He points to my small suitcase and my over-the-shoulder leather bag with my digital tethers.

"Yup, I travel light."

He smiles leaning on the door and says, "My kind of woman. Welcome to Chicago." The door closes and the noises of the world are forced into silence.

I tell him where we are going, and he raises the partition. We coast through the city of big shoulders. The highway is empty this time of early morning. The windows are tinted, and it looks darker than it is outside. I lay my head against the soft leather; my eyes grow heavy and the gentle steady rhythm of the car seals them shut.

Bright light floods around me. The hot humid air lies on top of me, pressing on me like a weight.

"Ms. Marci... We're here now."

I smile and clear my throat. "That's Dr. Marci—"

"My apologies." His smile fades into an embarrassed frown. "Dr. Marci, we are here now."

I step out of the car and squeeze Bill's shoulder. "You can call me Marci."

Bill smiles again. "Yes, Marci." He reaches into the car and pulls out my bags and my cup of coffee.

"Thanks, Bill."

He closes the door and tips his hat. "Just doing my job." He holds out a business card, and adds, "Remember, just call me if you need a ride. Anytime, anyplace you need to go."

I take the card. Bill tips his hat again and runs ahead of me to grab the door to the clinic.

"Thanks again, Bill."

"Just doing my job, Dr. Marci."

We exchange a smile; I wink and walk into the quiet lobby. I toss my cold coffee into the garbage can and dig through my bag for my ID. I approach the security desk and flash my badge.

"You're here early on a Sunday, Dr. Marci."

"Science never sleeps."

"Have a nice day."

I nod and walk toward the offices, opposite the communal areas and patients. The *tap, tap* of my shoes echo in the quiet hallway, and lights flicker on, announcing my arrival. I stop at the door with my name on it and tap my badge to the black box next to the handle. The indicator flickers between red and green, settling on green, the lock retracts, and I push into my home away from home.

I slip out of my shoes and put them in the shoe cubby by the door. I had plush carpet installed because scrunching my toes in the soft material relaxes me. Because I walk barefoot in my office, everyone must take their shoes off.

I made the Mayor and his staff takes their shoes off when they came to discuss the new research park we are planning. Plans that may come crashing down if it's determined that something we did is responsible for this mass memory loss.

My head starts to pound again. I need more coffee and sleep. I sit my bags on the desk and ease into my soft leather desk chair. I pull out a bottle of ibuprofen from the top drawer. I shake out three pills and realize I have no water. No coffee.

I force myself out of the chair and to the mini fridge and pull out a can of fizzy water. I pop the tab and ease into the chair and swallow the pills and half the can of water. I think about Eric and I cannot help but smile, my tense shoulder muscles relax. I recline in the chair, propping my feet up on the desk and close my eyes.

The faint glowing outline of my office fades into Eric's smiling face. We are dancing around a tiny point of white light. The light grows larger and we dance in a larger circle. Laughing and singing. The light keeps growing until we are swallowed by the brightness.

A tin-roofed farmhouse, surrounded by a field of incandescent yellow flowers, fills the space around me. I think about Alexi—

I was younger; Alexi and I had been dating for a year or so. He was dropping hints about proposing. While looking for sunscreen, I found the ring in his luggage by accident.

I was not ready to be married. I was pregnant, but I decided not to tell him. I did not want to say yes for the wrong reason. This was shitty timing for him to propose, for me to be pregnant. I was close to becoming the woman I always dreamed of becoming—

A light breeze blew through the open window and the scent of rain, ozone, and peppery weeds hung in the air. Alexi was fretting in the kitchen when his voice called out, "All ready?"

"All ready for what?" I stop tapping keys on my computer and looked toward the kitchen.

"You promised no work this weekend. Don't make me come back there."

I shook my head and continued to work on my simulation. His footsteps stomped against the wooden floor, and the bedroom door banged open.

"No work." He grabbed my shoulders. *"You promised me a weekend away from work. A weekend of picnics and frolicking in the woods."*

I held up my hand to say, "One second," and pressed enter. I jumped out of my seat and into his arms, wrapping my legs around his body.

"I did promise. And now I'll stop working. You still love me?"

He nods his head. "Yes, now come on!"

I was wearing a flowery dress, feet bare, hair flowing over my shoulder. The picnic was not far from the house, but it was Alexi's favorite spot. A small grassy knoll decorated with the purple flowers of creeping Charlie or creeping Jenny. I could never tell the difference, but I liked the peppery fragrance they released as their tiny leaves tore underfoot. I looked back at the house, the yellow peeling paint, the rusting red roof, and the flicker of the computer screen in the bedroom window.

"No work, Marci!" Alexi handed me a glass of wine that smelled like oak and tasted like dusty air after a hard rain.

"I promise just one more iteration to confirm that the synthetic nano construct is stable." I took a sip of wine, "Sweetie, if this works it will—"

Alexi nudged me with his foot, toes bare. He joked, "Will you stop it! I have to hear you all day at work. Just reserve your ticket for Stockholm—"

I ran a finger along the sole of his foot, he giggled, and droplets of wine spattered onto his shirt. His hand rubbed at the wine, "Look what you made me do! Now hand me a towel to clean this off."

I held out a paper towel. He reached for it, but I pulled it away.

"Give me—"

He lunged for the towel; my glass of wine tipped into the weedy grass. His glass tipped, spilling onto my hand, in between my fingers.

"Careful, sweetie, you will get wine over everything. It'll get sticky, and we'll have ants."

"We can't have ants." He grabbed my hand and began licking the fruity wine off each finger.

"Stop it, my hands are dirty—" I teased.

Alexi let go of my hand and then kissed my chest. Pulling at the fabric of my dress, I tipped my head, watching white puffy clouds dance in the blue sky.

Alexi kissed my neck; the fabric of my dress pulled to expose my collarbone. He was kissing my breast as he pulled off his shirt. Kissing my navel, my dress slid off and was thrown into the basket. He kissed my waist and pulled off his shorts. The clouds gathered overhead and watched as we tumbled into each other.

We stayed on that small mound of earth, limbs twisted around each other, until the sun was a yellow orange speck on the horizon. Sharp blurs of pink and purple smeared into the gray clouds. I felt the tingle of tiny raindrops on my warm skin, like wine spilling from a lover's cup.

We ran naked to the farmhouse, the damp blanket draped across our shoulders sitting on the porch, eating cut fruit and cheese, sharing sips of wine straight from the bottle.

Alexi wrapped his arm around me and pulled me into him. Lightning stabbed the horizon and the boom of thunder rattled the windows.

I lifted my head off his shoulder, listening to the squeaking chain of the porch swing, but then I heard the ding-ding of the computer. I squeezed Alexi's leg. He nodded with a smile, understanding. I ran into the house, pulling the blanket from Alexi and around my naked body. The fabric scratched me, or was it Alexi's absence?

"Alexi, it worked!" My voice boomed like thunder. I ran outside, shedding the blanket and dancing naked in the warm summer rain.

A smile stabbed across Alexi's face, and he took a long drink from the bottle. That was the moment I decided I was going to leave him.

Alexi sat the bottle on a porch table and joined me in the rain. I pulled him into a hug. "I'm so happy right now. My idea worked!"

"Champagne? We should celebrate."

I nodded my head yes. He walked to the house, smiled at me, and then stepped into the black of that tiny farmhouse. I was alone, happy, dancing to the rain tap-tap-tapping on that old tin roof—

I jerk awake at the soft tapping on my door.

"It's open. Come in!" I yell, rubbing my temple.

The door cracks and Mark's head pokes in. "Good morning, Marci."

"What's so good about it?"

"I bought you coffee and donuts." Mark steps into the office, kicks off his shoes, and sits the white paper bag and coffee cup on my desk.

"Wow, two chocolate glazed donuts." I look up at Mark. "Must be some really fucked-up news."

Mark nods his head in affirmation and sits.

"How you want it, Marci? Bad to worse or worse to bad?"

"Considering I have not had coffee or food yet this morning...start with the bad." I pull a donut out the bag, then continue. "And that way, I'll have a little caffeine and sugar in me when the stuff hits the fan."

Mark leans forward and starts speaking. "My team and I examined all 111 passengers of the plane, and 110 have retrograde amnesia. The one passenger, Alex, seems to have his memory intact, but—"

Mark stands and opens the mini fridge pulling out a can of soda water. The tab pops and he takes three gulps before continuing, "But it seems his memories are fragmented and surprisingly he seems to have the memories of other passengers."

"So does Alexi realize he has all these memories?"

"I don't think so—"

I clear my throat. "Does he remember himself at all?"

"Oh, he responds to Alex, and he knows facts about his life at times. But he flips back and forth. Sometimes he's someone else, another passenger or..." Mark shakes his head, mumbling as he takes a drink of water and continues. "Fuck, Marci, it's strange. It's like multiple personality disorder, but these personalities match the other passengers."

"Have you confirmed how many other passengers?"

"Still testing but so far it seems to be all of them. Dr. Shirley came by and gave Alex a quick assessment. She said—"

I wave my hand not wanting to get into the weeds yet. I swallow the last bite of donut and chase it down with coffee. "So what is the worse news, how are we involved?"

Mark takes a slow drink of his water, closes his eyes, and murmurs something to himself before audible words starts flowing out his mouth. "Well, it appears that Shannon's solution of experimental nano-receivers and transmitters were spilled onto Alex while visiting your lab."

I think about the other day with Alexi in the laboratory and remember something spilled on Alexi's pants. "I thought that was a harmless buffer. You mean that fucking moron, who called in sick that day, had an experimental solution sitting on the edge of a lab bench, and didn't label it? I told you that guy was a fucking moron, and he is on you, Mark!"

Mark sits straight and waves his hand. "Technically, Shannon is employed by you and works in your lab—"

"Mark, I'll jump over this desk and put all nine inches of my foot up your ass if you even try to pin that moron on me." I slam my fist of the desk. Mark jumps a bit and starts waving his hands.

"Marci, calm down—"

"Don't tell me to calm down, Mark."

"All I'm saying is that he is part of your funding contract—"

"You think people are going to make that nuanced distinction? No, my friend, you and I are going to be on the hook for this, not some idiotic postdoc!"

I spin the chair away from Mark. My head is throbbing at the same pace as my heart. *Think Marci, think*, I repeat in my head.

"How many people know about the spilled solution?" I ask.

"No one, except Shannon, you, and me... As far as I know, why?"

"Great, keep this between us. No one else needs to know. Let's get the formula of those nano-constructs and maybe we can just reverse this really quick."

"I thought of this, and—"

"So, if you thought of this, why aren't we making more constructs and reversing this? Problem solved."

"Marci, remember that Alex locked all the formulas in that program of his with three levels of password security. We don't know what was in this formula or how to remake it. I asked Shannon, and he said Alex coded the synthesis. That's why he had the solution out to show him and ask what to do next with it."

"Oh, we are fucked then."

"I was hoping you had something. Like you knew what Alex was working on."

"Fuck me, fuck you, fucking shit."

I lay my crossed arm on the desk and rest my head in the space. I close my eyes, trying to figure out our next move, but my mind keeps reminding me of Eric's smiling face, my skin breaks out in gooseflesh, his kiss, his—

"Marci, you okay?"

I lift my head. "You said Alexi still had his memories, right?" Mark nods. "So we just need to get him to tell us that password or the last thing he was working on."

"Good luck with that." Mark chuckles. "His head is a mess—"

"Makes sense he just had 110 other minds merge into his. There must be some way to help coax memories into their context."

"Like I was trying to tell you, Dr. Shirley said we probably should go along with the memories he is living out, but he should have periods where he is Alex. Touch, smell, or something may trigger him to be him. She said she'd need more time to work with him, but may be able to compartmentalize the personalities and memories..."

"Touch or smell?"

"Yes, like when I talked about Leslie, he seemed to be more himself, Alex—"

"Damn it—Leslie, I forgot about her. We need to get her to play along for a little bit so we can fix all this."

"What should I say to her?" Mark adjusts his glasses on his nose.

"Just keep playing dumb until I talk with her."

"Okay."

I sip my coffee and stare at Mark fidgeting with his glasses. A smile smears across his face.

"What are you all smiles about?"

"Marci, you realize what Alex did?"

"Yeah, fucked us really good."

"Besides that, he figured out how to remove memories and transfer them to someone else. This would revolutionize memory science forever."

Mark's words repeat in my head, *...revolutionize memory science forever...*

"Mark, we have to get scans of all the passengers. We will need as much of their brain maps as possible to remap their memories, hopefully soon." I take a sip of coffee. "We need to get the departments of Energy and Defense on board. We need their muscle. So you're going to fire Shannon in a show of laying the law down on incompetence."

"What? Why do I have to—"

"'Cause you hired him, and I have bigger fish to fry."

I stand, pacing behind my desk. "You know, Mark, this may be a real good thing. Bad to worse to awesome. Fuck, we may be onto something big."

"Yeah, if we can fix things."

"I will—"

"Marci, why do you call him, Alexi?"

"None of your business. Why?"

"No reason, just his name is Alex. I know there is history between—"

"Don't you have something to do now, beside pester me?"

"Yes, Mom!"

"Oh, God, I'd hate to be the mother to something so ugly."

Mark laughs and I laugh along with him.

"There you go. I'm good for something." Mark runs his hand through his hair and continues, "Admit it, that's why you keep me around."

I hold the donut up. "That and the donuts. Thanks."

Mark makes a puppy-dog face.

"Okay, don't push it. Now get things done before I stop liking you."

Mark bends down to put on his shoes. "If you need anything, you know how to find me."

Someone pounds on the door. "Marci, you in there?" a voice booms.

"Come in."

The door opens and three men in suits push through the door, past Mark, to my desk with badges extended.

"We're from the DOD. Jack sent us." The larger of the two men announces, walking across my office and plopping into a chair.

My head starts pounding. They did not take off their shoes and, by the shit-eating grins on their faces, that may be least of my problems.

CHAPTER 18

*Brenda/Leslie:
4 Days after Event*

My eyes are closed, but a glowing light hovers over me. Dr. Greene's voice is a whisper against rhythmic beating. A mechanical harmony of legato pings and staccato beeps.

I open my eyes and his blurry face is smiling, pen light in hand. My eyes fixate on the gap in between his bottom coffee-stained teeth. His glasses are crooked. His nose is bulbous and cartoonish. He looks away and straightens his glasses. I try to talk, but a croak of a voice comes out. I move my tongue around my mouth to stimulate saliva. My tongue sticks to the roof of my mouth. I pull it away. A foul, sour liquid fills my mouth. I swallow, but the rancid taste lingers. I try to lift up—

"Take it easy, Brend—" He reads the clipboard. "I mean, Leslie. This whole mess is very confusing. Your husband thinks your name is—" He takes his glasses off and rubs his eyes. He takes a nervous swallow of air and says, "Well, never mind all that. How are you feeling?"

He gives my arm a little squeeze. I follow his eyes to the IV needles poking out from my arm. I follow the tubes, connected to two large, solution-filled bags. One is clear. The other has a pinkish tint.

My voice is a whisper escaping my dry throat. "What's going on?"

"Oh, you were pretty dehydrated and pregnant—" His words fade into a monosyllabic word. Maybe he said, "Congratulations," or "Did you know?"

I decide to acknowledge both queries. "Thank you, and yes: I know I'm pregnant. I have had terrible morning sickness the past week."

"That would explain the dehydration. You should see your OBGYN about that."

"How long have I been sleeping?" I try to bend my legs. Stiff. Muscles tight and lazy.

"Three days. You were in and out of a deep sleep."

My mind hangs on the word three. Three minutes? Three hours? Three—it clicks to days. Seventy-two hours of lost time. Work? Oh shit, I had a case.

Dr. Greene, reading my thoughts, says, "Someone from your office stopped by yesterday." I follow his finger pointing across the room. "They left some things for you to read. I asked them not to, but they need your opinion. You must be important."

My eyes glance at the stack of several folders and a legal note pad or two, but settle on the woman stretched out in the recliner in the corner of the room.

I try to talk louder than a whisper, but my mouth is still dry, lips cracked. Dr. Greene pushes a plastic cup of water into my hand. I start to take greedy gulps.

"Slow down there."

I take a final drink and glance again at the woman sleeping in the corner, to be sure she is there and not a figment of my imagination. "What is she doing here?" My voice is still hoarse. I take another drink.

Dr. Greene looks at the woman. "There were no open beds, so she decided to sleep in here."

"No, I mean, why is she in Chicago? What's she—" I take another swallow of the water. "What the hell is she doing here?" I lift out of the bed glaring at Dr. Greene.

Dr. Greene steps back. "Um, well... You see..."

"I was asked to come here by the Department of Energy, Department of Defense, Department of Homeland Security, FBI, CIA counter-terrorist unit, and the local authorities."

Her voice is like a sucker punch. I turn from Dr. Greene and watch her long; slender limbs unfold out of the chair like a lazy spider approaching its prey. In two quick steps she is leaning over my bed. "I'm here to help. Help Alexi and the other passengers on that plane."

"His name is Alex, Marci. And what kind of help does Alex need from you?"

She stands erect. Her eyes closed. She starts rotating her neck. Soft pops of cartilage slipping into place. Her arms stretching and twisting over her head, more cartilage popping. Her body returns to a neutral position. Eyes open and she leans in close. The faint aroma of old spicy perfume causes my stomach to knot.

"For the record, when I met him, he told me to call him Alexi. But I don't want to get into that with you." She looks across the room. "His memory has been compromised."

I turn my head, and there he is lying on a bed. "What are you saying, Marci?"

"All of their memories have been corrupted."

I study Alex, and he appears so different. His face still sagging, tubes dangling from his body. I close my eyes trying to remember his face before he was staggering at the door like a drunk. I think about the other time that I did not recognize him—

He went to a conference for two weeks in Japan. We had been dating for a few months, and he was going to move into my condo when he returned.

I went to the airport to pick him up. I blended into the hive of bodies moving with determination. I had a book to read, but the words were not as interesting as the people standing, waiting, and moving from here to there.

My cell phone dinged with a message from him. A simple message, "I have arrived!" I stood and walked to the edge of security, waiting, twirling my hair around my finger. Studying every face, my heart beating fast with anticipation of seeing him. I was staring into the distance, having dismissed the faces that already passed, when I noticed a figure standing at the edge of my visions.

His head shaved clean; the fine stubble of a beard shades the sides of his face. His cologne was spicy, top buttons of his shirt open, suit jacket folded over his arm, standing there smiling at me.

I stood as tall as I could, my fight-or-flight mind coming alive. "Can I help you?"

He smiled. "You forget me already?"

It was his voice that I recognized, but—his beard and large, round afro were shaved off to the skin. He looked like a teenager, but the more I studied his brown eyes, his lips. I leaned into him—

"Alex?" I whispered.

"Wow, just two weeks and you forgot me already?"

I stretched my neck, and he pecked me on the lips.

He pulled away. "Are you playing with me or did you not recognize me?"

"You shaved. I never saw you without hair."

He wrapped his arms around me pulling me close.

"What, you don't like it?"

I rubbed my hand along the top of his head. The fine stubble tickled the palm of my hand.

"I love it." Our lips met, hands pulling each other close.

Alex pulled away and smiled. "I cannot believe you forgot me already. I hope you still love me! Because I already terminated my lease and have movers coming tomorrow."

"Sweetie, I'd never forget you. No matter how much you change your face, I'd always love you."

We grabbed each other's hand, walking into the hive of the airport—

I open my eyes when she makes an audible huff. I turn to her. Her eyes are off in the distance, staring at my husband. I clear my throat. Marci looks down at me.

"What were you saying, Marci?"

She pats my shoulder. "Never mind all of that. You rest up. When you get out of bed, we can have a nice long chat." She spins and walks away before I can ask more questions.

"She sure does know how to leave you wanting." Dr. Greene smirks.

I nod in agreement. "Trust me, you can do better."

Dr. Greene shakes his head, cheeks flushed with red. "Thanks." He pats my leg and walks to the door. "I'll have the nurse check on you and get you ready for discharge."

"Thanks, but can I ask you a question?"

He turns, squinting as though he is trying to guess my question. "Yeah, sure."

"Why is Marci here?"

"You two have some history, I can tell. Funny how these things work. I mean, what are the chances that an airplane full of people would just, *pop*," he throws his hands above his head, wiggling his fingers, "just forget everything. And that man over there appears to remember everything. And to top it off, Marci, the expert on memory capture and retrieval, knows him, another memory expert, and his wife. Funny how life can work sometimes." He gives a fake chuckle, like he is telling a well-rehearsed story. He wipes his hand across his forehead and through his thinning hair. As he adjusts his crooked glasses, clutching the clipboard to his chest, his laugh fades. "Funny how life works."

"Funny?" I glare at Dr. Green. He swallows hard, wiping his sweating face. I can tell he is not telling the truth. Rambling like an idiot to change the subject, fidgeting with his badge, avoiding direct eye contact, and sweating buckets. The lawyer in me knows something in his story does not adding up. I smile and relax my tone. "Funny is not the way I'd put it. Is Marci here as a consultant? Or something else?"

"Not my place to tell. She will fill you in on details. But your guy over there is in good hands."

"Her hands are the least of my worries."

He looks at me, shaking his head. "Just relax, and everything will work out in the end."

"Dr. Greene, thank you for talking with me."

"No problem. That's my job."

"Dr. Green, can I ask a sciency question?"

"My favorite kind. Ask away." He smiles and his arms relax, holding the clipboard by his side.

"What did you mean, all of their memories?' Like they forgot everything? Or just what happened on the plane?"

"That's a good question." Dr. Greene's chest puffed out, and he spoke with a low steady tone. "Everyone seems to have their semantic memories intact, but they appear to have lost their episodic memories."

"The what and the who memories?"

"Exactly." He chuckles to himself, but my raised eyebrow tells him I did not get the punch line. "Sorry, just a nerdy joke."

He clears the chuckle with a cough. "Semantic memories are concepts and idea-type memories. Long-term memory. Things like how to tie your shoes or math facts. Episodic memories are memories of events, like how you felt the first time you put on makeup or how your first kiss made you feel." He adjusts his glasses. "Episodic memories are thought to make us who we are—the who, what, where, and why of our lives."

"So how did they lose their episodic memories? And how or why did Alex get them all, but did not lose his? And how are you going to fix—?"

He cuts me off with a wave of his hand. "I really should not talk about this. I'll let Marci explain all that. Try to get some more rest. I have to go now."

He pulls his phone out of his pocket and steps out the door.

Frustrated that Dr. Greene just walked out, I push the buzzer. I want answers, I need a cup of coffee. I turn my head and stare at him. My husband. My Alex. I close my eyes and pinch the bridge of my nose to stop myself from crying.

"Hey there, honey," a gentle Southern-tinted voice calls from the distance. Her accent dragging out each word, forming sentences on their own. "Whatcha need, sweetie?" A pause, then, "Pie?"

I love pie. Cherry pie is my favorite. A big flaky crust. A mix of tart and sweet cherries picked at the height of the season. A small scoop of homemade vanilla ice cream.

It's the nurse from the other day, pretty round face, and thin red lips. White teeth poke out in between the space of her red smile.

"You pressed the button, sugar." She rubs my arm like she is rubbing away a stain.

"Yes. I was wondering if I could have a coffee. My lack of caffeine is giving me a headache."

"Oh, mommas should not drink too much coffee." She pulls a wayward strand of hair off my forehead and behind my ear. "But a little coffee is okay. I'll go grab you a cup. Also, once you're ready, we can get you up and dressed. Dr. Marci wants to chat with you before you take Alex home."

"You called him Alex and not Brian."

"Alex, he's a doll. Real shame what happened. He is always poking around here in the institute." She laughs, folding the blanket that Marci used. "First time as a patient, but he comes in and uses the equipment we have and checks in on several memory-challenged patients. Same thing with Dr. Marci. She is often here visiting or sending her flunkies, like that Dr. Greene." She shakes her head in disgust. "Marci and Alex are like two peas in a pod around here." She stops talking when she looks at me. "Oh, I'm sorry, sugar."

I raise the bed to a sitting position. "You said Marci comes here often?"

"Oh, a few times this month..." she stops talking and counts on her fingers, "and a few last month. Alex and her are collaborating on a new project. I think. Have been for some time." She rolls her eyes and looks away. "Funny, I didn't know Alex was married." Her eyes accusing me.

"Yeah, I didn't know Alex spent so much time here. I thought he did most of his research at the university."

She grabs my hand and squeezes. "Oh sugar, no need to get worked up. Alex has only been visiting to check on work stuff. Nothing or nobody to get worked up about." She let go and starts pulling clothes out of a bag. "Get cleaned up, and then you can chat with Dr. Marci. They want you in the room when they test Alex again."

"Test for what?"

"I don't know much, but—" She glances around the room, leans in, whispering, "You didn't hear this from me, but something strange happened on that plane. They all came here the same day Alex showed up. And Marci arrived not too long after." She rubs her eyes. "Been busier than a beehive here. All of them losing their memories. Amnesia-like, but not like that. Except, Alex. He seems to have his memories, but also..." Her voice trails off into a whisper. She looks at Alex and leans in closer. The sweetness of donuts linger on her breath. "He has all of their memories—"

"Yes, I know that," I interrupt, "but do you know how it happened? Or why it happened?"

Her face is still close. If I shift my head, our lips will meet in an awkward embrace.

She pulls away, seemingly hurt by my question. "Please, relax."

"I'm sorry. Just been a long three...four days, and no one has told me anything."

She rubs my arm. "I understand, sugar. I don't know all the science talk. But I'll tell you what I know."

I nod my head in appreciation.

"Something happened with Alex in Marci's lab in Philadelphia that caused this memory transfer." She stands erect, waving her hands above her head. "I don't understand it, sweetie. I'm sure Dr. Marci will explain it to you." She shakes her head and starts for the door. "I'll be back with that coffee. Let me know if you're ready to get dressed and chat with Dr. Marci."

My eyes close. Darkness surrounds me.

My eyes open, reading the numbers on the wall clock. Two hours of sleep is all I managed, but that groggy fog has lifted. The cup of lukewarm coffee and toasted bagel are still on the tray by my bed. I eat the dry dough to help settle my stomach. I take a sip of the coffee. The sweet, acidic, burnt-orange coffee fills me with warmth. The burst of caffeine begins to clear the dull pain behind my eyes. The nurse, whose name I cannot remember, is unplugging me from the bags of fluid and monitors. She pats a pile of clothes and walks off.

Where are my clothes? Whose clothes are these? Where did they get them? I pick a pair of sweatpants and an oversized Nano Institute sweatshirt that hangs on me like a baggy dress.

Marci pokes her head into the door and waves me out into the hall. I follow the *tap-tap* of her heels echoing through the corridor. We turn into a small room with a small round table in the middle and two hot-pink plastic chairs. I imagine they got their furniture on clearance at a pre-school auction.

Marci drops into the seat. Her hands press on the tabletop to break her descent. She slumps forward, eyes heavy.

I sit with ease and grace, folding my hands.

"What's going on, Marci?"

She exhales like a balloon losing air. "We don't have much time to talk. Alexi—"

I hold up my hand cutting her off. "His name is Alex. Why do you insist on calling him Alexi? You..." I stop myself from finishing the sentence out loud. I have two choices: I can play nice or play the bitch. It's her choice, but for Alex I'm going to try and play nice. "You know he prefers to be called Alex."

She rubs her eyes. "I'm sorry. I have known Alexi—" She smiles and tips her head in apology. "I mean Alex. A lot of history. When he was lying on the street and I breathed life into him, he was Alexi, and in my mind, always Alexi. But that's a different story, and I need to get to current events rather than dwell on past memories. We need to work together on this. Truce?"

She holds out her hand, her eyes wide, head tilted like a puppy. I want to be a bitch and slap her across her pretty, tired face, but I grab her hand. Her fingers are long and delicate. Cold. I squeeze hard and decide to play nice. She pulls her hand away, forcing a smile through the grimace of pain.

A small chuckle vibrates through my body, but I swallow it.

Marci, rubbing her hands together, says, "We have a big problem. Everyone on the plane that Alex was on has a type of amnesia. Well," Marci rubs her head again, "except Alex."

"Dr. Greene explained that to me. It's good that Alex has his memories intact." Marci looks from her hands and scowls at me. Her eyes studying every detail of my face. Her judgmental eyes making me feel stupid, exposed, I paraphrase myself. "That's good, right?" My voice soft, unsure, looking for Marci's approval.

Marci looks at her hand. "Alex seems to be okay otherwise, but he also seems to know the most private details of everyone on that plane—"

"I know this already, Marci!" The words cut off Marci. She lifts her head, tears welling in the corners of her eyes. "What I need to know is how the hell did that happen?"

Marci shakes her head. "I..." she rubs her temples, her eyes, "we don't know what happened..." Her mouth moves but her voice is mute.

"I heard a solution was spilled on the plane and that caused this."

Marci's mouth twist into a half smile and she shakes her head. "I'm not sure who told you that but, like I said, we don't know what happened. I'm working hard to fix it, and rumors and speculation only get in the way of my progress."

I reach for her hand. I give a soft squeeze. "It will be okay. What do you think happened?"

Marci grabs my hand. Her eyes say thank you, and she smiles when she says, "I'm not sure how much Alex talks about our work—"

I shake my head and tilt my free hand in a so-so manner.

"Okay, I'll give you the quick version. So we have a way to target functional DNA nano-constructs to the brain and map memories, and we were in the final stages of testing to make maps of entire neural networks of memories. Alex was in my lab to have his entire memory mapped."

"You did what to Alex? What are the side effects? Can these nano-thingies be passed to other people? How the hell do you get nano stuff into the memories? Did Alex sign a consent form? Did the FDA approve—"

Marci cuts me off by waving her hand, and says with a soft chuckle, "Wow, do you sound like a lawyer—"

"Yes, I am. And did Alex give consent?"

Marci waves her hand. "Yes, Alex gave his consent. Yes, he willingly drank the nano-solution. Yes, we were approved for human testing. Yes, I have a fucking team of lawyers who can go over all of this with you. Listen, Leslie, do you want to fuck around with lawyers or get Alex better?"

"Sorry, you can take the girl out of the courtroom, but not the law out of the girl."

Marci laughs. "I see why he likes you." I raise my eyebrows. Her shoulders relax as she says, "Listen, everything worked as expected. We mapped all the memories in his mind. He is the first human to have every memory mapped, and we were going to catalog and process the information, but now this has happened." Marci looks past me.

"What happened, Marci?"

She shakes her head. "I don't really know. But I'll tell you what I can."

"I would appreciate that."

"The government was..." Marci pulls her hand from mine, then smiles. "A DOE postdoc working on experimental nanos may have caused this."

"And that's it? You think I'm an idiot?"

"I'm not sure I can say much more than that." She shakes her head. "I have told you as much as I can. I need to figure some things out."

I slam my hands on the table. Marci jumps in her seat. I yell, "What the hell do you mean, you've told me enough?"

"Leslie, please understand—"

"Fuck you, Marci."

Marci's face twists like I slapped her. I look away from Marci to calm myself. "I'm sorry, but I have a feeling you know more."

"It's okay, I'm sure this has been stressful on you. I told you the truth that I know, so far. I don't want to tell you something and then have to backtrack, or worse misinformation gets into the press."

"Well maybe I can give you a bit of info."

Marci's eyebrows rise.

"Not sure if this means anything, but Alex told me some material flaked off in the airplane bathroom before they took off."

Marci starts taping her fingers against the table. "Shit, that's bad. We cannot let the suits hear this."

I look toward the door. "And what does the government have to do with Alex?"

Marci waves her hand.

I lower my voice, begging, "Marci, please...for Alex."

Marci starts talking mid-thought. "If you can map the memories with nano-constructs, you can potentially have those memories broadcasted to a receiver..." Marci's voice fades into an internal thought.

"Marci, tell me what you think happened? Please tell me, in plain speak, not ESP, DOE, DNA nano-bullshit. Will Alex be okay?"

Marci ignores me and continues. "Leslie, I need you to work with me so I'm going to be on the level with you. The postdoc spilled a solution on Alex. And it may have been..." Marci's voice fades into silence.

"What was in the solution? Marci, tell me what you're thinking,"

"I'm not sure. The postdoc is being questioned. But the solution was experimental nano-transmitters. I'm not sure. But Alex would have been primed to receive—" Marci starts shaking her head. "No, there's no way this could have happened. No way, it could... Are you positive that is what he said—"

"I'm sure he said on the phone he rubbed a powder off his pants. In the plane bathroom—"

Marci jumps out of her seat, pacing like a caged animal. "Don't tell anyone this. They cannot know that Alex uploaded his memory. They cannot know this. They," her finger points to the door, "will try to use this technology for who knows what, and they could ruin everything I have...*we* have worked for." She sits and rubs her forehead, "It would ruin us. Alex was part of this also. He has as much to lose as I do. Maybe more, now."

Should I play the part, or float her down the river? How bad can Alex be? The memories of all those people in his head. Does not sound so bad. But Marci playing Frankenstein with my husband...

"So can you fix him? Them?"

"Yes, but I need some time."

"What can you do?"

"I don't have time to explain—"

"Give me the quick version or I talk to the agents out there."

She smiles and nods her head okay. "Listen, I have the map of his memories. If you tell folks about this, they will confiscate my data and his memories could be taken and compromised." Her voice softens to a whisper. "I can use his original memories to remove the others' and return them. I know it sounds crazy. I don't have all the details worked out, but I can do it. Give me a chance to fix this, please—"

The door opens, and two large men in black suits push into the small space. I cannot read Marci like Dr. Greene. She seems to be telling the truth or some well-rehearsed version of it. The agent's voice cuts into my thoughts.

"Doctor, it's time to talk."

Marci grabs my hand and squeezes. "She's his wife. Leslie can come to the testing."

The two men glance at each other, and the larger one says, "They didn't say anything about her."

"She can help validate the results."

They hunch their shoulders, and one says, "Come on, I want to go eat, and this is the last thing on the schedule for today. Move it, ladies."

Marci gives me a wink. She leans in close and whispers into my ear. "Our secret. I'll get our Alex back." She leans in a bit closer, her lips tickling my ear as she talks. "Just play along. Alex thinks his name is Brian. Please, if you want to get out of here, don't react. Say very little." She looks at me, squeezing my shoulder. She presses something metallic into my hand. I study the gold ring, and realize it's Alex's wedding band.

"Please, I beg you... Please. We can get our guy through this."

She leans away, and I nod my head, but that satisfied smile on her face when she handed me Alex's ring and the word "our" linger in my mind. A stab of anger runs through me. Maybe a slip of the tongue. Maybe I'm reading too much into this. Maybe the heat of the moment. Maybe she said it to annoy me. Maybe she is scared.

We walk into the room. Alex is studying pictures and reciting facts and figures. He smiles at me. I sit in a seat in the corner. Marci stands with her hands folded across her chest. Alex waves at Marci.

"Hey there, Nurse Marci."

Her lips twist into a smile. She waves. "Hello, Brian."

Who is Brian? When did Marci become a nurse? I'm still confused about what is going on. Alex blows me a kiss. I catch it and blow it back. Marci looks at me and raises her eyebrows. I'm confused but happy that he remembers me.

I think about what Marci told me. Memory mapping and extraction. Remote extraction. Government involvement. The facts connect. Marci winks—a nervous wink, a wink begging me to stay quiet.

"Okay, Brian, you can go home with your fiancée." The doctor stands and points to the men by the door, "These gentlemen and I will walk you out, and we can go over a few things. Then, you can go home."

The two men in suits turn to me and smile. "We'll be back to talk with you, separately, before you can leave."

After the men walk out the room, Marci pushes the door shut, leaning against it. "Listen, you have to go with it. You're now Brenda, I'm Nurse Marci, and Alex—" She shakes her head. "Alex thinks his name is Brian."

"What, Brian like his author name?"

"Just trust me. You cannot confuse him now. Let me work and get him back to himself. I have his memories mapped. I can fix this. Just play the part, and we will get through this." Marci spins and steps out the door.

"Marci!" I yell. She turns to me. "I don't know what game you're playing, but you better fix this or God help me, I'll—"

"Don't make threats you don't intend to keep, sweetheart!" She spins and walks out the door.

CHAPTER 19

Marci:
21 Days After Event

I log into the shared research servers to sort out what Alexi was working on. Most of the shared documents are grants on determining the molecular basis of memories, or artificial neural networks.

In the folder marked, "Crazy_Ideas", is a document started on "wetware_computer_interface". Trying to use mini-synthetic brains to replace computer chips. Most of the files and folders I know about, but there is one folder labeled, "Memory_Creation_Destruction_Transfer". I click on it. A box pops up asking for a password and if I want a text or email to verify this computer.

"Damn it, Alexi, and these stupid passwords."

I lean back in my chair and put my feet up on the desk, pushing at a water bottle with my toes. I ignore the computer and that taunting password box and admire the plaques on the wall. The loopy cursive writing blurs in and out of focus. I rub my eyes, but I still cannot make out the fine print. It's my undergraduate degree from MIT. Next to it is my PhD and MD from The University of Chicago. Below my degrees there is a picture of the former governor of Pennsylvania and I shaking hands, with golden shovels, breaking ground on the Institute for Memory and Nano Technology. Next to it is the picture when I broke ground here in Chicago. My eyes lose focus and it all blurs into nothing. My heart starts beating fast because I should be able to read my name.

What if it was all gone? What would my life weigh out to? Am I dreaming all of this? Did I do all those things?

I rub my eyes and everything comes into focus. I stand, walking to the wall and examining the framed papers. I'm relieved when I read my name in large black block letter print. I inhale and exhale. I sit on the edge of my desk. I wiggle my toes in the thick carpet. I close my eyes and try to relax.

My cell phone chimes, I see his name flashing—Eric.

I press answer. "Hey there!"

"Well hello, Marci." He laughs a bit and continues. "You're alive."

"Sorry, just all hell broke loose, and I have not—"

"I'm just busting your chops."

"You couldn't imagine the hell I have been digging out of—"

"You mean a plane full of passenger that have amnesia, except for one guy, who's a neuroscientist and works with you?" He makes a noise like a laugh, and adds, "I can imagine."

"I see the story made it to the east coast already."

"East, West, Middle—I haven't been to the South yet, but it is all over the news."

"Fuck me!"

"That's the idea." He laughs again but cuts it short when I don't laugh along. "I'm sorry, Marci. Actually, for such a thing, the coverage has been just a few blurbs. Lucky for you it's been buried by the pending trade deal and the political debate last night. If I weren't a news junkie, I'd have missed it."

I rub my temple, pressure building behind my eyes. "Well I'm heading home tonight—"

"Perfect, let me pick you up and take you out to dinner."

"As nice as that sounds, I have to decline. I need to have all my attention on this."

"Marci, you need to eat. You like Mexican food? I know the perfect spot downtown—"

"Eric, thanks for the offer, but—"

"No buts, Marci! I know where you live. I'll drive over and camp out in your yard until you have a meal with me."

"Whoa, it was that good."

"Oh, blew my mind. All I could think about since was Marci and quantitative analysis of real estate derivatives."

I chuckle. "Is that a compliment?"

"From a quant hedge fund manager, the highest."

"Okay, mister. I'll have dinner with you, but not some overpriced fake bullshit Mexican food. I know a place, where the food is great, the margaritas are luscious and the atmosphere is perfect for—"

"Love. I'm sold!" Eric finishes my sentence.

"I was going to say conversation."

The phone goes quiet. The quiet after an awkward comment, and a more awkward response. He exposed himself, and I blew it off like a joke.

"I'm sorry, Eric. Just been a long few days."

"No worries. I'll see you tonight. Text me the time and location."

"Yes," I pause moving the phone from my mouth to exhale, and continue, "I'm looking forward to seeing you. It will be nice to do something other than work."

"Safe travels."

Before I can say sorry one more time, the line goes silent.

I stand and walk around the desk to the window. Cars and people moving past in slow motion. My head is filled with ideas and stratagems, but the dots are not connecting. What the hell happened on that plane?

I turn to the screen. You're not smarter than me, Alexi. Or are you? Were you? I look at the plaques on the wall and reassure myself that I'm the best qualified to figure this out.

A knock on the office door startles me from my self-loathing and into the present.

"Yeah, come in." I fall into my chair, click the password box away, and close the data share.

The door opens and the Director of the Department of Defense steps in, kicks off his shoes, walks slowly across my office, and sits in the chair across from me.

"How bad is it, Marci?"

I stare at him for a moment. He has thinning gray hair, thin wire frames hanging low on his nose, and a wrinkled face. The years, and the job, have not been kind.

"Jack, you look old."

"Marci, we can't all be blessed with good genes. And shit like this just causes more gray hairs to grow and wrinkles to form under my eyes. Now how bad?"

I pull two tumblers out of my desk drawer. Jack exhales, "That bad—" I sit a bottle of 25-year-old single malt next to the glasses.

"Or that good, depending on how we play it."

Jack pushes his glasses up on his nose. "Marci, you're always dealing, but your goose may be cooked. We got 111 people that lost their memories on a commercial flight, where experimental nano-things were released. Where is the silver lining in that?" Jack grabs a tumbler, fills it half full, sniffs it, gulps it in one swallow, and fills his glass halfway again. He fills the second tumbler and slides the glass toward me and continues talking, "You can talk your way out of a lot of shit, but this may take us both out."

"Jack, that's the difference between you and me." I recline resting my feet on the desk, wiggling my toes for effect. I always noticed that stockinged feet either turns a guy on a little or a lot. I'm betting Jack is the latter.

"Jack, let me spin this for you. What happened on the plane is a demonstration of the first memory transfer and deletion on a large scale. Imagine agent number one slips a target or targets the transmitter solution and agent two is ready to receive and delete memories. Hell, Jack, maybe even able to transfer false memories."

Jack swallows his whiskey in one swallow, smacks the glass against the desk, and babbles a bit before spitting out a sentence. "You're telling me those 111 memories were not lost but transferred and deleted. Who has the memories?"

I push the bottle with my foot toward Jack. His hand brushes my foot as he grabs for the bottle, his lips turns into a half smile. He cuts his eyes at me. "Excuse the touch."

I wave it off and continue talking. "Jack, if you came yourself instead of sending those disinterested goons, that soiled my floor mind you, you would have known that only 110 people lost their memories and the 111th person on the flight now has them in his head."

Jack stands and starts pacing, swirling the amber liquor. "Marci, you..." he stops, takes a swallow of his drink and squints at me for a moment, letting the words build in his head, before continuing, "Marci, you're the luckiest or the smartest person in the world. I mean next time lead with that."

Jack grabs my foot and shakes it and plops into his seat. I smile. I bet he will sniff his hand when he leaves my office.

I take my feet off the desk and lean in. "Jack, here is what I need from you—"

"Anything, Marci. I'll open up a budget line for this."

"Perfect. I need every passenger scanned. I'm having Mark set up a mapping unit at that converted factory building. Any assistance in setting that up would be great. The sooner we get the maps, the sooner we can retransfer the memories. I need a couple agents—maybe those goons you sent—to follow Alexi, the passenger with all the memories. If something happens to him, we are toast." I glance at my computer screen. "And a computer expert. I need you to hack some files on my data server that are password protected, and the password is...let's say, inaccessible."

"What is the information contained in these files?"

"Is that important?"

"Marci, if it's sensitive or classified info, then the computer expert I assign you must have the proper clearance."

I take a pensive breath. "Jack, I'm going to be honest—"

"Fuck, Marci, I knew the 'let me be honest' bullshit was coming."

"Jack, the tech is real, but the person who designed it was on the plane and his memories have been compromised a bit."

"Compromised?"

"We never crammed 110 memories into another human's brain, so you see why I'm crossing everything off my list."

"I see. Makes sense. So, classified? And will the agents following Alexi freak him out and cause any issues?"

"Yes, about the classified computer expert. Mark and I will make up a story about the agents—" I take a sip of my drink, I snap my fingers and continue with my thought, "We can tell him he has some sort of densities in his brain scans, that way he will not mind us calling and probing for information. We can hit the problem from two sides."

Jack nods his head in agreement. "Sounds logical. Anything else?"

I take the last swallow of my drink. "I think that's all, but I have your number."

Jack pours another drink and slams it. "One for the road, and all the headaches you're causing me."

Jack stands and gives me a little wave.

"Thank you, Jack."

While slipping his shoes on, Jack looks at me. "As long as you deliver, Marci—"

Jack pulls the door and is about to step out.

"Oh, Jack?" He turns toward me. "Can you be a dear and get your people to clean or replace my rug that your goons soiled?"

Jacks flips his middle finger and walks out the door. As the door closes, Jack raises his hand to his nose and take a long sniff.

I should go to Vegas one of these days. I look at my watch and I still have three hours before I have to be at the airport. I pour another drink and get to the business of going through Alexi's files that I have access to.

A few sips in, my office phone rings. I pick the phone up, hoping it's Eric, but expecting Mark to be on the line. His voice is soft and mumbling, but I'd recognize it anywhere. "Alexi?" I whisper.

He clears his throat, and then talks louder, "Oh... I'm sorry... Is this Marci?"

"Yes, this is Marci. Is this Alexi?"

"Yes, and I need help."

"Anything, what's going on?"

"I'm at a diner, downtown Chicago. I have no clue how or why I'm here."

"Alexi, do you know what's going on?"

"Marci, my head is pounding, and I can't seem to think straight. I wanted to call Lee, but you answered."

"Okay, calm down and tell me where you're at. I have a couple hours before I go back home. Maybe we can sort things out a bit."

I scribble the address down and call Bill for a ride, stuffing all my notes into a bag, figuring I would not be back to this office for a week or so.

I slip on my heels and step out of my office. Remembering my date with Eric, I pull out my cell and text, "Still on schedule, but something has come up. Will keep you updated. I'll need a drink later."

A few steps later my phone dings with a text, "Marci, no worries. I'm not going to bed early. Whatever time you get in call me. I cannot wait to see you."

This is followed by a string of emojis, margarita glasses toasting, eggplants, and rainbow confetti colored donuts. I'm not sure what he is trying to say, but I can't help but laugh out loud.

INTERLUDE

Alex/Brian:
Tammy

My stomach sounds like crumpling paper. My legs are tight, burning. Throat dry, sandpaper tongue rubbing against the roof of my mouth. I lean my body onto the door, and cool air tinged with the aroma of bacon and coffee wafts past me. The bell jingles and every head turns, watching me stagger in.

"Take any seat you like, hon," a voice calls out.

My eyes search for an empty spot, a booth in the corner.

"Is this okay?"

"Be right there, menu is on the table. You want coffee?"

"Yes, and a water." I fall into the vinyl cushions, massaging the cramps out of my leg.

I pull the menu out and stare at it. Have I been here before? Mama's Diner. Name sounds familiar, but my grumbling stomach does not care where we eat.

I flip through the menu and am torn between the Trucker's Two special: two eggs, two bacon, two sausages, two pancakes and hash browns, and the Forman's special which is 4 of everything. I flip to the back and there is the story about Mama's Diner and a picture of Tammy—

I try to remember the last time I saw Tammy. It was my undergraduate graduation from Northwestern. She had just sold the farm and was expanding her businesses. She wanted me to help her and stay in the family business. I was headed to graduate school to become a scientist, moving in with my girlfriend, Marci. I reminded Tammy that we were not family, just had a working relationship. Her eyes welled up and she said she loved me like a son. I laughed, and she slapped me. How many years ago was that? Ten or fifteen years—

I blink my eyes several times to clear the vision.

"Welcome, my name is Mia," A cup of steaming coffee and ice water slaps the table. "What can I get you, hun?"

"Um... The Trucker's special and—"

"How do you want your eggs?"

"Over easy and—"

"What kind of toast?"

"Wheat, and is Tammy here?"

Mia finishes scratching my order across her pad and smiles at me. "You don't look like Tammy's type."

"Is she here or not?"

"Why are you so interested in Tammy?"

"She's my mom."

Mia gasps and then starts giggling. "Is this one of those hidden camera shows? Tammy ain't got no children."

"Why don't you go ask her?"

Mia hunches her shoulders and walks away. I follow her until she disappears in the back.

I chug the water in one continuous swallow. I sit the glass on the table and there she is.

She is wearing the same shirt as Mia, except her name tag is dangling off her collar, and the top buttons are undone revealing her deep cleavage.

"Some things never change. You still like em'?" Tammy chuckles, doing a little wiggle.

"What?"

She slides into the booth across from me. "What the hell are you doing here?"

"I don't know. I was out walking by the lake, got hot and thirsty, and I walked in."

"You have some nerve—"

"I'm sorry, Tammy."

"What, you think a sorry is going to... What?"

"I don't know, but I need to talk with someone—"

"Talk to your Marci."

"We're not like that. We broke up years ago. We just work together now."

Tammy taps her fingers on the table. "What do you need to talk about, after all these years?"

I grab at Tammy's hand. "Tammy, my head is a mess. I can't talk about it with my wife or Marci. I just need someone—"

Tammy pulls her hand away. "You know, I looked for you after that day. My heart ached. I would have given you anything. You wanted out the business. I would have let you go, but the way you stung me, and then you fell off the face of the earth—"

"Fuck, Tammy, I said I was sorry. I was running away—"

"Again!"

"Yes, again. I changed my name and tried to forget my past..." I hold my hand to my face, rubbing at my eyes. "But after The Event where I got all those memories—"

"That was you—"

"I don't know who I am anymore."

Tammy huffs, stands, and slips into the booth next to me. Her body presses close, the fragrance of greasy hamburgers and maple syrup relaxes my muscles. She pulls my head to rest on her shoulder. "Brian... Can I call you that or do you want to be called Alexi?"

"Alexi?"

Tammy grins. "Or whatever your new name is."

"No, Brian is fine." I wipe my eyes. "I'm sorry, Mom"

"Don't worry, son. I will take care you," her hand rubs through my hair, "you can always come home."

I nod my head, sucking in a sob. "Thanks."

"It's okay Brian, you are home now. Why don't you come to the back and talk after you've had your breakfast?"

"Ms. Tammy, I didn't know you had a son." Mia sits the plates of food on the table.

"Yeah, I do. He helped build all this you know?"

Mia leans in close, studying my face. "I know you. You're him?"

I nod my head, cutting into the pancakes. "Yeah, I'm from the plane and the memory transfer thing." I fork the food into my mouth.

"Oh yeah, sure." Mia smiles. "I was talking about your performances. They're the stuff of legend. I hope we can work together—"

I glance at Mia. "What performances?"

"You know what I'm talking about."

I drop my fork. "No, I don't know. Now tell me what performances."

Mia looks between Tammy and me.

I slam my fist on the table rattling the plates. "Tell me."

"You know, your videos."

"What?"

"Okay Mia, that's enough. Brian wants to eat, and you need to take care of other customers." Tammy stands pushing Mia away. "He's had a hard morning. Don't pester him about that stuff."

Mia rolls her eyes. "I was just being friendly."

"Go be friendly over there."

Mia peeks around Tammy and extends her hand. "It was real nice meeting you, Brian. Hope we get to do some work together."

I drop my fork and shake Mia's hand. "Yeah, nice meeting you."

Tammy squeezes my shoulder. "Come see me when you are done."

"Yeah. Sure." I shovel another forkful of food into my mouth thinking about these videos I was in. My head starts pounding, the room starts to corrugate. I drop my fork and grab my phone, dialing her number. She picks up on the second ring.

"Hello, Lee... I need help."

CHAPTER 20

Brenda/Leslie:
35 Days after Event

I would be lying if I said I understood everything Marci and Dr. Greene told me about what is going on. Their hushed conversations and scientific jargon, and explanations of the test results left more questions and Google searches than offered answers.

I would be lying if I told you I feel good about having Alex home. I would have to lie if someone asked me if I love my husband. I would have to lie if you asked me if I recognize the person in the mirror. I lie all the time now. I lie to Alex that his name is Brian. Lie to myself that my name is Brenda. I lie to Marci that I trust her. I look at my face in the mirror, my smiling face, and see nothing but a lie.

My eyes are swollen. Puffy purple bags hang from them. The whites of my eyes are streaked with red lines from lack of sleep, bouts of depressed crying...or both. A few drops of saline will help. My hair looks like a bird's nest, and I don't care. Should I care? A brush and a flat iron will help.

My face is dotted with acne. The doctor said this is the hormonal changes in my body. I am changing into the ugly teenager I hated. I step away from the mirror, studying my naked body.

I rub the small bulge of belly, imagining the skin stretching to accommodate the new person I'm creating. My body becoming disfigured. My body robbed of nutrients. My body playing host to an ungrateful symbiont. Maybe ungrateful is too strong a word. I stare at my face. Maybe I'm ungrateful for not embracing this gift. This privilege to reproduce. The unique gift of being the female of the species.

The idea of holding this new life, this pea-sized baby in my belly, and the thought of their skin against mine fills me with a warmth. The sadness melts away. A smile. A confident smile. A strong smile. Will I have to go through this every morning? Or will these feelings of doubt pass like the morning sickness?

He is yelling about something. My smile fades.

I turn the shower on, drowning out his voice. Not sure I'm ready to play personality roulette today. Maybe I could get up and out before he wakes up. I step into the shower. The water is still transitioning between icy cold and burning hot. I don't care. His name is Alex, the man I fell in love with. I still love that person. The others, I couldn't care less about. Their stories. Their pain. Their memories. Fuck that. I want my Alex.

Marci has a plan. I hate Marci for what she did to him. An accident. A research technician. A mistake. Can she fix it? I have to trust her, like he trusted her. Does he remember? He forgave her. But should I? Is it my job to carry the burdens of others? Is it?

I rub my belly with the soapy, lavender cloth. I'm a woman. Designed to carry burdens. Designed to struggle and break through glass ceilings. I'm going to get through this. We are going to get through this. All three of us.

Alex is in the kitchen, cooking. Meat and eggs, again. I'm not going to say anything. Last time it turned into a big blow up. He is someone else right now. Someone different than Brian? The who is anyone's guess. I have a folder of pictures, names, and other tidbits of information about the one hundred and ten other folks. I'm supposed to match Alex's activity to the names and people. Help match memories to the random assortment of faces. Yet, I cannot let Alex realize I'm doing it. I have to stay in character. Extract enough info to figure out who's-who, but not pull him out of character.

I should have talked with Alex about memory formation. I should have asked him more about his work. Why didn't he tell me he was working at that institute? Maybe he did. I can't remember. I should have asked him more about his past. Dealing with him now, watching him struggle with his memories, I have no clue which are his and which belong to others. I should have asked him more questions. More about his past life. But when you are falling in love you only dig deep enough to form a trusting bond; beyond that, you're just digging to mask your own insecurities and finding reasons to stop falling. Right? You will have your whole life together to unpack and sort the baggage of the past?

Now I have to rely on Marci. Did Marci ask the questions? She knows him. She is part of the baggage. She can help him. She can help him, and I cannot. I just have to play the part, and she gets to play the healer. I wipe away the tears forming in my eyes. My throat getting tight. Gagging. Coughing.

The greasy aroma of fried food makes my stomach turn. I have not eaten this morning, but the threat of dry heaves makes me hurry to leave. I walk out into the kitchen. Alex is sitting at the table. He is shoving yellow runny eggs into his mouth. Dark, red-brown strips of meat. Maybe bacon. Maybe sausage. Maybe I'm going to puke. I mix my protein drink without acknowledging him. That person eating like a hog. Who is he? Not my Alex. Not Brian, either.

Brian is Alex's pseudonym. Science-fiction and zombie novels. I find it fascinating that Alex's mind is using the memories of a made-up person to reconstruct his world. I wonder what I look like in his mind. What does this Brenda look like?

I put two pieces of bread into the toaster. I grab a banana. I take a sip of the protein drink. The chocolate-vanilla, chalky liquid coats my tongue. The stink of the grease and meat fill my nose. I cough. A dry, deep cough. My stomach clenches. I run to the sink. Nothing. I grab my drink and head for the door.

I walk past the dinner table avoiding eye contact with him. I don't want another scene.

"Where are you going, woman?"

His voice. An angry, sarcastic voice. Not Alex, but him. I met this person a week or so ago.

"I asked you a question, woman!" He pushes the plate away from him. The chair scrapes on the floor as he turns to me.

"I'm going to work." I keep my head down and my voice is quiet.

"You rubbing that you work in my face? You now too good to eat with me? Where is your breakfast?" His words slur together.

I hold my drink up. I take a step toward the door. He pushes his chair away from the table. "That's all you're eating? No wonder you skinny as a mouse." He slaps his thigh, gyrates his hips. "Come on over and grab a sausage."

"Maybe tomorrow. I'll be late for my meeting."

"Ha, late for a meeting. They got you shoveling slop and cleaning toilets at that dump hotel." He pulls his plate to him and forks a piece of meat into his mouth, mocking me in a whining voice. "You going to be late for a meeting. Don't make me laugh." He makes a snorting noise.

I make a mental note to check the photos in the folder for a spouse working in a hotel. Maybe I can find out who this asshole is.

He looks at the kitchen. "So you just leaving that mess?" He stands. "What, my food not good enough for you? What, they fixing high-class food at that dump you work at?"

"No, not that." My voice is softer than I intended. I'm unsure if I said anything out loud. The words echo in my own head like a thought. The way he is glaring at me—eyes wide, eyebrows raised—I'm not sure if he heard me, so I repeat myself a little louder. "No, not that."

"I'm not deaf, bitch. So tell me, what you having for lunch? What, woman?"

"Listen, just calm down." He moves closer to me. I hold my arm out. "Please."

He keeps moving until my palm presses against his chest. He keeps moving forward, and I step backwards until my back presses against the wall. My mind yells at him to stop. The yell in my mind funnels into a smaller and smaller space until it leaves my trembling lips, soft and weak. "Stop."

I close my eyes. I remind myself that I love him. *I love him. I love him.*

I open my eyes, and he is still an arm's length away. Grinning at me. Bits of chewed meat in between his teeth. His breath stinks of grease and coffee. The burn of bile stings my throat. I swallow and exhale out my nose.

Then a pop. A metallic ping from the kitchen. The toaster. He jerks away from me. I fall forward as he stops pushing against my extended arm.

He walks away from me. "Sweetie, I think your toast is ready."

Just like that, he is someone else, maybe Brian. I turn away. He cannot see me cry. I have to play the part. I'm a happy fiancée or wife.

I wipe my eyes, raising my head with a smile. "I'm not too hungry now. I'm running late. I have to go."

He turns to me, grinning. "You need to eat breakfast, you know. You can't work these long hours and not eat well."

I wave my hand. "Bye." I push my feet into my sneakers and put my heels into my bag. "I love you."

The words squeak out of my mouth. Quiet like a sneaky lie.

I examine myself in the mirror by the door. I wipe my eyes. I inhale deeply, holding it for three seconds. I exhale and hold for two seconds. I repeat this, and then whisper, "I love you," opening the door.

"Hey, Lee?"

His voice stops me. That's the nickname he calls me. The air pulls out of my lungs. I don't want to turn around. I don't want to answer. I don't want him to stop being him. I don't want to be disappointed.

"You okay, Lee? You forgot your lunch, and your purse."

I turn to face him. I move very slowly.

I'm hearing him for the first time since the event. I didn't know this was possible, that he would be my Alex. It has been weeks but feels like months since I have been playing the part. But what do I do now? Go back to being his Leslie? Can I tell him I'm pregnant? Should I run to him or walk away like nothing is out of the ordinary?

I need to breathe. I need to breathe. I can't remember how to breathe. I can't remember how to be Leslie.

"Leslie, what's going on?" His voice, full of concern. His voice, growing louder. He is moving. Running across the condo to me. "Leslie, please answer me!"

My body is paralyzed. The distance between us is closing. He grabs my arms. My mind takes control, and I cannot resist him. It is my Alex.

"Alex?"

"Lee, what's going on? You're working too hard. Eating like a bird and not sleeping. Up early, to bed late." He pulls me closer to him. "Lee, you've got to take it easy. Those cases, those people, and their problems, will consume you. You have to leave that stuff at work."

His voice calms me. My muscles relax. I play the part willingly, wrapping my arms around him, squeezing hard.

"There's my best girl!" He kisses me on the top of my head. He rubs my back. His hands remember the way I like my back rubbed. Slow, soft circles. I pull away. His face is close. Our lips meet. His lips. Not the lips of some impostor. Not some lips playing the part, but his lips.

"Alex, I missed you." I squeeze his arms.

"Yeah, you've not missed me that much." His lips part into a smile. "You're always here or there. Haven't seen you much since my trip to Philadelphia. I guess I've been busy also. Lots of interesting stuff happening at work."

"You've been to your lab?"

"Where else would I have been?"

I take a step back. I feel like a fool. I have not been playing the part but avoiding him. I should have talked with Marci about what has been happening. She never mentioned he could become Alex, but why not? I wonder if she knew. Did she know he has been living some of his life as himself? And I have been avoiding him. Has he called her? Did she know? And I have been missing these brief moments of him. Missing him.

I wipe the tears forming out the corner of my eyes

"Hey, what's wrong?"

"It's been so long since," I sniffle, "we talked."

He grabs my hand and pulls me to the couch. We sit, and I lay my head on his shoulder.

"No matter how busy I may seem, I always have time to be with you."

"I know."

"What do you want to talk about?"

A million questions run through my head, but all I can think about is that documentary that Marci and Alex made about memory permanence.

"Can I ask you a question about that documentary you made?"

Alex giggles. "How'd you find that?"

"Netflix."

"Marci and I did that thing years ago. I never knew you were that interested in my research." He runs his fingers through my hair. "Ask away."

"Marci mentioned something about memory permanence... Or was it synaptic plasticity...or memory solidification? I don't have my notes" I shake my head in confusion. "Anyway, it was about how memories are not fixed and could be changed. Am I understanding that correctly?"

Alex clears his throat. "Yeah, you're on the right path. You see, the old idea was that memories were fixed. Once you have a memory, it's permanently stored. Like a file cabinet, with many folders. You pull one out, read it, and put it back when you are done, and the memory is unchanged. But current research—at least, a couple years ago— found that memories are fluid. Memories, once they are recalled, can be influenced. Even changed..." Alex's words fade into a mumble.

This explains why Marci is adamant about playing along with Alex's personalities. If Alex is confused or confronted with conflicting memories, he will change these memories. Rewrite them as his own. Corrupt them, and they cannot be removed or—

"Marci said memories could be erased. Is that true?"

Alex laughs. "Oh, man, I remember that part of the video, when I said, that's a long way into the science-fiction future, Marci. We had a huge argument on camera." Alex mumbles something under his breath, then continues. "They edited it to just have us glaring at each other."

"I noticed the tension, but you are now thinking Marci was right and memories can be erased."

"Let's take a step back. There were these memory experiments with fluorescently tagged proteins—"

"What proteins?"

"Fluorescently tagged proteins, essentially a light tag. Proteins are really small, and the light tag helps us see where the protein is at in the cells."

"Ah. Light tag is so much easier on the tongue, why not just say that?"

"Scientists like fancy words."

"And acronyms."

"As I was saying, the researchers tagged different proteins, one green and one red. The green or red light-tagged memories would blink on a screen when the mice performed some task. Always the same lights for the same tasks, and they speculated the same memory."

"Wow, you could map all the memories that way?"

"In theory, yes."

"That's kind of scary, like *Minority Report* or something."

Alex giggles. "A little. But the worrisome thing in my mind is that, in theory, after you mapped the memories, you could potentially record them, monitor them, change them, and even—as Marci suggested—erase them."

I think back to the video and the way Marci had said, "Erase them," with a laugh. "So, besides mind reading, what good can this research be used for?"

"Hopefully, our research will lead to understanding the process of memory formation and could help people with memory disorders, or traumatic brain stresses and traumatic memory disorders like PTSD."

"Wow, that sounded well-rehearsed."

"We have to get money for research. Donors like to hear that kind of thing."

Alex wraps his arm around my shoulder and pulls me into a tight hug. "I like talking about my research with you."

"I like talking with you." I lift off his chest. "One more question: did you and Marci figure out how to erase memories?"

Alex pulls his hands into his lap and starts fidgeting his fingers together. His head starts nodding. "Yes, I think I figured it out."

"Marci doesn't know?"

Alex shakes his head side to side. "No, I don't..."

"Don't what?"

"Don't trust Marci's intentions. She is in bed with people that would weaponize this technology if it works." Alex sighs, then continues. "I mean, we can't tell what the memories are by mapping. But if you can transfer memories to someone else, then they can recall the memory. And...if it works..."

"If it works?" I repeat the question.

"We never got to testing it. We were going to test it while I was in Philly but the postdoc working with us was out sick."

"Oh."

"But can you imagine what would happen if this got into the wrong hands or accidently released."

I nod my head. "It would be bad."

Alex clears his throat. "Okay enough of that, what's been going on with you? What case has you working these crazy hours?"

My eyes well up with tears. There is so much I should tell him. I should ask him—

"Lee, what is wrong?"

I lower my head and whisper, "I've missed you."

"Me too." He pulls me into him. Our lips meet again. His hands run along my spine. A warm heat runs through my body. I close my eyes, hoping the moment will last. Playing this part is easy. We tug at each other, removing layers of ourselves. We fall into each other. I do love him. We can do this.

The alarm in my head is ringing. I had an appointment this morning. I lift my head, staring at the clock. The hands of the wall clock come into focus. I still can make it. I lift off him, and our eyes meet. He rubs my arm.

"You have to go?"

"Yeah, I have a meeting this morning."

I search the floor for my own clothes, squatting to pick up my skirt.

"Sure you can't play hooky from work today?" I shake my head no, and he says, "Well, you can't blame me for trying to spend time with my beautiful wife."

Adjusting my bra in the living room mirror, he is standing behind me. I did not hear him cross the room. He puts his hands on my shoulders. "Thanks, Lee, for not rushing out this morning."

I can't think of the right words to say. His reflection moves closer, wrapping his arms around me. I press into his body, hoping this moment will last. The past weeks just a nightmare. My Alex is home at last.

Alex pulls away from me. His eyes scanning my body.

"What are you looking at?" I say to him, nudging him with my elbow.

"Those big breakfasts you've been eating are catching up with you." He laughs, pinching my belly.

I spin away from him. "Excuse me?" I button my top around my body. I should tell him, but Marci said play the part. She never said what part.

"I'm just teasing. You look great, Lee."

"Well you have no room to talk, Mister Ice-cream-before-bed."

"Oh, I see we got the claws out this morning." He waves his hand through the air like a cat. I laugh.

"That's the smile I love." He kisses me on the cheek, then pinches my belly again. I smack his hand away. "I love my girls a little curvy."

"Leave me alone and get ready for work. I'm going to be late." Against every fiber in my body, I gently push him away. He pokes out his bottom lip and walks to the bedroom.

I'm a few months pregnant, and I am starting to show. I finish getting dressed and rush to the kitchen to grab my food.

Alex mumbles something about working out.

"What was that, sweetie?" I yell at him from the kitchen.

He pokes his head out of the bedroom door.

"What do you want?"

"What are you doing? I thought you had to go to the—" I look up at him, that twisted smirk on his face sucks the air out of my lungs. I have to go.

"I thought I'd hit the gym before meeting up with Jerry to talk about the new book."

He is already gone. He is already someone else. That twisted smirk.

"What?"

He walks behind me, licks then kisses my ear. A wet, sticky kiss. The kind of kiss I hate. I push him away. I cannot play this part. I want Alex back.

"Stop, I'm going to be late."

He paws at my arm. I pull away from him, walking fast out of the kitchen.

I think about Marci, and her advice. "Just avoid him, them, as much as possible. He will not always be himself."

I stare at myself in the mirror by the door, pulling my hair into order. I stare into my own eyes. The eyes of a fool.

I believed her. Has she been talking with Alex? Her private checkups and calls. What can I do? She is the only one who can fix this. But is she going to make me beg for her help? Apologize for taking him from her? She let him go. It was her fault. Why punish me for her loss? Why?

A burst of light sparkles in my eyes. I blink several times. A sharp pain pulses in my forehead. My moment is finished. Was that it? How many other times during the day does Alex come out? I'll have to follow him and find out. I need to be there. I need him to be here with me.

Without looking back or speaking, I rush to the door. My hand is on the handle when he calls out to me, "Have a good day!" His voice is high-pitched. Happy, but it's not him. He starts walking, footsteps stomping closer. I have to answer. I have to play the part.

"You too!"

I pull the door open. His footsteps stop. I wait for him to call out. I step out the door, hoping he will call my name. I turn and his face is scrunched into a frown. He is about to cry. I want to run to him, but I don't love this him. I'm not playing the part. I'm not a good liar.

"I love you." My voice is a strained whisper. I'm hoping that will do it. Could that bring him back to me? He just smiles and hangs his head, staring at his feet. I pull the door halfway shut. I'm halfway out. Halfway in. Halfway playing the part.

"Alex!" I had to try getting him back.

He looks at me. His eyebrows raise, and confusion wrinkles his forehead. His eyes, but not his eyes are searching my face. I'm searching his face for his unique expressions. His smile. But he is gone, and I'm left playing the part trying to love someone else.

He hunches his shoulders, blows me a kiss, and mumbles, "I love you, too—"

I shut the door, imagining he finished that sentence with my name. I pull out my cell phone and Ralphie has texted me to meet for breakfast. I wipe my eyes and text, *I'll be there in ten minutes.*

***

Sitting at this coffee shop waiting for Ralphie, I remember the first time I meet Alex—

It was one of those days in between summer and fall. The crunch of leaves underfoot, a bit of wetness hanging in the air, and the wind had a little sting when it blew across your face. The gloomy fall weather matched my feelings about going to the office that day.

I decided to go in a bit later, trying to convince myself not to just work from home. Not wanting to become a social hermit, trying to find my place in the world, in Chicago; I compromised and stepped into the coffee shop. I was warmed by that sweet rich scent of fresh ground coffee and baked cinnamon rolls. I was standing in line when the door opened, and he stepped in.

He had a full scraggly beard, a small unkempt afro, tan slacks, black Converse sneakers, and a leather jacket. A black bag was slung over his shoulder, bulging with papers. He was standing behind me, the fragrance of his spicy cologne tickling my nose. I turned around to comment that he was whistling one of my favorite songs, but he was staring out into space. I was staring at him when the barista called out to me.

"Miss, what do you want?"

I turned, embarrassed, and fumbled an answer. "A large coffee—"

"You want room for cream?"

"Yes, and a cinnamon roll—"

"You want that warmed?"

"Yes, and I'd like to buy him," I pointed at Alex, "a coffee, also."

The barista yelled at Alex, "Hey Mister, what you want?"

Alex looked around, confused. Then I waved. "It's my treat."

Alex smiled. "Must be my lucky day. I'll have a large coffee, black."

"That all?"

Alex grinned at me, and I nodded.

We stood there with our cups of coffee, exchanged names and made googly eyes at each other, wrapped in that awkward space between total strangers and what now.

"So why would a pretty lady like yourself buy a scruffy nerf herder a coffee?"

I smiled, brushing the hair out of my face. "Why don't we sit over there, and I'll explain how I made the Kessel Run in 12 parsecs."

He laughed. That high pitch snort of a laugh. We sat in a booth and talked for hours. It was around lunchtime when his phone went off and he had to run. His fingers brushed the back of my hand.

"Leslie, are you free for dinner tonight?"

"Yes, I'd love to get dinner with you." Why did I answer yes? I had dinner with clients that night? I answered yes because I was already in love with Alex.

He stood and pulled his leather jacket around his bulky frame. He leaned in close, grabbed my hand, lifted it to his mouth, and kissed it.

"Until tonight."

I could not help but smile. I could not stop the warm feelings bubbling inside my chest. Heart beating fast. "Yes, tonight."

My eyes followed him out the coffee shop, whistling a tune, whistling his love for me. Could it be this easy?

The door jingled close behind him. I follow him with my eyes, strolling down the street. I followed him until he was out of sight, promising myself not to fall too fast—

Her voice startles me. "Here's your coffee, ma'am."

I smile, turning to get cream and sugar, I see Ralphie walk in. I wave and nod at a booth.

He whispers his order to the waitress as they pass, then he flops into the booth across from me. He smells like freshly turned soil. He pulls off his hat. He looks at me.

"How are you doing today?"

I nod my head. "Okay."

"You look happy, what's going on?"

"Nothing. Alex was Alex before I left home, and I was just thinking about the day we met."

"Yeah, nice to think about the positive."

"I was kind of a mess at that point—"

"You, a mess? I don't believe it."

I pull a loose stand of hair out of my face. "Most people don't know this, but I had just moved back to Chicago a couple years before meeting Alex."

"And then what? You guys were married a few months later?"

"Something like that. We fell for each other pretty hard."

"Must be nice."

Ralphie watches the people walk past the coffee shop window, his smile has flattened into a pensive frown.

I reach out and grab his hand. "The right girl is out there. Take it from me, you will find it when you least expect it."

"Easy for you to say." He laughs.

"No, really. I had just gotten out of an unhealthy relationship and moved to Chicago to start my life over. Then I bought a coffee for a scruffy, bushy headed Alex, and the rest—as they say—is history."

"Well I'm stuck at the unhealthy relationship phase. Better start buying coffees for strange women."

I take a sip of my coffee and the waitress arrives sitting another mug of coffee on the table. Ralphie opens a cream and swirls it into the steaming liquid.

"So how bad was this relationship that you had to move to Chicago?"

Ralphie reads my face before I can speak. "Sorry, you don't have to talk about it. We can talk about something else."

"No, no. It's okay. Past history. He was my high school sweetheart. He moved with me to Boston, where I went to law school. I started working at a law firm afterwards. He fucked around in college and became a leech to my successes and money. First he was happy for me, but over time resentment crept in. Drinking crept in. Other women crept in—"

"He didn't hit you or anything?" Ralphie squeezes my hand.

"No, just verbal abuse. How ugly I was. How dumb I was. After a year of eating his shit, I took a job here in Chicago without telling him. Packed a bag and moved back home."

"Did he try to move out with you?"

"I never looked back. I did not tell him where I was going. And I figure he wouldn't have the balls or desire to come after me. I was living with my parents and my dad said he had a bullet with his name on it..."

"Shit, I'm sorry that happened to you."

"Don't be. I wouldn't have moved, and I would never have meet Alex."

Ralphie gazes out the window. The quiet of the coffee shop settles between us. The grinding of coffee, the chatter of forks on plates, and the pleasantries of small talk.

"Is that why you started that non-profit you work at? To help abused women?"

I nod my head. "I had made enough money to be comfortable, defending corporate assholes. Why not give back? And I knew firsthand how hard it is to break the cycle of domestic abuse. I had the smarts and resources to leave, but it took me a couple years to convince myself to leave."

"I'm sorry." Ralphie mumbles into his coffee.

"Why?"

Ralphie looks away from me. He plays with the spoon in his coffee. "Just you dealing with Alex. The way he treats you now—"

"Don't be sorry about that. That person is not my Alex. Alex is the sweetest person you could ever meet. Those people in his head are not him, and I don't confuse that." I tap Ralphie's hand. He looks at me, and I continue. "Promise me you won't, either. Don't give up on Alex or Granny. Plus, when you think about it, I'm probably the best prepared to deal with this. I was in an abusive relationship, and I help people through theirs."

Ralphie nods. "Sure, Leslie. As long as he does not lay a finger on you."

"I'm a big girl. I can handle myself."

Ralphie checks his watch. He grabs his hat and starts to shimmy out of the booth. "I hate to leave the conversation here, but we can talk later."

"Yeah, I'd like that."

He turns and starts to walk away, then pauses. "I forgot to ask. How is the baby?"

"He or she is doing well. Just ignoring the world and doing their thing."

"Well, if you need anything, just let me know."

"Oh, a cup of coffee and conversation is more than I can ask for."

"It's no problem, Leslie. I mean it. If you need anything, anytime, just let me—"

"I will. You're a good friend. I'm glad we got to meet. I'm sure your princess is out there."

He smiles. "All I have to do is buy her a coffee, right?"

I laugh.

"That smile looks good on you." He winks, then walks away.

"Maybe meet for dinner?" He calls out, turning, walking backwards.

"It depends on what is going on with Alex and how much work has piled up on my desk."

Ralphie nods, smiles at me. "Dessert?"

"Ralphie, stop it. I see you almost every day."

"Never can see enough of you."

I shake my head and half smile.

He spins on his heels and walks toward the door with purpose. My eyes follow him walking down the street into his truck and driving away. I contemplate what happened between Alex and me earlier in the day. What Alex is becoming? My sweet Alex that I fell in love with. Marci has to have answers soon.

My phone rings. Like thinking of the devil, Marci's name flashes across the screen. I suck in a lungful of air, tasting the roasted coffee and soil; I press answer as I exhale.

CHAPTER 21

Marci:
50 Days after Event

I forgot what it's like to wake up curled in someone else's space. Surrounded by their scent, by their noise, by their warmth. The faint light from a rising sun is throwing strange shadows onto the ceiling.

I ease out of bed trying not to disturb Eric. I press my feet against the cool wood floor and rise from the bed. I bend to pick his shirt off the floor—wanting his scent on me, draping it over my shoulders—and walk to the wall of windows.

I stare out into the sleepy city. It's Saturday; the chaotic mess of the early morning is condensed into a few homeless people shuffling along the streets, police cars speeding by, and the SEPTA buses creeping along the street, stopping just to waste time. I study the dark shadows in between the buildings for any signs of life.

I plop onto the loveseat. Eric put it here at my request. Eric hates it when I call it a love seat, he always corrects me. "Marci, it's a two-seat sofa by the Danish designer Hans Wegner..." I just call it a loveseat to see him shake his head and impress me with his knowledge of mid-century furniture.

The upholstery is cool on my bare legs and butt. My eyes are drawn to the orange light sneaking between the buildings, fading and reforming, connecting to reflect off the glass and steel buildings, then pulling away to leave only shadows of its existence. The way the light dances, connects, and fades away reminds me of connections in the brain. Memories form and then are reinforced or fade away. I wonder if the light remembers where it has been. Does it care? How would I remember where I'd been if I were light? Traveling that fast, would I care?

I close my eyes to let my random thoughts about light, memories, and the brain collect and organize into a more meaningful idea or fade away as garbage.

The quiet of the condo is broken by a series of soft dings. My cell phone is buzzing with life. I'm tempted to ignore it and tease out the ideas forming in my head. Instead, I like getting my weekly updates from the goons following Alexi. Also, I'm expecting Mark to update me on the memory mapping of the passengers and Alexi.

I thought I'd never be friends with Alexi again; but when he asked me to collaborate on that stupid outreach video, it opened a door that was sealed shut. I was excited and had daydreams of us falling into each other, falling in love again, especially as we started to collaborate on research projects. Then, after a couple years of us growing closer, he confessed he was in love, married or getting married—all the same to me. All he could talk about was his Leslie.

I stand to get my phone, still beeping away with updates.

"Turn that thing off and come back to bed. It's Saturday, for Christ's sake!" Eric calls out.

"Early bird catches the worm. Sleepyhead."

"Early bird can go get coffees and donuts."

I turn off the volume, leaning into the bedroom. "I'd have to put pants on to go out."

Eric lifts his head and talks into the pillow. "I'm all worn out. Put pants on and get coffee and donuts."

"If you say so." I turn and walk toward the windows, accentuating my movements like a runway model.

"On second thought, why don't we call that place that delivers coffee and donuts and we can—"

Eric's words flow into each other, as though traveling into a tube and mushing into noise, as I read the reports that were sent. I mumble under my breath, "Alexi spotted going into leather clubs, spending time with Ralphie and Granny, going out with a person named Tammy..."

The name Tammy hangs on the edge of a memory. "I've heard that name before, Tammy." Staring out the window, I whisper, "...not Tammy from before?"

A warm hand wraps around my waist. My hand jerks forward, and my phone flings out of my grip.

"Fuck!"

Eric laughs. He snorts and talks at the same time. "Marci, I'm sorry. I thought you knew I was there."

"Oh, this cannot be happening." I pick the phone off the floor, reading over the text messages again.

"What's wrong?" Eric grabs my hand.

"Nothing just work stuff." I wave my hand. "Let's not talk about it."

"You sure, you seem upset? Anything I can help with?"

"No."

"Okay."

"I'm sorry. Where were we?" I lean into Eric, kissing him on the lips.

"We were going to get donuts and coffee. Right?"

"I always have time for coffee and donuts with you."

Eric smiles and pulls me into a hug, my head resting on his chest.

"Great. Get dressed, and we can walk to the little bakery down the street that opens at this ungodly hour on a Saturday."

I nod, half listening to Eric, but the slap on my bare butt snaps me to reality. "Ouch!" I rub at the lingering sting.

"Get dressed or there's more of that waiting for you."

"Is that a promise?"

Eric laughs and I run into the bedroom, pushing him onto the bed, delaying our walk to get coffee and donuts.

The donut shop that Eric and I are going to is about one mile away. We are skipping around, and splashing puddles formed by a late-night drizzle. The morning air is cool and relaxing. Eric talks about his house on the shore and how we should take a longer vacation there.

The buzzing of my phone starts about halfway there, and I grab it. "Mark" flashes across the screen.

"Come on, Marci. Put the phone away for one day. The troubles of the world can manage without you."

"I don't know about that." I bump him with my hip.

"Let's make a deal: you can check in every hour. If it's not a matter of national security or zombies running loose eating brains, I get your undivided attention to spend the day anyway I choose."

"It's only a deal if I get to pick any movie, dinner, and we have to have ice cream before I save the world from zombies." I laugh.

Eric nods, and we shake hands. I put my phone on silent and shove it into my sweatpants pocket. He leans in, kissing me on the cheek. I turn, and our lips meet. He pulls me into a hug.

"Can we do this all day?" I say.

Eric pulls away but does not let go. "After coffee and donuts."

Eric orders two chocolate glazed donuts and a large coffee, black. He makes fun of me because I order a dozen donut holes and an orange juice.

"I cannot believe you got donut holes and an orange juice." He grabs one of the white balls of dough and pops it into his mouth.

"Whoa! You can't do that. Not nice, mister." I put my cell phone between our sides of the table. "No reaching across this line, stealing food."

He leans over the table and kisses me.

"Or kisses." I wag my finger.

He sticks out his tongue and shakes his head. "You're a sore sport."

"I haven't had my coffee yet."

"So why'd you order orange juice?"

"I need a glass of orange juice, and then I have coffee. Then you can steal kisses." We both giggle.

Silence settles between us and is filled with people talking, horns honking, the mechanical beeps and whistles of trucks, that sweet noise of the city. I turn my head and find Eric ogling me.

"What?"

"Nothing, I just find myself smitten for you."

"Stop it, mister."

"Marci, I'm going to come out and say this. You make me incredibly happy, and I love you."

My cell phone buzzes and flashes a series of text messages. My eyes glance at the cell phone screen, and Eric grabs my phone.

"Oh no you don't. I say I love you and you—" Eric begins reading the messages.

"Those could be top secret messages, you know."

Eric looks at me. His smile twists into a frown, like someone pissed in his punch. His hand squeezes into a fist around my phone, shakes it in my face, and slams it to the table. He pushes his chair away and stands to leave.

I grab his arm. "Eric, please stop. I don't know what happened. We were having a moment, and I love you—"

Eric slams his fist on the table. "Don't say that, Marci. Just don't insult my intelligence anymore." Eric shakes his head and continues, "All morning you were dying to look at your phone. Go ahead and look. Marci!" He spits my name at me.

There are several messages from Alexi:

Hey, Nurse Marci I wanted to know if we could talk more.

I thought about what you said, and that kiss.

I cannot stop thinking about that kiss the other day.

Maybe we can meet again. Soon!!

Eric's eyes are watering, my eyes watering. I start to blab. "It's not what you think. I need to explain—"

"Fuck you, Marci. This has been one big game, and I fell for it. You're still playing in fantasy land but count me out."

Eric turns and walks toward the door. I grab my phone. "Eric, wait!" I shout running after him.

I throw open the door and he is standing there, the sun glowing orange behind him, his arms crossed.

"Go ahead—explain, Marci." He spits my name at me like it hurts.

I grab his hand and he pulls away. "Eric, please let me say I'm falling in love with you too. And this is not what you think."

"Let me see if I understand, Marci. A person named Alexi said they enjoyed kissing you. Nurse Marci is what they said. If I remember that was your profile name, and the first fantasy meet-up we played out. Not much room for misinterpretation. Now is it, Marci?"

"I was—" Eric cuts me off.

"All you talk about is Alexi this and Brian that. And all these weeks you were telling me you had to go to Chicago for this memory bullshit, and you're hooking up with these guys. Fuck you!"

"Eric!" I yell his name, to stop him from talking. "Eric, sweetie, let me explain what and who Brian is. He and Alexi are the same person. And why I needed to kiss him. It was meaningless. It was before we were serious. Please give me that."

"Before we were serious? Give me a break." Eric shakes his head and continues. "I don't know, Marci. Even if I knew this before we were serious, shit probably wouldn't add up. I bet if you showed me your messages, I'd see you and this Alexi have been texting non-stop. I'd bet every time you take a break to check that damn phone, I'd find some message between you and him. Am I right or wrong?"

"No, it's not..."

"If I'm wrong, I will apologize for being a jealous shit, but am I wrong?"

My mind is whirling like crazy. It is kind of like everything is spinning around us, and we are standing still. I can't do this. I reach out to grab Eric's arm, but he moves it. Just when I found love again, I do something stupid like this. His voice snaps at me.

"Marci! Am I wrong?"

I shake my head. "But please—" My eyes welling with tears and my voice cracks. "Please, it's just work stuff. Not what you think. Eric, please, let me explain—"

"Marci, I don't know what to think. Until you learn to leave your work at that laboratory of yours, you will not be happy." He turns and starts to walk away. "Maybe we can talk later, but I need time to process."

I watch him walk away. I want to yell his name. I want to run after him and scream how much I have fallen in love with him. That Alexi means nothing to me. But if he meant nothing, why did I kiss him? For a password?

Eric is a couple blocks away, and I still cannot yell his name. My throat is swollen and raw. I try to run after him, but my legs are lead weights. My stomach is in tight knots. Small throbs radiate from behind my eyes. The noises of the city, mocking me. My phone buzzes, Leslie is texting me:

Hey, Marci. I'm just wondering if you have time to chat. I been doing some research and had questions about the stuff you and Dr. Greene been talking about. Also, Alex was himself for a bit. Do you know if there is a way to predict when he will be himself vs the others? Well just give me a ring when you can. Thanks.

I wipe my eyes, ignoring Leslie's text. I dial Eric. It goes to voice mail. "Sweetie, I'm sorry. Please can we meet in a little bit and I can try to explain? Lay all my cards out and if we are done, we are done. But not like this. Please."

I stare at the phone, willing him to call me. Or text me. Or Snapchat. Any of the silly ways we communicated these last weeks, falling for each other.

I realize my purse, computer, and notes are at Eric's place. How am I going to get home? I order an Uber off my phone and pay with the card on file.

I get home, take a shower, and pour a cup of coffee. The doorbell rings. I run to the door, hoping it's Eric, ready to jump into his arms, but there was just a uniformed man with a box, asking for my signature.

I take the box to the kitchen table and tear it open. I smile, seeing my purse and other stuff. Eric is a true gentleman, and I fucked it up. *Nice going, Marci.*

Marci, the old fucking maid.

There was an envelope on top, my heart beating fast, hoping this is a letter to meet or give me a chance to explain. I pull the card out and read the loopy cursive. "No need to go to waste." Inside the inner envelope there are two theater tickets for a play I have been talking about going to.

My eyes tear up when the doorbell rings again. I wipe them and run to the door, certain this time it's Eric. I throw the door open, and it's two men with the Hans Wegner sofa.

"Where do you want this?"

I slam the door shut and as hard as I try not to, tears stream from my eyes. The doorbell rings again, and the men are shouting, "Ma'am we are going to leave this on your porch if you don't open back up."

INTERLUDE

Alex/Brian:
Marci

I am never alone, but she is not here. Where is she? She is with her mom. I drove her to the airport. Am I alone? I am surrounded by shadows. Long dark shadows wiggling along the walls. I rub my eyes and grab my cell phone off the nightstand. I dial her number.

"Hello." Her voice is hoarse. "Who's this?"

"Marci, it's me Alex."

She clears her throat. "Oh my gosh, Alexi. Is everything alright?"

"Yes, I'm just all alone—"

"What? Lee left? Like she moved out?"

"No, nothing that dramatic. Lee went to visit her mom."

"Oh, I didn't know she planned a trip."

"She had planned this trip before to help her mom settle some legal things."

"Oh."

In the background I hear a muffled voice. "Marci, you have company. Oh my gosh, I can call back."

"No, unfortunately I am all alone. It's just the radio. Anyway, you can call me anytime."

"You sure?"

"Alexi, yes. It's *NPR*. Now what's up?"

"I keep having this dream."

"What about?"

"Well it's hard to explain."

"Try me."

"Okay. So I'm on a train or bus, sitting next to this woman from the plane. All the other seats are empty. I study her features, but I can't remember her name. Our conversation is short; she always asks to borrow my book. The cover is always out of focus until I hand it to her. As she grabs it, a jolt of energy travels through the book and stings my hand. At that moment, the cover comes into focus, and it's her face on the cover. A voice announces that it's my stop. I snatch the book and hurry out the door. As it closes, I notice the bus has filled beyond capacity. They're all saying something. I chase after the bus, their voices shout in concert, 'You have our books!' Then the dream fades away."

"Have you told Dr. Shirley about this dream?"

"No."

"Why not?"

"I don't know why. It never comes up. What, are you my mom now?"

"Okay, Alexi. Just relax."

"I'm sorry, Marci."

"Don't be sorry."

"Well I am. And I'm sorry for Lee."

"I understand. Maybe you can help."

"How?"

"Give me the files you were working on, and I can create the nano-construct and maybe—"

"Is that all you want from me?"

"No, I want to help you all get better."

"You think I'm a stupid shit. Well fuck you, Brenda."

"What?"

"You heard me! You can go fuck yourself."

"Alexi, please—"

"Stop calling me Alexi. My name is—" What is my name? My head is pounding.

"What's your name?" Marci whispers.

"I don't know."

"Okay, let's calm—"

"Stop telling me to calm down, you stupid bitch."

"Okay."

"And stop saying okay, when things are not okay. My head is pounding, white fucking lights are flashing in my eyes."

"What can I do to help?"

"Fuck you, Brenda"

"I'm not Brenda, I'm Mar—"

"You can suck on these nuts, bitch."

Brenda gasps, and the line goes quiet. I look at the phone and it says, "Disconnected." I throw the phone on the nightstand, and the dark shadows creep back around me. Their voices call out to me.

I don't need her. I am never alone.

CHAPTER 22

Brenda/Leslie:
80 Days after Event

The mornings are the worst. I never know who he will wake up as. I tip-toe around the bedroom so I do not disturb him. He is changing. His face is the same, but he is changing. Morphing into something. Change can be scary. Is he changing into himself? My love. My Alex. Since he has been meeting with Dr. Shirley, he has been stabilizing into himself more often.

I step out the bathroom, towel wrapped around my body. His voice startles me. "Lee, come back to bed for a little, do you have to leave this early?" I look at the clock.

"Okay, ten more minutes."

"Ten, I need a little more than that."

I drop the towel. Gooseflesh prickles along my body, and I slip under the covers. His warm body snuggles against mine. The press of him, kissing my sensitive skin. His hands remembering where they should be.

"Oh, Alex." I comb my hand through his hair as he kisses along my collarbone, my breast, my thighs. As pleasure tingles along my body, it's easy to convince myself, no matter who he becomes, I will still love him.

These rare mornings with Alex make my life with the others easier. These fleeting moments make me yearn for more. But I am often interacting with one of the others—Brian usually, and that's not so bad. But I miss the other moments of Alex. The times he is talking with Marci. I'm missing moments where I could be with Alex.

I'm still not sure what I'm going to do is a smart thing. Could it make it worse? Maybe, but it may make it better. Better for whom?

Today is the day, I have decided. I have nothing important going on at work. He always meets with his friend, Jerry, at a fancy restaurant downtown on Fridays, and it's pretty close to my office. I plan on getting there early and, maybe if he spots me, he will be Alex.

I watch the hours on the clock tick by. I flip through the case file on my desk. It's a girl we helped before. Abusive brother. She loved him. After we helped her, she had moved out and on with her life, but love is a powerful thing. I fidget with the pages, not reading any of the details of how she managed to get into this situation again. It's always the same: counting on a change that never happens.

I try to remember what I am going to do this afternoon and try not to think about poor... I glance at her photo. A pale, freckled redhead. Amanda. Her face brings a flood of memories. A brother who hates women. Hates blacks. Hates Jews. Hates gays. Hates the world—

My cellphone chimes an alert. I close the folder. Time to go and play private detective. I got out of my other afternoon meeting with a pregnancy checkup excuse and a promise to reach out to... I forget her name. I have been forgetting trivial things. Pregnancy causes that, I read. I glance at her picture again, and her name pops into my head—Amanda.

I put her folder into my briefcase. A little light reading before bed. I force her image out of my head. Her story. I walk out of my office with a small wave to the faces in the conference room.

I decide to walk. It's not far, and I have plenty of time to get there before him. Pushing into the restaurant, I am met with a wave of onion and garlic aromas. My stomach knots, my throat burns with stabs of indigestion. I ignore my gastrointestinal warning and think about him. I have played the scene in my mind a thousand times, and each scenario ends with Alex and me exchanging a glance and falling into a lengthy conversation. Could I finally tell him that I'm pregnant? It's becoming more difficult to hide. Will he be excited or—

"Welcome to Speckled. Dining in or lunch pickup?"

Her voice startles me. A tall woman. Thin arms extend out of a white pinstripe, sleeveless, collared top. Hair pulled into a tight bun, pulling the skin on her forehead smooth. Looks painful. Her large, fake, toothy smile, pink gums showing, makes me nervous.

"Dine in, please."

She follows my gaze into the space. "Expecting someone? You can join them if they're already at a table."

A large man is sitting out on the patio, cackling. Sounds like Jerry.

"No, a table for one, please."

"I thought you were with him out there." She lets out a small laugh. Or maybe it was a sigh which trails into the words. "Follow me."

"May I have a booth along that wall?"

"Anything you want, princess!"

"Excuse me?"

"Is this booth good enough for you?"

She grins at me. I'm unsure what I did to her. Should I apologize? But for what? I hate these gastro places. Alex and I both hate them. Overpriced food and an oversized attitude. I hope it's worth it. I will play nice, so no one spits in my food and calls it special sauce. I smile.

"Yes, this is fine."

Her lips struggle into a smile.

I notice a couple men in suits ducking behind their menus, maybe a shy couple exchanging a sexy secret. I slide into the cold leather booth and maintain eye contact with my greeter. Maintain friendliness. Trying to ignore her teeth poking through her lips, I say, "Thank you."

Her fake smile widens, showing teeth and her pink gums.

She points across the empty sunlit space at a woman leaning against the bar. "Your server will be Angela, enjoy."

"Thanks," I say to my menu, trying to avoid her gaze.

I glance over at Angela, who is a curvy, short woman. Attractive. Skin the shade of a sun-kissed, sandy beach. Her long, straight black hair flows behind her like a superwoman's cape. Her smile is natural, genuine, and her voice is soothing, with hints of a Southern California accent.

She sits a sweating glass of water and a plate of macerated vegetables on the table.

"Welcome to Speckled. Please relax and start your dining experience with a glass of deconstructed cucumber water." She rolls her eyes, sarcastically explaining the process. "You drizzle water over the crisp sticks of freshly harvested cucumbers. Feeling the heat of the summer's warmth trapped in the fruit and being embraced by the refreshing coolness of the water..."

I am pulled into her deep brown eyes, like a picture I have seen. "Sounds complicated." I look between the shredded vegetables and her wide smile.

"They pay me to say that. Just stick the cucumber in the water and enjoy. That's what I do." She laughs and touches my shoulder, exchanging some of her warmth, some of her spirit.

"Yes, I may just do that."

"Take your time and look over the menu. It's pretty empty, so just call if you need anything. My name is Angela." She turns to walk away.

"Thank you. My name is Leslie."

She turns her head, hair flowing over her shoulders. "I know." She winks and walks away.

Her words repeat in my head, *I know. I know—*

How does she know my name? Did our office help her family? Did we help her? So many women and families have been through our office. I remember many of them. I would have remembered that face of hers.

The greeter's voice grates into my ears. Who is she talking to? I glance up and see those pink gums and white teeth. He steps out of the shadows. I listen to his voice, he is not Alex, maybe Brian. He laughs and flirts with her. Those pink gums and that hoarse laugh. They walk past me, outside. I switch sides in the booth. Alex sits across from Jerry. What is his story again? Did he play football? No, he's that strange, creepy agent. I think he does porn movies.

Angela flashes me a smile as she breezes from here to there, serving drinks and mumbling something every time she comes from the patio. She stops at my table.

"Some men. Just because they have some money, think they own the world and everyone who tries to live in it." She pulls her hair into twisty ponytail. "You need anything?"

"No, I'm fine." She turns to walk away, but I say, "One thing, do you know those two out there?"

She nods and then flops into the seat across from me. "Really?" She sucks her teeth. "Okay, I'll play along. Yeah, I know them. The gross fat asshole is Jerry Johnson, pinching my butt, thinking he is a big shot agent, but mostly does fetish porn..." Her voice fades into a mumble of curse words, some in English, others in Spanish.

"Why do they meet here?"

She raises her eyebrow and smirks. "Stop playing stupid."

"I, um...Wha—"

"They," her eyes dart to men in in the corner, "told me everything. They said you would show up eventually. You already know why he is here. My lover is in there. He has been coming here to see me. This is," her voice softens, "my time to be with him. My Eduardo. Don't take this from me." She wipes at her face. Her soft voice trembles. "Don't take him away from me, 'cause without this, all I'd have left is that shell I take care of at home."

I reach out to her, but I stop, gripping the table instead. I understand. Her lover is in there. He is in there with my Alex. Marci's use of the word "our" echoes in my head.

"It will be okay," I whisper. She nods and walks away into the darker shadows of the restroom hallway.

I watch Angela run from the kitchen to the bar, delivering drinks and food. She drops my plate on the table. No descriptions about the secret life of plants that made it into my salad. No remarks about heat and the summer's dew refreshing my pallet. Nothing. She just drops the plate and walks out to the patio, wrapping her arms around him. My Alex. Her Eduardo. Their memories.

I tap my fingers against the table, gritting my teeth, huffing out my nose holding in a yell. Are they watching me? Are they laughing at me? Tight knots of hunger grip my stomach. I stab my salad and chew the bitter greens with violence. Stab. Chew. Stab. Chew.

The two men stand, nodding at me, grinning as they stroll through the restaurant. What do they know? Do they work with, or for, Marci? Have I been playing the part, the sucker? My eyes squint and lips purse, ready to strike out with angry words. They pass into the shadows and out the door before I can explode.

I take a sip of my cucumber water. My shoulders relax. What's in this water?

I study their every movement. Angela and him. She leans in close, sharing a secret joke. He laughs and squeezes her arm. Flirting like old lovers. Should I go out there? Go out there and get him from her?

Marci's warning about compromising memories—corrupting and merging memories—pops into my head. I punch the seat and switch to the other side of the booth. I don't have to be a witness to his infidelity. It was foolish to do this. I will finish my lunch and leave.

I begin poking at my salad that has begun to wilt and look unappetizing. Even the cucumber water has a sour, bitter flavor. Anxious to leave, I glance around for a server. The patio door opens, and he saunters in from the patio. Our eyes meet. I smile.

"Lee, what are you doing here?"

His voice. It is him. I pinch at the bridge of my nose, trying to hold back tears.

"Hey." I say with a smile.

"What are you doing here?"

"It's lunch time, and everyone was talking about the food here. Thought I'd give it a try. A little uppity, if you ask me."

Alex grins. My Alex slides into the booth across from me.

"You okay?"

"Perfect." I smile. "Something was in my eye."

I reach across the booth and grab his hand.

"Well, always nice to see you unexpectedly." He squeezes my hand in response.

We gaze into each other's eyes. I am afraid to blink, not wanting to miss a moment with him. A pleasant quietness settles in between us. He rubs circles on the palm of my hand.

His voice breaks the quiet between us. "You have to go back to work? Maybe we can walk along the lake."

"I'd like that. Do you have to say goodbye to your friend?" I nod my head toward the patio.

"What?"

"Your friend Jer—" I stop myself from finishing the sentence. I have him. Alex is here now. It's my turn. "Nothing, let's get the check and go."

"Funny, I don't even like this place, but I feel like I keep coming here." He glances at Angela, then winks at me. "Maybe it's the cute waitresses."

I nudge him with my foot. "Very funny."

He rubs my arm. "Just teasing." He waves at Angela to get here attention.

In several long strides, Angela is squeezing his shoulder. "What can I get for you, darling?" Her accent blurs the words into a seductive language. She winks at me.

"Can we have our checks?" Alex asks.

"Anything for you, darling," Angela says and walks away.

"Is she a friend of yours, Lee?"

"Something like that." I squeeze Alex's hand. "Give me a second to say goodbye."

Alex nods.

Easing out of the booth, I call out to her, "Angela."

She turns and looks at me. "Yes?"

"Can I have a word, in private?"

She says something under her breath, then waves for me to follow. We turn into a small hallway. I want to be angry at her. I want to tell her to leave Alex alone. But her dejected smirk stops me. Eyes welling up with tears. I have seen this face. Every time I stare in the mirror. I cannot take him away from her. But do I have to share?

Her voice cuts into my thoughts. "What are we going to do?" Every word is annuciated with a staccato sharpness.

"Alex and I are going to go for a walk, and this will be the last time I'll come to this restaurant."

She shifts her weight from one leg to the other, hands on her hips. She wrinkles her mouth like she is sniffing something rotten. "Sounds like a good idea. Those guys that were here say there's a way to fix them. Give back memories with some sort of transfer."

"Why did they tell you that? That's confidential information."

"Oh chica, a little cleavage and a fake Spanish accent, you can get anything you want." She wiggles her hips. "Oh, and a little sugar on top."

I can't help but laugh. "I hear you, sister."

She extends her hand. "Until we get our men back, we have to share. *Entente*?"

"What? I don't speak Spanish."

"Entente is from French, and it means," she rocks her hand, "more or less, a truce." She winks.

We shake hands and walk into the main room. I stop short. Angela runs into me, pushing me off balance. I grab onto a table to stop myself from falling. He is gone. My eyes scan the room, and then I spot him, on the patio, laughing with Jerry.

"You okay?"

"No!"

She follows my eyes out to the patio. Her arms wrap around me. "I'm sorry."

I shrug out of her arms. I grab my purse, pulling out two twenties. I throw them on the table and run for the exit. The lady with the fake smile and pink gums steps in front of me and starts talking.

"Was everything satisfying?"

"Fuck off!"

"Well fuck you, too, bitch."

I push past her through the black curtains.

Standing in the hallway, I turn into the coat nook and slump against the wall. Tears flowing out of my eyes. I think about Alex. His voice. His hands. His body, pressing against mine. His playful teases.

My muscles dissolve and I slide along the wall to the floor. When will I get my Alex again? Another chance to hold him? My Alex...

Marci knows more than she has told me. Those guards know more than me. Angela knows more than me. Marci and her "play the part." *Just give me a couple days. A couple weeks. Just play your part,* she keeps telling me. That was a couple months ago.

My phone starts buzzing. I stare at my phone. At her name, Marci. I press the green accept button and put the phone to my ear.

"Hello, Leslie." Her voice is loud with a hint of agitation.

Beeps and mechanical devices whirl in the background. Marci's voice calls out louder, "Are you there, Leslie?" Her voice, pitchy and annoyed. "Can you hear me? One second, I'll go into my office."

The background noise subsides. "Hello, Leslie. Can you hear me now?"

I want to laugh. I want to let her go on talking to herself. I find humor in her struggle, her worry. Has the stimulus in my life sunk so low that I find pleasure in first grade humor?

I clear my throat. "Hey, Marci."

"There you are. I wasn't sure you could hear me. The technician turned the centrifuge on right when you picked up."

"Yes, I can hear you, Marci."

"How are things going? Are Alex's visits with the psychiatrist helping?"

"No, they're not helping," I lie.

"Well, Dr. Shirley thinks Alex is making satisfactory progress. She is helping him compartmentalize the personalities. That will help with the memory—" Marci pauses, murmuring, and then she continues in a whisper. "I can't talk about this over the phone."

"Not over the phone? Why not?"

"They could be listening."

She did not have to say any more. They are the same people following me around. They are always around. They were at the restaurant watching me. *They*.

"I understand, Marci." The line goes quiet.

"You should come to Philadelphia for a few days, and we can talk."

"And leave Alex?"

"They're watching him. Also, we can keep him busy with Granny and that hunk of a man, Ralphie."

A tingle goes through my body when she says his name. Why? He is attractive. Strong hands, but his touch is gentle. His smile melts the tension out of my shoulders. Or were those *his* hands, my Alex, messaging the tension out in small circles. But why do I care what Marci thinks about Ralphie? I unclench my fists and exhale through my nose.

"Yes, Ralphie is nice." Another tingle runs along my spine. I can't help smiling. "He has been a good friend to me." Warmth fills me, and I add, "Alex and me. I mean both of us."

Marci coughs into the phone. "Well, sounds like Ralphie has made a big impression on you," she says.

"No, it's not like that. He just offers support and words of encouragement when things are going bad with Alex," I cover my mouth, "and with Granny!"

"Well, I wish he would wrap those strong biceps around me. I know I could use that about now. Take my mind of things. Know what I mean?" Marci laughs. A high-pitched laugh. A sincere, sultry laugh. Why am I getting angry?

"Not to spoil your wet dreams, but I don't think you're his type."

Marci's voice is quiet. "Oh." My insult struck a nerve.

I continue speaking. "So can I come out next weekend? Maybe Friday evening until Sunday?"

"Yes, that can work. The lab will be empty, and I can show you the data without interruptions."

"Sounds good."

"Perfect. I'll give Ralphie a call and set—"

"No, I'll call him. I can stop by on my way home and make sure he has a key to our place and stuff like that."

"Oh... Okay, sounds like you have everything under control."

"I'll let you know my flight info."

"See you soon, Leslie." She says my name like it hurts.

"Marci, this is not a social visit. I just want to find out what's going on and what you're doing to fix things." The line is too quiet. "Marci, you there? Marci?"

I realize, after yelling into the phone for a minute, that she already disconnected. A ping of disgust rises up my throat. I can't get him out of my mind. He, Ralphie, has become my rock in this storm. What would he think about this trip to visit Marci? Does she want him? She can't take them both, Alex and Ralphie, away from me.

Marci has neither of them, and I intend to keep it that way. I click on contacts and find his name. I press the dial button, close my eyes, and imagine his face.

"Hey, Leslie."

I wipe the tears out of my eyes and smile. "Hey—"

CHAPTER 23

Marci:
86 Days after Event

The words on the screen blur into a smear of black. I squint my eyes, leaning my head closer to the screen and then farther away, but that words refuse to focus. My head starts pounding. I rub my eyes and focus on the clock across the room. I've been running simulations for 6 hours. Did I eat dinner? I will keep working until I figure out how Alexi did it. Maybe I got lazy relying on him to solve my problem. Maybe I'm not as intelligent as I think. Maybe I'm a fraud. Maybe Eric was smart to cut me loose. Maybe I was smart to cut Alexi loose before he could hurt me. Maybe I never loved Eric. Maybe I never loved Alexi—

I push my chair away from the desk and walk to my kitchen and grab the bottle of Tres Generaciones from the cabinet. I pour a glass and sip slowly. I walk into the living room and lay out on his fancy loveseat. Eric was a nice distraction. Something to take my mind of things and clear the cobwebs. I pick up my cell phone and read through his text messages. He accepted my apology, but did he forgive me? My finger hovers over the dial button, but he said he would be in Europe for an extended trip. He'd call me when he returns. I toss the phone back on the table.

I take another swallow of the smooth tequila and close my eyes. Chemical compounds, amino acids, and equations flash, wiggling together to form his image—

Eric's face was close. We were snuggled together under silky sheets. He was talking. "Do you regret any choices you made in life?"

"No, nothing."

He laughed. "You don't get to where we are in life without cutting someone or something's loose. You're either lying to me or yourself, and I hope for your sake it's the first."

"Nope, I'd do it all the same. I'm happy with the outcome. Respected researcher, comfortable life, and a warm bed to snuggle with you in. All the boxes checked off."

Eric kissed the top of my head. "Interesting."

"Interesting, how?"

He shook his head. "No, it's just that I got a girl pregnant in high school, but I denied it for years as I made my way through my life to get here. Feeling guilty a year or so ago, I went looking for the truth, my son. I went back to my old neighborhood, and found my old girlfriend Betsy. She told me that Jason—that was his name—dropped out of high school and overdosed in a crack house."

"Shit, Eric. I'm sorry"

"What if I was in his life? Maybe things would have turned out different. Maybe I could have told him how sorry I was—"

His eyes squeezed shut, tears escaping out the corners. I wiped his cheek.

"What if we could erase those memories?"

His eyes opened. "Marci, never." He wiped his watery eyes and then continued. "After that happened, I took it as a sign to slow down and smell the roses. To give back to the community. I started a foundation in my son's name. An after-school program to provide kids a place to go, people to talk to when life gets hard. Keep kids off the streets." He laughed and added, "I'd have had a heart attack by now. If I kept working that hard. All the stress I was putting on myself. And for what, money to buy more useless shit? Every time life starts to go too fast, I think about my son, Jason."

"Still, if we faded those memories—"

He cut me off. "Without our memories, good or bad, who would we be?"

I open my eyes, and the vision disappears.

"Fuck regret," I whisper into my empty house. "I know who I am!" I wipe the tears from my eyes. Am I happy with where I'm at? What if I made a different decision? I raise my glass. "Here is to all the right decisions! Here's to Eric!" And I finished my tequila in one long swallow.

My cell phone *bings* to life; I pick it up, and the blurry letters form into words. It's a text message from Leslie. Her travel plans. I have to pull my shit together. I have to stop pondering what could have been between Eric and me. I need to get my head into the game and figure this out. Maybe Eric leaving for a bit will help clear the distractions. Maybe it was for the best. I need those passwords. I need some good fucking news. My cell phone *bings* again. Another text from Leslie:

Marci, thanks for everything. I'm looking forward to coming out to see you. Sorry, if I was a bitch on the phone, but I blame hormones.

Dammit Leslie, let me be mad at you. Let me hate you for having what I want. What do I want? I stand and walk to the kitchen. I pour another glass of tequila and take a quick swallow. No, I don't want what she has. I couldn't care less about love and babies. I want power and respect. There are apps for loneliness and good times.

I look around the shadowy room and realize my house is a dump. One more thing I need to worry about, cleaning my house for Leslie. I swallow the rest of the tequila and put the bottle in the cabinet. I turn the tap on and start loading dishes in the dishwasher.

Three hours later, my house is vacuumed and smells Pine Sol fresh. I'm sticky and hot. I decide to run a bath and soak for a bit. Wash the grime off my body. Wash the stink of self-pity away.

I pour a glass of wine, light a few vanilla-scented candles and ease into the hot bath water. The flames flicker and throw strange wiggling shadows on the wall. I close my eyes and dip my head below the water.

I'm drifting in a dark void. He is calling my name. Where is he? I stretch my arms out. He is close. He is behind me. He wraps his arms around my waist, pulling me to him. The air is wet and heavy. I inhale his spicy rum scent. He turns me to face him. His face is close. His lips press against mine. My mouth opens, his rough tongue probing, and that sour metallic tang makes me gag. I try to pull away, but my muscles are rigid. He grips my arms tighter, pulling me into him. I'm squirming to break free. He is laughing. He is teasing me. *You still love me, don't you, Marci? You still want me?*

My mouth opens to scream at him, but fills with bitter metallic soapy fluid. Flickering lights fill the space. He is gone, and I'm floating. I break the surface of the water, gasping for air. The bath water is cold. A shiver runs along my spine, tensing my back muscles.

I wrap my arms around myself and whisper, "Get it together, Marci." I step out of the tub and wrap a towel around my body.

I grab my phone off the sink counter and find a voicemail from Mark. "Marci, call when you get this. I got some news."

"Better be good." I whisper to my reflection in the mirror. I press dial and put the call on speaker as I get dried and dressed.

"Marci, where have you been? I called an hour ago."

"Mark, don't start. Just cut to the point, please."

"I finished mapping all the memories in Alex's head." He takes a pause, waiting for me to congratulate him.

"And—"

"Oh yeah, you were right. It seems that the memories are not tangling together, and we can resolve the individual passengers. I have compared the maps and can see trace memories in the passenger scans to trace back to those in Alex's. Just like you predicted. Except..."

"Except what?"

"Except for Leslie... I mean, Brenda..."

"What?"

Mark clears his throat. "Well Alex's original memories are tangling in with these new memories he is creating with Granny and Brenda—"

"How is that—"

"I don't know, but I ran the simulations, and it's still possible to separate them out. I'm thinking if we get Ralphie's scan. You know Ralphie is Granny's grandson—"

"I know who he is."

"Oh right, sorry... We can use Ralphie's and Leslie's memory maps as anchors to be sure we can separate Granny's and this Brenda's memories enough to transfer Granny's back and minimize any corruptions to Alex's memories of Leslie."

The line goes quiet as I contemplate Mark's hypothesis. How are we going to erase and transfer these memories? What if I can't figure it out? What if I'm not—

"Marci, you there?"

"Yeah, Mark, just thinking. Leslie will be here tomorrow, and we can grab her scan. I have to go to Chicago next week and update Jack. I'll set up an appointment with Ralphie. Maybe, I can get him to agree to let us try the memory transfer on Granny first. Take care of that before it becomes a bigger problem."

"Great idea, Marci. One more thing. Comparing Alex's old scan with this new one and subtracting out the background 110 mind melt, there's a strengthening of some connections and a fading of others. I'm not sure what happens if this trend continues."

"That's interesting. We better get this fixed, right?"

"Yup, did you figure out something to try? Because I haven't." Mark sighs.

"Yeah, maybe." That metallic taste still lingers in my mouth. "Have we tried to attach a conductive metal to the nano-construct, like iron." I think about the solution spilled on Alexi, and it did not smell like rotten eggs, but freshly butchered meat.

"Marci, did you say iron." Mark laughs.

"Yeah, what's so funny?"

"Marci, that's what Shannon did his PhD work in, synthetic metalloprotein complexes—"

"Well, great. Get him in the lab, run the simulation, and start cooking this construct idea I'll be sending you."

"Funny, Marci. I fired him."

"Why the hell you do that?"

"Because you said to get ahead of the DOE and chop some heads. He was the guy that left the solution out that spilled on Alex." Marks clears his throat.

"Damn it, we have to get him back."

Mark chuckles.

"What the hell is so funny?"

"Well, I didn't fire him—"

"What? I'm confused."

"I couldn't fire him, he has three kids. I just put him on probation and moved him to the prep lab until things cooled down or he found another job. He's been begging to come back into the lab and help to make things right."

"Mark, you know how to turn a fuck-up into a win. Reinstate Shannon... I like a desperate man. Get him in ASAP. He better be in the lab tomorrow."

"Sure thing, boss!"

I click the phone off and wink at my reflection. "You can do this Marci."

I chew my bottom lip and dial his number. Like calling Dr. Jekyll and talking with Mr. Hyde.

"Alexi, is this you?"

"Sorry you have the wrong number." He answers, panting into the phone.

I listen and someone is whimpering in the background. I'm unsure if it's a man or woman. Alexi's voice yells, "You want some more of this. You've been a bad girl."

I hold the phone away from my ear, but I can overhear the sound of flesh being whacked and a muffled scream before the phone goes silent.

"Damn it."

I dial the "goons" trailing Alexi.

"What the hell? Are you guys even doing your job?"

"Hello, who is this?"

"Stop fucking around. Can you go splash some cold water on whatever is going on, so I can talk with Alexi?"

"You want us to go and break up that sausage fest?"

"I didn't realize you two were so sensitive. Maybe I need to talk to Jack about getting you both replaced."

"First we are not babysitters, and second we were given specific instructions not to interfere unless it was life threatening."

"Listen, this will be life threatening to you, if you don't get Alexi on the phone."

"Okay, don't get your panties in a bunch. We'll go break it up and call you back."

The phone buzzes, and I answer, "What's going on?"

"Well one guy is hog-tied, wearing lacy lingerie and..."

The second agent chimes in. "Ah, gross. I didn't need to see that."

"Hey Alexi, Marci wants to talk with you—"

"She'll have to wait. I'm not finished with this bad girl yet—" Gagging and moaning fill the earpiece. I hang up.

I should not have interfered. I should not have pulled him out of character, but Alexi has information I need right now.

An hour later, my phone rings. It's Alexi.

"Marci, I did it again. I can't control myself. I need this to stop. I want my life back."

A ping of nervousness goes through me. He is remembering the other personalities and actions, even when he is Alexi. I'm it sure how much time I have, so I dive in with questions.

"Alexi, sweetie, it's metal on the nano-construct that will transmit and receive?"

Alexi laughs for a bit and then speaks. "I knew you'd figure it out soon enough. Yup, it's the metal." He chuckles a bit. "You still don't know which one and how to put it together."

"We don't have time, Alexi. I need your help to fix you. Everyone from that plane—"

"I know you and your ambitions, Marci. You have to promise me you will put the genie back in the bottle once this is fixed. Back under the lock and key of all three of us."

"Alexi, I promise to do what is right. We don't have time. Leslie is suffering. You're suffering. Let me fix this."

"Okay, Marci. But promise me. Give me your word."

"Alexi, I promise to do the right thing."

The line goes quiet. I have gotten this close before and then he switches to someone else and offers me his nuts to suck.

"Alexi, please stay with me."

"I love you, Marci"

"What?" My heart starts beating fast. Even when I was with Eric, I could imagine Alexi's voice.

"I love you, Marci. Capital I and M, the Os are zeros. The password. Il0vey0uMarci. I knew you'd never guess that. And if you did, it has two-factor security."

All I hear are those words echoing in my head, *I love you Marci*.

"Marci, you listening? The push will go to Leslie's phone. She will be the gatekeeper. My love. Bye now."

The line goes silent. My heart drops into my stomach. Does he love Leslie or me? Or both?

I pull my sweatpants and top on. So much for a relaxing night. I have to go over my notes. I have to spin this right. Have my story straight before Leslie gets here. She is always probing for weak spots, always on the offensive. The way Leslie asks questions and figures things out. I cannot be caught off guard.

My phone *bings* with a text. What now?

Hey, just got to Spain. You'd love it. Come visit soon. Miss you more than I want to. Hope you're well. Cheers, E

I put the phone on the table and rub at the tears forming in my eyes. I go to the kitchen and pull the bottle of wine out and fill my glass. Fucking shit. I walk into the living room glaring at the phone. I take a sip of wine and text Eric, "I miss you too!" Followed by an eggplant and donut emoji.

I laugh out loud and take another long swallow of wine.

INTERLUDE

Brian/Alex:
Leslie

"Hey, wake up!" I open my eyes and Leslie steps out of the shadows into the light, her face glowing and smiling.

"Lee... What's wrong—?" My voice is raw and hoarse, so I cough, trying to clear my throat. "What time is it, sweetie?"

"Time for you to get up." She grabs and tugs at my foot. "Out of bed, sleepyhead."

"You're already dressed, so it must be late." I stretch, sitting on the edge of the bed.

Lee plops down next to me. She lays her hand on my thigh and squeezes. "You were sleeping so soundly, I couldn't bring myself to wake you. How are you feeling?"

"Good."

"See, the sessions are helping."

"I dreamed of this woman—" Lee pulls her hand off my thigh and cradles it in her lap.

"No, not like that. She seemed abused and hurt. I found her picture in the photos. Maybe I can help her."

"Help?"

"Maybe reach out and see how she is doing."

"You're not thinking of doing anything dumb?"

The question catches me off guard. How does one define dumb, and what justifies something as dumb? If it works, it will be considered great. Lee raises her eyebrow at the silence growing between us.

My mouth starts moving, and words spill out. "Maybe it will help, like with Ralphie and Granny. I can make notes and stuff. For my memoir."

"Memoir about what?" Lee studies my eyes.

I look away, into my hands, remembering a lie works better with some bits of truth. "About the event; it was Jerry's idea."

Lee stands, laughing. She leans in, kisses me on the forehead, and turns to walk away. I pull her arm, and she falls next to me. I wrap my arm around her and kiss her on the neck.

"That feels good, but I have a meeting this morning." Lee pulls away a bit.

"Come on, it's been weeks. You promised we'd have relations when you got back from visiting your mom."

"You're a funny guy. Weeks? We did it yesterday." She kisses me on the cheek.

"Can I make you a cup of coffee and talk with you?"

Lee smiles. "Yes, I'd like that."

I swing my legs out of the bed and kiss Lee on the cheek. I rub my hand along the gooseflesh on her arm.

"No funny business. Let's have that coffee and talk."

Lee stands pulling on my arm. Lee said I was getting better, but are those sessions with Dr. Shirley helping? Lee said we had sex yesterday, but I can't remember. Maybe my memories are being placed into the wrong compartments. I have to get this stuff out of my head. I think about the girl in my vision, Amanda.

"Lee, listen I'm pretty sure I am slipping in and out of personalities because of those recordings I have to make for therapy."

"Oh, Alex—"

"No, I have things to tell you. Let me get them out, before—"

I grab Lee's hand and guide her to the table.

"Lee, listen, our research was about recording and mapping memories, but I stumbled on an idea to transfer, implant, and even erase memories."

"What—"

"Please, Lee, listen. Marci cannot have all of this information. I'm not sure anyone should have it. But she needs some of this to fix our memories. I have made a summary of all the files in my private storage. Only give Marci what she needs to complete the transfer. Do you understand?"

"Yes, but why can't you give her the files she needs?"

"I'm not stable enough. I think she has tried to get the password from me, but I must revert back into someone."

"Oh, I see."

"Lee, only the files I have marked should go to Marci. The others keep away from her and Mark."

Lee nods.

"Please don't cry." I wipe the tears on her cheeks. "Lee, I love you so much and we will make it through this."

Lee jumps out of her seat and wraps her arms around me. "I love you, Alex."

"It's going to be okay. I put the information along with some other things in our safe deposit box." I rub Lee's back. "Come on, let's have that coffee."

Lee stands and goes back to working on the coffee, wiping her eyes and sobbing.

"You want anything else with your coffee, Alex."

"Who the fuck is Alex?"

Brenda spins around and glares at me. "What?"

"You called me Alex. Is that your new friend?"

"No...um... He is a new guy at work. Slip of the tongue, I have to train him today." Brenda shuffles her feet, grabbing her purse.

"Oh, you have to stop making me breakfast and go run to your new friend, Alex."

"I don't want to be late."

"Fuck you and your new friend."

I glare at Brenda as she runs out the door, not bothering to put on her shoes.

"Fucking ungrateful bitch," I yell at the door. "Didn't finish making my breakfast."

I open the fridge. "Slip of the tongue... Fuck her... She can slip that tongue on these nuts."

I slam the fridge. "Nothing good in here anyway. I'll go to Mama's Diner and get a bite."

CHAPTER 24

Brenda/Leslie:
91 Days after Event

I study all the faces on the plane. As the plane jerks forward gaining speed, I grip the armrests, squeeze my eyes tight, and mumble a prayer. The plane lifts off the ground. My heart is thumping against my chest. Will I have my memories when we land? Will I have everyone else's? The plane's pull against Earth's gravity causes my stomach to clench like a fist. I push against the seat. I push my feet into the floor. Toes scrunching, my teeth grinding. Hurting. Eyes shut tight. Then the pressure subsides. I am still me. My memories. Hopefully, I am still me when we land.

I listen to my music and try to sleep. No chitchat with my seatmates. No recipes or other interesting life tidbits exchanged. Just a hello, and a goodbye forever.

After the plane lands, I stand in the bathroom for ten minutes, staring at myself in the mirror. Just me. No one else in my head haunting me. Just me, Leslie. Not even Brenda came along for the trip. I splash water on my face and smile. It's just me. Walking out the restroom, I dial Marci.

"Hey, Marci. I've arrived."

"Leslie, welcome to the City of Brotherly Love. How was the flight? Are you hungry? I'm starving."

She seems happy. Relaxed. Her voice inviting. What does Marci want from me? I came here for answers, not to be friends. "It was a good flight. We went up and came down. And I still remember who I am. So that's a plus."

"That's great. Want to get a bite to eat?"

She ignores my dig at her. She is playing nice. Why am I playing the part? I am always playing a part.

"Dinner would be nice. I have to check in at the hotel, and—"

"Hotel? Over my dead body. I made the guest bed for you and everything. You're staying at my place. We can really chat, and I can explain everything to you."

I stop walking. The person behind me bumps into me. My bag falls off my shoulder. No excuse me or sorry. Just a smirk and the flow of people step around me.

"What was that?" I ask.

"Oh sorry... I didn't mention it, but you can stay with me if you like."

"I guess. Sure"

She makes a small noise, a happy squeal. "Great! I'll come and get you at the airport, and we can go to dinner." Keys jingle in the background. Has she been waiting all this time, ready to get me? Her voice cuts into my thoughts. "You like Mexican food?"

"Yeah, that's fine." The line goes quiet. I don't bother checking if she has disconnected and put the phone in my pocket. I squat grabbing my bag and start walking, blending into the mob moving as one. Moving as ourselves. I find the pickup doors and ease into a chair to rest my sore hips and swollen feet.

I'm nodding off in the seat when a woman squeezes my shoulder. She is wearing sweatpants and a plain gray t-shirt with a low neck. Hair pulled into a sloppy ponytail. She bends, grabbing my bag, and I notice she is not wearing a bra. No makeup on her face. But it is her. It's Marci like I have never seen her before. An unpolished version of herself. She is laying herself bare.

I came here ready to knock her off her pedestal. Why have I given her so much power over my life? It's always easier to knock someone off their pedestal than to keep them on display. She is playing nice. Is she playing the part? Should I play the part?

Be nice. Be nice. Be nice.

Alex's words replay in my head, *Don't trust Marci—*

Don't trust her with what?

I try to swallow the words before the vibrated air leaves my throat. "Casual Friday at work today?" I cover my mouth.

Marci stands erect and tilts her head. "What?"

Standing, I clear my throat. "Nothing, I have just never seen you dress so causal."

"Oh yeah. I was working in the lab all day, and then a quick workout. Do I smell?" She sniffs her pits, then laughs. "Just kidding. I showered. I'm not always dressed to the nines." She winks. "We all have our comfy clothes." Her eyes scan over me. "You want to change into something more comfortable?"

I'm standing in my heels, wearing a pencil skirt. Black stockings strangling my pregnant legs. Only thing I'm wearing of true comfort is my top, and this maternity support bra. I nod. "Yes, I would like to change into my," I squeeze Marci's arm, "comfy clothes."

She does a little clap. "Great. To the bat cave."

She spins and leads the way.

I pull the car door and gag on the strong scent of spearmint. The passenger seat is filled with papers, a laptop, and a backpack bulging at the seams.

"Just move that stuff out of your way." Marci reaches past me grabbing handfuls of her stuff and tossing it into the back seat.

"Wanna open the trunk so I can put my bag in?"

Marci laughs. "Good luck with that. Just throw your bag into the backseat."

The entire image I had of Marci—clean, sophisticated, and well-organized—is coming apart. Maybe I had her all wrong. I study her face as she drives. She pulls her hair back off her face revealing her smooth skin, lips curling into a smile. One thing I did not get wrong is how beautiful she is. Even in this relaxed, thrown together state, she still has that attractive vibe. The type of woman who can pull off the "I don't care" attitude. She smiles at me.

"What?" Her voice has a friendly, teenager quality. Like I'm her mother judging her by the neatness of her car.

"Nothing. You just surprised me."

"That's me, keeping everyone on their toes. Maybe that's why I'm sort-of-kind-of single." She giggles.

I squeeze her arm. "No, Marci, that's not it." She smirks, looking sideways at me. "What I mean is, you're a very lovely person and I'm sure you will find the one. I remember thinking the same thing until I met Alex."

Why did I say his name? I do not want to go there. I want to stay focused on why I came here.

The car stops with a jerk. Marci eyes are wide and glossy. Maybe tears. Maybe just the way the light is reflecting off the gray in her eyes.

Her mouth moves, but nothing comes out. I squeeze her arm again. "I'm sorry, Marci."

She nods, looks away, and starts driving again.

Her voice is cracking and soft when she says, "No worries. What do you want to eat?" She rubs her eyes, smearing tears across her face.

"Anything, you had mentioned Mexican. We can do that."

A smile flashes on Marci's face. She wipes her cheek, her voice a decibel above a whisper. "Yeah, I know the best place for Mexican food, and they have great margaritas."

We arrive at Marci's bungalow, and I change into more comfortable clothes. A pair of sweatpants to give my belly a little bit more room. We walk to the restaurant in silence, but a comfortable silence. Under different circumstances, I could be friends with Marci. I want to reach out and grab her hand. I want to wrap my arm around her and say, "Everything will be okay." Maybe it's just the hormones, the maternal instinct kicking in. Maybe it's just that I have no one else to turn to. Maybe if I can't have Alex, I can have the person who knows him the best.

The restaurant is a small. A galley of tables in the middle and five booths along each wall. A voice yells out with a thick Mexican accent, "Sit where you like. Be out with waters, chips, and salsa!"

Marci waves her hand for me to choose. I slip into the second booth on the right. The waitress sits waters, menus, salsa, and chips on the table. She smiles at me, leans in and kisses Marci on the cheek, promising to return for our orders. Marci winks at me.

"What?" I ask her in a playful voice.

"He talks about you all the time." She pulls her hair into a ponytail. "He always wanted us to go out and have drinks and get to know each other and be best friends." She grabs a menu. "Funny how things work."

"That's funny. Alex never mentioned that we should all hang out."

"That's interesting—" Marci holds the menu to hide her face.

I shake my head and search the menu for the least spicy, indigestion-inducing thing on the menu. Even though the morning sickness passed after my third month, the list of foods that cause some sort of gastrointestinal irritation keeps growing as the months pass. The cheese quesadilla with rice and beans seems like the safest bet. I glance at Marci. Her eyes are scanning my face. Her eyes search for the truth. Why did I lie? Does she know that I lied? Alex said we would be great friends.

"What are you going to have?"

"I'm sorry, Marci—Alex did say we should all be friends. I don't know all the details of how it ended between you two, but I know he still cares for you, and I just never..." I take a drink of my water, "never trusted you, with him."

"Well I'm having the California burrito." Marci lays her menu on the table and grabs my hand. I want to pull it away, but I don't. Her hand is warm and sweaty. I want to pull away, but her eyes hold my attention.

Marci squeezes my hand as she talks. "I love Alex, but I moved on a long time ago." She rolls her eyes and continues,

"I wish I was with Alex, instead of playing boyfriend-roulette, but that ship has sailed."

"Oh." I sigh, just to fill the awkward silence after Marci's confession of loneliness.

Marci, adds, "Sounds like he didn't tell you the whole story about us, and why should he? You would hate me more if he told you how it ended. Did he tell you?"

I shake my head no. "Not really. He just said you up and left one day for Philadelphia to pursue your career. Other than that, I didn't pry into the details."

Marci nods and looks away. I follow her eyes and the server is approaching. She sits a large, colored cactus motif glass in front of Marci. A large glass of water for me. We take turns ordering. The server nods and leaves.

"So what happened?" I take a sip of my water.

"Well..." Marci takes a swallow of her drink. Her mouth puckers, and then she shakes her head. "Damn that's strong. You eat at a place enough times you get the good drinks." Marci gazes at me sympathetically.

I smile acknowledging the unspoken question. "Yeah, I can't wait to have a margarita again!"

"First round is on me." She flashes a toothy grin.

Her teeth are white and perfect. Her lips have a natural, sexy red hue. Her eyes reflect a pretty grayish green. She is a beautiful woman. No airbrushing here. I gaze at her, waiting for an imperfection to slip. But even with no makeup and in sweats, she is goddamn beautiful.

"The second is on me."

She laughs. We both laugh.

"It's a date," she says.

The word date ends the laughter. A silence falls in between us. We both take a sip of our drinks. Both of us waiting for the other to speak. I'm pregnant and impatient.

"So what happened between you two?"

"Let's not get into that, we are just starting to," Marci takes a sip of her drink, "get along. Let me fill you in on the progress we made with Alex's memories."

"You're a memory of his. Let's just clear the air between us."

Marci's eyes narrow, squeezing out the green and leaving tiny, angry dark slits. "Like he told you, I left him for my career." She takes another swallow of her drink and shakes the almost empty glass. Ice rattles, signaling to the observant waitress to bring another. Signaling to me that she is angry.

I squeeze Marci's hand. "Come on, Marci. I'm trying to be friendly."

She taps the glass to the table and continues talking mid-thought, "I had my career and Alexi, and I was happy. I was young. I was in love. I wanted to do important things. But I got pregnant, and that scared the hell out of me. I never told Alexi; he would not have..." Marci's words blur together into one long slur. She shakes her glass, then finishes the rest of her drink. "He would not have let me keep pushing myself so hard. So I left one night. I had a major research paper coming out and found a position in Philadelphia. It was a couple years before I had the courage to apologize and ask for his forgiveness. That's the story. I picked my career over love, over Alexi, over our baby."

The waitress sits another margarita on the table and takes the empty one away.

Marci continues, "Now you know. You happy? You want to know if I made the right choice? If I'm happy?"

I shake my head no, realizing I should not have opened this can of caterpillars.

"I tell you, I've been thinking about that decision recently, and I hate to admit it, but I'd go back and..." Marci's voice fades talking into her drink, mouth teasing to sip "And do things the same. No regrets." She sighs. "Maybe."

Marci chugs her drink. I realize her flush, sweaty brow wasn't from working out, but probably for having a drink before arriving at the airport. All these years I have hated her, resented the fact that she held a place in Alex's heart. I never understood why. Now, I have what I want. My attractive, successful, nemesis is getting drunk and emotionally frayed. Should I take advantage of her? Not like this. Not now. Alex is right. We could be friends. But Alex said don't trust her. Which Alex should I listen to?

"I'm sorry I pushed you into telling."

She just nods, shaking her almost empty glass, the rattling ice signaling for another.

The waitress sits two plates of food on the table and gives Marci another glass of margarita.

Marci shovels three quick forkfuls of beans into her mouth, washes them down with a chug of her margarita, and then starts waving her fork in a circle between us.

"You and I are a lot alike."

"How so?"

Marci takes another bite, swallows, and starts talking. "Successful careers. Fell in love with the same guy." She giggles into her drink.

I giggle to myself, contemplating this.

Marci waves her fork again. "But you did it right, waiting to be more established and then having kids." She looks at me with sober eyes. "If you're wondering about the kid, I had a miscarriage. Doctors said it was the stress that caused the miscarriage. I should have slowed down, took a break, but I couldn't. I should've, but I just had my big breakthrough and..." Her voice trails into a mumble of words.

She wipes her eyes with a napkin.

"You did what you thought was right. No need to beat yourself up over things you can't change."

Marci nods her head. "Yeah, I know. I'm not usually this emotional, but..." She squeezes her eyes and shakes her head, "Whoa." Her eyes pop open. "I'm sorry about that. Still stings a bit thinking about it. Took me a long time to apologize to Alex and a longer time for him to forgive me."

The mention of Alex gives me an opening to change the subject. To talk about getting my husband back.

"So it's been a couple months since I last asked. Any progress on the memory sorting?"

"Yeah, lots. You think you know someone, but when you begin to read their memories, you realize you don't know that much about them."

I put my fork down. "What do you mean?"

"We know what people want us to know about them," she pokes her fork at me "but what about all the stuff that made them," she grins, "them?"

Not following Marci's drunken logic, I say, "All the stuff that makes them, them? I don't get it."

Marci starts shaking her head. "We have good memories. The memories we share. But we have shit memories, too. The ones we repress. But both memories shape who we are. What if we..." her words drift into a whisper.

"What, Marci? What are you saying about Alex?"

"What if we erased repressed bad memories? Would that change the individual? What if we erased good memories? Would that change the future person?"

"I don't think it would work that way. Just because you erase the past. Maybe people need their past to remind them of who they are and where they are going." I take a sip of my water. "We are talking hypotheticals, right?"

"You sound like him!" Marci pokes me.

"Alex?"

Marci shakes her head, "There you go, thinking I'm after your man. No silly, my boyfriend—" She pauses. "Kind of boyfriend. His name is Eric."

I turn my head away from Marci, staring at the mural of a matador hanging on the wall. "Oh, I didn't know you were seeing anyone."

"There's a lot you don't know about me, Leslie."

I glance back at Marci's face. "I'm sure. That's why we are spending time together. To become friends."

"Yeah, friends." Marci smirks. "Look, if you have a memory map, you can go in and edit out things... Maybe. Put memories in. That's what happened to Alex. All those other folks' memories were edited into his brain. In a little time, hopefully, for Alex's sake, I can edit them out."

I slump in the booth, pondering about what Marci is saying. I can get my Alex back. A flood of questions enters my mind, but before I can say anything, Marci starts talking again.

"Like I was saying, our boy has some pretty interesting memories. Tomorrow in the lab I'll show you. And we can decide if we want to edit more than just the passengers out."

"Is that our decision?"

"No, but I talked with Alex. He said if you're okay with it, we could do it."

"You talked with Alex about this?"

She takes another drink and rattles the empty glass. "One for the road." She eats the last bites of her food. "Yeah, we talk a couple times a week. He calls, and we chat about his situation—"

"What?" I pitch my voice and throw my hands in the air to act surprised, since I've not told anyone about my mornings with Alex. "So you're having a regular schedule of communication, and you didn't let me know?"

"Sorry, but I needed his help to fix this. Please, stay calm. It's not what you think. It's five or ten minutes, if that, and then he reverts into someone other than—"

"I'm calm, Marci. I wish you'd told me this and let me in on that time. You know how crazy it is living with those random people he has in his head?"

"I'm sorry for not sharing, but it was such a fleeting thing, and I needed him to concentrate on the science. I didn't want to get your hopes and then nothing. And, yeah, I do know something about those random people."

"How do you know?"

The server appears, clearing the table and sitting a fresh drink in front of Marci.

"I know because I think some of those memories are his memories."

"What?"

"It's better if I show you, and you can confirm everything. Tomorrow." She takes my hand.

My head is spinning with ideas and the insanity of it all. "Okay, Marci."

Marci laughs and takes a sip of her drink. She smiles at me. "We are going to be good friends when this is over. Alex is always right."

I nod my head. My shoulders tense as a wave of anxiety. My stomach tightens like a fist. I close my eyes, willing the nausea to go away. My stomach relaxes. I open my eyes and a toothy drunk grin is plastered on her face.

"Feeling better?"

I take a drink of my water. "Yes, just a bit overwhelmed."

"Just a few more months. At most. I'll have everything worked out by then."

I nod. "Why are you pushing Granny and Alex together?"

Marci makes a sarcastic sigh. "Because I like looking at that Ralphie." She giggles. "I could curl up in his arms any day." Marci raises her eyebrows. "I see you feel the same way."

Guiltily, I blurt out, "No!" I realize my voice has betrayed me. I think about Ralphie often, especially when Alex is acting out.

"Just teasing you, Leslie. I need to be sure I can exclude Alex's original memories from the new ones. Also, by him interacting with her, I can tease out her memories from the others." She finishes her drink. "Maybe I can help all the others also. He seems to have made a close bond with Granny and Ralphie, so it's easy to work with them."

I nod my head, so my voice will not betray me again.

"FYI," she says, "If you even think about messing around with Ralphie—" She squints, glaring at me over the rim of her glass.

I don't know what Marci is implying, but I think about Ralphie's visit a few nights ago—

Alex was away, and I was alone in the quiet of the house. Relaxing in the sweet fragrance of vanilla and lavender. I liked those times, alone in the quiet. I imagined I was in my life before the event. Before Alex's head was filled with 110 other people. I ran a warm bath and was just about to slip into the water when my cell phone rang. I saw his name and pressed answer.

"Hey, Ralphie. What's going on?"

I tapped speaker, and studied my body in the mirror, drawing along my expanding curves with my hands. My abdomen stretching to accommodate my growing baby. I rubbed my hands over my stretching skin, gooseflesh broke out on my arms. How long has it been since I was caressed? Not the rough pawing in the hurried space between Alex and whoever he becomes. I was barely listening to Ralphie, but the excited pitch of his voice pulled me to the conversation.

"So I'm in your neighborhood, giving a client a quote. Can I stop by and say hello?"

"Sure, I'm just—" The words caught in my throat as I contemplated my choice of words. Choice of actions, standing here naked, about to invite a handsome man to my house. But I imagine how his hands would feel on my body and answered,

"Well, you have to give me thirty minutes or so to get dressed, I was just taking a bath—"

"Oh my gosh, Leslie. Why didn't you say that? We can meet tomorrow. I know how sad you get at night when Alex runs off doing whatever." Ralphie's voice faded into a huff. Then he continued. "Leslie, just relax and enjoy your alone time. I'll see you tomorrow."

Still rubbing my hands along my breasts, my neck, and my belly, I decided. "No, please come over. It would be nice to see you."

What the hell am I doing? I turned away from the mirror and grabbed my robe.

"Okay, if you're sure. I'll be there in about one hour. To give you time."

"Okay, see you then."

The phone goes quiet. I set an alarm for thirty minutes and slipped into the warm water. My hands rubbed along my body thinking of Alex.

The buzz of my door rang.

My heart started to beat against my chest. I moved as fast as I could, grabbed my towel, and dried off. Throwing on my robe and walking fast to the door.

I pressed the intercom. "Who's there?"

"It's me, Ralphie."

"Oh, Okay. You're a bit early."

"Sorry, I can come back."

I pressed the buzzer. Asking myself what I'm doing?

Seconds later he knocked on the door. I pulled it open.

"Leslie—" His smile widened, and I shook my head.

"Come on in. I should have made you wait outside until I got dressed."

"Oh, I'm so sorry Leslie."

"Make a pregnant woman run for the door."

Ralphie walked into my house. I did not move, so he would have to brush against me.

"Make yourself at home. I'm going to finish getting dressed."

When I came out the bedroom, Ralphie was sitting on the couch, flipping through a photo book. I plopped on the couch pressing my body to him.

Ralphie shut the book and said, "I'm sorry again, you can throw me out anytime."

"No worries. You have been such a good friend to me."

I leaned into him, wrapping my arms around him. The aroma of soil and mulch filling my nose. The picture book fell from his hands, and I pulled away.

"I'm sorry."

"No, don't be. I caught you by surprise." He picked the jar of lotion off the coffee table. "Let me make it up to you. I can massage your feet. You were complaining this morning."

A small voice in my head said no, but my swollen feet said, "Hell yes."

I leaned against the arm of the couch and rested my legs in Ralphie's lap. As he massaged small circles of lotion into my sore, swollen feet he talked about his day. His dealing with Granny. Dealing with difficult customers. Dealing with his mounting debt because Granny was not working. I shut my *eyes and enjoyed the small pleasure of having his strong hands rub the knots out of my toes. Rub the knots out of my calf. Rub the knots out of my—I opened my eyes and placed my hand on top of Ralphie's, he pulled his hand off my thigh. I smiled and retracted my legs off his lap.*

"I'm sorry—" Ralphie shifted his body away from me.

I grabbed his shoulder. "Don't be. It was nice, but I'm... still married. Maybe we shouldn't—"

Ralphie stood and started pacing. "Leslie, you're an attractive, smart woman. I want to be more than friends, but I value your friendship. I apologize if I crossed the line. I won't let it happen again."

I stood and grabbed Ralphie's hand and pulled him to me. "Sweetie, you did not cross any line that I did not put in front of you. I love my husband, but I must admit it's nice to be cared for. But maybe I need to do a better job not taking your friendship for granted. So we don't have any misunderstandings."

I pulled Ralphie into a hug. The strong scent of cedar calmed me, and he squeezed me into him. I imagined Alex holding me like this. We stood holding each other for seconds, minutes, until Ralphie's phone started to ring.

"It's Granny's sitter."

I nodded as he walked to the kitchen to take the call.

He walked out the kitchen with a raised eyebrow. "That's strange."

"What?"

"The sitter was leaving."

"Why?"

"Alex took Granny out for dinner."

"That's nice. Better than what I imagined him doing."

Ralphie walked to the door. "Yeah, well I better get home before they get back. See you later." He stepped out and pulled the door closed behind him.

I opened the door and popped my head out.

"Ralphie, wait." He turned, and I stepped into his space. His earthy musk scent intoxicating me, I ignored the voice in my head, stood on my toes, and kissed his cheek.

"What?"

"That's for being a good friend."

He smiled, wagging his finger. "I'm going to go before we cross a line."

"Remember, I'm a big girl."

"You still love him, don't you?"

I nod. "Yes."

"Then I'm going to respect that line."

"Thank you."

Ralphie started to walk away when he stopped. "You ever think about what you're going to do if Alex stays this way?"

"What?"

"You know, what if Marci can't fix his memories and he keeps acting out these other personalities?"

I shake my head no. "For better or worse is what I promised. No matter who Alex becomes, I'll try to love him."

Ralphie nodded. "You're a good person, Leslie. But no matter how much you want to love someone you may have to let them go. I know you know this, but I'll always be there for you."

My mouth opened but my voice was gone. I was focused on holding it together and not bursting into tears, imagining my life living with this Alex forever.

Ralphie continued talking. "We all have our crosses to bear though, right? No need to bear them alone."

I nodded in agreement and closed the door as he walked off.

I leaned against the door and started to sob. My stomach twisted in guilt for trying to replace that ache in my heart, my mind for Alex's love, with Ralphie's. That's when I decided—

I open my eyes and scowl at Marci. "I'd never do anything to hurt Alex, Marci. I love Alex. I want him back."

"What if you don't get him back?" She staccatos the words, pointing at me.

"I'll love him no matter what."

"Great! I'm glad to hear you say that because I'll need scans of your head, and you have to authorize access to Alex's files."

"What?"

"It will make more sense tomorrow."

Marci smiles at me as she slips out of the booth. "I need to use the ladies' room. We can get the check and head home. We have a long day tomorrow."

I follow Marci with my eyes until she disappears in the restroom. No drunken stumbling. I exam her glass on the table. I hold it to my nose, expecting the pungent scent of tequila. Nothing. I stick my straw into the drink. I take a taste.

Just carbonated lemon lime sweetness. No alcohol. Was this all an act? Why? My heart starts pounding in my chest. There is a pulse behind my eyes, pushing. My vision flashes with light.

"How is everything going?" The server's words are slow and deliberate.

"Everything was lovely, but why don't her drinks have alcohol in them?" I hold the glass out for the server to exam. "Is Marci playing a joke on me?"

The waitress appears shocked. "No, never." Her large brown eyes search for the correct phrase. She grabs the glass out of my hand. Her thick accent seeps through her broad smile. "Don't tell Ma, but her last two drinks did not have alcohol. She came in earlier and had a couple drinks. She was excited that you," she points at me, and her smile widens, "her good friend, was coming to visit. We know how Ma can get, so we cut her off without her knowing it."

I wipe my eyes. "What? Who is Ma?"

"We have known Ma," she winks, "*Marcina*, for many years, and we call her Ma because she is so serious with the world. We still look after her like family so she does not get into trouble."

"Trouble?"

"You know, being a single lady and everything." The server giggles.

"Marcina?"

"Oh, she may kill me. She said you were her good friend. She was Marcina when she was pregnant and had just broken off her engagement to... I forget his name—"

"Alexi?" I answer.

She opens her eyes, shaking her head. "No, that was not his real name. He changed it to Alexi, but she always called him," she snaps her fingers a couple times, "Brian! That's it. Ever since they—" She looks over her shoulder, and continues, "...broke up, she now goes by Marci. I think Marcina is a much prettier name. Don't you think?"

The name Brian hit me like a punch. "What?"

"Oh, I'm embarrassing our girl. That was past history. Forgotten memories. This meal is on the house. Just get Ma, I mean Marci, home safe."

"Thank you. Everything was delicious. I'll make sure Marci gets home safe."

"She makes such bad luck with men. Her new boyfriend," the server winks at me, then continues, "they were getting serious and then *poof* he moves away. I told her to go with him, but you know Ma." She taps the table. "You just make sure she gets home, okay."

I nod. "Yes, I'll make sure she's okay."

The server hugs Marci as they pass and speak to each other in Spanish. I only catch a few words, but as they hugged and kissed each other's cheek the server said, "Tienes una buena amiga."

Marci, glancing at me, replies, "Si, ella es una muy buena amiga."

INTERLUDE

Brian/Eduardo:
Angela

She invited me here for drinks. Who is she? Who am I? I stare at my reflection in the mirror behind the bar. My face blurs. I rub my eyes. I swallow my tumbler of tequila in one swallow. I recognize the face in the mirror. I'm Eduardo.

"Sweetie, you came."

I spin on the bar stool to face her.

"Of course. It was meet you here or sit in the quiet house staring at the wall."

She lunges for me, stumbling into my embrace. My arms wrap around her. Her scent, like wet, fragrant earth after a good rain. She presses into me, pecking me on the cheek. I remember holding her like this. I close my eyes and a vision swirls out of the fog—

I looked at her through the lens of my camera. She twirled between sunflowers, the filtered light danced along her naked body. Her feet digging into the ground, sweat beading on her forehead. Her skin melting into the ground. Her image disappeared from the camera frame. My arms were wrapped around her—

Her lips peck me on the cheek, breaking the vision. The fog dissipates around her head, and I can see her smiling face.

"What are you thinking about?" She slips out of my grasp and sits on the stool next to me.

"Just that photo shot we did last summer in New Mexico."

"Oh, I loved that casita with the hot tub, the pool and garden—"

I rub my hand along her thigh. "And that garden with those giant sunflowers. Those golden yellow leaves and massive heads that curved down watching you dance."

Her cheeks redden. She turns away waving at the bartender. "Hey, could I have a Casamigos Reposado—straight up."

"Make that two, please," I add.

Angela leans into me, our lips meet, tongues meet—

The bartender clears his throat and smacks the bar with the crystal lead tumblers. "Let's keep it PG, please."

Angela and I both giggle. Her hand rubs at my beard. "I like this."

"I like you."

I kiss her lips. The bartender clears his throat again.

I glare at him. "Okay, Dad. Give it a fucking rest. There is no one in this dump, and you're acting like a kiss is going to ruin your business."

"Sir, I'm not going to serve you if you cannot control your temper."

"Fuck you and—"

Angela rubs her hand on my chest. "Eduardo." She slaps her hand on the bar. "Eduardo, look at me and calm down."

I turn my head and face her. "He is just doing his job."

"What?"

"Let's just enjoy our drink, and then go back to my place."

I nod. She is holding her glass out. Her body, her face, the bartender, the cherry wood of the bar begins to smear into that matte-black fog. Her glass hovers in the void. Voices call out, taunting me. Where am I? Who am I?

Her voice calls, "Eduardo! Just breathe—"

Am I Eduardo? Am I Alex? Am I Brian? I blink my eyes and shake my head. The black fades away like an Etch A Sketch, and there is her face. Brenda.

She kisses me. "You had me worried. I thought you changed."

I study her face. Is she Brenda?

"Yeah, I'm okay. Just a headache coming on." I blink, and her face flickers. It's my Lee.

I grab my tequila, holding my glass out. "To us."

Our glasses clink together. "Forever," she adds.

She closes her eyes as she gulps the smooth tequila. I smile. I haven't seen Lee this happy in weeks.

I can't help myself. I kiss her. Her breath is hot with tequila. My hand rubs along her thigh, her hand squeezes my waist, and I'm squeezing her breast—

The bartender slaps the countertop with his rag. "Get the hell out of here, both of you."

I scowl at the bartender and flip my middle finger.

Lee pulls my arm. "Come on, babe. We can have a drink at my place."

I nod, glancing from the bartender to my own reflection. Eyes squinted, brows narrowed, my lips like thin lines scrawled across my face. Who am I?

She tugs on my arm.

"Come on."

I glance at her. Who is she? The voices yelling in my head. Where am I? Who am I? A woman is singing in my head, *I got my new lover, and he don't know...*

I shake my head and follow behind my lover.

CHAPTER 25

Brenda/Leslie:
92 Days after Event

Marci drums her fingers on the steering wheel, looking at me sideways. I want to tell Marci that I am sorry, but am I? I want to tell her we can still be friends, but should we? I open my mouth to speak, but the hum of the air conditioner fills the space. I wish I took a taxi. She is still upset about the consent papers I had her sign earlier, but I'm sure she would have done the same thing if in my position. Why did she offer me this ride? Why did I take it?

I am still processing all the information Marci showed me about Alex. You think you know something about someone, then their mind is peeled back revealing all of them and you realize you know nothing—

"Do you know what airline you're taking?" Marci's voice is soft, blending into the drone of the blowing cool air.

"Um, I think it's United."

"Okay, I'll park and help you to the terminal."

"Oh... that's okay, Marci. I think I can manage."

"No, you need to take it easy and not put too much stress on the baby."

"Really, you can just drop me off at the curb—"

"Leslie, please let me do this."

Why is Marci insisting on parking and walking me into the terminal? It was cute at first, her fussing over me. Maybe it's because she had a miscarriage from working too hard. "Okay Marci, if you insist."

"I do."

"Thank you." The quiet drone of the air conditioner washes over us.

Marci's sideways glances are making me self-conscious. Every minute asking me about my water consumption. Asking about my caloric intake. Lecturing me on prenatal nutrition and vitamins. I'm already nervous without Mother Hen clucking in my ear.

She is trying to help. She keeps saying we are friends. I don't want to be her friend. I don't want her guilt about her miscarriage laid on me. She is trying to right her mistake, not taking care of herself when she was pregnant. She blames herself for losing her baby, her family. I have enough burden to carry.

Marci walks behind me pulling my suitcase. I walk fast. I have no words to share, and I want no advice. Once in the terminal, I reach for my suitcase, Marci tries to embrace me.

"What are you doing?"

Marci recoils like she was snake bitten. "Oh sorry, here's your bag." She holds the handle like refusing a diseased fruit.

"Thanks, Marci. Thanks for everything." I start to walk away.

"Leslie, please don't walk away like that. I'm trying to be friendly," Marci rubs her eyes. "I'm trying to change."

I step toward her. "This is hard for me, too."

She extends her arms for a hug. I extend my hand for a shake. We settle on a fist bump.

"Don't worry, Leslie. I'm going to fix this."

I wasn't sure what thing she was talking about fixing, our friendship or Alex. "I know you will. I'll call once I land."

"Drink plenty of water on the flight."

I nod and wave.

"Leslie, I'll be in Chicago in a month or so and we should get together. Hopefully, I'm close to fixing all of this."

"I can only pray you are. I have to go, Marci, or I'll have to run for my flight."

"No running. You go."

"See you, Marci."

She spins and her heels *click-clack* against the floors. Even when she walks outside, the *click-clack* of her shoes striking the ground with purpose filters into the terminal. *Click-clack, click-clack, click-clack.*

I make my way through the airport and settle into a hard, plastic seat. My eyes grow heavy, watching the people buzzing around. Everything blurs into swirls of darkness as I close my eyes. I think about the previous day that Marci and I spent in her lab—

***

Her shoes *click-clacked* against the polished white lab floors. She plopped into a leather office chair, wiggled a mouse, and the screen came alive with an interconnected maze of dots and lines.

"This is Alex!" Marci beamed at me. She traced her finger across the maze of interconnected lines. "Lovely, isn't it?"

"Yes, I think so." I'm looking over Marci shoulder, staring at the mess on the screen like abstract art.

"Look" she clicked on the mouse "these are his memories of you." She turned to face me. "Notice anything?"

I stared at the screen harder, shaking my head no. "I don't know. Are the dots bigger with more lines radiating out?"

Marci grins. "This one is a smarty pants!" She started clicking at the lines. "These are just representations of memories. And..." Marci's voice trailed off into the clicking of the mouse. The hum of lab equipment filled the space between us. The noise was relaxing—Marci's clicking, the hum of the machines. My eyes started closing.

Marci's voice interrupted the fuzzy noise. "And this is the keystone memory."

"The what?"

"That's what I call them. The root memory. The memory that anchors all the others. It has the biggest dot and is interconnected to the other associated memories." Marci cut her eyes at me. Her lips curled into a grin. "These are the dots, I think, that tether you to Alex." She pointed at the screen.

My entire life with Alex condensed to a bunch of lines and dots. Our life together bound by one dot on this screen. "Wow, that's amazing."

She clicked on the dot, and all our dots and lines flickered out leaving the screen blank.

I gasped. "Marci, what did you do?"

Marci looked at me with a toothy, childish grin. "I erased your keystone—"

I jumped out of my seat. "You did what?"

"Leslie, calm down. This is a digital representation. Just experimenting with the connectivity of Alex's mind. Here, look." She clicked on the screen again. The dots and the lines reappeared filling the screen. She clicked again and a flood of multicolored lines and dots flooded the screen. Our keystone glowed bright in the middle of many other keystones. I slumped into my seat, angry that I got so excited about a bunch of dots on a screen.

Marci laughed. She gave me a wink. She was always winking at me. Maybe a nervous tic. Maybe she got pleasure out of irritating me. How did she know that would irritate me? Something he said? Something in these dots?

"Can you see the actual memory?"

Marci squinted at me. "What?"

"You know, can you watch the memories like a movie, or read them?"

Marci shook her head and studied the screen.

She started talking but her eyes were tracking something in the distance behind me. "No, these are just representations of the interactions between neurons, glial cells, and all the other cells in the brain." She waved her hand, like she was saying hi to someone.

I turned my head to see if someone or something was behind me.

"Oh, sorry, Leslie. Just thinking about something." Her eyes bored into my face. She had that fake smile, like she was tolerating me and my questions.

"How do you know which memories are connected to me, or you?" I asked to the computer screen.

"Good questions! The short answer is, we don't know yet..."

"So how do you know those are my dots?"

Marci cleared her throat. "Uh-hum! As I was saying, we don't know which dots are which specific memories, but we can infer."

"How's that?"

"Where are my manners, did you need some water?"

"Water...what? No, I'm just trying to understand all these dots."

Marci rolled her eyes and huffed. "So, after the nano-constructs have saturated the brain, we can scan for their signatures and link them to memories, by association..."

"Oh." Once again, I was not sure what to say. I should have been impressed, but by what? Marci could have been lying and throwing just enough science mumble-jumble at me to keep me from getting at the truth.

Marci glared, but I ignored her by studying the dots.

"Hey, you need water!" She jumped out of her seat and rushed out of the office space. The *click-clack* of her shoes faded into the humming noise of the lab.

The dots started to blur into a mosaic of colors. The lines swirling streaked across the screen like a screen saver. A hand touched my shoulder I jumped, squealing, and turning to see that familiar crooked nose.

"Dr. Greene, you scared me."

"Oh, I'm sorry." He nodded his head, adjusting his glasses. "I just wanted to check in on you guys. Where's Marci?"

"Getting me some water."

His eyebrows raised, and I caught him taking a quick peek into the lab.

"Here, did she show you this?" He leaned over me and clicked the mouse a couple times, and tens of thousands of red dots and lines overlaid the original yellowish dots.

"What did you do?" I asked, my voice full of more alarm than I intended.

"This is the one hundred and ten other folks in Alexi's head. We just reconstructed the scan the other day."

"You mean, Alex?"

"Oh yeah. Marci just calls him Alexi all the time. I guess when they first met, she called him—"

I cut him off by waving my hand. "Yes, I know the story."

"I guess you do." He adjusted his glasses, looked at the computer screen.

"So these nano-things, how do they work exactly?" I asked.

Dr. Greene looked at me, raising one eyebrow.

"Sorry, I'm not a scientist. I mean, how do the nanos saturate the brain? Marci was just explaining when she left."

He smiled, straightening his glasses, and I could tell he was going to try to impress me with his knowledge. I reached out and caressed his hand and smiled a thank you.

"So Alex was given a drink of the nano-constructs that specifically target the region of the brain used for memory creation. The main parts are the amygdala, the hippocampus, the cerebellum, and prefrontal cortex." He paused to tap the top of his head while he explained. "Not going into much more detail, we find that the hippocampus and amygdala—which is involved with episodic memories—are heavily saturated with the nanos. Only sucky thing is that the drink tastes like sulfur because of, well," he waved his hands, scrunching his nose "science stuff that would take too long to explain."

I nodded, not understanding but getting the idea; you drink a nasty drink, and these nanoparticles go to the brain. "What happens after you drink the nano stuff?"

"Well, we take a scan and ask questions. In simple terms, the nano-constructs light up, and we get a faint brain scan. We ask questions and certain groups of neurons light up, and we assign those to that particular memory. You follow?"

Dr. Greene smiled at me. I nodded, unsure what to say.

"Great. Look." He started clicking on the screen. "Here is Alexi—" He coughed. "I mean Alex and everyone. When we ask questions about Granny, all of these dots light up." He clicked on the screen and a separate set of dots and lines flash on the screen. "This is Granny. We completed her scan after the accident. Some of her memories are faded, but the outline of the memories are still there. We can use the keystone memories to match between Alex and the passengers to reconstruct the memories—"

His words faded into *wha-wha-wha* as he goes off on a science textbook lecture like Marci, talking about erasing memories. I interrupted his monologue. "How did it happen? Granny's memories being erased?"

Dr. Greene shrugged his shoulders. "Not sure, but we know Alex accidentally dispersed an experimental nano-construct on the plane, and it caused a memory transfer to him while fading it out of the others." Dr. Greene leaned in close whispering in my ear. "We are trying to perfect the process, but without Alex's notes—"

"What are you talking about?" Marci's voice cut him off.

Dr. Green jerked up. "Oh nothing, just talking about how the victims on the plane got—"

"We shouldn't talk about that with," Marci gave me a crooked glance, eyes darting between Dr. Greene and I, "anyone."

Marci handed me the glass of water. She scowled at Dr. Greene who started to retreat out the office. Marci smiled and mumbled through her clenched teeth. "Don't you have someplace to be? A report to finish writing? A solution to prepare?"

Dr. Greene nodded and shuffled out the room. I took a greedy drink of the water. "Thanks, I was thirsty."

"You have to stay hydrated for the baby."

I grinned, nodding my head.

"What's wrong?" Marci towered over me and massaged my shoulder.

"Nothing, everything is fine, just taking it all in."

Dr. Greene walked in holding a glass with a milky solution.

"What's that?" I ask.

"I need you to drink that so I can map your memories."

"What?" I thought about all this talk about erasing and transferring.

"Leslie," Marci squatted down squeezing my thigh. "I'm not going to hurt you. We need the scan to compare the keystone memories between you and Alex so we can sort his memories and the passengers."

I nodded my head. I sniffed the glass that Dr. Greene handed to me. It stunk like rotten eggs, and I hesitated, but Dr. Greene gave me a reassuring nod, and I took a drink. I followed it with a drink of water to wash out the foul chalky aftertaste.

"Nasty, stuff there." I twisted my face in disgust.

"Thanks, Leslie." Marci winked, and a shiver tingled my spine; the skin on my arms goose-fleshed.

"So when do you scan me?"

"It takes a while for the solution to work. Maybe 30-90 minutes from now."

"Oh."

"Just relax, you're in good hands"

I nodded, but a million questions enter my mind. *What about privacy? Is this like posting pictures on Facebook and your data is sold without you knowing? How many times was Alex scanned, and the passengers? With their consent? Will I have to give mine?*

Marci's voice cut into my thoughts. "Enjoying yourself?"

I nodded, my brain throbbing with information.

Marci clicked off the computer, maybe sensing that I have had enough science for one day. "We don't need to keep staring at those dots and lines." Marci massaged her temples. "It's enough to give you a headache."

"Yeah, right. Last night you said you had information about Alex's memories. You remember."

"About the different personalities Alex is exhibiting. I mentioned they were not all different people, but some are his own repressed memories. Do you know what that means?"

"I'm not sure about these being his memories and personalities. I thought you were just a bit drunk last night when you hinted at this."

Marci rolled her eyes. "Yes, I had a bit to drink, but I remember every word. And I don't make up stuff just because I'm drinking."

"Oh, I'm sorry... I didn't mean to imply—"

Marci started talking over me. "Not sure how much you know about Alex's past. It took him some years before he told me but, from what you told me, some of these outbursts are definitely from his past. I'll help you sort it out as much as I can."

How much do I know about Alex's past? How much do you ever know about another person's past? Does it matter? If they are a good person, does it matter?

"We all have those things..." I pointed to the blank computer screen. "But you've known Alex a lot longer than I have, so I'm sure you know a lot more than me."

"I'm only going to tell you about what I know, nothing about what was on that screen. Some of those are unassigned, and I don't want to tell you anything false."

"Okay. Makes sense."

"Alex's name was Brian. He changed it to escape his past. I teased him in private with it, and that may be why he never told you about this." Marci grabbed my hand. "Let me know if you want me to stop telling you anything. Alex's past is kind of dark." Marci's eyes glanced down to my belly. "You okay?"

"It's okay. I'm fine."

"Alex's parents died in a car accident when he was young, and he grew up with foster parents. His foster dad was abusive, and he ran away when he was a teenager. I don't know all the gory details, but he met a woman named Tammy. She was a dominatrix and turned tricks she picked up at a diner where she worked."

"And what did Alex do?"

"He helped out."

"What do you mean helped out?"

"Some of the clients liked it rough."

"You mean women liked to go and get roughed up?"

"Some women, but mostly men."

"So that asshole he turns into...is really some repressed part of him?"

Marci hunched her shoulders. "Probably. I think most of the people you have been interacting with are just jumbles of his past personalities."

"You mean..." My voice trailed into my thoughts, and I picked the thread out loud, "I can understand him being Brian, but there's no way he is this asshole abusive person."

Marci ignored my comments and continued with her memorized remarks. "Alex is acting out parts of his repressed personas. It's like he is living in flashbacks. He is filtering his world through his past memories and experiences."

Marci leaned back in her seat. "You think you know someone and then bam."

"Yeah, think how I feel. Does he still... you know?" I can feel my cheeks blushing.

"Oh!" Marci smiled and winked at me. "Work with Tammy?"

I nod.

"I'm positive before the event—and even before we started dating—he had cut all ties with her and that lifestyle. But the agents that have been following Alex saw him in a diner with various men and women. And when I checked, a woman named Tammy is the owner of the diner."

"Oh." I took a drink of the water. Tiny specks of light flashed behind my eyes. Pulsating taps of pressure. I closed my eyes.

"You okay, Leslie?" Marci's hand gripped my arm.

Her hand was cold and clammy, I shuddered, and she let go. "So let me get this straight, Marci. You're saying all these personalities I'm living with are just Alex's secret memories and not the one hundred and ten other folks in there?"

"Well, I'm not saying that. They're leaking out and mixing with his old memories. Maybe even amplifying his memories. That's why I asked you to play along with this. Like this asshole. It may be repressed memories, but it could be someone on the plane, and we don't want the memories to become entangled."

"Why'd you tell me all these things if they may not be his memories, but someone else's?"

"I just wanted you to know the truth so you can make decisions when it's time."

Confused, I asked, "Decisions?"

"Don't worry about that, now."

"When should I be worried about it?"

"Leslie, please calm down. You don't want to get too agitated. Think about the—"

"If you say baby, I will smack the shit out of you, Marci." I huffed

"Leslie, please. Okay, I'll tell you—"

"If you want to tell me something, tell me about you and Alex. Tell me," I stood looming over Marci, "How did you and Alex meet?"

She giggled. That drunk giggle. "Leslie, you are so dramatic. That happens when you are pregnant and blood sugar is low. Hey, let's get some lunch."

"What? Lunch?"

Marci stood and wrapped her arms around me. "Come on Leslie. We are getting off track. Let's eat. We can do the scan afterwards."

I staggered backwards out of Marci's embrace. "Yes, I can use some food. I'm getting a bit lightheaded."

"Oh, Leslie," Marci said, voice deep and maternal. "We need to get you something to eat. Finish that water and we can go."

***

The vivid memory fades as the captain drones on about preparing for landing.

As the plane descends, my stomach scrunches like an accordion. All I can imagine is walking off this plane and forgetting who I am or becoming consumed with memories of others. Consumed by my own repressed memories.

Who am I? Leslie. I'm married to Alex.

The plane slams into the ground. My diaphragm begins to spasm. I grab the vomit bag. I hold it to my mouth. I burp, nothing but the sensation, the hot bile burning my throat. I hold my fist to my mouth and swallow hard as the plane comes to a stop. The clicking, the 'excuse-mes', the beeping of cellphones coming to life focuses my attention on everyone leaving the plane.

Once off the plane, I rush into the bathroom. Splashing water on my face. Studying the woman, the face, in the mirror.

"Who am I?" I whisper. "Leslie." I repeat the question in my head. *Who am I?* I whisper louder. "Leslie." I shiver, thinking that I could look in the mirror and see someone else's face.

I splash my face with water again. "Who is Brenda?" Marci never answered that question. Is she an ex-girlfriend? One of Alex's tricks? Damn it, she never told me. I never asked.

"How did Marci and Alex meet?" I did ask that question, but once we got to the restaurant, she was more excited to tell me her plan to get Alex's memories restored and how to help everyone else. She never told me how she met Alex. Is that important? Why am I crying?

My phone buzzes with life. I jump a bit at the sudden jarring noise cutting through the silence. My non-profit partner's name flashes across the screen.

I suck in a sob. "Hello."

"Leslie, I'm glad that you're okay. You had me worried that something happened at home again or with the baby. Where are you?"

"Hey, Ben, I took off for Philadelphia."

"Philadelphia? You didn't mention that you were leaving."

"I'm a grown woman. I don't have to tell you my every move."

"Don't get mad. I just want—" He sniffles. "I just care about you, as a friend. We have worked together for what...?" The line goes quiet.

Should I answer?

He continues with a cough. "Five years. We built this non-profit together. Don't push me away. Please."

I hold the phone away from my face as I inhale and exhale, preparing to tell some version of the truth. "Everything is fine with the baby and with me at home. I just needed some answers, and I had to go to Philadelphia to get them."

"Leslie, I know when someone has been crying. Even over the phone."

"Please, just drop it. I'm okay. Hormones and stuff."

"Okay, if you say so. I would not do this to you, but that girl is here, and she is in pretty bad shape."

"What girl? They're always in bad shape."

"You know that girl from the plane who lost her memory, with the abusive brother."

I think about Alex. His plane. Is she in there, in his head? "What?"

"A few years ago, we helped her. Her name is—" The crinkle of pages turning fills the silence.

I blurt out, "Amanda Conner. Parents died. Stepbrother abused her. We got her legal protection with the help of her neighbor, and we moved her out. Things turned out okay. One of our early success stories. Went to that dinner party. She met a nice guy. They had a kid. Remember?"

"Yes, her."

"What's the issue?" I snap.

"She's in our office, and I need you to—"

"You know how to handle this one. Call the police and get a restraining order. Why bother me now? I've had a long day and—"

Ben snickers. "We have all had long days. If it were that simple, I would have handled it already, but it has some complications surrounding that plane event." His voice fades as he says "event." I'm not sure if he said it at all.

"Damn it. I'll be right there."

"I would normally handle it, but—"

I cut him off. "Tell me, Ben, why can't you handle it? I'm still at the airport, and I wanted to go check on Alex. I just want to go home and eat ice cream. Be pregnant and happy for one damn minute."

"Leslie, calm down—"

"If one more person tells me to calm down, I'm going to... Fuck off!"

"Okay, Leslie. Listen I know you are frustrated, but you have to come in. It was the neighbor that bought her in, and she only wants to talk with you. There's something else—"

"Why, Ben? Why me? Please tell me why?"

"If I could do this without you, I would." Ben lets out a sigh. "Listen, Alex is involved. He's missing. You have to come in and talk with the neighbor, and the police once I bring them in, which is going to be soon."

"Alex is missing?"

"Sorry, I didn't know you were out of town. I thought he may have been at the clinic with you."

"Why the fuck didn't you say that at the beginning? I could give two shits about this girl. Alex is missing?"

"Leslie, please..."

"Ben, I'm sorry. I'll be there as soon as possible. I'll try and find Alex." A stab of guilt radiates through my stomach.

Ben's voice pitches higher. "I'll stall things here. I'll play the pregnant card."

"Oh Ben, why didn't you tell me you were pregnant?"

Ben giggles. "Very funny. Leslie, you know I care about you, and I'm sorry about what you have been going through."

"I know."

"Now get your butt here. ASAP."

Walking to the taxi stand, I wonder if I should call Marci. Phone in my hand, I scroll to her name. My finger will not press the large green dial button. My fingers hover over the call button. What am I going to say? Beg her for more help? I'm sure Alex is fine. Is he turning tricks? Would Marci's agents tell her about his every move? If he were in real trouble, she would know. Would she call me? Are we friendly now? She will call me if Alex is in trouble.

I put the phone into my bag. Like a loaded gun. What would she say anyway: *Toe the line. Hold the act. I almost have this figured out. Fascinating. A couple more weeks.*

I got all the answers she is going to give. I pull the phone back out and call the one person that I trust. I try his number. He answers on the second ring, and before he can say anything, words spill out.

"Hey, Ralphie, it's me, Leslie. I'm at the airport. Something happened with a client from the plane, and Alex is missing. Could you give me a ride, and I can fill you in on my time with Marci?"

There is a silent pause. His deep voice fills my space. "I'm on my way."

CHAPTER 26

Marci:
220 Days after Event

I'm flying into Chicago to start plans for the memory transfers. I lean back in the seat and think about Leslie and the hell she has put me through the last few weeks. I close my eyes trying to relax. Felling the pressure of the plane lifting. I think about dealing with Leslie again, especially after the last time I was in Chicago. I thought we were getting along and then she ambushed me. She has been a thorn in my ass ever since she got access to Alex's files.

But Marci is one step ahead, sweet Leslie.

Leslie thinks she is being cute with her consent forms and privacy of data bullshit. Friends of the passengers, her lawyer bullshit. Fuck, I don't need to deal with this shit. But I needed her to push that approve button after I enter that password. I had to agree to it.

We could have handled that stuff in private, but she had to make a show out of it. She made me look silly in front of Mark and that postdoc, Shannon. I close my eyes and think about what Leslie did to me—

***

It was during lunch before I scanned her the second time in Chicago. The question was from left field, such an innocent question that I had stepped into it before realizing I was holding a live grenade.

"Tell me more about this memory technology you and Alex developed and its applications," she said, picking at her salad.

"Well, everything is in the early phases. Alexi is the true mastermind. I developed the core technology, but his research on memory mapping led him to the transfer and editing of memories."

"Interesting. So are there documented lines of intellectual property?"

"What? We're all collaborators, so—"

"I'm sorry, Marci, Alex had pretty secure files. Not even the DOE computer guys could breach them. So whatever he locked up, he wanted it out of your hands. And, with his memory comprised, I have been asked to speak on his behalf."

"What are you saying, Leslie?"

Leslie reached into her bag and pulled out a stack of papers. "You'll see here, Marci, that all my ducks are in a row. I have Power of Attorney over Alex's financials, health, and intellectual properties." She flipped through several pages, and continued, "And this includes the files that are secured by Alex on any file share services."

"Wow... I thought we were friends, Leslie."

"Really, Marci. Nothing to worry about. You can trust me. Like I trust you. I drink that nasty nano-solution and let you scan my memories. This is just standard lawyer stuff. I'm sure you advise all the passenger on the plane to seek legal counsel and go over that consent form you were handing out."

"No, the government handled getting those forms signed."

She waved her hand and spoke with a confidence I'd not seen from her. "Those passengers on the plane and their families are not my matter—except Alex, Granny, Ralphie, and myself. I now represent the interest of all four of us. Moving forward, there will be a new consent form and all preceding forms will be null and void."

"Yeah, I'm sorry. You can't just bust in here and tell me what to do. I'm sorry, but you can take a hike with all that noise."

Leslie laughed at me. That's what sticks in my head, the way her lips curled into a devilish grin, her shrill staccato laugh. That high-pitched, defiant hyena laugh. Everyone in the restaurant glared at us. Smiled at us. Smiling at Marci, the clown. Mark and that idiot Shannon, who seemed disinterested in the conversation, had shit-eating grins on their faces.

"Oh, my dear Marci. You're up shit's creek without a paddle. Your friend Jack is a snake, but useful. His computer nerds could not get into the computer. So he asked me if I could help you. I said I had conditions—"

"Conditions?"

"Yeah, conditions. A big stack of them. Consent, intellectual property rights, a cut of the profits. You and Mark were going to cut Alex out. Not on my watch. We get 50% moving forward."

I stood ready to leave when Leslie forked a tomato and waved it at me.

"Stuck like a bug. Don't make a scene, Marci. Sit, eat, enjoy. Did you think a Harvard law graduate would just cow down to everything you said? You run all this jargon a mile a minute out your mouth, but you're not the only expert in the world. Hell, your own people turned on you."

I scowled at that yellow-bellied Shannon, who just shook his head. I smirked at Mark; his face was beet red, stuffing food into his mouth, shaking his head in disagreement with Leslie's accusations.

"Marci, I don't want to play this game any longer. I know you need more scans of my head. I actually want you to have my scans. I know you need Alex's files." Leslie rubbed her hand over her rounding belly. "I want you to fix Alex, Granny, and everyone else. But not on your terms. On mine."

I had no choice but to eat crow. I had no choice. She had all the cards I needed. I could not do it without Alex's notes. I had no choice but to yield my pride.

I must give it to her. She didn't gloat or rub it in my face any further. I signed the papers without much pomp and circumstance.

I had one bullet in the gun, and I played it.

"Leslie, do you regret giving up on working at a top law firm? What, a U of Chicago and Harvard graduate? One day becoming a judge, maybe politics. Do you regret meeting Alexi and getting pregnant? Just working at some non-profit, wasting your talent?"

For all her tough exterior, people are all the same inside. Insecure of our choices. Always filtering them through the lens of someone else's approval. That's why her answer stung more than everything else she did.

"Marci, I actually stepped down from partner because I wanted to give back to the community. Meeting Alex and getting pregnant was icing on the cake. Do you regret running like a coward from your love and baby for what, something so easily lost?" She smiled at me, like a mouse that belled a cat.

We glared at each other for a few minutes. I needed her scan. I needed the two-factor key. What I did not need or want was her approval. What I didn't want was her pity.

"Fuck you, Leslie. Mark can do the scan, and I expect the two-factor key turned off by tomorrow morning."

I walked out. Found this little bar, ordered a double tequila, and replayed what had happened. Was she right? I did regret my choices. Maybe, I should call Eric and fly out to Europe when this is resolved. Take an extended vacation and smell the roses—ah, fuck Eric; lovers always got in the way of whatever I tried to accomplish. Alexi and Eric—I want to check that love-shit off my list.

After my second drink, I got a text from Mark that the scans were done. I paid my tab and walked to the lab. Leslie was waiting for a taxi home. To show there were no hurt feelings, I offered her a ride. She refused, like last time, but I insisted.

"We can't end things like this, Leslie."

Leslie got into my car, and most of the ride we sat in silence.

I asked for a truce until we were through this. She told me I needed to learn how to self-validate.

As we pulled up to her condo, I asked her if she could love Alexi knowing that he was cheating on her. She insisted that she loved him still, and it was not him that was cheating, it wasn't Alex. I offered to fix her memories also. She wiped at the tears flowing from her eyes. She asked, "Is this the game you're playing now? Are you happy now, Marci?"

I wish I could have said yes, but I could not let her get away with showing me up. I wanted her to know how powerful I was—

"I'm going to do you a favor, Leslie. I'm going to fix your Alex, but only because he's a friend and—" the words hung in my throat. I coughed, adding, "But maybe you'll consider letting me wipe these last months away from your memories. The struggle with an unfaithful husband, the struggles of your pregnancy, and anyone you had to run to for emotional support and comfort."

Leslie snapped her head, finger pointing at me. "I never—"

"I'm not judging you for any of it. Just putting that out there"

"Why, Marci? Why say such things to me? Why go down this rabbit hole? I told you I would be fine. We all have our burdens, and these past six months with Alex will be mine." Leslie's eyes welled up with tears, her voice cracked, "This will be my burden to bear, and you..." Her voice faded into the door being yanked open. She wiggled out, slamming the door hard.

I watched her waddle up the steps and disappear into her building. Was I wrong? I was trying to be a friend, put what happened behind us. She got one in and I got one in. Even-steven. Couldn't we still be friends?

That was a few weeks ago, but it still grated on me. Gaining access to Alexi's notes had been a game changer. I had a lunch date with Eric, about business and investment stratagems. We may not have been a hot item—now or ever again—but I trusted him. I still desired him. Desired his hands on my body. Did he still want me? Could it still work between us? But he said, as long as the lab was first in my life, he did not want to be second. He said we could be friends.

"With benefits?" I asked. He smiled and kissed me on the cheek. I told him I'd meet him in Spain when this was over.

He said he would believe it when we are drinking sangria at a little place he knew in Valencia. That was yesterday.

He texted me an emoji of an eggplant and donut. That made me smile. That made me happy—

***

My eyes open, my body jerking as the plane touches down. I ignore the pilot's blabbing about weather and connections. I plan what I need to do. My first stop is to meet with Ralphie.

When I get to the clinic, Ralphie's landscaping truck is in the parking lot. I walk into the lobby. The perfumed, lemony cleaner mingles with his earthy, mulch aroma.

He stands, a foot taller than me, broad shoulders, his meaty hand extends. "Marci, so nice to see you, again."

I ignore his hand and spread my arms wide. "Everything we've been through, we're at hug level." He smiles and steps into my space wrapping his arms around me. The fragrance of cedar relaxes me. "How's Granny?"

He releases me and talks about Granny as we walk to my office.

"You guys are running a procedure today. Had to get her here and then I got your text to meet."

I nod my head. "Yup, I think we can get your Granny back sooner than I thought. It will be the first try, and that's what I needed to talk to you about."

I push my office door and, as planned, Jack and his lawyer are waiting for us. Ralphie pauses.

I pull Ralphie's muscular arm. "It's okay, Ralphie. None of us bite. I want to clear things up before the procedure."

Ralphie looks down at me, and whispers under his breath pulling his arm away. "You slimy bitch. Leslie warned me about you."

"It's not what you think. Please, take off your shoes. Thanks." I wink at him walking to my desk.

"We're just going over the procedure and how it will work."

As we go over the paperwork and the details Ralphie relaxes. Jack and the lawyer exchange a glance and excuse themselves.

Ralphie pulls his mouth into a smile. "Should I be worried?"

"No, it will be over soon."

Jack and the lawyer come into the office with a stack of documents.

"Hot off the presses. We had a legal carrier bike them over from our Chicago office." Jack says, laying the documents in front of Ralphie.

"Here, Ralphie. We need you to release Granny into our care and sign a new set of consent forms. These are standard, experimental drug consent forms." The lawyer points to the line for Ralphie's signature.

"I'm not signing anything without Leslie."

"You and Leslie make all your decisions together?" I ask.

"What? No. She's my lawyer."

"A lawyer you seem to comfort a lot. Got to pay for that free legal service," Jack responds.

Ralphie's forehead twists between embarrassment and anger. His hands grip and squeeze the arms of the chair. He looks at me. "It's not like that." His voice deepens with anger.

"Guys, come on. Let's keep this professional. None of this schoolyard BS." I warn Jack and the lawyer.

Ralphie smiles at me, but he does not release his grip on the chair.

"Listen, Ralphie, I believe you. What I want is what is best for everyone. Leslie has been through a lot, and you have been a good friend. I think that's what these two are getting at. A bit childish, but the sentiment is that. I want to make sure that you and Granny are also cared for." I pause for effect, waving my hands in a rainbow arch, and continue. "All the passengers affected in this event."

Ralphie starts nodding in agreement. The lawyer slides a paper toward him.

I explain the form. "Ralphie, this is the experimental release form. We need this signed to help Granny. We are setting up to go, within the next few days. I thought you'd like to be first in line. Granny, Alexi, and even Leslie."

"Leslie?" Ralphie blurts out.

"Ralphie, she has been through a lot. Some things and some people are worth forgetting, right?"

"I guess. Who is she forgetting?"

"Patient confidentiality!" The lawyer pipes in.

Ralphie mumbles, "She didn't say anything about this."

"It's okay, Ralphie. Like you said, there was nothing between you two." I slide a pen across the desk.

Ralphie reads the paper, tears forming in his eyes. He starts scribbling his name across the bottom. "I want this to be over."

The lawyer and Jack scoop the documents off the desk and stand. "We have 110 other people to get signatures from."

The two men slip on their shoes, wave goodbye, and exit the office.

Ralphie stands to leave, but I say, "Ralphie, level with me. The suits are gone. You and Leslie got closer than friends."

Ralphie sits and leans across the desk. "Marci, it doesn't matter. She wants..." Ralphie shakes his head. "She needs to forget about me and move back with her life."

"Maybe not."

"What game are you playing, Marci?"

"No game. I offered to remove you from her memories, and she told me to fuck off. I did not want to say that in front of those guys."

Ralphie chuckles, "That sounds like Leslie."

"I knew you two were an item."

"I'd not go as far as an item. Like I said, good friends—"

"You took her to Lamaze classes, I heard."

Ralphie leans back and shakes his head. "You're a piece of work. You had us followed?"

"Not me, the suits. You guys are national security risks. I argued that this was an intrusion in private citizens' lives. But, you know, I'm just one little voice."

Ralphie nods his head. "Whatever. Yeah, I took her to Lamaze classes and gave her a shoulder to cry on. You know when Alex was... you know."

"As you know, Leslie and I are not the best of friends. But I think she should get the last several months removed from her memories. Imagine her living with the fact Alexi slept around with everyone and anyone for the past seven months. Could you live with that burden?"

Ralphie shakes his head no. "But Leslie is determined."

"Leslie wants things to go back to as they were. I think she will come around to this point of view."

"Yeah, good luck with that."

I smile in agreement. "Let me worry about Leslie. What I need from you is your word that you will help Leslie if she is freed of these memories of Alex and something goes wrong."

"Goes wrong?"

"Memories can be tangled. When you subtract memories, it may not be an exact science. She will need a trusted friend, someone she has known for some time like you, to help."

"What? No not like that. Friendship is not something you check off on a box or inject into someone's mind"

"You're misunderstanding me. Ralphie, you would be compensated. Start your own business, pay off those loans, and that home re-fi loan you had to take out because Granny was out of work."

"What, you—"

"Just a thought. You need the money."

"I don't need money that bad. I care about Leslie, and I couldn't do this to her."

"I think Leslie would want you—"

Ralphie cuts me off. "Why can't you just erase the past eight months, and she can go back with Alex?"

"That's what I hope will happen. I'll try my best. It's technical. I just want to cover all bases. Do you understand?"

"Yeah, I don't know, Marci. This feels like you're playing—"

I cut him off before he can finish. "The memory thing only happens if she goes through with it. And it doesn't work. Plus, remember she's at fuck off right now. Also, there's no reason to think that the procedure would fail. We moved 110 memories!"

Ralphie raises an eyebrow of doubt.

I lean forward, and reach for his hand, giving it a little squeeze. "Look, here is the paperwork. Just sign it. Leslie doesn't go through the procedure you get compensated. She goes though the procedure and she remembers Alex, you get compensated. She forgets Alex, you get Leslie and compensated."

Ralphie pulls his hand away, like I stung him. "That sounds sleazy. I get Leslie." Ralphie rolls his eyes and sucks his teeth. "What, like you're selling meat?"

"Sorry, you know what I mean. You will be a friend and maybe more. I know there was more looking at the overlap in your maps."

Ralphie studies the papers. His fingers and eyes trace the amount several times. He mumbles, "That's a lot of landscaping companies." His eyes continue to read the document.

He smirks at me. "She did tell you to fuck off. I'm sure she would tell me to sign it. This would be giving up free money."

"Win, win, win!"

He grabs at the pen, glancing between me and the paper several times. He scribbles his name on the line.

I stand and extend my hand. He grabs it, squeezes hard. "Why does this feel like I'm shaking the hand of Mephistopheles?"

I smile, thinking. "Ralphie, I'm getting more than your soul."

Ralphie's phone buzzes to life, and he fumbles to answer it. He talks in a hushed, mumbling voice as he picks up his boots and steps out the door. I know it's Leslie. I overhear that they are meeting at the Clinic.

Ralphie does not wave as his truck drives past my window.

I slip on my shoes and make my way to the clinic. A few more screws to tighten and Leslie will be begging me for forgiveness. No one makes a fool of Marci. No one threatens to take what I worked hard and sacrificed to build.

"Look at me now, Leslie. I'll show you self-verification!"

INTERLUDE

Brian/George:
Sara

I stop typing and recite the last few lines I wrote:

"...You close your eyes, hoping you're being gaslighted, because that's the only way you can convince yourself to sleep—"

My cell phone buzzes breaking my concentration.

"Hello."

"Hey, it's me Sara. You wanna go for a run?"

I think about running, my body still sore and achy—

Her voice cuts in, "Don't think, just say yes. It's a nice day to get out, and I'll buy you lunch at that place you like."

"Yeah, but... I need to finish—"

"Please..."

I close my eyes, imaging her lips twisting into a pout.

She pleads, "I really need to talk with you."

There is something in her voice, like when we were kids and she needed her big brother.

"Okay, but only if you promise not to be annoying."

She laughs. "I'll pick you up in five minutes."

"Okay, see ya."

"See ya."

I push away from my desk. A sharp pain radiates out from my chest as I stand. I think about Sara and her fruity smelling hair. I grab my shoes and jog out to the street.

We run for a mile without talking. My lungs are burning. Panting. She stops running, hands on her hips.

"You okay?"

"Yeah... Just out... of—"

"Shape." She lunges and pokes me in the belly.

"Stop that." I swat her hand.

She leans away and looks me over. "My gosh, you're ticklish like him."

"What—"

She wiggles her fingers and starts kneading my stomach.

"Come on! Stop it, sis."

I twist my body and start giggling as her fingers poke into me. I grab her wrist and pull her away. She stumbles and falls laughing.

"You brute, beating up on your sister. I'm going to call mom."

I reach out my arm. "Come on tattletale, let's go eat."

Sara wraps her arm around mine and lays her head on my shoulder.

"Thanks."

"What are big brothers for?"

We get to the restaurant. It was a place our parent would take us to when we got good grades on our report cards. They would give you a pack of bubblegum for every 'A.'

"I love this place." I pop a French fry into my mouth.

"I know. Remember when I snuck out the house to go to that party and got super drunk?"

"Yeah, I remember. You puked all over my shoes."

Sara reaches out and grabs my hand. "You are the best—" She pulls her hand to her face and rubs her eyes.

"What's wrong, sis?"

She shakes her head and leans back. "Nothing, I'm just being silly."

"Let me guess, guy trouble? What happened now?"

"Nothing. Everything is great in that department." She sips her drink. "What about you?"

What about me? Am I seeing anyone? Am I dating Marci, or Granny, or Lee, or Brenda?

"Yeah, you know I'm engaged to Brenda."

"Who?" Sara's brow scrunches.

"You know, Brenda."

Sara shakes her head. "Well, doesn't matter as long as you are happy."

Am I happy? Why doesn't Sara know Brenda? Is Sara my sister?

"What the fuck. You don't know Brenda?"

"George, calm down—"

"My name isn't George. It's Brian. Why are we here?"

"Okay, remember when we were little and—"

"Fuck lady, I don't know who you are. How did I get here?"

She reaches out—

"Don't touch me." I stand and fish money out of my wallet, throwing a twenty on the table. "I don't know what game you're playing."

Her eyes are welled up with tears. "George, I—"

"I told you," I slap the table, "my name isn't George."

I brush past the waitress, who runs over to the table.

"Is everything okay?"

I spin around. "Fuck you!"

The waitress staggers back, gasping like she was slapped. I look back at the woman in the booth sobbing. Who is she? Do I know her?

A voice, louder than the others, start calling out in my head, *Fuck her. Fuck her. Fuck her.*

I throw the door open and strut out.

CHAPTER 27

Brenda/Leslie:
227 Days after Event

"Ralphie, I don't know what I'm going to do. I don't know how much longer I can go through this."

Ralphie nods his head. "We'll get through this. Marci said she is almost ready to fix things."

I roll my eyes. "I'm tired of hearing Marci's bullshit. I just want my Alex back."

"Back before everything, and everything he put you through?"

"I can forgive him."

"You sure?" Ralphie raises his eyebrows.

"I guess I'll find out soon enough."

"Do you want to leave it to guesswork?"

I snap back. "What's that supposed to mean?"

"I'm sorry to keep bringing this idea up, but what if Marci could erase these months out?"

"I told you I didn't want that."

"But you and Alex could pick up where you left off. Forget all this madness and even—" Ralphie's voice fades in a mumble. "Me."

I shake my head. "No, stop it. Memories make us who we are. That's one thing I've learned out of all this. How precious our time is and the way we remember those moments. Plus, there were some good things that came out of these last few months." I smile at Ralphie and he winks at me.

"Yeah, it hasn't been all bad."

"No, it hasn't. I got to know you better and Granny. And surprisingly, I've had sweet moments with Alex that reminded me how much I love him."

"How's that?"

"I remember that night I got back from Marci's lab. I had cried myself to sleep wondering where Alex could be. I was at my wits end and thinking about leaving Alex until this was over. I heard a crash in the kitchen. I ran out and there was Alex. I didn't recognize his face, swollen with black and purple splotches. His left eye a tiny slit where an eye should be. Standing in a pile of tomato sauce. Spaghetti splattered down and around his legs. He took two shaky steps and flopped into the kitchen chair.

"We talked that night. Alex and I. Something about the pain medication made him be himself. Something about focusing on the nagging pain of each breath stopped him from being the others, being his repressed selves. At that moment I knew he was the same man I fell in love with. And now that Marci has Alex's notes, I'm sure I'll get back my Alex and we can raise this thing inside of me together." I rub my hands over my belly and laugh.

Ralphie sighs. "Yeah, I know he was Alex more, because you seemed to lose my number, but I was happy for you."

"Yeah, a few fucking weeks of happiness. A few weeks of mostly Alex with a smear of that asshole. As he stopped taking the pain medication and the purple-black splotches faded and the ribs healed, he became the people I hated. I had to follow him around for those briefest of moments. A couple hours here. A few minutes there. This is not sustainable. The last couple months have used me up."

Ralphie reaches out and grabs my hand, and I continue speaking before he can start. "Well, you know. The brief moments I spend with Alex are not enough. I need my husband back. I want my husband back. I want to be loved and cared for, not going through emotional hell every few hours. I'm going to have a baby soon. I don't know what to do. She's got the files and my memory scan. I'm tired of this madness. It's wearing me down."

I take a sip of my orange juice, creating a pause in my monologue to let him speak. He is living it with me. I stare at his beautiful, smiling face. He has held me when I cried. He has been there helping me hold the pieces together. Ralphie is the sole constant in my life. We share a common bond—people we love tormented by their own memories. Marci has pushed Alex and Granny together; she says it will help remove or extract Granny's memories out of Alex.

By pushing Granny and Alex together, Marci has pushed Ralphie into my life. I'm thankful for that. He has been my lighthouse in these turbulent months. The person who massaged my feet when I spent the day chasing after Alex. The person who went with me to my Lamaze classes. The person who held me together when everything seemed to be falling apart. The person whose shoulder I cried myself to sleep on. I wish it were my husband, but it was not my husband; it was him. I study his blurring face, his smile.

"So we did have an English class together in college, and I have proof!" The random statement catches me off guard, but I should not be surprised. Ralphie always changes the subject when I go on one of my hormone rage rants. I'm not sure what to say, so he continues the story.

"Funny, I was showing old photos to Granny, and I saw a Polaroid of a group of us after a class project." He pulls the photo out of his shirt pocket and slides it across the table. "Here, look for yourself."

I exam the picture. It is me. I'm younger, my hair is longer, and my arm is roped in between his.

"Well, pictures never lie." I cut my eyes at him, grinning. "If you never showed me this picture, I'd still be calling you a liar. But I'm starting to remember this class."

Ralphie shakes his head, smiling. "You should see the other pictures I have of you."

I nudge his leg with my foot under the table. "I know you're lying now."

"Yeah, just joking. I always wanted to ask you out but never had the chance. We did spend some time together working on that project—"

"With two other people. You're making it sound like we had romantic nights together." I laugh.

"Wow, you know how to crush someone down."

I reach across the table and grab Ralphie's hand again, squeezing it a bit this time. "I'd never crush you. Wish I got to know you better back then. You're one of the kindest, sweetest men I know. You have helped me so much."

"Right back at you." Ralphie grins. "I mean, sweetest woman I know."

I pull my hand away, holding it to my chest. Embarrassed, I whisper, "What do you think I should do?"

My stomach twists with guilt. I'm holding hands and flirting with Ralphie. I'm not wearing my wedding band. It is not because of Alex, but it hurts my swollen fingers. Should I be guilty because I have more love, at this moment, for Ralphie than my husband?

Ralphie shifts his body in the seat. "I don't know, sweetie."

A shiver tingles along my spine when the nickname "sweetie" slips out of his mouth like a well-worn leather jacket.

"I talked with Dr. Greene a bit, and he explained the procedure." Ralphie rubs his face with his hands. "I don't know what to think. It feels like he wants to use Granny as a lab rat. They mapped her head, and now they're using molecular subtraction to determine which memories belong to her and not Alex." Ralphie stops talking. He looks out into the restaurant, his eyes scanning for something, he shakes his head and turns to me. "What the hell is molecular subtraction? Is that safe? Can we get a second opinion?"

The questions hangs in the space between us. I hunch my shoulders, as I don't have any great answers either.

Ralphie continues. "Do you trust her?"

"Yes, I do." My voice is quieter than I expected.

"That was convincing." He grins raising his eyebrows.

I put my hand over his, squeezing a little. "What other choice do we have but to trust her? Plus, I have a stack of documents with her signature on it."

He nods his head. "Yeah, we have documents." His voice fades into a pensive sigh.

"What is it?"

"It's probably nothing, but Marci had me come to her office last week and talk—"

"You two need anything else?" The waitress' voice barks at us.

I look up at the bosomy waitress towers over my shoulder. Her steel-gray hair frames her youthful face, but the wrinkles that crisscross under her eyes give her secrets away. Name tag dangling, I read it and answer, "No thanks, Tammy. We can have the check."

"Here you two go. No rush." She glances between Ralphie and I. "You two make the cutest couple. You two remind me of my son and daughter-in-law." She cackles a hoarse, throaty laugh at us, turns, and walks off into the kitchen.

I think about her name, Tammy... Could it be the woman Marci told me about? No, it was Tabby or something else. I'm sure Marci would have told me. *The diner that Alex is turning tricks in is near your condo.* Or would she?

I close my eyes to stop the white flashes from become brighter. Head pounding. His voice is calling from the void. Calling my name. My real name, soft at first, growing louder as the pounding subsides.

Leslie... Leslie... Leslie...

My eyes blink open and his face, brow wrinkled with concern. "Leslie, you okay?"

I nod my head and rub my belly as the baby starts moving, kicking.

"You want to feel the baby moving?"

Ralphie nods. He scoots next to me and slides his hand under my oversized shirt, placing his cool hand on my belly. He glides his hand over the stretched skin, applying a little pressure. "Does that hurt?"

"No."

He keeps probing until a satisfied cooing noise escapes his mouth. "I can feel it." He pulls his hand from under my shirt and goes back to his seat. "Wow, that is cool. Does it happen all the time?"

"Off and on. Usually at night when I'm trying to sleep. Little bugger already causing me trouble."

"So Marci wants to do this procedure soon?" he asks.

"Hopefully, I'm ready for this nightmare to end."

Ralphie grins. "I haven't been that bad, have I?"

I shake my head. "If there was any positive in this mess, it was you. But—"

I swallow my words. What do I want? Would I still spend time with Ralphie? Should I spend time with Ralphie? Before I can finish my thoughts, Tammy returns to collect the check.

She scoops the pile of cash Ralphie laid on top of the bill. "Need change?"

"Nope, all yours!" Ralphie answers.

Tammy squeezes my shoulder. "Good luck! And when it's time," she points to my belly "take the drugs!"

We all laugh, and I nod a thank you.

Our phones beep to life at the same time. A text message from Alex on my phone. "Hey, Lee, wanna meet for lunch?" My heart thumps against my chest. I want to say yes, but in an hour Alex may not be there. I could find some other version of him. Someone I don't love or can never love. I created a method to ensure that Alex shows up and not some random character. We meet at some place only Alex knows about.

I text: *Sure, let's meet at place we had our first date.*

My phone beeps: *Okay, see you in 2 hours.*

Ralphie looks from his phone. "This woman has got to be losing her mind."

Caught off guard, I mumble, "What?"

"Did you get this text from Marci?"

I shake my head no. Ralphie sucks air between his teeth. "Well, she wants Granny to come in for another scan in preparation for the," Ralphie laughs, holding his fingers in a *V* shape, "mind melt! Live long and prosper."

I smile at his silly face.

"Crap." He snaps his fingers. "I can drop her off, but I may be a little late getting back. Have to supervise at a job site. You think Alex could wait with Granny?"

"Maybe, but I'm meeting him in a couple hours."

Ralphie's smile fades into a frown. "Oh, I see."

"No, not like that, Ralphie. It's my birthday today, and I'm hoping he remembers."

Ralphie slinks against the booth seat. "Oh, I didn't know it was your birthday." He leans forward. "Well, happy birthday, you. I'm sure once you get home there will be a bunch of flowers, from Alex, waiting for you." He wipes the tears streaming from my eyes.

Embarrassed, I cover my eyes with my hand. Embarrassed that I'm making a fuss about Alex forgetting my birthday. "I'll be okay."

I wipe my face with a napkin on the table. The aroma of maple syrup and bacon fill my nose.

"Forget about me and my stupid birthday," I snort out. "Let's make a plan for getting Granny picked up."

Ralphie shakes his head. "That's why I—"

A tray of dishes clatter to the floor. The restaurant becomes quiet, and I can imagine him finishing that sentence. My body fills with a warmth that I have not felt in months.

Ralphie continues speaking. "No worries. I can try to work something out."

"Don't be silly. If you drop her off, I'm sure Alex and I can go pick her up." I reach for Ralphie's hand, but he moves it out of my reach.

"Leslie, I don't want to interfere with your Alex time."

"Don't be like that, Ralphie. I know it's silly, but what if he remembers my birthday and wants to surprise me? I don't get much time with him. You understand?"

"Leslie, I think he will remember." He nods, his mouth scrunching into a smirk. "I'll remember," he puffs out his bottom lip, "When I'm in my most desperate hour, you abandon me to find love."

I stick my tongue out. "You spoiled brat. You need all the attention like a little baby? Alex and I can pick up Granny after we meet. You just drop her off."

"You'd do that for me?" He reaches out for my hand.

I grab his hand with a squeeze. "Anytime."

The way he looks at me, I'm falling. The way he looks at me, he is falling. His mouth is moving. His voice is full of reluctance. "Go be happy with," he pauses, takes a drink of water, "with Alex. I know he will remember your birthday. I'm sure you will be surprised today."

My mind goes through all the reasons why Ralphie and I cannot be. All the reasons we are not together. Will we be friends, after this is over? There is enough room in my heart for both Ralphie and Alex.

Yes, we will be the best of friends. I'm lucky to have him in my life at this moment. The rest will fall into place when the time comes.

***

I rush to the office to finish some work before I have to meet Alex. I waddle into my office and plop into my desk chair. I flip through Amanda's folder. The photo of her bruised face is paper clipped to a police report. I close my eyes and think about how much I love Alex. Even when he was inches from my face, threatening me—hot breath and wet spit on my cheek, my back pressed against the wall, his words smacking into me—I thought about how much I loved him.

That's what Amanda said to me when I asked her to press charges. She said she loved him too much, and he's not always like that. Who is not always like that? She does not remember who she is. She does not remember who he is. She does not remember what he did to her. She lost her memory on that damn plane. Marci's experiment gone wrong. I rub my fingers over the photo, over her swollen, purple-black eyes and nod with understanding.

That's the thing about love. I think of Alex and his bruised ribs. Who was he when he went to find her? What was he thinking? Does he remember? Does Alex remember? Even though she would not press charges, the beating Alex took from Amanda's stepbrother was enough for him to be arrested and Amanda saved again. I pray that Marci has figured out this memory transfer thing and everything will reset to normal.

I close the folder. Alex cannot save them all, but he is determined to try.

My cellphone dings with an alarm. I grab my purse, turn the light off in the office, and drive to our restaurant. I push open the door, and I spot him in the corner. He waves. I wave and start zigzagging around the tables.

As I get closer to the booth where he is sitting, I notice a woman, slumped into the booth across from Alex. It is the woman from the gastro-pub. When she looks at me, her name pops into my mind. Angela.

"Alex, what are you doing with her?"

He looks at me, eyebrows raised. She squinted at me, lips pursed into an angry frown. I glance between them both, confused. Marci's voice drums in my head, *Play the part, you're almost there. I'll get your Alex back.*

I put my hands on the table to catch my balance.

"I'm sorry. I feel a bit faint."

Angela hops out of the booth, wrapping her arm around me.

Her Southern California accent wraps around her every word. "Oh dear, please sit down. You should take it easy."

I slip into the booth, and she snuggles close to Alex. No this is not Alex. Who is he? Why did he text me? How did my system fail?

I close my eyes and try to prevent the specks from becoming squiggly flashing lights. I close my eyes tighter, trying to stop the tapping in my head from becoming vibrating bangs. The pounding in my head drowns out the words he says to me. As my stomach knots, I squeeze my eyes harder, trying to force the white flashes to go away. I take several deep Lamaze breaths. The pounding softens to a gentle tapping. The white flashes fade into pinpricks. I open my eyes, hearing his voice.

"Sweetie, you okay?" His voice is quiet, an unfamiliar voice.

I nod my head; still unsure I can speak. They are not as close as I imagined. Angela's face is smeared with concern. Her hand grabs me. I want to pull away, but I let her hold my arm. Her hand is cold but refreshing against my hot skin.

"I didn't know you would be with your friend." My voice is soft.

"Oh, Angela just happened to be at the bar when I got here." He gestures across the restaurant to the bar. "She was telling me about Eduardo and Nurse Marci's tests."

"Well Granny is at the clinic today getting scanned. I told Ralphie we could go pick her up after."

He nods at me. Angela's hand releases my arm, and she leans against his shoulder.

"Okay, do you need some food? I already ate." His voice has a sarcastic tone.

I shake my head, still unsure about my voice. Still unsure about what I should say. His hand moving below the table. She is grinning and kisses his ear. I stand, turning away from them.

"I'm going to go and let you two finish chatting."

He starts to protest, but Angela cuts him off with, "Yes, I'll see he gets to Granny."

I wipe my hand across my face, walking out.

I dig my phone out of my purse and call him. Ralphie answers on the first ring. I can say nothing, sobbing and snorting into the phone.

"Leslie, calm down. Tell me where you are." Ralphie is whispering.

I cannot speak. I have forgotten how to speak. I don't know.

"Listen, just meet me at the hospital. I think I can leave early. We can grab Granny and go out to dinner for your birthday."

I nod.

"Leslie, please answer. Do I need to come get you? Did he hurt you? Just calm down and let me know you're okay."

I close my eyes.

"Inhale and exhale. Inhale and exhale. Inhale and exhale." Ralphie's voice coaches me like in Lamaze class.

"Thank...you..." I whisper.

"You're doing good."

After a few minutes of this, I regain my composure.

"Yes, I'm okay. He did not hurt me. He was just—" The words escape me. I breathe deeply again. "He was not himself and was with another woman."

"Ah shit, I'm sorry, sweetie. Can you meet me at the clinic?"

"Yes, I'll meet you there. I may go and clear my head for a bit"

"Leslie, sure you are okay? I can come and—"

"Ralphie, I'm fine. Really. I'm fine."

"I'm sorry."

"Don't be—"

"It will be over soon."

"I know. I'll see you in a bit."

I sit in the car, pondering what just happened. I'm not sure how much longer I can go through this. This roller coaster of emotions. The soft tapping starts in my head. The cars in the parking lot begin to vibrate. The colors fade into shades of gray, fade into a dull shade of white.

I close my eyes, screaming as loud as I can, but I don't hear anything but the thumping of my heart between my ears. Should I take Marci's offer? Can I forgive Alex? What about Ralphie and his friendship? It means the world to me, but I want my Alex.

My head pounds with anger. I smack my hands against the steering wheel. Maybe Marci was—

"Fuck you, Marci," I scream. But maybe she is right.

***

I get to the clinic and park next to Ralphie's landscaping truck. Is that Alex's car at the end of the lot? Can't be, I rush out of the summer's heat into the cool air of the clinic. Soft music dangles around my head.

"Have a lovely day, Ms. Leslie."

I wave at the security guard. "Thanks, Charlie."

He hands me a visitor's badge, and I head to the scanning area.

Ralphie is standing in the examination area lobby.

"They're not done yet." He starts talking before I get to him. He is moving to me. We meet in a hug somewhere in the middle of the hall.

He pulls me closer. His body still has the scent of raw earth and flowers. I pull away a bit and study his face. He leans into me, and our cheeks rub together. Our lips press together. My lips part, our tongues touch. Gooseflesh tingles along my arms. I never want to forget him.

I'm not sure how long our kiss was, our moment of passion. All the built-up tension releasing in a single kiss. I'm not sure how long she was standing there.

When I pull away from Ralphie, I see her. Eyes scrunched into tiny angry slits and lips pulling into a frown. Before I can say anything to her, Marci spins on her heels and walks away. Her steps are heavy, like she is taking her anger out on the floor. The *click-clack* of her shoes matches the pounding in my head.

I try to move but my stomach clenches and releases. The baby's kicking my diaphragm. My legs wobble, and I would have unspooled onto the floor if Ralphie was not holding me. I hold on to him a little tighter, closing my eyes, trying to hold off the inevitable.

Ralphie's voice calls to me. "I'm sorry, sweetie."

I shake my head. "No need to be sorry. We can find Marci and explain."

We walk off together in the direction Marci stomped off. As we pass an exam room, we hear voices, and moaning. Curious, I knock and push the door open.

"Marci, you in here?"

I gasp, raising my hand to my mouth. Granny and Alex stripped naked, pawing at each other like horny teenagers. The movement of sweaty flesh flickers in between Ralphie brushing past me, lunging, fist balled and winding up to strike.

Granny's screaming causes Alex to stop thrusting and turn to us. Granny looks away, grabbing at her clothes and trying to cover her body. The wet smack of Ralphie's fists on Alex's lips snaps Alex's head back. Granny screams, clawing at Ralphie, throwing herself in between Ralphie's fury and Alex's body. Ralphie pushes his grandmother away, the woman that raised him, so he can continue beating Alex.

I scream for him to stop, but a pain stabs my abdomen and my voice fades into a painful yelp. I lean against the wall to stop from falling. Ralphie stands over Alex's crumpled body. Like that day, all I can do is scream for help. I close my eyes, arms wrapping around me as the muscles in my legs fail to support my weight. Tears are welling in Ralphie's eyes, his mouth moving in the form of a sorry. People rush into the room, pushing past us. Marci is kneeling next to Alex's body, flashing a pen light into his eyes.

"Come on, stay with me. What's your name?" Her voice is stern.

His voice is groggy, confused, but it is his voice. My Alex. "Recuerdos llenan el vacio."

Ralphie helps me into a seat, the pain in my abdomen is subsiding. Granny is still scrambling to get dressed. Alex is on the floor, smiling at me. Marci is kneeling next to him. She glances at me and winks. She stands, barking orders at the nurses rushing into the room. "Get them prepped for the procedure."

Confused, I mumble, "It's ready?"

Marci glares at me. "Yes, it's time!" Turns away, helping gather Granny and Alex onto the gurneys. Her shoes *click-clacking* drum between my ears. I close my eyes, hopeful, praying, that everything will be as I remember.

PART 3:
RECUERDOS LLENAN EL VAĆIO

CHAPTER 28

*Brian/Alex's Memory:
227 Days after Event*

Memories Fill in the Void

*I don't remember,
The fine details of that day.
Was it sunny or did it rain?
Did we splash in puddles or lay
on soft green weeds,
with yellow flowers?
Did we name animals in the clouds?*

*I don't remember,
The fine details in your hair.
What was the color you streaked in?
Red or blond?
Or some shades of brown and gray?*

*I don't remember,
Your voice.
Was it deep and sweet?
Or high and whiny?
Did you snort when you laughed?
What did I say?*

*I don't remember,
Holding you close.
Tears like raindrops?
Did I squeeze you too tight?
Am I the reason you cried?*

I don't remember.
Please tell me.
The truth would be best,
But lies can fill in the void.

Paint me a pretty picture.
A sunset full of the pink in your hair.
A red picnic blanket,
A wicker basket full of cheese and wine.
Summer rain.
Forgotten, black rubber boots.
Forgotten, yellow raincoats.
Holding hands, running for cover.
Our picnic feast forgotten.

You're not crying,
Your face is wet with warm raindrops.
Laughing at the scene we left behind.
We pull each other close.
You smell like ripe fruit.
Watermelon or tomato.
Our lips exchange a secret.

I can hear it.
I remember,
I can hear it,
Echoing in the void,
"I'll love you, always."

CHAPTER 29

Marci:
228 Days after Event

I lift my head out of my glass and wave at the bartender for another tequila on the rocks. Larry, the bartender, looks at me, wondering where I'm at on the scale of drunkenness.

"I'm all right, barkeep. I could drink you under the table!"

He laughs and sits two glasses on the bar. "My dear Mar, I'd like to see that."

He pours two glasses of tequila. The alcoholic fragrance cuts through the perfume of stale beer and lemon disinfectant that fills this small, dark pub.

We clank our glasses, and after one quick gulp, I slam mine against the bar.

"You want another?"

I wink, and Larry fills my glass again. He puts his glass into the sink of water. A quick rinse and it's on the shelf again. Contents forgotten; its usefulness forgotten.

"What's on your mind, Mar?"

I hate that nickname—Mar. Always reminds me of some cheesy coastal town, but he is attractive. Top button on his shirt is always unbuttoned, proving his bulging pecs refuse to be contained. He leans on the bar. His white teeth shine in the dim light. His jet black, shiny hair slicked back like a 50s movie star. Perfect for this place. Perfect for confessing one's sins.

"Do you really want to know, hun?" Not sure why I call him hun, but it seems to fit the mood, and he leans in closer. His fruity cologne tickles my nose. Cheap, like the tequila, but sometimes you need the cheap to appreciate the good stuff.

His deep voice blends into the whine of the bar fridge. He is trying to be sexy. "Mar, I always want to know." He stands, moistening his lips with his tongue. His washrag wipes the bar, filling the air with more artificial lemon perfume.

I take another sip of my drink. I hold the pungent alcohol in my mouth, stinging my throat as I swallow.

"I'm lonely, Larry. And lonely people do stupid things."

He lifts an eyebrow. I can imagine a camera panning in on his square jaw. The audience laughing at his boyish confusion, and the cougar going in for the kill.

"Well, you will always have me, Mar." The way he says that name. The *r* rolls off his tongue and fills the space between us. Maybe I like this nickname after all. I repeat the name in my head. Mar. Mar. Mar. Imagining him saying this in my ear as we find pleasure in each other's embrace.

A sharp beam of light slices through the dark bar, illuminating the eddies of dust swirling around the small space. A figure strolls in from the brightness. As the door closes the slit of light is consumed again by shadows. Larry jumps to attention and wipes along the bar to greet this new customer. A ping of jealousy fills my mind, and I swallow the rest of my drink in one gulp, ensuring he will repeat my name.

"Have a seat anywhere. Can I get something started for you?"

"I can sit at the bar, and just a glass of club soda with a lime." Her voice pulls my head out of my empty glass. It's her.

"You can't have him!" I shout. My voice is slurred, loud and uneven.

Leslie goes to answer, but Larry's voice cuts her off. "Calm down, Mar. I'll get you another round in a sec."

I wave at him and watch him grab a glass, for her. I watch him fill her glass with ice. I watch him fill the glass with a carbonated liquid. I hate her for taking him away from me. I tap my glass against the bar.

"One second, Mar!" My name does not roll out of his mouth, but shoots at me like a frustrated command.

"Hey, Marci. Mind if I sit next to you and talk?" She pulls the stool out and wiggles onto it.

I shrug my shoulder. "Do I have a choice?"

Her voice is small in my ears. "We need to talk."

"We have nothing to talk about. Nothing!" I tap my glass again. Larry grabs my glass and prepares a new drink for me.

"Let's go over there and talk in private." Leslie points.

I turn, following her outstretched hand, and shake my head. "Too far from the booze." I take a sip of the drink Larry gave me. "And definitely too far from my friend, Larry. Look at that body."

He smiles at the mention of his name, running his fingers through his hair. Teasing me with desire.

"Okay, we can talk here."

"I prefer we not talk at all. I've seen all I need to know."

I study Leslie's face. Her skin is smooth and shimmers in the dim bar lights. It is true that a pregnant woman's skin glows with the sweat of an angel. I shake my head at Larry pretending to be busy.

"Well, I just need a few answers before I let you finish..." She pauses. I cut my eyes at her. She grins and lifts her eyebrows, eyes darting between Larry and I, then continues, "...doing whatever you were doing."

I swallow the rest of the drink and slam the glass on the bar. I lean in close to Leslie's face. "Listen, bitch. You just don't get it. You can't have your cake and eat it, too. You think all the pieces are just going to fall back into place," I snap my fingers, "and boom, your perfect life will be restored?" I shake my head. "Oh no, sister. All those repressed memories have bubbled back to the surface. Old demons are going to haunt you and him."

"What are you talking about, Marci?"

"You don't know shit about Alexi. Do you?"

Leslie wipes her face as I spray her with drunken beads of spittle. "I don't know what you're talking about. We've been through this before. I don't care, Marci."

I laugh through my nose. "Did you know I saved Alexi's life? He'd just changed his name from Brian to Alexi. And after us, he changed it to Alex. He always changes his name when he moves on." I take a sip of water that Larry pours for me without asking. I nod at him and tap my empty glass of tequila.

"He was hit by a car, lying in the street like a lost child. It was me," I tap my chest, "*me* that breathed life back into him. It was me," my voice starts to crack and fade, "that nursed him back to health. I was his Nurse Marci."

"I didn't know that—"

"Like I said, you don't know shit. Going to come in here like you're the boss. Demanding things from me." I gulp the water, soothing my raw, scratchy throat. "Do you know why Brian changed his name to Alexi?"

"Yes, we've been over this. He was adopted and was abused. Then he—"

I raise my hand to cut her off. "If you would stop pretending to be angry, maybe you'd learn something."

"I'm sorry. I just thought there was no need for you to tell me something I already knew."

"So you know about Tammy and that bit of history, remember?"

"Yes, I remember you telling me about her business."

"Funny thing, you actually know Tammy. She serves good eggs and bacon, don't you think?"

Leslie gags on the swallow of soda she was drinking. I pat her on the back. "It's okay, sweetie. The pieces of the puzzle are starting to click together in that brain of yours."

"You mean, she—"

I wave at Larry. "I need another drink."

"Tammy, who works at the dinner by my condo?"

"You know he was having sex for money, private fetish play."

"I don't know what you're talking about, Marci." Leslie takes a sip of her water.

"If you really want to know what that lifestyle is about, there's a private club called Leather and Lace. Hard to find if you're not looking for it. Take a peek in there if you want to see what type of life you will have to deal with if Alex's past several months are not erased."

"What the hell is Leather and Lace?"

"It is a leather and fetish bar for... Well, I'm not going to spell it out for you, but you can imagine the types of things that go on in there."

Leslie's face distorts in disgust and horror.

"Maybe I'm wrong about you, but you don't seem to be into leather or BSDM fetishes." I take the last swallow of my drink, hold the glass out and wiggle it to get Larry's attention. "But I could be wrong, and Alex will be ready to help you satisfy those urges."

I pull a folder out of my bag and lay it in the bar. I flip it to a picture of Alexi in his leather chaps, spanking a man in lacy lingerie. "Look, here are some photos the agents took because I had a hard time believing Alexi would do such things."

Leslie starts to gag and cough, grabbing at the folder, closing it, and shoving it away like poison.

"If you're going to throw up, go that way."

She starts shaking her head, and a small squeak escape. "Oh god, oh god, oh god. No, this can't be true. You sick bitch."

"I'm just trying to make sure you have all the evidence. I know how you lawyer types are. Look at his pictures—"

Leslie smacks my hand.

"Marci, stop it. Stop it! I don't need to hear or see any of this. I know Alex's mind was messed up and he would never do these things to hurt me. You don't know..." Leslie's words fade into babble.

"I can put Alex back to before the event. All you have to do is ask me."

"Marci, why are you doing this?"

"Oh, what happened between you and Ralphie will stay between us girls. Our little secret."

"What?" Leslie shouts. Larry, trying to ignore us turns his head in our direction.

"Can I have another, Larry?"

"Why are you doing this, Marci?"

"I know everything. I even know about you and Ralphie."

Leslie starts shaking her head side to side. "Nothing is going on between—" She starts coughing and grabs her drink.

"You can't even get the lie out. Like I said, those agents have been useful." I tap my temple and point at her. "And your scans have been very revealing."

Leslie slips off the stool in an awkward bow-legged stand. "I've heard enough, Marci!"

"And what, you going to tell momma? Sit down and let's finish talking—" I take a sip of my warm tequila. "Hey, Larry—does ice cost extra?" He drops a scoopful of ice into the glass, and Leslie straddles the stool again.

"Good girl," I say. "Take all your medicine."

"Marci, when this is over—which thankfully is soon—we will never speak again."

I hold my glass out. "Cheers to that! But remember you fired the first shot."

"If that's what this is about, then bring it!"

I clank my glass into Leslie's and take a long swallow, finishing the drink.

"I just need you to give me permission to perform the memory subtraction on Alex..." Marci shakes the ice in the glass. "You could also say, 'I'm sorry, Marci.'"

"You want to do what? And why the hell would I be sorry?"

I slide the folder toward Leslie, who stares at it like a venomous snake sneaking up to her.

"I want to fade out some of these unsavory memories, like what is in this folder."

"You think you can just wind me up, and I'll fold like a wet bag?"

"No, I think you'll think about what I've been saying and make the logical conclusion. Stop thinking about the friction between us, and think about Alex. You think he'll forgive himself after what he put you through?"

Leslie, sips her water. I can tell she is moving the pieces in her head. She looks at me. "And what happens afterward? Will he remember any of this?"

"What—the way you and Ralphie have been lip locking over the past weeks?"

"Lip locking? Listen. We... Nothing... Just a moment of weakness, nothing more. Nothing less. I admit it was wrong but stop holding this over my head!"

"I'm sorry, I have to ask one more time about you and Ralphie's relationship, since you say it was nothing."

"Okay, what do you want to know? But I'm done playing this game."

"Did you have sex with Ralphie?"

"No, never. Besides that kiss, we had no physical contact."

"One more question, Leslie. Do you love him?"

"I told you to stop it with this Ralphie mess. There's nothing between us. Now drop it." Leslie slams her fist on the bar.

"So when you think of love, you defend your feelings for Ralphie and not Alexi. Very interesting."

"You little snake in the grass. What do you want me to say? My husband has been haunting me with wild personalities. He is sleeping with who knows what or who," Leslie points at the folder, "and you're pestering me about one kiss? One lapse in judgment? Fuck you, Marci!"

I remember that morning with Eric, and how that one text about a kiss derailed us. Leslie stands off the stool and waddles to the door. She turns pointing a finger at me. "Marci, do it. Help Alex get better. But you better pray this procedure works, because so help me," she raises her fist in the air, "you're not the only one that can talk to agents. So help me, you will be finished! Everything you've given up would be for nothing!"

She is halfway out the door when I yell at her, "Hey, before you walk off thinking you know everything..."

She turns, a silhouette in the sunlight, her free hand resting on her hip.

"Two questions, Leslie, and then you can go sulk with Ralphie about me. One, how long will it take you to forgive him? Remember, I can help you too."

Leslie shakes her head. "I told you, I can forgive."

"Just putting that out there. And two, do you know who Brenda is?"

Leslie's steps into the bar. Her hand slips off the door handle, and the door closes with a muted click. I can't hear her, but I can read her lips, asking, "Who?"

I laugh, slapping the stool she was sitting in. "Come on over and let Marci tell you, sweetie." I wink at her. "Like I said before, you don't know shit!"

Leslie yells, "I'm done being humiliated, Marci. After this is done, I hope you go crawl in a hole and rot." She rubs her watery eyes and waves me off. She throws the door open and disappears into the hot light that slips in behind her.

I grin at myself in the mirror, holding my glass of ice out, toasting to the great Marci, and all things remembered.

CHAPTER 30

Leslie:
230 Days after Event

I pause before walking into Alex's room. Marci will be in there. I have been dreaming of this moment. Walking into the room and Alex opening his eyes and ending this nightmare. Opening his eyes and remembering who I am. Not Brenda, but Leslie; his wife. His pregnant wife. I'm going to walk into this room, and everything will be back to normal. I still have not decided what to do about my own head, but I can always decide later. I can try counseling or something. I am sure there is no expiration on erasing memories.

I will walk into the room, praying for the best. Or rather, I will waddle into the room. I'm eight months pregnant, and it's been tough hiding this beach ball of a belly. But I'll take advantage of the pregnant status as much as possible. I'm wearing sweatpants, flip-flops, and a t-shirt. I showered, but I didn't bother with makeup. When you're this pregnant, it's all about comfort.

I walk into the dim room. A machine is beeping. I follow the tubes from the machine to the bed. He's still sleeping. Tight white sheets pulled to his neck. Like a mummy. Like a ghost with a real face. Next to the bed, she's folded in the chair. That should be me. His wife. Not his ex-fiancée. She uncoils out of the chair, holding a finger to her lips. I stop moving. She moves across the room and wraps her arms around me.

I hesitate but wrap my arm around her. Just the other day we were threatening to kill each other and now she's hugging me. Maybe she is an angry drunk. Maybe she's plotting something. I want to pull away, but she pulls me closer into her space. She leans in as if she'll whisper a secret into my ear.

Our cheeks touch. Her cheek is cold. Wet. Has she been crying? My mind goes to the worst. The procedure didn't work. That's why she is being nice. The great Marci failed, and I have to live with Jekyll and Hyde until death do us part.

Marci pulls away. She smiles at me. She is beautiful. I wish I could find a flaw in her face. She's been here for two days straight. Hospital food and coffee. Folded in that chair. Comfortable, but still a chair. Even in this dim, unflattering light she looks stunning.

Her voice, matching the rhythm and volume of the beeping machine, calls to me. "Leslie, I think our boy is going to be okay."

The phrase "our boy" makes me cringe. My hands ball into fists, and I imagine punching her in that perfect face. Maybe I am an angry sober. I want to scream at her, *It's not our boy! He is my husband.* I want to correct her, but I do not want to fight.

I grab her hands and squeeze.

"I hope this works, Marci." She lays her head on my shoulder.

She whispers into my ear. "I hope it works out, too."

I wonder if we are talking about the same thing working out. Can we still be friends after all this? We've been through so much. I respect Marci more than I did several months ago. She still makes me want to vomit but, for the past seven months, most things have not sat well in my stomach. I laugh at my own joke. Marci looks at me.

"I'm glad you're in a good mood. I have been worried about you. Probably more than you think. I wanted to say I'm sorry for the way I treated you the other day. I didn't want that. I didn't want any of this." She walks to the opposite side of the bed. "You want to wake our man up?"

Why does she do this? I bite my tongue and nod my head.

I rub his shoulder, tugging and pulling at his body. "Alex, my love. Time to wake up."

After a few gentle tugs, his eyes flicker open. He smiles at me. His smile. My Alex. It is him. Marci did it. I glance at her, she flashes a toothy grin. I comb my hand through his hair.

"How do you feel, Alex?"

He smiles at me. "I feel okay. My head is a little groggy." He rubs his forehead. "Feels like I have been sleeping too long. Strange dreams."

"Take it easy. I'm here for you." I lay my palm on the side of his face. He jerks away from me.

"Sorry, Lee—" His eyebrows raise, and he grabs my hand. He starts shaking his head and blinking his eyes. "I'm sorry. It's just I feel all tingly, and there are white spots on my eyes."

I step away and glance between him and Marci. Marci with that wink and smirk.

He stops blinking and turns his head away from me to Marci. "Brenda, how are you, my love?"

Marci seems surprised, at first, and hunches her shoulders. Then she leans in and kisses Alex on the cheek. "I'm doing okay."

The air is sucked out of my lungs like a punch to the gut. "What's going on?" My legs wobble, and I grab the edge of the bed to stabilize myself. "Marci, why did he call you Brenda?"

They both turn to me.

Marci stands, shaking her head. "Leslie, please sit down. I think I can explain."

I try to catch my balance. My arms are flailing. The uncomfortable weight of my belly causes me to stumble backward. Marci gets to me before I fall to the ground, helping me into a chair. Alex is sitting, ready to come to my rescue.

"Alexi, stay in bed." Marci commands him.

"Leslie, relax. Please calm down and breathe!"

I take uneven gulps of air, but my head is still pounding. The white flashes pulse in my eyes. "What is going on, Marci?"

As my world starts spinning, I close my eyes, listening to Marci's voice.

"Leslie, I wanted to tell you this earlier, but the truth is my middle name is Brenda. I'm Brenda."

The voice in my head is screaming, but what comes out is a whisper. "What?"

Marci speaks in a calm, even voice, "Leslie, Alexi used it as a nickname for me." She squats, squeezing my knee, smiling. "Leslie, the procedure worked!"

My eyes flicker open, glaring at Marci. I couldn't care less that her middle name is Brenda, and it was her nickname. I spit words at her. "Why does he remember you but not me?" Her face fades into a blur across my eyes. I close my eyes again, listening to her voice chip at the blackness.

"The memories were too tangled. Erasing the past few months probably caused some of your memories to be faded. I didn't realize... And obviously, we haven't done the follow up scans yet. I'm sorry, Leslie. I truly am." Marci shakes her head. "I didn't want this."

"Well, put them back."

"It's not that simple."

"You said you were going to make this right."

"I tried to minimize the memory erasures, Leslie. You have to believe me, Leslie."

She keeps saying my name like I might forget. Every time she says my name, the white flashes at the edge of my vision spark brighter. "What?" My voice is shaky.

"Silver lining in all this is that you and Ralphie can still be together. I can help Alex get back to normal. Everyone can be happy, right?" Marci's voice was shaky, like she was trying to convince herself of the lie.

"I'm not happy, Marci! You lying piece of shit."

I lunge out of the chair pushing past Marci. "Alex, look at me. It's me, Leslie—your wife, remember?"

His eyes search my face for recognition. But his lips curl into a frown and he shakes his head. "No, I don't remember. Sorry."

I fall back into the chair. This is worse than when he was Brian or that other BDSM abusive asshole. At least he recognized me. I'm nothing but a stranger now.

"This doesn't make sense. You said it would work. Things would be back to normal. How could you do this to me, Marci?"

"Leslie, calm down please. I'm not lying. I didn't want this."

I think about Alex and our life together, and my head is pounding. I am blinded by a migraine, and I close my eyes. Wetness seeps between my legs. A warm, soothing sensation.

Marci smiles at me. "Leslie, I think your baby is coming."

"What?" I follow her eyes into my lap. Sweatpants soaked through.

"Your water just broke. You're probably going into labor."

Alex calls out, "Brenda, what's happening?"

I glare at him. "Stop calling her Brenda. Her name is Marci."

"Leslie, please calm down. Everything is going to be okay." She winks at me. That annoying wink. I hate her. I hate her. I hate her.

"How is this okay? I'm about to have our baby, and he doesn't fucking remember me at all."

"Leslie, I'm sorry." Marci stands and runs out the room yelling for help.

The white flashes in my eyes start throbbing. The pounding in my head fills my ears with drumming. I clench my fingers into tight fists and punch the chair. My abdominal muscles are contracting and relaxing. A sensation fills my abdomen like I'm having a bowel movement. I squeeze my thighs tight. Between the strobes of light, he reaches for me. My eyes fill with white. The white turns into black—

When I open my eyes, He is standing over me.

"Hey, Alex." I reach out for him, and he takes my hand.

"Hey, Leslie."

It's still not him. Not my Alex. I pull my hand out of his grasp. "How are you feeling, Alex?"

"I feel great. Good to be myself and getting my life back in order."

"Is our baby okay?"

He looks behind him. I follow his eyes. Marci is standing by the door. He looks back at me and nods.

"Yes, your baby is okay, Lee—" He stops mid-sentence, remembering. "Leslie, everything is going to be okay."

The room begins to corrugate outward from his face. I close my eyes as throbbing pulses start behind my eyes.

"I don't understand what happened," I say. "Marci, you told me this procedure would work."

Marci moves to me, but it's his voice saying, "I have to thank you so much for caring for me these past months, and while being pregnant. I can kind of remember the time we spent, but those memories have been faded." He takes hold of Marci's hand. "Marci told me of the sacrifices you made to accommodate me when I was acting out my past memories. We dated so long ago, and I thank you for loving me again. I'll never forget you."

"We are married, Alex. We have a baby now. We had a life. More than just a casual date. I love you, Alex!"

I lift out of bed. A pain tears at my abdomen. "Woah, Leslie!" His hand pushes on my chest. I let him guide my body. I stare at him. They are his eyes. His hands. His smile. It's my Alex. She erased me, screams in my head, but a loud sob is all that escapes my mouth. He wipes the tears running down my cheeks.

"Don't cry, Leslie. I owe you my life. We will make this right." He turns to Marci. "We have to make this right with Leslie and Ralphie. Marci even went to your home and removed all signs I was there."

"You did what?"

Marci steps in. "We thought it was best to remove any artifacts from the past seven months. Alexi had his key and with his memory restored your power of attorney is null and void at this moment."

"What about our marriage certificate and court documents showing we are married, Alex?"

He looks away from me. Marci answers, "We didn't find any such documents. But once you're back home, you'll settle back into your life. Your mind needs time to reset after a stressful time like you had. You start to believe the fiction is reality. I think Ralphie is waiting for you."

"What? Ralphie?"

Hearing his name, the throbbing in my head fades. Hearing his name with mine stops the walls from buckling. The white flashes fade.

Alex and Marci are whispering. Alex stares at me while giving Marci an awkward kiss on the cheek. That's my kiss. That's my Alex. He smiles at me. I miss that smile. I miss those kisses. I'll never forget him.

Marci rubs my arm. "Get some rest, sweetie. We'll bring your son by in a little."

Alex pats my leg and heads to the door, holding hands with Marci. I follow him with my eyes. He pulls the door open and she winks at me. They step out into the hallway. The door closes, and I'm all alone whimpering to myself.

My mind is processing this flood of new information. Processing the role I played in this madness. I fought so hard to keep living with him, my Alex, and for what? The door swings open, and the *click-clack* of Marci's shoes fills the small room.

"Cheer up, sweetie. You will see this is all for the best."

"You bitch. I'll make you pay for this."

"And how do you plan on doing that?" She waves at me and grins. "I'm going to do you a favor. Just drink this solution. In a few hours, everything will be right as rain." She sits the glass on the nightstand.

"What is that, Marci?"

"I never thought of you as a friend before. I hated you for taking Alex, but the way you stood by him over these past months I had—" Marci wipes her eyes. "I forgave you when you stayed with me at my house. I changed my mind about you." She starts pacing around my bed. "But you just played me. You made me like you. I let my guard down, and you kicked me in the gut."

"What the hell are you talking about, Marci?"

"You trying to take my future away, my life, everything I worked for. And then you and Ralphie!" Marci stops pacing and punches the foot of the bed. "How long have you been going at it with him? Tell me, is that really Alex's baby you had?"

The thought of my baby crosses my mind. My breasts full and painful. Is there a baby? Can I see him? Can I hold him?

"Where's my baby?"

"I need to know. Leslie, be honest. You and Ralphie have been together for some time."

"What the hell are you talking about? Do you need this Ralphie relationship narrative to justify what you did?"

"No, Leslie, I want the truth. Like I said I didn't intend for this to happen."

"Whatever. Like I said I did not meet Ralphie until that first night in the clinic." Is that true? My mind flashes to moments we shared the past several weeks. A moment further back in time where we worked together in college.

"That's not what your scans said. Ralphie's memories mapped similarly to Alex's memories, but there were ones from a while ago. You knew him for some time longer than at the hospital."

"Ralphie and I did know each other in college. We worked on a project freshman year and went out for beers as a group. I forgot about it until Ralphie showed me a photo the other day. Ralphie tried to act like there was more, but you know how guys are—"

Marci snorts. "I know how guys are, and how silly girls can be. You thought about him often in your dreams. Admit it, you're in love with him, aren't you?"

I hesitate, thinking about what Marci is asking me. "No—"

Marci throws her hands up, cutting me off. "You don't have to answer that question. Just drink that solution and everything will be okay..." Marci paces around the room, talking fast, "It was easy. You and Alex didn't know each other that long. I was surprised that your memories were not that embedded. Only one keystone memory needed to be removed, and poof!" She throws her hands up. "I'm not sure Alex even loved you."

Those words hit me like a slap across the face. She violated my memories. My eyes water, and my body shakes with anger.

"You had no right to explore all that. I never gave you permission. I have documents signed by you prohibiting this type of intrusion." I try to sit up, but the sharp stab of pain pulls me to the bed. "You never had permission."

"Like I said, Leslie, you don't know anything. I have everything buttoned up for your pretty lawyer head. You may have heard of all the security acts put in place after 9/11. After you made me look like a fool that day, I had a conversation with my friends in DC and... well, my stick turned out to be bigger. And at the bar a few days ago, you verbally gave me permission and we have a witness." She towers over me. "But back to the question at hand. You do love him, don't you? Easy how those things happen. How we fall into the arms of another. Always accidentally." She leans away, grinning.

"No, I told you! Ralphie and I are no more than friends."

"You tell nothing but lies. First, you never met him, and now you're confessing you met some time ago." Marci throws her hands up and snorts a laugh. "Whatever, Leslie you don't have to be honest with me, but be honest with yourself. Look, I want you to be happy. That's why I'm giving you a way out. Just drink the solution I gave you. Trust me one more time."

"All this over a kiss and making you look bad?"

"Oh, I know the penalty for a kiss. One less meaningful than between you and Ralphie."

"You're a piece of work—"

"Listen, Leslie, you have a couple options. Go and try to bring me down. I have the US government behind me, lawyers, and a shit ton of money. They are tripping over themselves to get this tech. You cannot get in my way now. Or you can take the solution, and live the rest of your life, happy and well-compensated."

"Money is not the same as love and having what's yours."

"I'm truly sorry. I didn't intend for this to happen, but I can make it right."

"Two wrongs don't make a right, Marci."

She shakes her head and waves her hands.

"You're right. But then you will have a sad life, fighting a hopeless cause, chasing someone who doesn't remembers you and will never love you again." Marci winks and walks to the door. "If he ever loved you. Just drink that over there. When you wake up, you and Ralphie can ride off into the sunset."

"What about my baby?"

Marci turns. "What about him? He's all yours."

I shake my head. Would she take my baby? "Does the memory thing affect the baby?"

All those times I studied her face, I could not find any flaws, and now I see it. The one thing I could have used against her in my mind to etch at her perfect image. I see me. I see her flaw; she looks like me. The sister I never had. I'm Leslie, and she is Brenda. I wish I would have realized this earlier; maybe things would have been different.

Marci's voice cuts into my thoughts. I forgot I asked her a question, and I missed the first part of the response.

"—nothing worth worrying about, but how do I know what influence nano-tracers can have on a developing mind? Maybe we can do some scans. I'll make a note about it, and you and I can get together and chat after you drink that."

I turn my head to the glass of milky white solution. I remember the taste. "Why, Marci?"

"I promise we will be the best of friends. You, me, Alexi, and Ralphie."

A searing white pain burns behind my eyes. My mind shouts, "I'll never be your friend." But my voice betrays me, and a defeated whimper slips out. Marci winks and walks to the door, stops, and spins around, wagging her finger like she realized something.

"Funny thing is none of this would have happened if Alexi just let me sell this technology. But you know how he is. Once he gets on his moral high horse, poor Marci be damned. He wanted tests," Marci's smile widens, "and now we have the mother of all tests."

I shake my head, confused. "What?"

Marci continues without acknowledging my confusion, like she is talking to a ghost, "One hundred and ten memories transmitted. It was a lucky break when that idiot Shannon spilled that experimental nano-solution on Alexi. Then we get a call that everyone has lost their memories, except Alexi. I couldn't figure it out at first. Then when you told me that he brushed the dry particles off his pants in the plane's restroom, I realized the experimental transmitters must have recirculated in the air system of the airplane. The speed at which it worked was impressive, but I guess when you do the math, hundreds of trillions of nano-particles could fit," Marci holds up her pinky finger, "on my fingertip. And, by your account, he could see the dried powder. That would mean..." Marci's voice fades into a mumble, closing her eyes.

I assume she is thinking, she continues mid-sentence, "...but it was not a complete transfer for everyone. More like pulling random pages out of a series of files and stuffing them back into a random folder in Alexi's mind. The surprising thing was that the files were erased in the donor brain. I speculate that it was because they only had transmitters, and Alexi had both transmitter and receiver. But, for the people sitting closest, the transfer was complete. Then Alexi started to exhibit their personalities. The problem was if a root memory was pulled from the donor and erased, they would still be impaired." Marci smiles with satisfaction.

My mind swirls with questions. "I still don't understand how the transfer happened. It makes no sense."

Marci's eyes widen. "That's the thirty-million-dollar answer. Our boy Alexi had that clue. In an oversaturation situation, with a metallo-protein complex, the donor could have their memories mapped, and then the nanos would be re-released into the environment. If you have a receiver nearby, like Alexi was, you get transference. He has the specifics locked in another set of encrypted files. Once I have those files, I'll be able to add new memories, not just move them..." Marci does that lazy eye wink, and continues her monologue. "The government agencies could not throw enough money at us. All I wanted was a passcode, to get things back to normal. Look at me now." Marci nods her head in agreement with herself.

"What about me, now that I know everything?"

Marci looks at me, then to the glass of water on the table. "Oh, don't worry, Leslie. After you drink that, you will forget we even talked. Also, Ralphie has agreed to help us out in all of this. He loves his Granny so much... We worked out a little deal where I fix Granny first, and he promises to take care of you. I know he loves you. You do love him, right?"

"What?"

But, like talking with a ghost, Marci ignores me and steps out of the door before I can inconvenience her anymore. Do I still love him? Do I want to go through more of this memory game? Is Marci right? I did love him. No, I do love him. Which him was she talking about? Alex or Ralphie? Which him do I love? Both. What about my baby? Will I forget him? Will I forget everything? I'll never forget him. I promise.

I lift the glass to my mouth. The foul stink of rotten eggs fills my nose.

I remember everything. I close my eyes, trying not to forget him. I promise, I'll remember.

CHAPTER 31

Alex:
260 Days after Event

Marci insists I asked for this. Memories of my past to be removed; she showed me the consent forms. My name. My signature. My idea she said. Yet, the memory maps she showed me were wrong. Marci keeps showing me the images of me doing all sorts of sexual acts with men and women and asks if I'd rather have these images stuck in my head. I don't want that in my head, but I don't trust Marci. I should trust Marci, but there is something forced together that would separate.

Marci is not around much. We have separate homes. I'm living in an apartment Marci rented for me in Chicago, and she lives in Philadelphia. This seems strange for a couple in love—inseparable is the term Marci uses, about to be married—to live like this. Marci seems interested in these personal encrypted files on wetware and memory transplantation. I studied them, and I can't give that info to anyone—not to Marci and her questionable entanglements.

I went into the lab at night and made the nano-construct, in secret, to help speed up the memory restoration of the passengers. I said I had a solution made from before the Event, but I should delete these files. No, I can't do it. I don't have many of my memories, so I'm trying to hold on to the brilliant ones.

I told Marci I couldn't remember the passwords. I wanted to call things off with Marci and sort my own life without out her intrusions. I need space to figure things out without her lies about data and wondering what she does during the weeks she spends in Philadelphia and Europe.

What was taken from me? There's a void in my head. A pain that has no source. No focal point. I don't know who I am. I'm not sure what I was or where I came from. I'm a scientist. I'm engaged to Marci.

But what about Leslie? Leslie... I don't remember, but there is something about her smile. She makes me smile. I think I'm falling for her. Or is that because I lived with her during my memory overload?

Leslie is part of that void in my head. She should fit in, but I'm not sure what puzzle her piece fits in. I want to spend more time with her, but she's in some sort of relationship with Ralphie. They seem awkward together, like Marci and me. When she comes to the clinic, I can't take my eyes off her. The dresses she wears, her perfume fills me with warmth. Should I say something to her? Should I tell her how I'm feeling?

And there is the ghost of Brian still in my head. Who is he? What is he? A writer, I guess. I am Brian, a pseudonym.

I logged into my computer and found a file with a novel outlined and chapters started. I don't remember writing any of it. But one part stands out in my mind; it fits into the void. It fills me with hope that I can figure out what happened and fix it. All I can do is soldier on and figure out who I am. Maybe I will finish this novel, or start a new one. Or maybe I'll do something different. Make new memories and forget the past.

I found the name of a psychiatrist, Dr. Shirley, in my notes. Maybe I'll give her a call.

I close my eyes and let the fuzzy, pixelated shades of black swallow me; white sparky caterpillars eat the edges, and a voice starts reading from the ether.

When you walk through the belly of hell you expect to find the soothing gates of heaven at the end of your arduous journey. The fiery red-hot sun will cool into a white ball of restorative jelly. A cool drink in hand and weary feet massaged by the eternal springs. The scars that crisscross my body, and these thick dry callouses on my hands and feet, would be smoothed flat into soft baby skin. I could lay down my weapons and finally sleep. The reward for traversing and surviving the journey through life, this hell. But here I'm. Still struggling on my journey. My sleepless enemy, tugging at my calloused hands. I'm still alive and therefore my journey continues.

I guess that's the small-print part: you can't be alive and enter heaven. You can see the faint, white glow at the end of the hellish tunnel, but you have to keep pressing on. All the others that died on our unexpected journey through this hell were forced to take the shortcut. That's the worst part of the journey, remembering. Remembering what life was like before the gates unleashed its restless souls. Remembering the lives cut short during the journey and, though sad, a bit of happiness fills you. They found their exit. You carry their stories, their incomplete stories, a lover's story, a son's story, and a stranger's story.

I'm still living so it's my job to fill in the blanks and pretend I knew them and the lives they lived—or would have lived. One day someone will pretend to have known me and finish my story.

Remembering, that every time you think you reached the Gates of Heaven, there are many more miles of Hell. That hot red ball in the sky always fades into something less menacing, less painful. You close your eyes, hoping you're being gaslighted, because that's the only way you can convince yourself to sleep. You have to forget that zombie night keeps fading into another zombie day...

"Zombie Day," Brian Watson.

CHAPTER 32

Leslie:
290 Days after Event

I open my eyes, and the darkness is unsettling. The blackness resting like a heavy mass on my chest. My heart is beating fast. My arms are tingling. My feet are stabs of pins and needles. My head is full of white, angry noise. Am I dying? I want to die. I am not sure what to think anymore. I close my eyes and try to relax. I try not to think about what is coming next.

Pings of light decorate the blackness, leaving remnants of streaky, fading light. The pace of the flashes quickens, and the whiteness overtakes me and fills my space. I push through the white fog, and I see him. I can't remember his name, but I know him. Were we lovers? We are on a train. This man is sitting with a small child. I recognize the man and the child, but their names elude me. Even though the train car is empty, I sit in the seat in front of them, trying to remember their names.

The tap on my shoulder startles me. I turn my head, and I recognize his face. His familiar face, too close to mine. Any closer, and we would embrace in a lover's kiss.

"Can I borrow your book?" His voice has an echo. So close, but miles away.

"What?"

His finger is pointing. "Your book. It has information in it that I need. Can I look for it while riding the train?"

I glance at my lap, and there is the book he is referring to. I don't remember holding a book. The title blurs into fuzz. I move the book, trying to focus the images.

His impatient voice breaks my staring contest with the book. "So can I?"

There's something about his face that I find comforting. "Sure."

I pass the book to him. The moment his hand contacts the book, a jolt of energy surges through me. The blurry cover focuses, and my face is on the cover. The book has my picture on it. I pull the book out of his grasp but, with a determined pull, he snatches it out of my hand. The cover blurs out again.

I plead, "Wait, I need to see it again."

"I'll be quick, I promise." He opens the book and starts reading, despite my desperate plea.

I look at the baby next to him. The boy's face is blurry. Like he is vibrating with energy. I reach my hand out to him, but I turn away from him before I become nauseous. I rub the sweat forming on my forehead. My shirt grows wet with rings of perspiration.

A voice booms overhead, announcing that my stop is next. I stand and walk off the train. As the doors close, the man is still reading my book. The cover is blurry, but I remember my face on the cover. As the train pulls away, the man waves at me. He has my book. I remember. The boy's face stops vibrating. It is my son.

"He has my son!" I start screaming. I run after the train. I stop running as the train fades into the horizon. I stop screaming once I realize there is no one around. Still, I give one last fading plea, "Help, he has my son."

Her voice startles me. I turn my head and see her face.

"He has something more important than your son," she says.

I walk closer to her, rubbing my eyes. "What? Who are you?"

"Oh, my dear, you never know anything." She shakes her head, walking to me. She grabs me by the shoulders, her face like mine, but not me. Her eyes, like mine, but not mine, boring into my mind. "You never learn, Leslie." She winks at me. "You forgot your book."

She starts shaking me. Calling my name. The scene erases like an Etch A Sketch. Whiteness, blackness, I open my eyes.

He is shaking me, calling my name, "Leslie, wake up, sweetie. Leslie! The baby is crying."

My eyes concentrate on his face, his large smile, and it takes me a second to remember that I'm in this life with, Ralphie.

Ralphie smiles. "You'll probably be gone when I get back home tonight."

I nod.

"Granny is going to miss you."

"I know, but—"

"You don't have to say anything more." Ralphie leans in and kisses me on the cheek. "Goodbye, Leslie."

***

This past month or so has been a whirlwind. Marci's story was smooth—an accident, head trauma, memory loss, baby survived. She had pictures and everything. I never consented to another memory scan. Marci assumed I drank the solution, so she did not push the issue. I went along with it, and I asked and begged my friends and family to stop inquiring about what happened. My law and business partner, who kept a copy of those signed documents that Marci stole, is the only other person who knows I am still me.

The documents are worthless because Marci's government contacts had my—our—public records changed or erased to match Marci's story, Marci's lies. Marci did manage to steal my life, but not my memories. I'll have to build my case against her, from scraps of my life. Marci does not realize what a mistake it was for her to underestimate me, and she will pay. But I want Alex more than seeing her fall.

It was easier to play this part than I expected. I had been playing a part for months so playing an amnesiac and falling into Ralphie's caring arms was easy. I can't imagine he had anything to do with Marci's planning, but I am not one hundred percent sure he is innocent. He also thinks I drank the memory-erasing solution.

I have not slept with him. He never asked. I am leaving now. He is a gentleman with a good heart, a good friend and is giving me all the space necessary to recover. He had no choice. I still have my condo.

As much as I enjoy the coziness and comfort of Granny's house, I spend my time alone at my condo organizing my thoughts. I was biding my time to leave for good. I wanted to make sure Marci wouldn't get suspicious if things ended between Ralphie and I suddenly.

I owned the condo before I meet Alex, so it fit into the narrative Marci had constructed. Marci tried to clean out all of Alex's artifacts from my life, but she only got the obvious stuff. I still have the small reminders of his to fill my space. His favorite coffee mug. His threadbare college sweatshirt. His wedding ring—

I pull my baby to my chest, and he starts to nurse. I see in his face the man on the train. I remember who he is, my Alex. Alex's memories were only faded, Marci said. I knew how to play this part. I would see him at the clinic, ogling me from the distance. I could tell he remembered this from our past. I would wear dresses I knew he liked, and perfume that turned him on. I was playing the part.

By coincidence, we saw each other at a coffee shop, and I bought him a coffee. He confessed that Marci was not around much, and asked if we could hang out, be friends. I gave him my number and told him to call me. That was a month ago.

We've been seeing each other several times a week. Alex ended things with Marci last week when she went to Spain without him and said she didn't know when she would be back. Alex asked if he could stay at my condo while he sorted things out in his head.

He asked me if I loved Ralphie, I shook my head.

He leaned in and kissed me.

He asked me to tell him everything.

I did.

He said he remembered that he loved me.

He asked if I would move back into the condo with him. I nodded and kissed him.

That was a week ago. I am moving back home today.

Alex is taking his son and I out to dinner tonight to celebrate. We're going to a restaurant by Buckingham Fountain. The same restaurant we went to before he proposed. Does he remember? Should I care?

I lay our baby in the cradle and close my eyes, trying to remember being in his arms, again.

The End

ACKNOWLEDGEMENTS

NO BOOK IS EVER written in a vacuum, and this book, being my debut novel, has a long trail of memories; I want to start at the end and make my way back to the beginning.

I want to thank—You, the reader, for trusting me with your time. You made it to the end of this crazy adventure, and I hope you will trust me again in the future, to twist words into a tale. If you enjoyed this book and want to see more from me, please leave a review and tell a friend!

I want to thank my publisher RhetAskew—Mandy and Dusty—who took a chance on my #DivPit pitch on Twitter and worked with me to put this novel into your hands! It has been an amazing journey, and I look forward too many more. Special shout out to the RA editors, Emma T. who pushed more out of the story than I thought possible, and Jennifer Soucy who helped push the book over the finish line! Editors are the eyes in the authors blind spots. One of the pleasures of working with a small press like RhetAskew is the instant network of fellow authors and supporters, who I have become friends with over my publication journey.

I want to thank my Beta Readers: Jay, Tera, Connie, and Maria, who read early drafts, listened, and offered advice and moral support as this tale went from an idea to the story you just finished. I want to thank Hannah Sandoval at Purple Ink Pen (If you need a developmental or line edit, she is awesome!) who worked with me on early drafts of this story.

I want to thank the folks who kept me sane and asked every week when the book was being published, my Tuesday Drinking Buddies: HamRock, Snuggles, Punch-it Paul, Stabbin' Captain, M.I.A., D-Bone, and my favorite bartender at Danny Z, Amanda!

I have a number of friends (I remember who you are) from my graduate school days at Arizona State University, who would come and listen to me read poetry (Mary McCann—KNKX jazz host, gave me a microphone and the rest was history) and my artistic partner back then, Robby Roberson—we need to do a Jacaranda's Paradise reunion tour. (Robby is a wonderful musician, and if you are in the Tempe/Phoenix AZ area, you should go check him out. Tell him Jotham sent you).

As we get to the end of this winding road, thanks to my sons for making life interesting, Max and Xavier, don't give up on your dreams.

Big thanks to my wife, Georgia Geis (if you follow my newsletter you have seen her cool print art, if not go check her out at atomicnumber14.com), who also gave me a microphone to perform at her weekly variety show in Phoenix, AZ, "Take out", and then got stuck with me! Georgia read the very first draft of "Will You Still Love Me…" and gave advice and support as I babbled on about every plot twist, and who celebrated with me when I got that email from RhetAskew! Thanks!

And last but not least, this road started in a row house in West Philadelphia—"Born and raised…" (I had to do it, LOL)—Love you Mom, Dad, Ta, and Nim! You guys always believed in me.

And here we are at the beginning—Thank you again, for going on this journey, and hopefully you will tag along on the next!

Note: Some of the science is real and some isn't, yet. LOL Maybe I'll put my own story under the microscope and take it down the Rabbit Hole of Research—(My newsletter that explores the Science in Science Fiction and Fantasy).

ABOUT THE AUTHOR

JOTHAM AUSTIN, II lives in Chicagoland with his wife and two sons. He has his PhD in Botany, and can be found taking electron micrographs of cells at The University of Chicago.

When Jotham is not in the lab or writing, he splits his free time between gardening, woodworking, and home-brewing.

Check out his Rom-Com Novella, **Tomorrow May Be Too Late**, part of the *Askew Ever After Box Set*, available to order at: **https://www.Books2read.com/askeweverafter**

Follow Jotham Online

LinkTree:	https://linktr.ee/Jothamaustin
Twitter:	https://www.twitter.com/jomega22
Instagram:	https://www.instagram.com/jomega22
Facebook:	https://www.facebook.com/jomega22
Amazon:	https://amazon.com/author/jothamaustin
Goodreads:	https://www.goodreads.com/jomega22
BookBub:	https://www.bookbub.com/profile/jotham-austin-ii
Newsletter:	http://eepurl.com/gFCTXv

WWW.RHETASKEWPUBLISHING.COM

Made in the USA
Monee, IL
22 July 2021